I0766077

WELCOME

THE
DAMNED

THEIR CHAMPION COMPANION NOVEL

K.A. KNIGHT

The Damned (Their Champion Companion Novel).

Edited By Jess from Elemental Editing and Proofreading.
Formatted by The Nutty Formatter
Art by Annteya
Cover by JV Arts

N
WORSHIPPERS OF THE SUN
THE FORGOTTEN
THE LOST
PARADIS
TOWN OF SPRING
DEAD SEA
THE
WASTELAND
THEIR CHAMPION SERIES

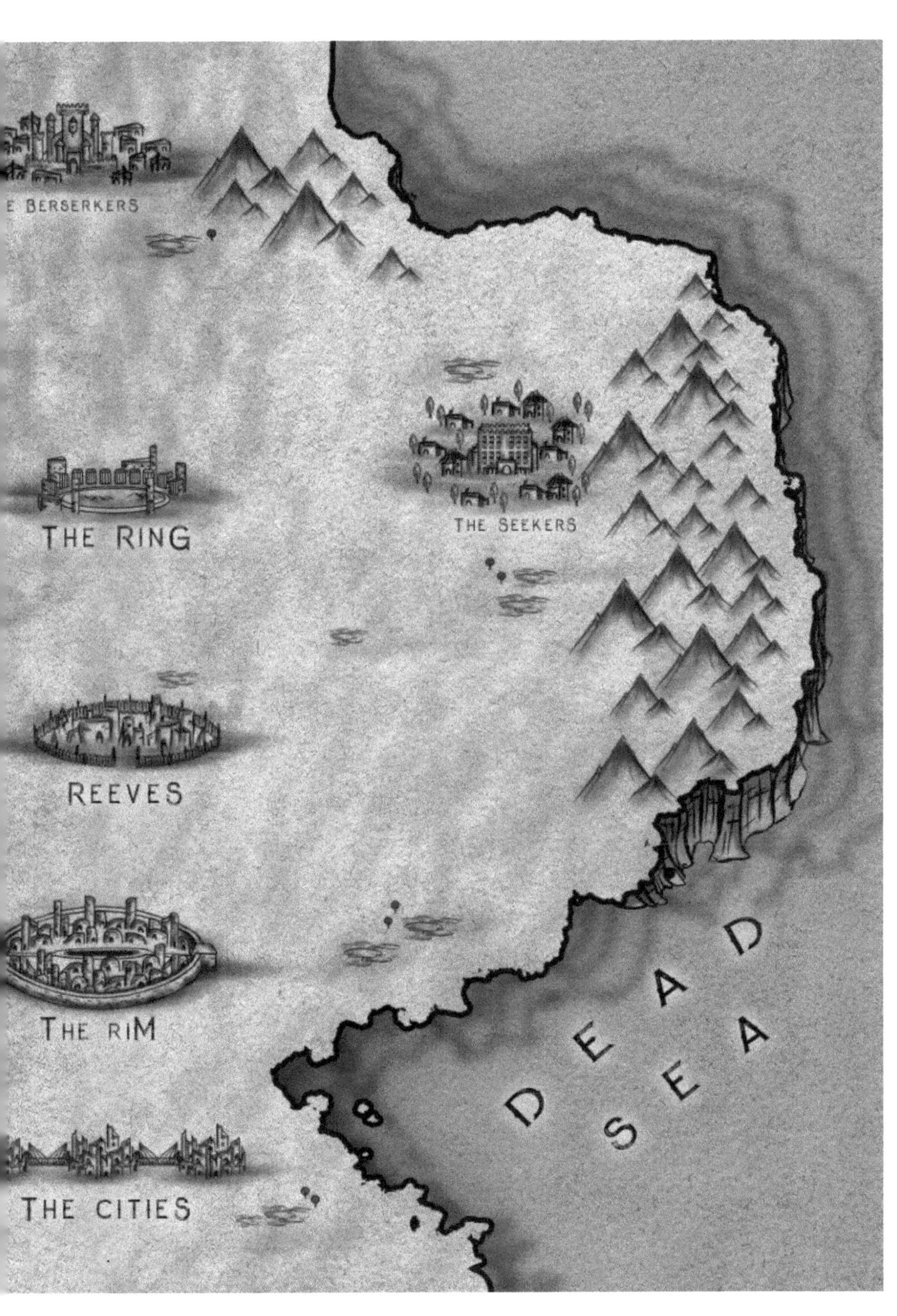

E BERSERKERS
THE RING
THE SEEKERS
REEVES
THE RIM
THE CITIES
DEAD
SEA

THE NATION'S LAWS

NO ONE WILL EVER BE TRULY FORGOTTEN WHEN THERE
ARE THOSE WHO LOVE YOU STILL LIVING.

AND NOT ALL WHO WANDER ARE LOST.

TO BE DAMNED ISN'T ALWAYS A BAD THING…

NO EATING PEOPLE.

NO RAPING.

YOU KEEP WHAT YOU KILL.

NO SLAVERY.

NO TORTURE.

DON'T LIKE IT?
GET THE FUCK OUT OF THE NORTH.

THE QUEEN OF THE WASTELAND,
TAZANNA WORTH

ENFORCED BY HER GENERAL, PIPER.
(WHO RULES!)

Chapter 1
No Pants Club

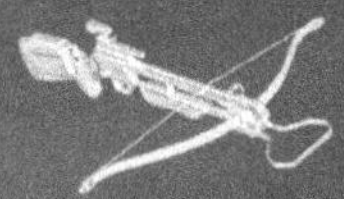

The sun hasn't even risen, yet I am awake, sitting on the steps of the building in The Ring by myself, preparing for what is to come. I know Archel is hovering somewhere behind and above me, stalking me like my shadow always does. The rest of my men are still asleep. Evan is snoring away, Clay is fighting in his dreams, and Jago is dozing. The latter briefly watched me as I readied to leave, but once he saw Archel come after me, he went back to sleep.

All of us are aware that we don't know when we will be able to rest next.

Why is that thought so exciting?

I've loved being here with Worth, seeing her heal and reign, but I'm getting antsy, getting bored. I want to get back out there. My men and I are not the type to sit still and live idly. We need the fight. We need the open road. Worth saw that and gave me the opportunity for adventure. I can't thank her enough.

We have been at The Ring since the war ended over a week ago… which is still strange to think about. It hasn't been long since I was still Pip, the sheltered girl from Paradise. Now I'm a pascha, a general, a leader, and I fought and won a war with some incredible warriors behind a queen I would die for.

Everything she does is for someone else, for The Wastes and its people. They protect us to make us better, to give us a home and safety. That was only proven when she took a blade to stop The Cities. When I saw her fall...

I had been with my men, fighting back-to-back. Jago was ripping through their masses with Clay alongside him, roaring in their faces. They fought like animals, while Clay tossed bombs every now and again. Evan stayed with me with his knives as I protected him as best as I could. Even though he's not a warrior like Jago and Clay or even me, he held his own. He killed, he protected me. Archel, of course, never left my back, but whenever I looked at the bodies piled at his feet, he had more than anyone else.

My shadow assassin.

We moved across the land as one, killing as many as we could. We knew we might die, we knew what we were sacrificing, but it was worth it. I would do it again to be where we are now.

With a home, with a future for our land, and freedom. But Worth... Worth almost paid the ultimate price.

Both armies stopped when we saw her fall. We waited with our hearts in our throats as her men sprinted to her, but we didn't know if it would be too late. Luckily, Evan was on the ball. What he lacks in fighting skills, he makes up for in medical knowledge. He didn't panic once, and he was at her side in a moment, dragging her back to life.

When we got back to The Ring, he nursed her and brought her through an infection and even more injuries without a complaint... Well, okay, without much complaining. That's why I left him sleeping—he's exhausted. He didn't sleep for two days as he looked after those injured from the war, going from amputations and surgeries to setting broken bones and covering lost eyes. After that, he went to check on our queen, and then he would do it all over again.

So I need to let him rest. I also need to remember to tell and show him how proud I am of him. He acted with such grace and strength under pressure, and without him, I have no doubt our queen would be dead. She knows that too. They are friends, after all, and I've seen her thank him more than once.

In her own way of course.

But she's well enough to let us go now, to send us on our first mission to get more supplies for the injured and those who will be injured in the future. We are going right into the cannibal heart- land. It sends both fear and exhilaration through me. All night, my men and I looked over maps with comments from locals and those who know the path. It seems no one goes near the hospital due to eaters, but that's our destination.

We planned our route carefully, each having duties to fulfil before the journey. Jago sorted out supplies, Evan organised medical and food provisions, Clay and I handled weapons, and Archel procured the bikes.

Now we are ready to go. Ready to ride into our future.

"Princess," Archel murmurs, the sound almost whispered on the wind as I turn my head to try and see him. He blends into the shadows cast by the moon until he steps forward. His blond hair glistens under the moonlight, and those blue eyes lock me in place just like they did the first time I ever met him. He still takes my breath away, still makes my heart race. I know if he didn't want me to, I wouldn't be able to see him. My shadow is the best assassin in The Wastes, but he's also *my* shadow, my love, the man who danced with me, helped me heal, and taught me to survive.

No one else knows him like I do, and no one ever will. "Hmm?" I ask, distracted by my own thoughts.

Here I am, the pascha. I'm a leader with people looking to me for guidance, and once I sent The Lost and Forgotten home, that pressure lessened but didn't disappear. At least out on the road, that weight will disperse until I'm just me.

Just Piper.

"It's going to be sunrise in about an hour," he informs me. "Do you want to get ready?"

I nod. "Right, don't want to be caught with our pants down," I tease as I climb to my feet and take his outstretched hand.

He smirks at me and drags his eyes down my body. "Uh, Princess, you're not wearing pants, remember? You said, and I quote, 'they were too restricting, pants are the work of the devil. And not the good devil with the parties and sins and orgies, but a real, evil kind of devil.'"

I look down with a grin. "I'm not wrong though. This is why I'm the leader—I'm smart like that. I would ban pants in my cults."

"You mean clans?"

"Nope, I mean cults. The Cult of Piper, worshippers of the great and mighty. We would have hymns about penises and big men, even one for a Disney princess for Jago. We would get trashed, and being awesome would be an entry question," I ramble as we head inside, hand in hand.

We are staying in the rooms on the bottom floor, and that is where we head now. It's split with a hole in the wall, making a window into the other room where we pushed three beds together. My men are still asleep, apart from Jago, who is sharpening his blade at the table. He nods at Archel when we come in, and I blow him a kiss as I walk through the other room to the en suite.

I push open the door and step into the dirty bathroom. The place where the mirror once hung is dark and empty, and since the light doesn't work, we have lanterns placed around the room. The toilet doesn't flush, so we have a bowl of water to make it happen, and to the left is a walk-in shower, which is the reason I chose these rooms. The shower works, and it even gets hot every now and again. I strip off my shirt—which belongs to Jago and is so long, it might as well be a dress that allowed for a nice breeze on my lady parts because...no pants, am I right?—then turn on the shower. I carefully step over the lip where the glass screen clearly used to be. A groan has me looking over my shoulder. I didn't even hear Archel come in, but he's there, leaning against the doorframe as he watches me. His eyes run down my body and begin to smoulder. That look alone makes me shiver and stand taller. He sees me as beautiful, desirable, so much so, he struggles to stay away from me. Even with my scars, even after all that has happened to me, he still wants me.

"Always, Princess," he murmurs. I blink, clearly I said that out loud. He steps inside and shuts the door behind him. "Would you like me to show you? I gladly will, again and again, for the rest of our lives."

"Is that right?" I grin, turning and stepping into the lukewarm spray. Ducking my head, I slick my hair back with my hands and wash my face before I meet his eyes. He watches me with his intense, all-consuming gaze. To others, he's a killer, an untouchable shadow. To me, he's the man who brought me coffee because he knew I missed it, who gave me his shirt when he left so I could smell him and feel safe.

He gave me the room and support I needed to heal, and although healing is not a straight line and sometimes I struggle, he is always there in that darkness with me. Not with a light, but with a hand. He endures it with me.

"Going to just stand and stare?" I tease. "Is my poor little shadow unsure where to start? Want me to explain? See, these are boobs, fun bags, tits, milk jugs—" I giggle as he rips off his shirt and shucks his pants before storming into the shower after me. A moment later, he wraps his lips around my nipple and his hands cup my ass, yanking me closer as water flows over us.

I grip his hair with a groan as he flicks, nips, and licks my nipple before releasing the tight bud from his mouth. "What were you saying, Princess? Feel free to continue," he teases before turning his head and sucking my other nipple into his mouth.

The pleasure from his lips arcs down, creating a line directly to my clit, which starts throbbing, begging for his attention like a needy bitch. My pussy basically runs a fan club now and is also my shadow's biggest supporter, especially for his magical dick, which makes me see stars.

I would worship at his cult altar. The Cult of Cock. I would drink from a cock-shaped goblet and sing songs of his penis. Never mind Cult of Piper, it's all about the dick cult. We could have ball cushions and penis—

"Piper," he says as he laughs, pressing his head against my chest. "You know you're saying that all out loud, right?"

Blinking, I peer down at him. "Really? Huh, what do you think though? Would you join?"

"The Cult of Cock?" He grins. "Or just a cult specifically for my cock?"

"Both." I shrug.

Leaning up, he presses his lips to mine, silencing my constantly rambling thoughts and mouth. I groan and press my body against his as he backs me into the wall, propping his hand next to my head to pin me in place. His thick, hard cock presses against my stomach, making my pussy quiver at the thought of what's to come.

He pulls away, leaving me panting with desire. "Only if you're the only member," he murmurs.

"Boy, you better get busy with your member after that kiss," I mutter.

"This member?" he teases, reaching between us and sliding his fingers along my pussy. "Yeah, that," I breathe.

He hooks his hand around my leg and pulls it up, wrapping it around his hip. I press my lips to his. No more talking. I need him, and he needs me. We have a very unsure path before us. We don't know what will happen tomorrow or a year from now, so we have to live in every moment, and when the end comes, we won't have any regrets.

His fingers trace up my inner thigh, making me moan against his lips as he swallows the sound and presses closer. His talented fingers find my center and stroke down my already wet pussy before dipping inside me. With sure, strong strokes, he starts to fuck me with them. No holding back, no teasing. We don't have time for that.

His thumb rubs my clit as he brings me higher and higher to that place of pleasure. My body trembles as I bite his lips, letting him take all my noises. He presses his thumb to my clit, holding it there as his fingers curl and rub along my walls. Archel wrenches my pleasure from me, not allowing me to get there but forcing it.

I love it. I love how easily he makes me weak. How easily I tumble over that edge, crying out into his mouth as my pussy clamps around his fingers in release. He fucks me through it, not even letting me breathe or come down from the high. I rip my mouth away, turning my head to suck in desperate breaths as his lips trail down my neck.

Kissing, licking, biting.

"Princess, I want to taste you, to spend the next hour licking your pussy," he growls out.

"But we don't have time," I reply on a moan. "Stupid time.

Instead, you will have to dick me real good."

His shoulders shake in laughter, even as he pulls his fingers from my channel. He pulls back, keeping his eyes on me, and sucks them clean with a groan. "That will have to do, though I will never get used to how fucking amazing you taste."

"Dick. Now," I snap.

His hands dart out, and I flinch, so he slows his movements. We share a look in which he silently asks if I'm okay, and I nod. Those fingers, which were just inside me, wrap around both thighs and lift me. His hard cock presses against my pussy, so I wiggle, trying to get him inside me, but he grips me tighter, holding me still, just on the edge of him being inside me. I narrow my eyes, and he smirks before pushing my back against the wall, balancing me as his right hand grabs his cock. He drags it back and forth along my pussy, bumping my clit before notching the tip at my hole and gliding back again.

"You cunty bitch. I swear if you don't—fuck me in the ass!" I yell as he slams inside of me in one smooth move.

He smirks. "Maybe later. I want your pussy too much right now."

Crossing my ankles at the base of his spine and using the wall, I start to ride him, and soon, we find a rhythm. Our breaths join before us, our slick bodies moving together. The water is cold now, flowing over our overheated skin.

He groans my name, the sound sending a spike through my heart as love explodes within me. "Love you," I pant as I press my face against his shoulder, trying to hold off the next orgasm I feel building.

I want to stay in this moment forever, just us together in our slice of heaven. His grip tightens on my thigh, and his thrusts speed up until he's slamming me against the wall. His thick, long cock fills me again and again, each stroke pushing me higher and higher.

"Love you too, Princess," he grinds out, biting my shoulder for a moment. "Fuck, fuck, fuck," he mutters, and the fact he's struggling to hold off is what sends me over the edge, knowing how weak and helpless I make him.

"Princess," he yells as I scratch my nails down his back and explode around him, dragging him after me. He grunts, his hips stilling as he comes, and we stand there breathing heavily, our bodies locked together. Raising my head, I pull back and kiss his lips.

"What would I do without you, my shadow?" I murmur. "You will never have to find out," he vows.

A knock comes at the door. "Hurry the fuck up. I want to shower. Stop distracting her with your penis," Evan yells, making both of us snigger.

We hear Clay then. "Leave Pascha to it, she has needs," he rumbles. His dark, deep voice still has an unused quality to it.

"Uh-huh, like the need to get drunk, strip off, and try to run through the camp?" Evan laughs as they move away. It's nice they are getting on. There have been a few times where they have butted heads, mainly Jago and Evvie, but other than that, we are getting along well.

I hope that doesn't change. This is a complicated relationship, and it's not like there is a book on it. *Woman and Four Cocks*, or *How to Control Your Dicks...* that kind of thing.

Breaking away, Archel lets me down, pulls free of my body, and turns me into the spray. He helps me wash my hair, his long fingers feeling magical as he rubs and scrubs and gets me ready for the day. He worships me like the princess he calls me.

When we are done, I don't bother putting on clothes. Instead, I strut out of the bathroom to get my clean ones, which are laid out and ready to ride in. I walk past Evan, who is putting medical supplies in his bag, and Clay, who has a bomb splayed on the table as he works to construct it. Jago is peeling an apple with his knife, his boots propped up on the table.

I hear the bang as Jago's boots drop, and he leans forward, those fiery eyes burning as they track down my body. Clay grins at me as he stands as if to chase me, while Evan groans.

"Fuck, good thing there is no warm water left, I need a cold shower anyway," he mutters.

"Pascha, you get more beautiful every day, and your clothes only hide the sensual goddess hidden beneath," Clay murmurs, his head lowered as if in reverence.

I point at him and meet the others' eyes. "And that is how you sweet talk a lady, take note," I announce.

"Brawler, I call you hot all the time, plus I show you with my hands and mouth." Jago smirks, his usually impassive face filling with lust and arrogance.

"Yeah, well, that's why I call you Beast." I wink as I slip into the other room.

Men. Who knew they could be so much fun?

Chapter 2
Cock Rings and Tampons

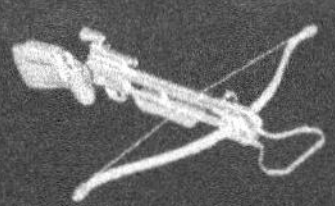

I get dressed quickly, itching to hit the road. I slip into some black jeans with some rips up the front—I need to sew them at some point, since they let in too much sand—and I add my bra that Clay made me. It has material on the side closest to my skin, but the outer layer has metal on it to protect me. Out there in the heat, I need to be as naked as possible to stay cool. Once I add my pascha marks, I will look like the leader I am.

And badass, totally badass.

I grab my old jacket. I need to get another of these too, but there's not much I can do about the holes now, so I start to strap on my weapons. My crossbow goes over my shoulder, my swords are sheathed at my sides, and two knives are slid into my boots. I shove the remainder of my things in my bag, including my coffee that my shadow got me, which I take everywhere. Once done, I turn to see them all just staring at me.

"Pervs," I tease. "Ya ready to ride?"

"If you are referring to you riding my cock, then yes." Archel winks.

"You wish, pal." I grin. "I'm talking about a true beast—"

"So me?" Jago offers. "That rumbles—" "Me?" Clay interjects.

"And is made of metal—my bike," I finish, and Evan sighs. "So not me," he grumbles.

"All of you bastards are dirty. Get ready and let's go, and if you are good and kill lots of people and get all sweaty and dirty, I'll ride you later," I promise, hoisting my bag over my shoulder as I turn and head out of the door. There is a moment of silence, and then I hear them scrambling to follow me as I laugh and march down the stairs and outside into the rising sun. The heat hits me instantly. Fuck, I'm going to be sweating in places no one should ever sweat.

For a moment I just breathe in the quiet air. Everyone is still asleep, so it's silent for once. No clank of weapons, no fighting, yelling, or fucking. Just silence, the sun, and me. I close my eyes as a smile curves my lips. I don't think I will ever be as happy as I am in this moment. I have a job, and I have a friend who trusts me to help her protect and save our people. I have four men who love me and want to fight and die by my side. Whatever is to come in my life, whatever I have to face out there on the road, this is the moment I will remember. When my heart is light, my scars are not quite as heavy, and the world is supporting me. In my darkest moments, I will come back to this memory of utter brilliance and peace and remember that no matter what, it gets better. There is such beauty in this world if you are willing to fight for it.

I have been since I first stepped foot—er, wheels on this sand, and that won't stop now. Worth might have settled down into her role as queen with her men, but I'm just starting out on my own adventure, and there is so much to see.

To do.

"Are you sleeping standing up or pushing out a fart?" Evan calls as he stops next to me. I flutter open my eyes to meet his, his lip ring shining in the light.

"Lovely. You just ruined the moment, Evvie." I sigh and then grin as I walk past him. "That was me pushing out a fart. I crop dusted you for being a douche."

"What the fuck is crop—Oh, Pip, that's nasty!" he calls after me as I giggle.

"You asked for it, douche!" I move along the path and weave through the waking warriors. Some nod at me, others ignore me. Hopefully one day, I can inspire as much fear and loyalty in them as Worth, though I doubt it. That bish is one terrifyingly sexy queen. Ah shit, now I'm thinking about Worth in weird ways again. Only the guards are at the gate, and they let me through with barely a glance. Our bikes are on the other side, ready to go. Jago and Clay ensured they were safe and topped them up on gas last night. I sling my bag over the back of mine, attaching it and tying it down as I yank out my goggles and push them onto my head.

"No way, Worth would lose," I hear Archel joke, and I look back to see him jesting and laughing with Clay, who mainly grunts but goes along with it. It makes me smile to see my men getting along. We are finally a family. We fight and don't always get on, but we all love each other.

"Lose against who?" I ask, turning and leaning back against my bike.

"Ten mountain men," Archel answers as he pulls up his black hood, obscuring his face.

"No way, she would win. She's a boss ass bitch," I state calmly. "That boss ass bitch is currently heading this way," Evan inter-

jects, and I follow his gaze to see her strolling to the gate with her men.

Licking my lips, I ignore the guys as I meet her at the gate. She smiles at me warmly, her hair pushed back and plaited to the side. Worth is in her usual leather leggings and a white tank top, showing off the roses and brands and scars on her arms. She has knives along her side and a coiled whip secured to her waist. She looks like the queen she is. Before I even get to make a joke, she pulls me into a tight embrace. I blink, unused to the gesture, but the warmth of friendship flows through me from it, as does pride. I know it's hard for her to trust other people, to reach out, and yet she does for me. When she pulls back, I can't help but grin at her.

"Be careful out there. Trust no one but your men and come back to us, General. That's an order," she demands, her voice strong. She holds my gaze until I nod.

"Yes, my queen," I reply and grin wider, enjoying her concern. This will always be home to me, but she was right—I still want to be out on the sand. I hear someone head my way and glance back to see Evan joining me.

She follows my gaze. "Take care of her for me, Doc. I'll try not to hurt myself before you get back."

I laugh, and even Evan grins before he hugs her. I was once jealous of how close they are, but not now. I'm happy he made more friends, and she needs someone like Evan in her life, not just to put her back together after kicking ass but as a non-fighter. A healer. It connects our family in more ways than one. "I'll bring back extra supplies just for you," he teases her, and with a wink at me, he heads back over to the others, who are watching us, leaving me with Worth and her men, who are speaking between themselves as they stand behind her.

I meet her eyes. She has this magnetism that holds a person captive, unable to look away. Being in her presence is enough to make you feel inspired, stronger, and confident. It's just who she is and the energy she emits.

"I have a present for you," she tells me. "It's a token for my general, wear it with pride."

A present? I almost jump up and down, but I manage to act cool...ish. She turns to her man, Maxen, and grabs something black from him before handing it to me. I frown as I shake it out and hold it up, and then my breath hitches and my eyes widen as I stare at it. It's a leather jacket in perfect condition, but it's the symbol on the back that leaves me speechless.

It's stitched boldly, jaggedly, under a skull with a bolt coming from its mouth and roses for eyes. She even found us a name—The

Damned. I look up at her, unsure what to say as I clutch it to my chest. No one has ever really given me a gift before, especially one so thoughtful. She did it just because, for no reason, and I will trea- sure it. Fuck, I may even sleep in it. Maybe screw in it—

"When you get back, we will have one for each of your men," she informs me, interrupting my inner thoughts, which is probably for the best.

I know I need to thank her, to say something, but for the first time in my life, I'm speechless. "Worth," I whisper, looking down at the jacket again before meeting her eyes. I swallow, trying not to make a joke, but I can't help it, it slips free. "This is so much better than pied piper."

She laughs, and that darkness that lingers in her eyes lightens for a moment. I stand taller at that, at being able to make her laugh. "You know it. You damn those souls who betray us. Now get going, General, it's time to turn the sands red."

I grab the jacket and put my arms through the sleeves before tugging it into place. It fits perfectly, and I feel stronger, like I am wearing armour, the symbol of our people. She is with me, they all are. I will never be alone again.

"Thank you, Worth. I will wear it with honour," I squeeze out before turning to leave so she can't see the tears forming in my eyes at her thoughtfulness.

I yank down my goggles and start to walk away before her voice stops me. "Piper?" I spin to look back at her with a smile, ignoring the feelings welling inside me.

"Yes, hot stuff?" I retort, the sand stretching between us. "Fight like the champion you are," she demands.

She has said it to me before, but it almost staggers me that she believes in me so much, that she thinks I am on par with her skills. She is wrong of course. I could never beat her, I'm not the cham- pion. This wasteland only has room for one, and it's her, but I'm happy to be her right-hand woman, her hunter...her damned.

Nodding, I turn away and climb onto my bike, ignoring the looks my men throw my way as I start the engine. I have a job to do, we all do. A job for our queen, our people, and our land. As the pascha, they look to me for guidance, and in every one of those eyes, I see honesty, love, and respect. They would follow me to hell and back, and I know before this journey is through, that is exactly where we will go.

"Let's go, Damned... How badass does that sound?" I laugh, and with a lowering of my head, I skid through the gravel and roar off into the sands, my men following and my queen watching after me. I glance back to see her waving goodbye, but only for now, not forever. I know I will see her again, and when I do, I will have earned this title and the honour she has bestowed upon me through blood and death.

I will become The Damned.

The sun is shining down on us, the heat almost unbearable. Sand fills my mouth, nose, and every crevice on my body, yet I'm grin- ning like an idiot. My heart is filled with excitement, and adrenaline is pumping through my veins. I'm ready to be back out here, to see what the sands have to offer, to see everything.

My men ride with me. We know the path we are taking, and when we stop for the night, we will orientate ourselves. I chose a route through feral territory to add some excitement.

Because why not?

We have been riding for hours. We stopped briefly for the toilet and food, and then we carried on. It should take us just two days at this rate to reach the hospital. The added time is mostly due to the main bridge across a sandy chasm apparently being ruined, so we have to go around it, which adds hours onto our trip. Oh well. More time on the road, more time with my men.

We need it after the war. Although we got to spend time together at The Ring, it wasn't the same. Jago likes his space. He was like, well, a caged animal there. Pun intended. Even Archel was getting restless, and Clay couldn't blow anything up. Evan was happy, but he wants to go wherever I do.

We drive along what used to be a main road in a small town by the looks of things. Half the shops are blown up and falling down. Others are covered in layers of dirt, sand, and dust that will never be removed. At the end of the holey, cobbled street, though, lies a pharmacy. I whistle to my men and pull to a stop inside the four bays outside, the old white lines faded and cracked. The pavement before the store is cracked and dotted with holes and dirt, and paper and old food cans are littered around. Graffiti covers the boarded-up window and the front door is missing, but you never know. We might get lucky, and with more mouths to feed and bodies to look after, we need as many supplies as we can get. Pulling up my goggles, I look at my men. "Let's check it out." I swing my leg over, groaning when my thighs and back ache. I do some quick lunges and star jumps to limber up and get the blood flowing, ignoring their incredulous looks, and then I pull my crossbow.

"Fine, me first," Jago rumbles and stands, machete in hand as he storms towards the door. I follow after him.

"I'll go round back and check for other entrances," Archel calls. "Doc, you're with me. Clay, watch the bikes."

"Good plan, we know you like a good backdoor," I tease, making him stumble as laughter bursts from him before Jago throws us all a glare.

"Shh, Brawler. Haven't I taught you anything?" he hisses.

"It was him," I protest, and he rolls his eyes before leaning down and gripping my chin, even as he smiles and those fiery eyes heat.

"It's always you, Brawler," he murmurs before kissing me soundly and pulling away, leaving me panting and hoping for another kind of backdoor fun. He, however, has different plans and saunters into the building, plunging himself into the darkness.

I follow after him, lips closed and silent, pointing my crossbow at the floor so I don't accidently shoot Jago. He flicks on his torch, and I grab a can from the floor, gently roll it down the aisles, and wait.

When no snarls or shouts reach us, I relax a little. I don't think anyone is here. The once tiled white floor is covered in sand and blood splatters, our boot prints leaving impressions as we step farther in.

It's a small store, only two aisles, with broken, empty shelves in the middle leaning against each other. There are discarded shampoo bottles and boxes littering the floor. Jago points left and goes right. Raising my bow, I head down the left aisle, careful to step over anything that makes too much noise. I keep my footsteps light and my finger ready on the trigger. I run my eyes over the shelves as I go. They are mostly empty, but I spot a pack of condoms on one and grab it, shoving it into my bag. Even at the end of the world, you can never be too careful. Farther down, I grab some deodorant, soap, and tampons, which I nearly weep over. It's the one thing I miss from Paradise—tampons. Who knew?

I reach the end of the aisle, and it opens up into a pharmacy counter. It has a door to the right which is shut. Jago emerges a moment later and nods at me. For a moment, a mischievous smirk covers his lips as he silently shows me a box. My eyes widen and my mouth drops open as I try to contain my laughter.

A cock ring.

He picked up a cock ring.

With a wink, he pockets it and acts like nothing has happened, like we didn't just raid a pharmacy and the only thing he collected was a fucking vibrating purple cock ring. I drag my gaze back to the counter. A steel shutter separates it from the rest of the store, and it has a few bullet holes in it, but it seems locked. Jago heads towards it, so I press my back to his, keeping watch. There's a clank as he tries to pull it up, but it remains firmly in place.

"Bolted. We need a way around," he murmurs.

Just then, the door rips open, and both of us raise our weapons, ready to fire, when Archel's grinning face pops around. "Hurry up, would you? Jeez, what took you so long?" he teases.

Snorting, I step past Jago. "Just tampons and cock rings," I remark.

He nods with an understanding expression. "Sure, sure. I found the door to the pharmacy section, looks untouched. People have tried to get through, but it's locked tight. Evan thinks he can get in." I follow him into the small, cramped back corridor with only two doors. One leads to the employee area and the backdoor loading dock, which is empty. The next is locked tight and just to the left of where the pharmacy is. I see the bullet holes and hack marks he was talking about. People have tried to get in, but it seems it was to no avail. Evan is on his knees, fiddling with the doorknob, as I rest my crossbow on my shoulder.

He mutters to himself, and just as I am about to ask what he said, he exclaims and sits back, twists the knob, and swings the door open. "Holy fuck, when did you learn that?"

He grins over at me. "I'm not completely useless to have around, Pip. I have my...better qualities," he comments, running his gaze over me suggestively.

"You are totally getting a blow job for that," I tell him, and his eyes widen, making me laugh. "Not now, Evvie, later. First, let's check the drugs."

"Drugs, got it," he mutters, but seems stuck on the blow job offer as he gets to his feet. Archel passes him, chuckling, and slaps his shoulder as he goes.

"Thanks, man. I won't be sucking your dick to show you my gratitude though."

"Me either," Jago rumbles. What a touching moment.

Chapter 3
Dance Party Bitches

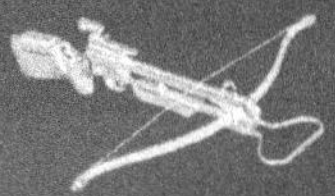

After clearing out the pharmacy, which we manage to get an impressive haul from, we strap it on our bikes, sharing the loads so we won't lose it all if anything happens to one of our rides. With the afternoon sun high in the sky, we race across the sand, trying to cover as much ground as we can before sunset.

We ride into the night for a while, but even with our headlights, it's hard to traverse the rough ground, so we decide to find a place to crash, not wanting to risk wrecking any of our equipment just for an extra mile or two. After searching the surrounding area and destroyed buildings, we ride for ten more minutes before I notice the shadow of a structure on the horizon. I whistle, and we circle around the abandoned tanks and burnt-out cars. Across what looks to be an old parking lot, which is now covered in sand and skulls, there's an old sign with paint across it, which reads, *The end is nigh.* Nice.

When we pull up outside the building, I step off my bike, crossbow in hand, and walk towards the large front doors. The glass is missing, of course, but the building is still standing and appears to be in decent condition, which is rare. Flicking the light of my crossbow on, I raise it and point it at the sign to see the writing.

Student Halls.

Huh, this must have been near a university. I peek inside and shine my light around before rapping on the doors. It's silent, apart from the bikes humming behind me. I turn when nothing appears and nod. The bikes shut off, and the guys grab our gear. I wait for Jago, and when he's at my side, he pulls a blade from his sheath, one the size of my forearm, and grabs the handle. I nod, signalling I'm ready, and he yanks it open as I follow him inside. The entrance is covered in sand and debris, and there is another set of doors, this one wooden, with windows next on either side. I open it and Jago slides past me. I trail behind him, my back to his as we move silently across the floor. It's cleaner in here, not spotless—nowhere is unsoiled in The Wastes—but the sand isn't as bad. By the looks of it, it's one large common room. At the back is another doorway with a stairwell on it, and Jago heads that way as I move around the large square space. There is an old desk to the right, long abandoned, and behind it is a tipped over office chair, some scattered papers, and even a half open can of Coke covered in a bloody handprint. I move back, my boots scraping across the floor as I walk to the other side of the room.

The once white walls are now tan, each corner is coated in cobwebs, and there is graffiti covering most of the walls with unreadable text drawn over each other. I can only make out a few names and words apart from one set of large red letters boldly stencilled across them that reads, *We are the left behind.* Cute.

Jago comes back and blocks off the stairs by pulling an old-style letter rack across it and jamming a piece of metal through the handle. "Just in case." He shrugs. "But it seems clear."

I nod and wander over to the last door, which has the wooden plate half hanging off it, declaring it's 'Maintenance.' I try the handle, but it doesn't budge. With a sigh, I pull back and smash my crossbow down on it repeatedly, the sound echoing loudly. The handle breaks and drops to the ground with a clank. Kicking open the door, I surge in and swing my torch around before grinning. There's an old fridge and two desks with cameras above it, an ancient filing cupboard, and what seems to be a tea and coffee station with the kettle and mugs still there. Everything is left untouched, forgotten.

Left behind.

There is another door at the back, so I tread over on silent feet and open it, peeking in to see a bathroom complete with toilet, sink, mirror, and a small step-in shower with an old white curtain pulled across it. Nice. Good score for the night.

"Clear!" I call.

I hear the others moving around as I open the drawers and search through them, finding some sweets at the bottom and then glancing at the date. I snort when I see they expired a while ago, but my stomach is used to that by now, so I pop them into my mouth and take the bag with me as I head back, my crossbow slung over my shoulder.

"Block the door," Jago orders. "One awake at the desk at all times. I want the bikes brought in and stored in the corner."

"There is a barrel out front, bring it so we can get a fire going, Clay," I insert, automatically adding to Jago's command. "Evan, get the food out, we need to eat and bed down. I want to set off before first light."

They all move away to do as bid. I prop my crossbow up against the wall next to the door and stretch out as the bikes and barrel are brought inside. I unload my sleeping bag and lay it down with the feet to the fire and the head away from the door. I slip a knife under my balled-up jacket I use for a pillow before stripping off my goggles and jacket, and carefully folding and placing them over my bike, ready for tomorrow. I take my boots off next, flipping them over and shaking all the sand out before removing my socks and draping them over my footwear. The floor is clean, and I wouldn't do this in most places, but there aren't any glass, needles, or weapons, so I can stretch out and let my feet breathe for now.

Clay gets the fire going quickly and angles it near the beds, his muscles bulging as he effortlessly moves the huge barrel—I'm almost drooling from the show. His mask is still in place, but then his bright eyes flicker up and lock on me, and he winks when he catches me staring. I grin as he slowly pulls his braid around and lets it free as I watch. It's like hair porn, and only the crack of food opening distracts me.

The others arrange their beds, and we sit on them as we share the canned food and dried meat strips before sipping on the home-brewed vodka from The Ring. It makes Evan cough, and Archel laughs and teases him as I lean back on my elbows, closing my eyes as I absorb the warmth and comfort, the feeling of freedom, of just being with my men with nothing but the road and unexplored land around us.

"You hear me, Brawler?" Jago interrupts.

I tilt my head and open my eyes to see him scooting closer. His arm slips behind me, propping me up as Archel reclines with his head in my lap. "Hmm?" I ask.

"Tomorrow we should cover nearly all the terrain, but I'm not comfortable going in the dark, there are too many places to hide. We were thinking about waiting until the next morning, watching to see the comings and goings before we head in," he repeats, smiling at me. Those fire eyes shine with the actual fire reflecting in them. His shoulder-length hair is pulled back, framing his thick, handsome face. His shirt is off, and I run my eyes across his impres- sive shoulders, remembering how it feels when he holds me, pulls me closer, and pins me, like when we used to practice fighting. "Stop ogling, Brawler, unless you plan on following through," he teases.

Laughing, I pull my gaze from his man boobs and meet his eyes. "Sounds good to me."

"What does?" he inquires, his eyebrow raised.

"Both." I wink, stroking my fingers through Archel's hair as he hums and closes his eyes. Clay frowns and scoots over, knocking Archel away.

"Pascha, will you braid my hair?" he requests, his mask gone, exposing his thick, plump lips. "It is too long for me to reach."

I want to tease him, knowing he's lying, but I don't because it's an honour, and honestly, I like playing with their hair. Even Evan has started growing his out so I can play with it, plus there's more to grab onto when you ride them. Am I right, ladies?

Accepting the twine he hands me, I run my fingers through the long, icy blond locks, combing out the knots as he groans and leans into me. I start to plait it down the middle, leaving strands out on the sides—it's the warrior braid he taught me. It doesn't take long. I tie off the end, then add his usual beads and feathers to it so he looks like a Viking warrior again, and my pussy pulses in appre- ciation.

I hear a flick, and a moment later, static flows softly through the room before it switches to a low, soft slow song. I look around and spot Evan playing with a handheld radio. He glances up and smiles at me.

"I found it at the pharmacy, it still works."

He carefully sets it down, and we all become silent as we listen to the slow notes of the music. It's an old song—jazz, I think. It's surprising how much I missed music from Paradise. I can live without TV, but music still has a way of transporting me away, even for a moment.

A hand descends before my eyes, and I follow it up to Archel's smiling face. I see the memory of when we last danced in his gaze. Grinning, I let him help me to my feet. His other hand slips down my arm to my hip as I lean into his chest, and we start to sway with the music. The notes take us away from here, just us and the tune. "Want to play our game?" he whispers, and I laugh.

"Can I cut in?" Evan asks, and with a sigh, Archel twirls me into his arms.

He catches me and pulls me closer, so my body is pressed against his, and starts to spin me around the room as he smiles down at me, his lip ring glinting in the firelight. "Hi, Pip."

"Hi, Evvie." I grin. "Nice moves."

"You know it." He winks, and then a minute later, I'm twirled, and I land against a hard chest with a grunt. Looking up, I meet

Clay's eyes. He glances back at the guys as if he doesn't understand how to dance before he simply picks me up and starts to move slowly to the beat. My toes don't even touch the floor as he dances me around, making me laugh until, with a kiss on my head, I'm passed to Jago. He holds me close, pressing his head to mine as he hums along to the music and sways. Our hips are pressed together so tightly, there isn't even an inch between our bodies.

"I love you, Brawler," he whispers. "I'm so glad you came into my life and brought me along."

"I knew it," I whisper, before leaning up and kissing his lips as we stop. "I love you too, Beast."

"All right, love birds, let's bed down for the night. We need some sleep," Archel calls, and with one last lingering kiss, Jago walks me back to the sleeping bags. They fight over who gets to lie next to me. I ignore the punching and tackling and slip into the bag. A moment later, two bodies join me on either side—Jago on one, Archel on the other.

"Night," I mumble.

"Good night, Pascha," Clay calls.

"Night, Pip!" Evan says, taking first watch.

"Good night, Archel. Good night, Jago." I giggle.

"Stop, or we will be here all night," Archel grumbles and pulls me closer. "Sleep."

I let the silence relax me, and not too long after, the snores begin, but I remain in a state of semi-consciousness, trapped between being awake and asleep, and sometime later, I hear shuf- fling and then quiet footsteps. I open my eyes and see Evan grab- bing a candle before heading to the bathroom as he cups the flame.

Grinning, I silently slip from my loves' arms and pad after him—after all, I have a promise to keep. He doesn't seem to hear me as he moves into the bathroom, gently putting the candle in a holder before stepping back. I kick the door shut behind me, and he turns with a girlie scream before it cuts off, his hand on his chest.

"Jesus, Pip," he exclaims.

"Gotcha," I tease, and stride towards him.

"Yeah, you—" I kiss him hard, and his words cut off in a groan. He kisses me back, but I pull away a moment later and drop to my knees. "What the—"

I quickly undo his jeans, shove my hand inside, wrap it around his rapidly hardening cock, and pull it free. I lick my lips at the sight of his piercing and rigid, long length. Meeting his gaze, I flick out my tongue and lick his tip as he watches. He stumbles back into the sink, spreading his hands on either side of him, and grips the dusty porcelain as he shakes his head.

"Piper—"

"A promise is a promise, Evvie," I murmur as I lick down his cock and back up again, loving the feel of him becoming fully hard in my hand. Laving my tongue up and down his length, I tease him, sucking at the tip as the taste of his salty pre-cum fills my mouth, making me moan and suck him farther in. He groans and moves his hips as he tries to resist me. Fine, he wants to play like that? I swallow him all the way down, my hand curled around the base of his cock, until the tip of his dick hits the back of my throat.

He cries out softly, thrusting deeper before I pull back and suck him down, bobbing on his cock quicker and quicker. His panting is loud in the small space as I clench my thighs together to try and gain some friction on my pulsing, wet pussy.

"Pip, fuck," he moans, the sound going straight to my already throbbing clit. The suppressed desire, and the need and worship in those two words makes me increase my rhythm as I circle and twist my hand at the bottom. With a groan, he explodes in my mouth. I swallow it, and when he starts to soften, I pull back and lave the tip of his cock, wanting the last of his release before I sit on my heels and wipe my mouth with a finger. His eyes are closed, his mouth is open in pleasure, and his hands are white-knuckling the sink to keep him upright.

Standing, I drag my hand up his body and grip his chin until his eyes open and lock on me. I kiss him softly, licking his lips before I twine my tongue with his.

"Good night, Evvie," I whisper, just like old times, as he pants against my lips, tasting his release there.

"Good night, Pip," he responds.

Chapter 4
My Baby

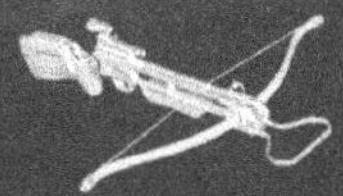

The next morning, I'm on watch, and I wake them up before the sun rises. We have some food and water, and then hit the head and wash as much as we can before we pack up. We work effortlessly as a team until we are dressed, the bikes are outside and ready, and the only proof we were here are the clean marks from our sleeping bags.

I pull down my goggles as I start my engine, and after checking the map, we set off for the day. Like Jago suggested, we decided to camp close to the hospital, which we should reach just before nightfall. This way, we can watch the comings and goings and not stumble around in the dark building and fall through the floors or get ourselves killed.

Jago takes point today, and I stay at the rear, my crossbow mounted and ready. You never know who you're going to run into, after all. We stay out of the major cannibal and feral areas, avoiding the subway, the old aquarium, and stadium. I see them in the distance, the sun blazing over the horizon as we speed across the sand. We drive hard and fast until Jago gestures, and then we pull into an old parking bay next to what used to be a lake, if the sign is anything to go by. Now, it's just a dried-up, sand-filled crater. Turning off my engine, I wipe my face and push up my goggles before stripping from my jacket and stretching, ignoring the sweat coating my body as I accept a bottle of water from Archel.

He leans next to me as Jago and Clay check the area, and then Evan gets the food out, and we sit on the ground between our bikes and share it. After we eat, I lean into Archel's side, eyes closed, just letting his warmth flow through me as I rest.

A noise has me sitting upright and scanning the horizon. The others must not hear it, but my reaction has them grabbing their weapons and looking around.

"What is it, Pasc—"

I put my finger to my lips and strain to hear anything else. I'm just beginning to wonder if I'm going crazy when it comes again.

A cry splits the air.

I leap to my feet and grab my crossbow, and then without waiting, I rush towards it. I slide down the sand dune into the crater and look around. When I spot a large pipe to the right I head in that direction. I hear my guys behind me as I flick on my torch and look inside. The cry comes again, this time alerting me to the fact it's definitely not human.

Leaning in so I can see better, I scan the edges of the rounded tunnel where the sand hasn't reached, and the cry comes again as something moves—something I mistook for a sand pile. I feel the guys around me, watching my back.

"Pip," Evan hisses, "what are you doing?"

"Wait a minute, there's something here," I murmur, and being brave, I stretch my hand until I feel something matted but soft, and then I grab it and pull it out into the light. My mouth drops open when I realise the tiny thing in my hand is a puppy, a baby feral. It looks like a cross between a German Shepherd and a Husky, with big brown eyes, a wet nose, two big, droopy ears, and thick fur. Its little cry comes again as it wiggles in my grip, and my heart instantly shatters. I can't help but pull it against my chest and cuddle it.

"Shh, baby, it's okay, you're safe." I look down, stroking its back as it wiggles to get closer. "Oh my gosh, you are the cutest little thing! Look at your large eyes and these huge paws for such a tiny baby," I coo, and when I look around, I see the guys glancing from the puppy to me.

"Oh fuck, I know that look." Evan groans as he drops his head back. "It's the same look she got when she adopted me."

"It's all alone," I whine, and Jago snorts.

"It's probably got a mum around here somewhere." He gazes around doubtfully, noticing the endless stretch of wasteland on either side of us. "Shit, Brawler, what are we going to do with a puppy?"

I notice the blood and claw marks on the tunnel leading away, and then put two and two together. "I think its mum put it in here while she was hurt."

"Probably ferals." Archel sighs. "It is cute."

"Yes, you are. We can't leave you here alone, can we, Beast Jr.?" I coo down at it as it yips happily.

"Beast Jr.?" Jago repeats painfully, while Clay laughs and comes over, petting the puppy gently for such a big guy.

"He can be our good luck mascot," Archel offers.

"Beast Jr., Brawler?" Jago sighs loudly.

I hold it up against my face, both of us staring at him. "He has your eyes," I reply.

"Dear fucking God," he snaps. "Fine, keep the puppy, but I'm not cleaning up after the thing."

I cuddle him closer. "Don't you listen to Daddy, Beast baby, he's just mardy unless I'm touching his cock. Yes, he is! Oh yes, he is," I coo, and they all laugh as we head back to our bikes with the newest member of our crew held safely in my arms, nipping at my fingers.

Chapter 5
Disappearing Act

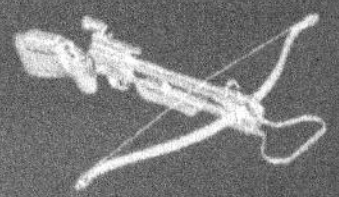

We tuck Beast Jr. into a shirt and strap it to Jago, who holds him as he drives, even if he does throw me glares. We don't stop anymore, heading right for the hospital. We find the signs on what used to be the motorway and pull off, driving until the huge building rises out of the sand like a beacon. I stop and look around for a place we can watch from. Archel points at an old store front. The door is covered in sand, but we pull around the side and conceal our bikes as he heads to investigate. When he comes back, he smiles.

"It's a good spot. Come on, Princess." He grabs my hand, and I follow with my bag. He's kicked in the front door, but Jago slides it shut behind us, and as we wait, he sets down a string with cans tied to it to alert us in case anyone tries to get in. Evan drops the huge bottle of water there as we head up the dusty, creaky stairs, not wanting to carry it up.

We find a few open doorways, but he leads me to the one on the left, which opens into an empty-ish room. There's an old, dirty mattress pressed up against one wall, but the best bit is the huge windows looking out over the hospital. "Yep, we'll stay here tonight.

Archel, set up the sniper." He kisses me and goes to do just that as I check the floor for anything that might harm Beast Jr.

"Okay, he can come down."

"Thank fuck," Jago mutters and places the puppy on the floor. He instantly starts running around, sniffing everything as I explore the other rooms. There is a bathroom with no sink or toilet, just an old, filthy bath and rusted taps. There's another bedroom with an actual bedframe, all wood and half snapped and broken, but no mattress. That's it. I try the taps, but they groan, and a moment later, brown liquid spits out, so I quickly turn them off and grab my water bottle instead and place it on the side.

Heading into the other room, I grab Beast Jr., kissing and fussing over him while placing him in the bath before kneeling at his side. "It's okay, baby, let's get you clean," I coo and carefully start to clean him, tipping the water bottle and working it into his fur.

It takes me a good hour to get him clean, and then I dry him with Jago's shirt and leave him to nap on my bag while I sit down with the others. Jago is at the window, looking through the scope, while Evan checks over our supplies and Archel naps, sitting against the wall with his eyes closed, but I know he's listening to everything.

"Anything?" I ask Jago as I sit down and watch him.

"Nothing yet," he murmurs, then glances back. "Front doors are closed, no sign of movement in any windows. Seems structurally safe." He looks over at his wet shirt and narrows his eyes. "Brawler," he growls.

"Yes, baby?" I reply sweetly, blinking at him.

He throws me a glare and then returns to observing as I grin at Evan, who just shakes his head at me. "One day, he's going to kill you, Pip."

"Nah, he likes my pussy too much," I tease, and Jago snorts.

"And she keeps him from being a mardy serial killer," Archel scoffs.

"She will be the reason I become a serial killer if she carries on," Jago mutters.

"Asshole," I retort as I lift my puppy into my lap and cuddle him. "Your daddy is an asshole."

"Which one?" Evan grins, and I wink at him.

"Not you right now, you're pretty," I murmur as we relax.

We pass the hours by talking and swapping roles for keeping watch. I'm up next, and after a few hours, Clay relieves me and Jago passes around the food. We don't make a fire, which would give away our position as the sun sets.

When I nip to the toilet, I come back to find Jago loving on the puppy, and I point in his face. "Ah-ha! I knew it!"

He glares at me and passes me the dog and huffs, leaving me grinning down at him.

"I knew he loved you already, just you wait."

I get out my bedroll and tuck my puppy in at my side as I lie down and relax, but I can't sleep. I'm too excited for tomorrow and what we might find, so after a while, I give up and sit upright. Clay is watching me, Jago is asleep, Archel too, and Evan is on the rifle.

I run my gaze over Clay. His mask is off, his kissable lips are on display, and his eyes are locked on me.

I keep my eyes on him as he slowly grins at me. "Need something, Pascha?"

"You," I answer honestly.

His eyes widen, and I stand, checking on the others before I extend my hand to him. He follows it up to my face and then takes it, getting to his feet. I lead him silently from the room.

"Pascha," he murmurs, and I grin over at him.

"Shh, big guy," I hush, as I open the door to the other room, drag him in, and then kick it shut behind us.

Smiling at him in the dark, I yank off my shirt and throw it on the wooden bedframe.

Clay groans, running his eyes across me hungrily. "Pascha, we don't have to—"

"Shut up." I grin and push him into the wall, reaching for his trousers. "I want you," I murmur and lean up onto my tiptoes. I kiss his chin until his head tilts down. He gives in and kisses me back. A growl vibrates through him as his hands come down, grip my ass, and lift me. Giggling against his lips, I wrap my legs around his waist as he turns and presses me to the wall. His huge muscles make me gasp as his fingers drag up my side and grip my breast in a hard, sure action. His tongue sweeps into my mouth and tangles with mine, dominating my mouth until he pulls back on a pant.

"You'll have to stay quiet, my queen. We are on a mission, after all," he rumbles, leaning down. My eyes roll back into my head as he sucks one of my nipples between his lips. I groan, the sensation of his wet mouth through the fabric causing me to rub against him.

The idea that we can be caught any minute by enemies has me wet as hell and grinding against him like a cat in heat. I want to blurt out all the very inappropriate things that come to mind, but like he knows, he lifts his hand and covers my mouth.

He grins against my skin as he drags his lips across my chest to my other nipple, tweaking it and giving it the same treatment before he pulls my bra down. I lick his hand as he chuckles.

"Either fuck me, or I'm going to start singing really loudly," I mumble, but his palm obscures my words. His head lifts, and he pulls his hand away.

"What was that, Pascha?" he asks, his hard body pressing against me. His other hand slides up my thigh and cups my pussy possessively.

"Fuck me," I murmur. His smile turns dangerous, his eyes flashing at me, reminding me of the wild mountain man he is.

"As you command, my pascha," he rumbles.

Without hesitation, he squeezes my pussy before pulling away and turning me around. My legs drop to the floor, and the side of my head rests against the wall. He presses his body against my back, letting me feel the strong thump of his heart and the solid, hard length of his cock as his big hands pull my legs apart, stroking and squeezing my thighs. His lips brush my ear. "Is this okay?"

I almost fucking cry with how sweet it is. This giant mountain man, my rough lover, is checking if it's okay. They all know what happened to me, and even now, in the throes of passion, he's checking in. It makes me relax that last inch, and I give myself over to him, knowing I'll enjoy whatever he does. My smart retort disappears under his rough touches and the promise of his body against mine.

"Yes," I whisper, knowing he needs verbal confirmation.

As soon as it leaves my lips, he bites my ear hard, tugging it as his hands glide up my ass to my waistband. He yanks my pants down over my ass and thighs, then he releases my lobe as I stifle my moan while he pulls them off one leg. He kicks open my legs, keeping me off balance, and my hands go to the wall.

"Hold on, baby girl," he murmurs, and I swear my fucking pussy gushes at that endearment. Be still, my beating vagina. I don't know who he heard it from, but he can call me that any-fucking- time. His fingers trace the edge of my panties, and knowing they are hard to come by, he pulls them off instead of ripping them.

A true fucking panty hero.

His fingers stroke my thigh, all the way up, until he cups my bare pussy. He applies pressure, making me grind into his touch. He has to feel how wet I am, I'm practically dripping, yet there are no cocky remarks, just pure lust for my feral mountain man.

His thick fingers drag down my folds, back and forth, teasing me before he parts my lips, and a moment later, I feel warm air blow across my sex. I can't help but close my eyes and lean into the wall, my knees weak.

"Clay," I whisper, and hearing his name on my lips seems to spur him on.

He flicks my clit, making me groan, before his lips are suddenly there, wrapping around the nub and sucking. There is no finesse, no cocky, sure teasing. He wants to give me pleasure, so he does.

What you see is what you get. His thick fingers trail down my sex, coated in my cream, then press against my entrance. As he pulls back, he nips my clit, then lashes it with his tongue, slowly thrusting his fingers inside of me. Clay stretches me to the point of delicious pain as I lift up with a groan and start to ride them, unashamedly chasing my release. His tongue never relents, I don't even know how he's breathing, but if he dies, at least he did it while doing something worthwhile.

Death by pussy.

His other hand grips my thigh, digging into my flesh to the point of pain. Those thick fingers twist inside me, stroking my walls, demanding my pleasure, pulling cries from my throat. He never stops, never gives up. He adds another finger and fucks me with them hard and fast as he alternates between lashing my clit with his tongue and nipping at it, until finally, I come with a yell. He surges to his feet, pulling his fingers free of my fluttering chan- nel, and covers my mouth. Shuddering against him, I almost fall as my legs give out, but he holds me up, and wave after wave of plea- sure storms through me.

When I stop shaking, he starts to pull his fingers away from me, but I grab hold of them and suck them clean, and he groans in my ear, grinding into my ass. "Inside of me, now," I mumble as I pull them from my mouth. He wastes no time, gripping my hips and yanking my ass out. My eyes close as I shiver with desire, my stomach clenching and pussy pulsing in aftershocks as I hear a zip, and then the huge head of his cock presses against my entrance.

He rests his head against mine, and from one breath to the next, he thrusts inside me. He isn't slow or soft, no, he slams his huge cock into me, forcing me to take it. A groan leaves my lips and my hips jerk from the force, but he keeps me there, pulling me back and impaling me on it before sliding out and slamming in. The wet slap of our bodies is loud in the quiet room. The others must be able to hear us, but I don't care, not with his breath on my back, his hands on my skin, and his fucking monster dick destroying my pussy like Worth in a sword fight.

I try to keep the noises inside, I really do, as he plunges in and out of me, pulling me farther out. He effortlessly holds me with his strength, hitting that spot inside me. He releases my hips and then tugs my hair sharply, making me cry out.

"Oh fuck."

He slides his hands down my arms and grips mine, holding them as he powers into me. It's too much, he's too big, too fucking good. A loud moan slips free. Without missing a beat, he releases my hand and covers my mouth again, giving me something to bite into.

I can feel my release building again, my greedy pussy clenching around his cock as I try to breathe through his hand. He moves closer, pinning me to the wall as he pistons in and out of me, his low groans spurring me on. I bite down on his palm, and he snarls and slams into me, grinding his cock, and it throws me off the edge once again.

I scream, the sound muffled as I explode around him. My pussy clamps and drags Clay's own orgasm from him. A low groan fills my ear as his hips stutter, and I feel his release fill me.

Panting, he leans against me as we both try to catch our breaths. The feel of his trembling body has me smiling widely against his hand. To know this big, bad warrior is weak because of me is a heady feeling. When we have recovered a little, he pulls out of my body, making me whimper. He turns me and grips my chin, forcing me to open my eyes, and then he leans down and kisses me.

"Forever, my pascha," is all he rumbles, but my heart does a somersault, and I go weak in the knees...again.

If they could bottle Clay, we would be fucking rich as hell.

After cleaning up and getting dressed, Clay follows me back to the other room, both of us grinning from ear to ear. Satisfaction and pleasure wind through me.

"Wait, where's Evvie?" I ask with a frown, looking around.

"He went to get some water," Jago replies, tugging on a string with Beast Jr. He lifts his head and frowns. "He should be back by now."

"I'll go look, Princess," Archel offers and kisses my cheek, trooping down the stairs. A moment later, he rushes back up, his eyes narrowed and his lips tilted down. "Don't freak out, Piper."

"What? Is he okay?" I almost yell, stepping closer, my hand going to my weapon.

He swallows. "He's gone. There's a blood trail outside and other footprints. Our can string was cut, we didn't even hear them. Someone took Evan."

My heart sinks, and then we all burst into action.

Chapter 6
Vegetarian

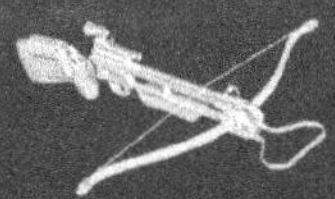

Evan is gone.

It's pitch-black outside, but Jago easily tracks the footprints. Archel forces me to stay inside with him to watch the scope and Jago's back as Clay accompanies him. Within a few minutes, they are back, wearing grim expressions. I can't stop pacing, wondering what's happening to Evan.

He's not a fighter.

Who took him and why? Don't they know The Nations' laws by now? Surely it has to be outlaws or bandits, which means we've stumbled into their camp or they have been tracking us. My mind refuses to stop until Jago grips my chin and forces me to look into his eyes.

"He's strong. Stop giving up on him already, Brawler." With that, he pulls me into his arms and carries on talking. "The tracks stop at the entrance to the hospital. Looks like we were wrong— people are clearly living in there, and they must have spotted us. We are going to have to go in and get him."

"Did you see him?" I ask hopefully.

I pull back as Clay and Jago share a look over my head. Jago sighs and nods as Clay steps forward. "Pascha, there were signs they might be cannibals."

My heart stops in my chest, and my body turns cold as I stare at him. "What do you mean?"

"There were skulls outside, rib cages and skeletons hung in warning, and blood everywhere. We even found discarded skin," he tells me soulfully.

I pull at my hair before spinning and smashing my fist into the wall. "Fuck! Get your guns, we have to go—"

"We will," Jago interjects, "but we'll go in smart. Evan can survive until we do, he's clever. Trust in that. But if we rush in guns blazing, we won't save him, and we'll end up dying ourselves. Get your weapons. Archel, lock the puppy in here with some water, he will be okay. We are going to go in silently and move through the bowels of the hospital until we find Evan. Understood?"

Right now, I'm glad for my beast because I'm too worried to think straight. He leans in and kisses my cheek like he knows my thoughts as I twist my shaking hands. I close my eyes for a moment to try and push back the fear surging through me, making my stomach roll. I have to focus and be smart, or Jago is right—my own fear will make us lose Evan.

Hang on, Evvie. I'm coming.

Breathing slowly to calm my racing heart, I methodically grab my weapons and start to strap them on. I add as many as I can carry, knowing if there are cannibals in there, then they aren't going down without a fight. Clay covers himself in bombs and slips his mask on. Archel and Jago are covered head to toe, and we make sure our clothing is dark. We even put on my pascha makeup to conceal my pale skin, and I wind my hair back so it won't get caught or be used against me. Once I'm ready, I close my eyes for a second and then turn.

"Let's go get Evvie," I order, my voice sharp, but it does nothing to hide the fear in my tone. It doesn't fool my men, but they say nothing, loyally following me. I lock up Beast Jr. after putting some food and water down, hoping we return, otherwise he will die up here. I pat him goodbye, and his whine follows me as I shut the door and troop downstairs.

We don't take the bikes, since we need to stay silent. "There has to be another way into the hospital other than the front door," I murmur as we move noiselessly across the sand, my boots slipping slightly on the dunes. Lights flicker on inside, shining through the broken, taped up windows, letting us know there are definitely people in there. They were either just hiding or not giving away their position.

Now, they don't care, and I don't know if that's a bad thing or a good thing.

"I overheard a lot of Evvie's studies. There should be a mortuary entrance behind it, or at least a loading bay door," I mutter.

"Then let's go around," Jago suggests, and before we reach the open, flat land leading up to the hospital, we circle to the left, avoiding the spotlights that were turned on. We can see a fire burning on the roof, and as we draw closer, we hear laughter and yelling coming from inside. We all share a look, knowing that means there are more than three people there, maybe even more than ten.

Shit, how many cannibals are there?

There is a fence to the side, and we have to keep going, trying to find a hole. Just when we are about to give up, we spot an opening in the fence. I pull my crossbow, and we all crouch and duck through the hole before following the downward slope. It leads into a small parking bay, where there is an abandoned ambulance. Its back doors are open, and it has a blood trail leading into the rear and gore covering it.

Lovely.

To the right is what looks like sliding glass doors. The glass is gone, of course, but the frame remains, leading to two dark blue wooden doors that have two very distinct bloody handprints on them. There's a light above that flickers on and off, buzzing with electricity. Jago goes first, pressing his back to the left door. Archel grabs the handle, and with a nod at Jago, he rips it open and we rush in, all taking different parts of the hallway. There are no doors or anywhere to hide, just a long corridor with what looks like a bank of elevators at the bottom and an entryway. There's a long, fresh, bloody drag mark leading down, criss-crossing over older, nearly black blood.

Shit, is that Evan's?

My stomach rolls, and I carefully step over it, not wanting to touch it as we move quickly to the end. Once there, we ignore the elevators, looking at our options. To the left is an open door with stairs, and to the right is a room that says 'Morgue.'

"Which way?" I whisper.

The bloody trail stops here. There are only a few droplets across the once white floor, letting me know the person must have been picked up. But were they taken to the stairs or morgue?

We can't split up, not with cannibals here. I won't lose another of my men, but if we spend hours searching, it could mean the difference between Evvie's life or death. Jago debates what to do, looking around before he turns to the morgue. "Let's check down here first, since it's the closest point to the blood."

Trusting his judgement, we follow him, all of us ready to face whatever is on the other side of the door. Luckily, the fear of the unknown keeps me on my feet and stops me from being a worried mess.

The door's electric lock has been broken, and with the barrel of his gun, Archel pushes it open for Jago to slide through. I slip in after him, refusing to wait, and luckily, no one shoots us. It's hard to see, though, and my eyes strain into the almost pitch-black space. It looks like an entryway, with a hallway to the left and doors leading off of it. There's more blood here, and skulls and bones litter the floor. When my vision finally adjusts, I almost gag—there are skins pinned to the wall.

Human fucking skins.

Their baggy eye sockets and open mouths make me turn away in horror. How long have they been killing, eating, and skinning people?

How many innocents have died here? My Evvie won't turn out like that.

Moving across the floor, we carefully follow Jago's path, avoiding bones and bits of chairs and tables left over so we don't make a sound. The hallway stretches on, but the door at the end is half pushed open, and from inside, we hear grunts and see the flicker of flames.

We manoeuvre down the hallway, with Jago in the lead, me in the middle, and Clay and Archel taking up the rear to protect our backs. Once we reach the doorway, we listen carefully. There is a loud sound, almost like chopping. As metal hits wood, I panic, pushing Jago back and sliding through the door. I freeze, bile rising in my throat as my blood runs cold.

There's a giant man with his back to me, and it takes me a few seconds for me to process what he's doing. He's swinging a cleaver down on what looks like meat, then tossing it into a barrel next to him, which is overflowing with scraps and gore. The scent of death and coppery blood makes me gag, but when I spot the hand falling off the table, I realise what he is cutting up.

Humans.

With a snarl, he reaches down and grabs it, slamming it onto the table before he continues to slice into it like Jago does his apple. Blood flies everywhere, and sweat pours from him. To his left is what I'm guessing used to be a cremation oven, but now it just holds a fire with a spit roast over the table. Every surface is covered with severed limbs, heads—fuck, I even spot hips. I almost throw up, but I swallow it down. I remain frozen to the spot, unable to register the horrors that have happened in this room. To my right is an empty, once silver slab with a partially chopped up human. His head is turned this way, his dead eyes are filled with blood, and his skin is almost blue.

Fuck.

A gagged scream has me looking to the left, and my eyes widen when I see Evan tied to a table. He's struggling against his restraints. His hands are tied above his head, and his legs are spread on a fucking mortuary table, ready to be chopped up and eaten. His shirt is missing, and his pants are bloody, but he seems okay. The cannibal has his back to me, and the sound of him butchering the body parts must have masked my entrance. I press a finger to my lips as Evan's eyes swivel around before coming back to me. He nods his head in understanding and quiets down. I crouch behind the closest table as the cannibal turns, throwing meat over the metal spike in the oven. I gaze through the crack in the door, shaking my head at the others and giving them the wait symbol. If they rush in now, we can't guarantee Evan's safety. I need to untie him first and be as sneaky as we can about it. These aren't the type of people to fuck around.

When he goes back to his manwich, I begin to creep along the floor, keeping my breathing quiet and sliding my feet across the blood-soaked tiles. It's slow going, and I have to freeze whenever he turns around to roast his meat, but I'm nearly there. My foot slips in a patch of blood, and my boot slips out, knocking into a wheeled table. It clanks as it rolls towards Evvie, stopping near the table he's tied to.

My eyes widen, and I grip my crossbow tighter as the chopping sound stops. Oh fuck, oh fuck. I can almost feel his gaze sweeping across the room before I hear footsteps as he heads around the table.

I freeze, and Evan starts to yell against the gag, making noise to cover my blunder. The footsteps stop and retreat for a moment. "Shut up!" he snarls, the sound giving me goosebumps. It's halfway between animal and human.

A few seconds later, the chopping starts again, and I relax. This time, I hurry. I rush those last few feet to Evvie and stand. Keeping my eyes on the cannibal, I start to untie his feet. His blue eyes are wide and panicked, and he turns his head to look at the door and back to me as if telling me to go.

This fucking moron.

When both feet are undone, I move to his head, my hands slipping on the bloody rope. It takes me a while to get one undone, then I have to reach over him to get the other. "Hold on," I murmur so quietly that it's barely audible.

Fuck, this one is even tighter. I struggle with the fraying strands, the table almost rocking from my movements. My gaze is locked on it, my breaths coming out faster and faster.

I've just finished untying the last rope when Evan's hands jerk up and rip out the gag. "Behind you!" he screams. I turn and duck just in time as the cleaver comes down on the table where my hand just was.

I fall back to the floor, staring up at the cannibal. His teeth are spiked, his head is shaved, and his eyes are sunken and dark. His face and body are splattered with blood, but it's the madness, the utter hunger and insanity across his face that makes me swallow.

"Hi, don't suppose you're a vegetarian?" I squeak out.

Chapter 7
Cannibal Party

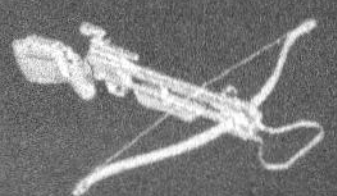

He roars and lunges at me. Panicking, I kick the rolling trolley at him and leap to my feet. The cleaver swings down again as Evan gets up, and I roll over the table until we're both on the other side, facing off with him.

I hear grunts and signs of combat from the hallway, and realise the others are probably fighting more cannibals, hence the lack of their presence.

Okay then, time to boss this.

"Guess not?" I grin as I grab the edge of the table. "I like meat, trust me, but I'm too skinny to eat, motherfucker, so eat this instead." I shove the table hard, and it smashes into him, pushing him back against the wall.

I leap over it while he's struggling, grab the cleaver, and slice upward. He howls as he blocks with his hand, his fingers severing. I ignore his other hand, which is trying to grab me, and kick his cock until he falls. Then, in one smooth move, I slice again, almost cleaving his head from his body. Leaving the blade stuck in his throat, I kick him back to the floor to die before looking over at Evan.

"You're my princess now, I rescued you." I wink.

He shakes his head, untying the rest of his restraints and coming around the table. Evan looks me over. "Are you okay?"

"I should be asking you that," I counter.

"I'm fine. Fuckers knocked me out while I was getting water, and I woke up in here. Pip, there are more of them, a lot more. They were upstairs...playing with humans. I heard it."

I nod just as the door smashes open and all three of my other men step through. "Nice of you to join us," I joke. "Sorry you missed the buffet."

"Oh God, stop with the puns." Jago groans. "You okay, Pasha?" Clay asks.

I nod and grab my crossbow. "Let's get the fuck out of here." I step closer to them, and Archel sighs.

"Might be a problem. They've blocked the door, so it looks like the only way out is up."

"Great," I mutter. "Looks like we are attending a cannibal party."

Checking my bolt is still loaded, I ready myself. "Let's do this."

I push past them, stepping over the five new bodies in the hallway. Once back in the entryway, I see what they mean. They have blocked the hallway to the back exit off by crashing the fucking ambulance into it. There's no way we are getting through.

So upstairs it is.

Smart little fucking cannibals, thinking they have trapped their food.

They are damned though.

Heading to the stairs, I keep my crossbow up as I turn the corner and aim. There is no one there, just more bloody marks leading up the stairs, as well as some nipples and penises pinned to the wall. Lovely. That can't be hygienic at all. Watching the top of the stairs, I continue to ascend, going slowly. Jago is at my side, Evan is in the middle with Clay, and Archel watches our backs from the bottom door until I reach the top. I glance at Jago and nod. He crouches and peers around the corner before looking back.

"Clear," he murmurs.

I follow him around the corner. It's another hallway with a ripped off door at the end. We press ourselves to the wall and peek around the frame. It's darker here, with only a few low fires burning in what looks like a reception area. There are banks of elevators to the right with handwritten signs saying 'Death Ride' and more stairs leading up.

There's an overturned desk in the middle of the entrance with chairs scattered everywhere, and even a broken vending machine. The walls are covered in blood and drawings and body parts, the floor is dirty and stained, and the tiles are peeling away. There are even a few holes in the ceiling that make me worry this whole place is about to come down.

The worst bit though?

The double front doors are chained and blocked off. There's no way we are getting out of them without alerting the cannibals and being killed. No, we need another way out. "Any ideas?" I whisper to Jago as he searches for an exit too.

"It seems we have to go up again. It's a hospital, they have to have more than one exit," he mutters. "We'll find it, but until then, we stay quiet and move silently. Don't draw their attention, we are not becoming their food."

I nod, and we slide out together, moving along the wall to the stairs as a group. Once there, I swing my arm out, stilling Jago as he goes to step around the corner.

"What?" he whispers, but I press my finger to my lips and kneel, pointing out the tripwire.

It's thin, really thin, almost too small to see, but it runs across the bottom of the doorframe. I peek around the corner to the wide double stairs, but I see no one, so I'm betting it's an alert system like ours.

Standing, I step over it, and when nothing happens, I look up, searching for the trigger. It's attached to the ceiling through a hole... and it looks like a fucking guillotine. It's not a warning system, it's a fucking booby trap.

Brilliant.

I gesture for them to follow me, and they do. We head up the stairs slowly, looking for any more wires or traps. When we reach the top and there aren't any, I open the door, wincing at the creak, but no one leaps out, so that's good.

I sigh as I look around. It's the upstairs balcony, and across the way are more stairs. The flooring is holey in some places and utterly filthy with clothes, burnt out fires, and body parts tossed everywhere. I slide my feet over the floor, and I'm halfway across when what I thought was a clothes pile moves. My eyes widen, but Archel is faster.

Within a second, he's on the cannibal, who is turning to us. He snaps his neck, lowers him back down, and covers him before he moves back to my side.

"That was hot," I murmur and then keep going, hating being out in the open. When we reach the stairs, I don't spot any more traps, so I guide them to the open doorway at the top. It feels wrong to be going deeper into the belly of the beast, but we don't have much choice.

This one is a full floor, with open doors to the left and right. It looks like a ward. I don't hear anyone, but that doesn't mean anything. Some of the lights are flickering, though, and I spot the door saying 'Fire Exit' across the way. Bingo! After pointing it out to the others, I slowly begin to move in that direction. I scan the area for any more cannibals disguised or ready to eat us.

I'm about halfway across when the floor starts to feel weak under my feet. I still, staring down at the floor with more holes in it than the rest. Probably from time, weather, and treatment. I slow down and slide my feet, not wanting to fall to my death.

That would suck.

My breathing seems loud up here, yet we are silent. I really hope this exit is an actual exit and we can get free of this cannibal labyrinth. I've just stepped out when the floor caves under me. I throw myself back, but the hole grows until I'm dangling through it, my legs kicking in mid-air. Jago catches me, and I pant as I gaze down…

Right into the eyes of a cannibal in a fur coat, wearing a crown made of fingers, who is sitting on the floor beneath us on a fucking throne made of skulls. He stares at me, I stare back.

Awkward.

"Erm, hi, we came for the party?" I squeak out.

His head tips back, and he lets out an inhuman screech. I hear it ricochet around the building, waking all of the cannibals.

I guess it's party time.

Chapter 8
Yippee-Ki-Yay Motherfucker

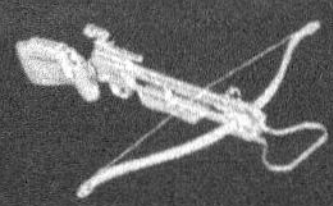

I scramble back through the roof, just as a spear is thrown in my direction, narrowly missing me as I fall into Jago. "Oops, guess they are ready for the three-course meal."

"Yeah, which course are you?" Evan queries nervously as he checks me over.

Archel and Clay prepare as we hear the thundering footsteps and yelling of the cannibals as they run up the stairs. Clay sets a tripwire bomb while Archel blocks off the other entrance.

"Dessert, obviously," I scoff as I leap to my feet, ignoring his complaints. I look around in confusion and start to panic. Where the fuck is my crossbow? Then I see it hanging from a rusted nail in the hole in the floor, dangling down right in front of the gap where the cannibal king is waiting.

Shit.

I hear a smash, and when I look around, cannibals are breaking through the door Archel is guarding. Jago snarls and rushes over, adding his weight and holding them back. A hand slips through the door, its dirty, black bloody nails scratching as it wiggles around.

With a growl, Jago and Archel work together and slam the door shut—right on the hand. There's a scream, and I look over to see Clay lighting sticks and throwing them down the stairs with a grin. I hear a bang and know he's holding them back.

But there are a lot of them. We need to get out of here. There is no other exit...apart from down.

Fuck it. I throw myself on the floor, crawl to the edge, and peek over. The king is still there, staring up at me, but I need my bow.

Hooking my finger through the strap, I wiggle it from the nail, my arm muscles straining. I hear a yell, and two seconds later, something whizzes through the air, grazing the top of my ear. Hiss- ing, I look down to see the king firing arrows at me...arrows of bone. I gag but focus on the crossbow. I tug and wiggle, my legs kicking on the dirty floor to give me more power. My face turns red and my ears ring with the force as he fires again. I have to duck, and then I yank the crossbow free.

Taking aim, I kneel and fire back at him. It connects, and he spits with a snarl, thrown into the throne with the force. He scrabbles at his chest where the bolt is protruding from his shoulder area. Gripping my weapon tighter, I look around for a way out. They are coming through the door, and more are surging to Clay, where Evan is now also throwing bombs.

We have no choice.

I glance back at my men and grin. "Going down?" I ask politely.

"Don't you dare," Jago yells.

I wink and look at the hole, ignoring their protests. "As soon as I'm through, run for it. I'll take on this fucker down here. Clay, throw as many bombs as you can. Evan, let's go," I order, and when they all nod, I strap my crossbow on, grip one of my stolen knives from Archel in my hand, and slip it into the leather to keep it there before I hook my hands on the edges of the tile and swing through.

I need to move fast before the king fucker recovers and tries to eat me, so I swing back and forth, lowering myself to the balcony as far as I can. When I hear him snarl, I drop.

I land on my feet and roll to prevent breaking my ankle. I pull the knife free as I roll, and when I come up, I swing as he lurches at me with a roar. I hear a crash and a swear and know Evan is through. I listen as more bombs and yells sound, and then I hear running above us before the clap of three more sets of feet land behind me.

But I ignore them, leaving them to deal with the cannibals above and any more around us as I focus on the king.

He throws his head back, and a howl escapes his lips, showing his sharpened black teeth, black mouth, and bloody lips and chin. Taking my opportunity, I rush him. When I stab him, the knife gets stuck, and I have to yank it out, but it still sticks. Fuck. He looks down at me, his mouth closing, and my eyes widen. He backhands me, and I'm flung to the side. I hear the others shout as I roll across the floor, nearly tumbling off the balcony, where half of the railing is ripped away before I jump to my feet, panting.

"I've got this bitch," I snarl, flashing the now bloodstained knife which he yanked free by the force of his hit.

With a war cry, I fly at him, dropping to my knees at the last minute and sliding right through his parted legs. I slice as I go, cutting across his knees. He stumbles with a roar, and I slash his ankles and then get to my feet before throwing myself on his back. He stumbles forward but stays upright, starting to spin with a growl as he tries to throw me off. I hold on, ducking my head when his hand comes back and swats at me. I ignore his disgusting stench, which is burrowing into my nose as it presses against—Fuck, is that a human skin cape?

He spins, and I almost throw up from the rapid pace, but then suddenly, we feel weightless. I lift my head as we tumble over the edge of the balcony. I reach out desperately, and my hand connects with part of the railing which is broken and hanging over the edge. I hold on tight, my fingers slipping on the rusted metal as we fall another inch. Our bodies dangle in the air as I scream, his hand wrapping around my ankle. The added weight makes the railing creak. Looking down, I snarl as he bites my ankle. He's trying to climb up my body, my grasp slipping down the metal from our combined weight. I can't hold us both.

Fucking cannibal.

I look to the ground below us, which is at least a fifty-foot drop. We won't survive it, so it's time to dethrone this king. I kick and kick, but he avoids it. I scream as my hand slips farther, almost to the end of the broken railing. I hear my men trying to get to me, but they are fighting their own battles. I need to save myself. With renewed vigour, I slam my foot down and connect with his face. Time seems to freeze as his hand loses its grip and he starts to fall. I watch, hanging there as he hits the ground with a sickening crunch, blood blossoming around him.

"Yippee-ki-yay, motherfucker," I call.

Turning back, I reach up, trying to pull myself up the railing. It's slow going, and I slip a few times before I near the cracked, crumbling edge of the balcony and grab it with my other hand. I start to pull myself up when suddenly there is a hand before me. I look up into Evan's terrified eyes and release the railing. I swallow my nerves as I hang from one hand for a moment before, with a grunt, I swing my other aching arm up and grab his hand. He tightens his hold and then yanks me over the edge and into his arms. His hands run down my body as I pant and shake from adrenaline, his eyes flickering between mine in fear.

"Are you okay?" he rushes out. "Awesome," I croak out.

"Good! Find us a way out, Princess!" Archel yells, and I look over to see the cannibals jumping through the opening, right on top of my men. They are winning, but there are too many, and they are starting to become overwhelmed.

Shit.

Time to go.

I leap to my feet, as does Evan, while my mind whirls, trying to find us an exit. Spinning around, I spot a door in the corner. My heart leaps as I look back at my men and grin, grab my crossbow, and start to fire into the horde while backing up at the same time.

"Got the exit! Let's go, boys, dinner is over!"

Chapter 9
Sick Bitch

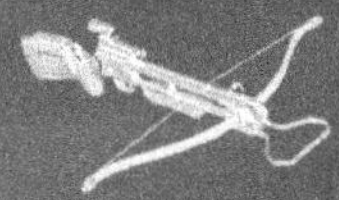

We rush down the stairs, firing into the throng of cannibals who are chasing us. Loading another bolt, I shoot and almost trip before righting myself and reaching the door. We smash through it and come out on the other side. Carts had been placed in front of it, which was why we probably didn't see it before. We step out next to the elevators in the entryway.

Fuck.

I rush to the front, slinging my crossbow over my shoulder as I tug on the chains. I ignore the snarls and shouts, trying to find us a way out. It's locked up tight, though, and without a key or a fucking chainsaw, we're trapped.

I glance over my shoulder to see my men backing towards me. They're still fighting, but the tide of cannibals is getting stronger. We are trapped. Licking my lips, I look around, but this is it, there's no other way out. We're out of time and options.

Apart from one. Fight.

We're strong, but there are a lot of them. We have no choice but to defeat them, however, because this is not where my men and I die.

We have a puppy to get back to and lots of sex to have. Swinging my crossbow around, I start firing into the masses.

"We are trapped. Fighting it is, boys!" I call.

I hear them swear, and with renewed vigour, they begin to attack. I hear Evan hiss in pain, and then Archel is up on a barrel, fighting and swinging while laughing crazily. Jago rips through them, as feral as they are. Evan holds his own, helping Clay toss bombs and taking out as many as they can.

It still won't be enough, so I draw my sword and rush in. Spinning and slicing, I listen to Worth's voice in my head, and I let my movements flow. I block out everything apart from my instincts, ducking and weaving, avoiding snapping jaws, teeth, and weapons as I take out as many as I can.

The surge increases, pushing us back. We are losing, but that can't fucking happen. We are not the damned, we are the damners. We won't die here, we will die of old age together on the road—or maybe from too much sex, I'm good with either.

"Not today, bitches," I snarl in one of their faces before I stab them through the heart, spinning to pull my blade free. I quickly look around as a plan comes to mind, a crazy plan. It's totally insane, utterly batshit...and it might just work.

"Trust me!" I scream as I rush towards Clay. I grab one of his three sticks and grin at him. "Get that elevator door open." He frowns, but without question, he fights his way to the elevators while I hold the cannibals back.

"Elevator!" I yell at the others. "Now!"

"Brawler," Jago shouts in warning and fights to my side. I hear a whistle and glance back to see Clay has it open. Thank fuck the actual elevator is still there, though a bit dirty. He tugs Evan in, and Archel stands at the entrance, fighting off those who have noticed. I light the match and toss the explosives at the front door.

Jago groans, grabs me, and tosses me over his shoulder as he barges through the cannibals. Some rush at the bomb, others try to keep pace with us, but Jago is too fast. He throws us into the elevator, and Archel rushes in after us. Clay slams the metal doors just as the explosion rocks through the room.

We hear crashing as screams and chunks of cannibals hit the door. Panting, I sit up and look around.

Clay grins. "That was incredible, Pascha."

Evan glares. "It was insane, Pip. What the hell?"

I shrug and get to my feet, looking them over. They have a few wounds, nothing too serious. We wait another minute before I nod, and then Jago and Clay pry open the doors and we look out. Some are still alive, hurt but alive. Some are missing limbs, and some are completely blown to smithereens. There is blood and gore everywhere.

The front doors are also blown open, and there are black scorch marks all over. Fuck, it worked. I can't believe it.

Jago and Archel step out and start finishing off those who are still alive. I help, and within ten minutes, all of the cannibals are dead. We are left standing in the massacre, panting, exhausted, and covered in blood and parts of people we don't think too hard about.

Evan joins me, and I look him over. "You okay?" I ask. "Peachy," he mutters as he gazes around and pales. "Fuck, I feel

sick."

"Really? I'm hungry," I remark.

He turns to me, his eyes widening in disbelief. "You can't be serious, Pip!" he hollers as the others join us.

"I am! It's like when we used to watch those zombie films, it made me hungry." I grin.

He gags and spins away. "Jesus, you're a sick bitch."

"Yup." I lean in and kiss his cheek. "And you're stuck with me." "Fucking hell, let's get those supplies and get out of here," Jago

grumbles, and I nod.

"Stay alert, there could be more. We go together, in and out," Archel adds.

"Let's do it! Let's go, Power Rangers!" I yell, and when I see their blank expressions, I sigh, realising they have probably never watched TV. "I have so much to teach you, padawan."

Archel was right—we find some cannibals hiding. They react like animals when we spot them, attacking on sight and foaming at the mouth. We kill them easily, and together, we follow Evan's lead. We search the wards, but there isn't much left. However, Evan finds a stockroom and locked medicine cart we manage to get open, filling our bags.

We also hit the pharmacy. Some of it is gone and parts are trashed, but we find some gems. We could spend the next year searching the hospital, but we don't want to be here that long, especially in case more cannibals show up. We do manage to get some equipment for Evan and supplies for the pregnant women and kids though, which is good.

We double-check as much as we can before we leave. Once back outside, I suck in a deep breath. The sun is starting to rise—it's a new day.

"Well, fuck." I sigh, rubbing my face. "That was fun. I wonder what the rest of our missions will be like."

They laugh. It's either that or break down. Who said they needed an adventure?

Oh, right, my dumb ass. I guess almost being eaten counts, though it was not in the way I would want to be eaten. "Let's get Beast Jr. and hit the road. I want to put some miles between us and here."

Chapter 10
Beast Bros

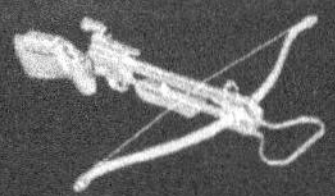

Tired, bloody, and sweaty, we quickly move back to the apartment building. I head straight upstairs and check on Beast Jr., who is snoring away softly. I pick him up while the others pack our stuff, and then we head back to our bikes, getting out of here as fast as we can. Jago sighs and holds out his hand. "I'll take him," he mutters, and I grin before handing the sleeping pup over.

"Aww, you're like beast bros now," I tease as I climb onto my bike. He flips me off, so I blow him a kiss as I rev the engine and pull down my goggles. "Let's get away from here and find a place to camp where we can shower and rest."

Archel nods and takes the lead. I drive after Archel, with Evan, Clay, and Jago following behind, watching our backs as the sand sprays from our bikes. We gun it from the cannibal hospital. I'll need to make sure to mark it for Worth so that we never go there again without a shit load of reinforcements.

We ride for a couple of hours and stop just before midday, not wanting to get heat stroke or sunburn. We find an old motorway service station and leave our bikes right outside before heading in.

We don't venture too far into the first destroyed shop. It's almost pitch-black, the shutters are down, and the only light seeping in is from a few holes. It's dirty as hell too, but it's somewhere to rest for a while.

It looks like an old burger place with a counter at the back and smashed, overhead boards hanging down before a kitchen. The tables and chairs are scattered around, some broken, and the lights are smashed, so I lie down on one of the old-style booth tables. Jago places the puppy on my chest and wanders away as I close my eyes, my feet hanging off the edge as I wiggle my toes.

Knowing I need to move before I fall asleep, I sigh and sit up, empty the sand from my boots, strip off my jacket and shirt, and head to the water they hauled in. Archel helps scrub the blood and dirt off me, and Clay braids my hair, and then we all sit on the floor. Puppy runs between us as we share some food.

"If we push it, we should get back to The Ring in two days," Archel murmurs.

"Good, I want a proper shower," Evan mutters.

"Such a princess," I tease, and he narrows his eyes on me, making me laugh. "But that sounds good. We'll refuel, rest, and see where Worth wants us to go next."

Clay grins. "I need to make more bombs." "Of course." I nod as I eat.

"Why is this such a normal conversation?" Evan exclaims, exasperated. We all just blink at him, and he grumbles as he looks at Beast Jr. "They are all crazy, don't let them fool you."

"If we are all the same, and you are different, doesn't that make you the crazy one?" Jago teases. Evan blinks and then swings his head to me.

"Look what you have created," he complains.

I look Jago over and wink. "Something fine, if I do say so myself, Beast."

"Fucking hell," Evan mutters. "It's always like a bad porno around here."

"You love it," I retort and pick up Beast Jr. as he runs by me. "Yes, he does, baby. Oh yes he does."

"On that note, it's time to get going." Archel laughs and gets to his feet. "Come on, Princess and Beast Jr."

Jago groans, and I laugh. Only a few hours ago, we could have been eaten, so fuck yeah I'm laughing. Let's hope every day is this exciting.

Or maybe, erm...less people eating. That would be fine too.

Chapter 11
I'm Like Mould Baby

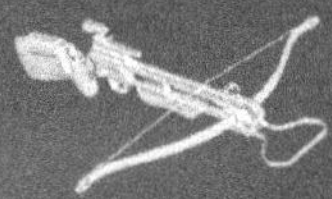

The rest of the ride back to The Ring is uneventful, thank fuck. As soon as we arrive, I'm rushed away to Worth. Evan kisses me goodbye and leaves to check on the patients and expectant mothers, while Clay and Jago come with me. Archel seeks out Dray to tell him about the cannibals and probably bro out over it. I swear if those two didn't meet Worth and me, they would have gotten married—probably would have killed each other in a bloody divorce, but married for sure.

She's waiting for me in her rooms, and once I'm let in, I stand there awkwardly watching her polish her sword. Shit, why is this so hot? *Don't look, Piper, stop staring like a weirdo,* I tell myself, but I can't look away. Watching her long, slender hands rub the cloth up and down the shaft of the blade—

Fuck.

I need to think about anything else—Evan's ass crack, Jago's man balls. Anything! She looks up, her eyebrows arched, and of course I panic because I was staring at the way her hand gripped the sword, wondering if that's what she did to her husbands, so I blurt the first thing that comes to mind. "Ass crack balls."

She blinks before looking at the sword. "I see, and how was the mission?"

I slump, rubbing my head. *Good one, Piper, call the queen of The Wastes an ass crack.* One of these days, she is probably going to murder me, or not. I am quite funny, and I like to think I keep her entertained the way Beast Jr. does me. Speaking of, I look back through the open door to see Beast glaring down at the dog, which is jumping on his legs.

"One sec, Your Majesty," I blurt, then turn back to him and narrow my eyes. "Pick up the fucking dog, or I swear I will never touch your dick again."

He snarls but scoops Beast Jr. up, holding him against his chest and giving me an uncomfortable stare, even as the pup licks his chin and cheek. I wink at them. "Seeing you like this gets me all hot and bothered," I purr.

"Piper," Worth says on a sigh.

"Shit, yeah. Mission. Okay." Kicking the door shut in a laughing Clay's face, I stride across the room and take a seat oppo- site her, kicking my feet up onto the table. She doesn't even look at them as she carries on rubbing her blade. Seriously, it's like a black- smith porno in here, no wonder she has so many men.

"It started off well. We raided a pharmacy—" An image of the cock ring flashes in my mind, and I cough and quickly carry on. "And reached the hospital in good time. We stayed the night near it to watch it, but, well, that's where it all went to shit."

"Explain," she says, still stroking the sword. I am both turned on and terrified. As if at any moment, she might kill me with it, but I think I would probably thank her with it sticking from my chest, because it would be an honour to die at her hand. *Okay, stop being weird Piper. Focus.*

"Well, I was busy entertaining my vagina, because she is hella needy and Clay was looking good, and then I came back after the big horizontal mambo game to find Evan gone. So we tracked him to the hospital and had to break in. There was this creepy dude cutting up bodies in the morgue with Evan tied to the table like some big meat kebab." I alternate between looking at her hands on the sword and her face. "Can you stop rubbing for one second? You are confusing my vagina. Anyway, as I was saying, we freed him and tried to get out, but those people eaters were smart. So we ended up fighting our way through the hospital—I almost fell off a balcony— and blowing ourselves up in an elevator before we killed them all. Then we found all the supplies and decided to get the fuck out of there." I suck in a deep breath and slump back in the chair.

She frowns, watching me.

"That was a lot to unpack," she comments, rubbing her head as she sits back in her chair, finally stopping that weirdly sexual rubbing. "Anything else?"

"Oh, I adopted a feral." I shrug.

"Of course you did." She laughs and then sighs. "Okay, first things first, are you all okay?"

"I mean, Evan's pretty pissed he almost became a manwich, but yeah, we are fine. We got all the supplies as well."

"That's good, but I'm more concerned you are okay though. I'm sorry you had to go into that situation." She shakes her head, smiling wanly. "Unfortunately, it's part of being in The Wastes. You never know what you are walking into. Ferals, cannibals, people trying to steal you, sell you, kill you. It's an occupational hazard, if you still want the job?"

"You bet I do," I growl out. "I can handle it. I eat meat for fun, no cannibal is going to scare me off."

We both stare at each and burst into laughter. "That came out so wrong," I mutter.

"It did. Okay, stay and rest for a few days. I have another situation that needs to be dealt with, but it can wait. Instead, why don't you come for a walk with me in the morning?"

"With the mother lady?" I groan. "She's fucking scary."

"She is, but she's also a good person. If you give her a chance, I think you'll like her, and you'll probably grow on her."

"Yes! That's me, like mould, I grow all over you." I wince again. "Again, dirtier than I meant it to sound."

Laughing, she jerks her head to the door. "Go on, get food and sleep. I mean it, Piper, rest."

I stand as the door opens to reveal her husbands, all but Dray, who is currently fighting Archel in the corridor. Sighing, I look back at her. "Men."

"Men," she agrees, and as I turn to leave, she calls out, "Piper, I mean it. If at any time it becomes too much, let me know. Your position is important, but you are more important to me than the job, understood? Even if you decide one day it's not for you, you will always be my right-hand woman."

"Thank you," I reply sincerely, and once in the hall, I narrow my eyes on Archel. "This is the way you are acting in front of your son?" I snap when I see Beast Jr. chasing after them, yipping and jumping at Dray's legs to bite him. "You are not setting a good example."

Archel freezes, looks at the dog, and grins. "Who's a good boy?" he coos and picks him up as he yips, stroking his back. "Yes, you are! Don't worry, we will make you a protection dog."

Dray snorts, smacks him on the back, and grins at me as he slips past to see his wife. I shake my head and look to the others. "Come on, I need to nap."

Jago starts to grin, and I point at him in warning. "I mean it, nap, no funny business. Keep little beast to yourself, and I don't mean our new son, but your wang-a-dang." They all start laughing, so with as much dignity as I can muster, I turn and storm away, my head held high.

I don't know if I won that little argument, but I definitely had the most style.

Chapter 12
Walking Is Hard

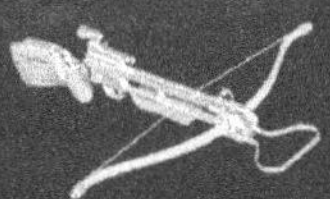

"Motherfucker, it's too hot for this shit. My thighs are sweaty and rubbing together," I grumble as I unstick them and do a little waddle to try and stop the chafing. "Bloody thick thighs betraying me."

Worth laughs as we wander around the complex of The Ring. Mother, or Clarissa, as she is called, walks alongside us silently. She throws me confused looks every once in a while, as if she doesn't know what to make of me.

I try to rein in the crazy as much as I can, I really do, but honestly, I don't know what is considered too much anymore. I'm used to speaking my mind, to never filtering my thoughts or actions, especially around Worth and my men. I must have gotten into bad habits, and they just end up slipping free.

When I make a comment about Worth's boobs, Clarissa surprises me by bursting into laughter. I blink at her in astonish- ment. I thought she hated me, but the more we walk, the more she warms up to me, and I realise she's just guarded. She's survived a lot and has had a ton of people lean on her. It made her strong, but with that came the struggle to trust and let people in.

I guess all three of us are the same.

"So you are a pascha?" she asks as we wander. The Ring is silent this early in the morning. I left my men sleeping, not even Archel stirred for once. "What does that mean?"

"Badass." I shrug. "I think it means I lead them, but honestly, I couldn't understand it. I just nodded and went along with it not to be rude."

"Don't let her fool you." Worth laughs. "She leads The Forgotten, The Lost, and now The Damned. She might seem easygoing, but under all those jokes is a true warrior, even better than I am sometimes. She's a born leader."

I almost blush as I look away from their appraising gazes. "Yeah, well, you still have better boobs. Like, seriously, how do you get them to stay up like that?"

She ignores me, of course, and winks at Clarissa. "You two will get along, I know it. She's a little crazy, but she's the most loyal friend you will ever meet, and she knows the darkness the men in this world are capable of. She's experienced it, bears the scars from it, and fights that much harder to protect innocents because of it. I trust her with my life, with my people."

"Thank you," I whisper, knowing that's a high honour. "I knew you liked me," I tack on, because I just can't resist.

Clarissa looks at me and nods. "I'm sorry, I didn't mean to come across cold. It's simply how I've always had to be. I hope we can be friends. Honestly, I don't have many."

I smile and slap her arm. "Well, now you have another, though I warn you, you'll probably never know when to laugh or scream with me around."

We carry on walking in silence, taking in the world. Every so often, we discuss what it's like to be a woman, weapons, men, or even the places we have been. There is no judgement, only friend- ship, and I find myself relaxing and genuinely enjoying it, even the sweaty thighs.

"I think we should make this a tradition," Worth suggests as we stand side by side, watching over The Ring and our people. "I agree," Clarissa replies.

"I second—wait, third that." I grin, and they laugh.

"There is a tiny dog and a man hiding in the tree behind us," Clarissa comments before wandering away, proving she is already adjusting to our level of insane.

Worth and I both turn to see Archel hiding in the branches like she said, watching us. The thing giving him away? My puppy is at the bottom, barking up at him as he glares and presses his fingers to his lips.

Crossing my arms, I can't help the smile flirting on my lips. "Baby, what are you doing?"

He looks up and smiles before leaping down, grabbing Beast Jr., and strolling over. I take my new best friend and cuddle him to my chest. "He was looking for you, so I volunteered to help him find you."

"And that involved spying on me from a tree?" I counter with an arched eyebrow.

"And with that, I'm out. I have enough crazy men to deal with myself. See you later, Piper," Worth calls and strolls away.

Archel just smirks at me and steps closer. "Okay, maybe I was missing you and looking for you."

"Uh-huh, come on, you two, let's go get breakfast." I take Archel's hand, and with my puppy in my arms, we set off in search of food.

❧

After breakfast, Worth has a surprise for me. She has me interviewing and testing some of her warriors to become part of my road team. That way I can order them to certain areas, for supplies or conflict resolution or trade, and not always have to go myself. It means I need to test them and their skills though, so with my men at my side, we hold auditions in three phases.

The first is face-to-face. I have to get along with them and understand why they want to do this so I can trust them.

The second is seeing them fight and ride so I know they can handle themselves.

The last? My favourite—a hunt.

I sent Jago, Clay, and Archel to hide some objects for me. I will give the warriors basic locations, with some wrong directions, and tell them to work as three teams to retrieve each one. Along the way, my men will watch and report back, and I'll judge them on time, teamwork, and aggression.

The first phase takes hours. I instantly dismiss five men for not respecting me. They looked to my men for orders and completely passed over me, even though they knew I was in charge. Sometimes being a douche is hard to grow from, and they clearly haven't, even though they have a queen now.

One of them gets annoyed, and Jago knocks him the fuck out for running his mouth. My dark little heart loves it. I focus back on the fifty or so men before me. I want to whittle it down to exactly thirty—ten in each team—so I need to be tough and strict. They are all huge warriors, with scars and weapons covering their bodies. In their eyes is knowledge of combat, they are used to this world. Some are scavs, and some are guards for The Ring. I even notice a Lost milling about, and a Forgotten who seems to have stayed behind.

"It's going to be a long day," I announce as I stand before them in The Ring. "Be prepared to wait, and be ready for the unexpected. Before this day is through, you will hate the fact you volunteered for this, but if chosen, you'll have a family for life, a new home, and a new crew to ride with. You'll have a purpose and a place within The Wastes to protect the innocent." I look through them then. "If that isn't something you want to do, leave now. This won't be easy. It's not just existing, this is a job, and it will be bloody and tiring, but it will be worth it."

There's a slight shuffle, and then one man walks away with his head down. I let him go. He's not Damned material if he can't handle the mere thought of it. There is no shame in bowing out when you know something is not for you.

"Okay then, let's begin. Line up, and I'll meet you one-on-one down below in the preparation area for warriors," I order and then turn, holding my head high as I walk down the steps to the room below.

I don't need them worrying about what others think or lying to show off. I need to know the real them, and I plan to do just that.

After setting up downstairs, which means we dragged a table and some chairs down, I sit behind it and wait for the first person. He's a big bastard, huge actually. He has to bend his head to get through the entrance, and when he sits, the chair creaks, making him wince.

"Name?" I ask.

"Vaughn, but all my friends call me Vin," he offers and reaches out to shake my hand. I raise my eyebrows at that and accept, noting he doesn't squeeze to assert dominance. In fact, he seems almost afraid of hurting me with his size, so he is extra careful.

"Where did you come from, what clan?" I inquire as I cross my legs.

"I was just a lowly scav roaming around." He shrugs. "Nothing exciting. I never fit anywhere. I didn't want to hurt anyone, and I was big enough that they couldn't force me to."

"Honest." I nod. "I like it. So why here? Why now?"

"You seem like good people, friendly enough, and I'm getting old. I need a place to rest my head and people to watch my back. Plus, I like helping people, it makes me happy." He smiles, showing his pearly whites, which I was not expecting. He seems like a big softie, and I instantly like him.

"Thank you, Vin, you may wait upstairs." I smile.

"Thank you, Pascha." He nods respectfully. "It would be an honour to serve you." He leaves as I blink after him.

So far, so good.

Chapter 13
Gladiator Style

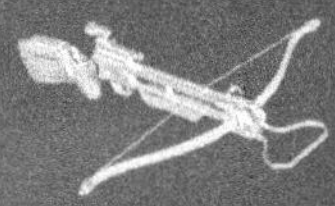

The next phase—fighting. I take a weird amount of pleasure in this.

Around forty-five men and women are left. I've noticed a few that really stick out. Like Vin and a woman named Sascha, who has one side of her head shaved and is covered in tattoos. She seems really strong and smart, maybe enough to lead a team. I just hope she can handle her own with the large men in the fighting ring, but by the look of her biceps and muscles, I would say so.

Another is a man named Abraham. He's quiet, almost too quiet, but he's willing to talk. He told me about his past, about losing his husband, and now all he wants is to forget. I can appreciate that. I keep my eyes on them the most, because in addition to picking thirty people to bring on, I need three team leaders, and right now, they're tied with another man named Reginald. However, the cocky look in his eyes and the way he speaks makes me hate him just a little, even if he is qualified.

Jago splits them until they are evenly matched, but I shake my head. I want them outmatched, caught off guard. I want to know what they are truly capable of when it comes down to the wire.

Instead, I team Vin and Sascha, Abraham and Reginald, and the rest so they are opposing. Brains, brawn, and speed. I want to see if they will survive out there during these missions. I couldn't live with myself if I didn't test them properly and then they never came back.

Jago, Clay, and Archel oversee the fights from below while I sit above with Evan. He's here to give me his opinion. He's good at understanding people, and as a doctor, he might spot something I don't.

"Begin!" I call as I sit and then look at him. "I feel like a gladiator from that film we watched the night the lights went out," I whisper, which makes him smile as he reaches over and lays his hand on my leg.

"You mean the night I got my first hard-on?" His eyes twinkle as he looks over at me, gripping my thigh harder. "You were lying on me, and I was a teenager, babe," he explains when I gape open-mouthed. "You were everything I wanted. That was why I rushed to the bathroom, red-faced. I was so upset, thinking you felt it."

"Well shit." I huff as I hear the commotion from below. "Now I'm curious how many other times you hid a boner...a flag of lust."

"Every fucking time," he mutters. "All you had to do was walk into a room, and don't even get me started on our sleepovers. Christ, Pip, you were torture in the best way."

Unsure what to say to that, I look back at the fighters, focusing on them as he chuckles and leans closer, running his tongue along my earlobe. "If you want, I can show you later."

"Deal," I whisper breathlessly, scanning the fighters but not seeing much. I just feel the warmth of his mouth and his breath across my skin causing goosebumps. How close he is, the feel of his talented hand—

Shit, two are out. Focus.

Ignoring his roaming hand, I watch the fights carefully. Jago, Clay, and Archel point things out for me, and I follow the ones they seem impressed by. Once the first round is over, six more are out.

The next round is one versus three. I want to see how they

handle insurmountable odds, like we faced with the cannibals, to see what solutions they can come up with, and in the worst case, if they are willing to lose for the cause.

We start with some of the men. The first manages to win, but barely, and he's limping. The second is adamant on not losing, so much so that it blinds him and he loses anyway. The third wins, but there was nothing...intelligent about it. He could have won it sooner, but he used his muscles, not his brain.

Next up is Sascha. She's the one that interests me the most. We pit her against three men, and although she is smaller, she holds her own. But three against one drives her back, farther and farther. She starts to get tired and winded, but she doesn't give up. Her eyes are hard and her face is contorted in a snarl, even as she glances around. I see what she is about to do a second before she moves. She's smart, really smart, and is using her obstacles to her advantage. She leaps up onto the fence, and when they follow, she flips back down, knocking one out and leaving two.

She uses the area around her, which is smart. We never said she couldn't, and before long, she has them both on their backs.

Vin is up next, against Reginald and Abraham and one other. The man might be a gentle giant, but when it comes to fighting? Not so much. He's a warrior through and through—feral, strong, and with no quit in him—but he has an edge. He's not too cocky, and he uses his brain to assess the situation rather than running in without thought. Recklessness can be a plus sometimes, but I've learned my lesson on that. If you can put thought into it, do it, because you are more likely to survive, and with Worth and my men around me now, I know I have to. No more rushing into danger unseen without a thought for Piper...well, not all the time anyway.

He wins using his brain, with Abraham only slightly losing, but I discard him as a leading candidate, although he will make a good runner. The rest of the fights are uninspiring. I pick out some good candidates, but I already know who I want for team leaders. However, I can't announce the names until all stages are complete.

They get no time to rest, since they wouldn't get it out in The Wastes. I order them to their bikes, with Archel and the others already on the road to watch them.

"Ride, and know that we will be watching and assessing. This isn't just for your job. Out there, it's about working together. It's about surviving the odds. Can you?"

Chapter 14
Ride Bitches Ride

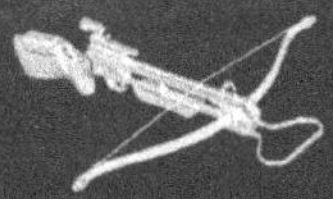

I wait at The Ring with Worth and Clarissa. We eat and laugh, while I watch the clock, wondering who will make it back. This position of power weighs on me, but today, I feel happy and a little smug. All those men who looked down at me, called me weak… yet now I have an army of men fighting to the death to try and follow me. I know a lot of it is because of Worth, but I got myself here. I won this position fair and square.

I wonder what the younger me would have thought. She was always itching for adventure, thinking there was more above ground than they let on. She was right, and now look at me, sitting with a queen as I help her rule the lands filled with thousands of people, places, and new experiences.

There is still so much out there to be explored, and I don't think I will truly settle until I have seen all of it. As Evan's parents told him, there is no feeling like that of seeing something no other has, to be the first human to set eyes on it. He told me that once when he wove me tales of castles and princesses above ground to help me sleep. It seems I am following in their footsteps, my parents too— though I wish they were here to see it. I barely remember them now though, since I was so young when they died on patrol. I wonder if they would be proud, or would they hate the person I've become?

I have no way of knowing, but I make myself proud every day for getting up, for continuing to move forward, for healing from what I experienced. There have been so many times in my life when I didn't know if I would make it. Yet even in the dark, I found the light, and I will continue to find it each day, even when it's hard, even when it hurts or I don't feel like it.

Because life is too fucking short.

I plan to live it to the max with my men at my side and plenty of orgasms—a lifetime's worth. An orgasmic world, you could say. Cum central. The big O. Just call me Sir Cums-A-Lot.

"Does she know she's speaking out loud?"

"You'll get used to it," Worth replies without even a blink.

"I really don't think I will," she mutters but smiles at me like I'm a crazy person, so what do I do back? I wave.

Fucking hell, no wonder I don't have many friends.

Luckily, I'm saved by the bell—er, well, technically the rev of engines, but you get my drift. Do people still say drift? Fuck, am I old?

"Piper, engines," Worth reminds me as she takes a bite of her food. Fuck yes! I jump up and wave as I rush away, probably leaving them wondering if I was dropped a lot at birth.

I wasn't. There was that time when Evan dropped me down some stairs when we were playing, but the doctors didn't think that had too much impact on my brain.

Much.

I rush through The Ring and make it back to the gate to see the first team coming in—led by Sascha. Fuck yes! Girl power! I want to scream it, but I swallow it back and keep it professional as she pulls off her helmet with a skull drawn on it and grins at me. She gets off and strolls up to me, handing me a note with a giant X on it. "Well done! You beat everyone."

I grin, and I really try not to say it, but it just slips out. "Pussy power!"

Luckily, she just laughs. "You know it. So what now?"

"Now we wait for the others. I'll make a decision tonight and announce it tomorrow."

She nods and looks back at the men from her team. "Free time, boys. Get lost." She turns back to me, winking. "Just a heads-up, that Reginald asshole tried to take my team out by smashing into my bike. I managed to bitch-slap him away, but we had to stop to fix it. He's not a team player, only out for himself. Thought you should know." She walks away, leaving me gawking after her. She managed to bitch-slap him, fix her bike, and beat everyone else back here?

Worth may have some competition for my girl crush of the month. Maybe I should make a rota or a calendar. Or maybe so many good-looking, incredible women should stop showing up.

Shaking my head, I remind myself to have a word with Reginald, the cunt-wit. He won't be welcome here if he can't play nice, and he's blown his chance on the team. All that remains is to see if he can handle the rejection or if it will get him kicked out.

Or worse, killed.

The next two teams come back with a two-minute difference. Honestly, they were all amazing, but I dismiss them and gather my men to have a meeting on what they saw and what they think, but I, of course, will make the final decision.

We assemble in our rooms, sitting on the floor with food and drink spread between us as I recline back into Archel's arms, my feet on Jago's lap as he eats.

"So, tell me everything," I say between bites.

"I like the two you did—Sascha and Vin. I think the third leader isn't here yet, but they would make good ones," Jago starts. "Vin's smart but strong. Sascha's fast and a good problem solver, so it could work to have a similar team to send out on certain missions."

"I agree, Pascha, very good warriors," Clay offers. "I did not like the Reginald character you pointed out. He was a sly snake in need of sacrificing."

"Agreed," Archel remarks. "There were a few other good ones we can point out. Relatable, proud, and will get the job done."

"I saw no medical issues with either leader candidates," Evan comments. "As for medical history, I noticed Sascha has scars," he observes with a wince.

"Everyone has scars, Evan. It's the apocalypse," I reply with a 'duh' look.

He sighs and gazes around and then his eyes fall back on me. "Very...distinct scars, Pip. Like yours."

I swallow. "Oh," I mumble and drop my food for a second. "That means she's stronger than we thought," is all I can say, and he smiles softly.

"That she is." I don't know if we mean her or me now, but I don't ask. "As for Vin, he's had some broken bones, some which didn't heal correctly, but it shouldn't hinder him at all."

"So Vin and Sascha as team leaders. Are we all in agreement?" They nod or say yes, and I smile. "Now to pick their teams."

"How does it feel to be in charge of the enforcers for the whole Wasteland?" Evan smirks as he passes me more meat with a narrowed-eyed look, demanding I eat. "You always said you would do something amazing, but I honestly always thought it would be starting a strip club."

"I mean...that's not a bad idea." I laugh, and Archel kisses my cheek with a chuckle. "It feels surreal that people will have to listen to my commands, my orders."

"Don't doubt yourself, Brawler," Jago cautions.

"The big man is right. You have an incredible mind, and you see the best way to deal with situations. You should not worry," Archel murmurs.

"What the skinny and small man said, Pascha." I see Jago's eyes narrow at the small comment, and I hide my smile. "I knew the type of woman you were within five minutes of meeting you."

"Which is?" I prompt.

He reaches over and kisses my hand. "A leader, a warrior. A pascha."

Well shit.

"Fucking hell, that's so sweet," I gush. "Okay, get your dick out and I'll suck it."

He laughs, in fact they all do, and I glance between them. "What?"

"Your response to a sweet, touching compliment is to suck his dick?" Evan wheezes as I shrug. "Oh, Pip, never change."

"So wait, I'm not sucking anyone's dick? Boring."

Chapter 15
Time To Go

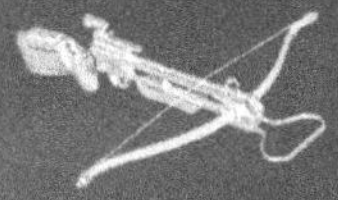

The next day, the warriors gather early, some nervous, some cocky as I jump onto the table in the early morning sun, ready to get them started.

"Not all of you made it," I begin. "I'm not like Worth, I don't have pretty speeches, just facts. Some failed, and some showed you cannot perform in teams, which doesn't work in this role. Some of you stood out so much, we have created a role within our new func- tioning leadership just for you." I scan the faces again. "Never forget why we are doing this—for our people, our lands, and to protect innocents. Not for notoriety or the fact you will probably get to kill people." I toss Reginald a look. "But I bet you are all ready to find out. When I call your name, move to the left." I pause, ensuring I still have every- one's attention.

"Rey, Gutter, Leaf, Sam, Vic, Derek, Bomber, Disciple, Freddy, Abraham, and finally, Sascha," I finish, and wait for them all to move —a total of ten men and one woman.

"Good. Sascha you will be leading this road team." Her mouth drops open before she covers it. "You will report to me, the people in your team will report to you, and I to Worth."

Looking back at the others, I meet their eyes. "If I call your name, move to the right." I call Vin and ten men, and watch as they move to the side, leaving the rest in the middle, around fifteen to be exact.

"Reginald, Clancy, Meat, and Rover, you have not made the cut, please leave. The rest of you will be stationed at The Ring for now as backup and to protect and refill our road teams. This won't be forever, and when we—"

"Fucking bullshit!" Reginald shouts, and I sigh and look at him. "It's rude to interrupt, you giant bumhole," I snarl, letting the insult slip as I jump from the table and get in his face. "You didn't get picked because you're cocky, arrogant, and unable to think past your own gains and actions. You can't work with a team, never mind beneath a woman who you clearly look down on. You'll be lucky if you fit anywhere in this fucking world. My suggestion, Reginald," I growl out as he glares, "is to bow your fucking head and learn respect or get the hell out of our way. This isn't a man's world anymore, it's a fucking woman's domain, baby, and you're just along for the ride."

I turn away, giving him my back, taking a page from Worth's book —never show them fear. My men watch carefully in case he tries something, but I don't need them to. I already know he wants to show off, show his strength, and for him, he probably thinks he's putting a woman in her place. He just doesn't realise that place is above misogynistic idiots like him.

I part my legs when I stop, ready to turn, listening for it. A second later, it comes. The sand crunches under his feet, and the air blows towards me. I turn, ducking the blade, and smash my fist into his chest, cracking his ribs. I do it again, and he stumbles back as I bring my arm down across his, snapping his wrist and forcing him to release the blade as he howls. Turning, I kick him in the face twice before he goes down. He hits the sand hard. I hear yells of encouragement, and my men coming towards me as I stop above Reginald.

Standing above him with my legs on either side, I stare down at his bleeding, shocked face. "I think it's time for you to go. If I see you tomorrow, you're dead." Stepping back, I watch as he gets to his feet, hesitating. "Now, asshole!" He turns and starts to run away, and I look at Vin and Sascha. "As my new enforcers, ensure he reaches the border before sunrise, won't you?"

"You've got it," Vin agrees.

"A pleasure," Sascha purrs. "With me," she calls to her team and winks at me. "Let's give him a good scare."

I watch them go with a laugh before turning back to the others. "Enjoy tonight's freedom, gentleman. Tomorrow, you start a new life as The Damned, the enforcers of The Wastes!"

"Hoorah!" they call, and when I turn to leave, I see Worth and her men watching me from the stairs. She smiles at me proudly and salutes, giving me her blessing.

The Damned just grew. Maybe it's not us who are damned... but those we hunt.

Chapter 16
Prettiest Princess

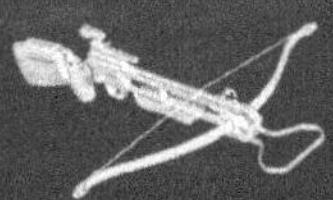

I catch up with Worth and discuss the idea of having a ceremony to welcome all the new enforcers. She likes it and leaves me in charge of preparing the celebration. So, of course, I rope my men into helping me. I put Evan on the location and drinks, and Archel on food and spreading the word. Clay is in charge of making sure Archel doesn't kill anyone, and Jago follows me with Beast Jr. jumping along at our feet.

I find the blacksmith in his shop at the back. Before Worth came along, he was in charge of sharpening the weapons for the fights and the soldiers. Now he works with Worth to create so much more, and I know he loves it. He creates jewellery and signs, and his talent and happiness are obvious in each creation.

"Yo, Willy," I call as I step into the shop. He turns with a glare. A huge mountain of a man, he has to duck to even work in his shop. He wears a leather apron, and his bare arms are covered in sweat and dirt. His bald head shines from the heat, and he has goggles perched on top.

"It is William, how many times do I have to tell you?"

"So, Willy, I need your help," I say with a smile. "Queen's orders."

He sighs, puts down the hammer, and crosses his arms. "Call me William and I will."

I wince but smile sweetly. "William, oh great bender of metal, the hardest hammerer in The Wastes, weapon maker extraordinaire, and a very tender lover, I heard, will you help me?"

"I'll ignore the sarcasm because Worth says if I try to kill you again, she'll put my head on a pike. Fine, what do you need?" he grumbles.

"See? Knew you didn't hate me all along." I clap. "Excellent, how many metal necklaces can you make before this evening?"

"It depends on how big—"

"That's what she said," I whisper, unable to help myself. He stops, and we just stare at each other before I clear my throat. "Size is up to you, make as many as you can."

"Uh-huh, and what goes on these necklaces?" he demands. "The Damned symbol of course." I toss a drawing at him, the

one Worth used for my jacket. "See you tonight!" I call, leaving him muttering death threats under his breath as Jago grins next to me.

"You really have a way with people, Brawler."

Turning, I walk backwards as I smile at him. "Worked on you, didn't it? You were obsessed, couldn't leave me alone."

"That's a bit extreme. You distracted me with your boobs, and I was helpless."

"Uh-huh, and then you stayed for the winning personality, and now you love me," I tease.

"That's it," he snaps. "You have gotten far too cocky."

I squeal and turn as he rushes at me, but as always, Jago is too fast for me. He snatches me and throws me over his shoulder, slapping my ass.

"I think it's time to remind you why you came back to my training every day."

"You're the boss," I chirp, then groan as his hand squeezes my ass, waking my vajayjay up.

He rushes to our room, kicking the door shut behind us and smashing me to the wall. Our lips meet hurriedly, and lust explodes between us until I'm trembling as he sucks my tongue. My fingers dig into his shoulder as I wrap my legs around his waist and grind against the hard cock I can feel through his pants.

Our desperate kiss breaks apart at the sound of a whine, and we both turn and see Beast Jr. as he tilts his head, watching us get it on. "That's so creepy," Jago whispers, our cheeks nearly pressed together.

"He can't see us doing it, that's like mentally scarring," I reply. "Then what the fuck do you want me to do?" he snarls, making

the puppy yip again.

"I don't know. Put him in the other room while we fuck... Wait, you can't leave him alone." I groan.

"That's babies, Brawler." Jago sighs. "Fine, next time Archel or one of your other idiots is taking the feral so I can get my dick wet without my bare ass being stared at by a puppy."

"Deal." I laugh as he puts me on my feet. With a sigh, he leans down and hoists the puppy up, kissing his head as he turns.

"Come on, little one, I need to fuck Mummy and it's weird if you watch," he mutters as he heads to the bedroom. Jago covers him in a blanket and slowly backs from the room, shutting the door before he can follow. He looks to me, his eyes dark, his lips tilted in a smirk. "Where were we, Brawler?"

"You were about to fuck my brains out and show me who is boss?" I offer sweetly, batting my lashes at him.

"Damn fucking right I was," he snaps and lunges towards me. My laugh cuts off into a moan as his lips smash into mine. He grabs my hips and hoists me up, pressing my back against the wall again as we pick up where we left off.

He holds me there as his hand moves to my trousers, unbuttoning and unzipping them quickly before burying right into the material.

He slides it down until he can cup my wet pussy, swallowing my moan as I grind into his hand.

I pull my mouth away and nip his lip. "Fuck me," I demand. "So impatient," Jago growls and turns us, tossing me onto the sofa before following me down. He blankets my body with his as he pauses above me. "I'll fuck you when I'm good and ready. Right now, I want to taste my cunt."

"Your cunt?" I grin.

"That's right, Brawler—my cunt. Now be a good girl for once and scream for me," he snarls, moving down my body and yanking off my trousers. He tosses them away before my underwear gets the same treatment.

Then he drops, forcing his massive shoulders between my thighs. I have no choice but to throw my legs over them, exposing my wet pussy. I feel his eyes on me before his tongue darts out and drags down my center, licking all of me before he groans at the first taste of my cream.

"Best fucking flavour in the world." He sighs against my pussy. "I could die down here. In fact, I think I will. Choke me," he orders as he finally lets go of his control and ravishes my pussy.

His tongue sweeps back and forth, up and down, before circling my clit and flicking. Jago's fingers press against my hole, and just as I inhale deeply, he spears me with them, forcing them into my pussy all the way to the knuckle before he strokes my walls. He doesn't let up, fucking me with his fingers, slamming them into me over and over as his tongue drags along my clit.

He sucks on the nub, biting gently. The pleasure storms through me, ordered by that talented mouth, and within moments, I'm screaming my release. I lift my hips, grinding my pussy into his mouth so he can't breathe, and my hands scramble on the fabric of the sofa. I throw my head back and squeeze my eyes shut as I ride wave after wave of pleasure. He fucks me through it, not even slowing down until I suck in a stuttering breath and push him away with weak hands.

He kisses my clit and pulls his fingers from me before sitting back. With his eyes locked on me, he sucks his fingers into his mouth and groans. The sound is carnal and dirty, and I can't take it anymore. I need him inside me.

Sitting up, I pull my shirt and bra off, and then I reach for him. He drops to me willingly, kissing me roughly and letting me taste my release on his tongue.

Pulling his lips from mine, he stands and quickly sheds his clothes before grabbing my hips and flipping me. Jago forces a gasp from my throat as my face hits the soft sofa, then he yanks my ass back and I feel him settle behind me. His huge cock presses against my pussy, warning me of what's to come.

Unashamedly, I push back into it, grinding, wanting it inside me. I only just came, yet I'm already ready for more. Ready for him. He wastes no time on pretty words, no, my beast grips my hips and thrusts into me, making me scream and writhe as he forces that huge cock into my still pulsing channel. With a snarl, he pulls out and slams back in.

My breathing is ragged, and my hands clench the material to hold on as he sets a hard, fast pace. He fucks me ruthlessly, the force pushing me forward and dragging my beaded, sensitive nipples along the sofa until I'm crying out. I clench around him, unable to speak or think as he replaces every thought with him.

"Fucking" —thrust— "love" —thrust— "you," he snarls, punctuating each word with a hard, quick thrust, driving my pleasure higher and higher. My next orgasm is already in reach, working its way through me.

It explodes when he slaps my pussy with an open hand, catching my clit and lips, making me scream as I come. With two more thrusts, he snarls and stills as his own release fills me.

Falling forward, he kisses my sweaty back as I shiver and shake, and drool definitely falls from my mouth. "Anytime you need a reminder, Brawler, just let me know," he teases, his voice breath- less, and I can't help but laugh, which in turn makes us both groan.

After Jago showed me well and truly who was boss, I showered and got dressed for the evening. I want my new enforcers to know they are important, and honestly, warriors use any excuse to celebrate.

By the time I get downstairs, the sun has started to set and the booze is already flowing. Someone is playing an old guitar they found, and Clarissa is singing along to it. It makes me stop and stare. Her voice is so raw, so fucking beautiful. It's unlike anything I've heard for a long time, reminding me of sultry singers from the fifties. Her eyes are closed, her head is tilted, and her hand is held out to her side as if she's projecting the memories into the song she sings about overcoming pain.

It almost brings a tear to my eye, and I catch Worth's man watching her lovingly, eyes wide and jaw slack, as if he's unable to look away.

Dragging my own gaze away, I shake off the haze her song has put me in and smile at a warrior as he thrusts a bottle of clear liquid at me. "Home brewed vodka, lass," he informs me and stumbles away to dance.

Grinning, I take a sip, then wince at the strength, but I swallow it back, not wanting to be rude, especially when they are all looking at me. My new recruits are sitting together, laughing and joking at a table. Sascha is arm wrestling Vin. I toast them with my bottle before making the rounds. I find Worth and her men sitting towards the back on the ground near a fire. She's lying in Thorn's arms with a lazy smile on her face as she watches the flames. I almost feel like I'm intruding as I stand there before she raises her eyes to me.

"There you are. Come sit and listen to this story Dray is telling us about the time he apparently swam in the Dead Sea," she jokes.

"I did!" He sighs.

I sit down in the open space between Dray and Jax, gasping when I'm suddenly picked up. Clay holds me as he sits and deposits me on his lap with a pat on my head, making me roll my eyes. Jago and Evan squeeze in next to Maxen, while Archel kicks Dray over and sits in his spot as he snarls and flips him off before crawling to Worth and lying in her lap.

"What was it like?" I ask with a tilt of my head. "I've always wanted to see it properly. I've seen glimpses, and Clay has told me stories about the creatures that inhabit it now and the wild waves."

"Dark, but not dead like they call it," Dray starts. "It's filled with life. I don't even have names for some of the animals. It was hot as well, and salty, but there was something about floating in it..."

"Not scared of being eaten from below?" I laugh.

He smirks and grins at me. "Any creature that thinks it can eat me is welcome to try, I'll kill them all." He looks up at Worth, who gazes down at him lovingly. "Apart from you, wife. Feel free to eat me anytime."

"Ew." Evan laughs. "Too much information."

"What, don't want me to eat you, Evvie?" I purr, and he looks over at me, his eyes darkening as he runs his gaze across my body.

"Shit, okay," he mutters, making us all laugh.

"I heard you pissed William off again today," Worth comments, quickly changing the subject.

"Nah, he loves me, he's just grumpy." I take a swig as I talk.

"Uh-huh. Is that why he told me if I don't stop you from annoying him, he is going to melt you down into a horseshoe?" She laughs.

"Wow, it's so nice of him to think that's all I would melt down into," I reply sweetly.

Clay chuckles in my ear, kissing my neck. "I would never let him, Pascha. I would blow him up first."

"No blowing things up in The Ring!" Worth and I say at the same time as we hear cheers and look over to see Sascha taking her winnings.

"I like her." Worth smirks. "She's crazy like us. Oh, Piper, better to make any announcements now before they all get too drunk, or you'll never get any sense out of them."

"Good point." I get to my feet and take Archel's hand to help him up. "Let's go get the necklaces and present them, then we can get trashed and fuck."

"Piper." Worth sighs, shaking her head.

"I mean, you're welcome to join," I joke, "but this is kind of a sausage party, if you get my drift."

"Just go," she tells me with a laugh.

I wink at her and wind through the crowd, my men on my heels as I search out William, who is drinking alone in a corner and glaring at anyone who gets too close. "No," he snaps.

"Necklaces please, Willy," I singsong.

He narrows his eyes before reaching back, grabbing a bag, and tossing it at me. "This was all I had time to make, now fuck off."

"Thanks, cutie. You can get started on making the twenty-eight others tomorrow." I turn then, ignoring his insults, and check the bag. He made two, but they are beautifully crafted, smooth, and clean, and even strung on black woven thread. I guess I know who I'm giving them to. It's a symbol, after all, of their station, uniting us so they won't ever feel alone, even if they are on the road.

Looking around, I try to find somewhere to stand to do the announcement, but every table and surface is taken. Sascha notices and jerks her head before looking at the table with The Damned. "Move your fucking drunken asses, our leader needs it," she barks, and I've never seen a group of men move so fast in my life. Grinning, I head over and leap onto the top. Jago is there to steady me, and Vin and Sascha stand on either side like bodyguards, their arms crossed, even though they don't know what is happening. They're simply being loyal, which makes me only more sure I have made the right decision. Even against our own, they are with me, which is exactly what I need, because we never know who we will be hunting out there.

"Listen up, scoundrels!" I call, and some cheers go up at that.

"We've got some new enforcers in town that I want you to meet." The music stops, and I gesture to Sascha and Vin. "These two,

Sascha and Vin, will be team leaders of The Damned, under my command. They are the law enforcers, so you answer to them. Show them respect, or you'll have Worth and me to answer to. Understand?" Some grumbles go up, but people nod. "Good. Without any pompous speech, here." I pass a necklace to each. "This shows who they are. All enforcers will wear one, and if you see them without it... well, kick their ass for me," I joke and grab my bottle and lift it into the air. "For The Nations! For our queen!"

A massive roar goes up, and feet stomp as I down some of the bottle, which others copy. I wink over at Worth and wipe my mouth. "Now let's get drunk and have fun!"

With that, I leap down and turn to face Sascha and Vin. "Enjoy tonight. Tomorrow, you work," I instruct.

"Yes, sir." Sascha nods.

"Understood, captain," Vin responds.

"Good, punishment for your own team is up to you. Watch them tonight and make sure they don't make fools of themselves or die. Now excuse me, I have four needy men and a whole lot of booze to drink."

Taking the bottle with me, I down it and mix into the crowd. For the next hour or so, I drink and dance with my men, laughing when Archel shakes his ass for me. I'm busy grinding with him when I realise I can't see Jago, Evan, or Clay anymore. "Come on, let's make sure they're not killing anyone," I grumble and pull him after me.

We eventually find them at a table with herbs and some hard pieces of, well, what I can only describe as wood-looking food. Archel chuckles as Jago pokes one. "Why not try it, man? They are really good," he encourages, but his voice is choked. I glare at him, and when Jago takes a bite, I wait to see if he was lying, but Jago groans in bliss and eats the whole thing, so Evan and Clay join in. I turn to Archel to see him struggling to contain his laughter.

"What?" I snap.

"You'll see, Princess," he wheezes.

Forty minutes later, he's right. I do see, and I'm going to kick his ass for not warning them.

"Jago, don't!" I yell as he downs the bottle and throws it, making me sigh. "Archel, you asshole, go stop Clay from pretending to be a bomb."

He laughs so hard he has tears dripping down his face as I glare at him. "Sorry, Princess, I couldn't resist. They needed to relax anyway."

"But drugs? Really? You could have warned me!" I stop abruptly when I spot Evan with his shirt around his head as he shimmies his chest to the music. Fucking hell, they will never live this down. Good job everyone else finds it hilarious. It seems it's a rite of passage to take Conian without being warned.

But still.

I prop my hands on my hips and get into his face. "I swear if you don't round those drugged idiots up, I'm going to dump your ass."

"Nah, you like my ass too much, Princess," he teases and kisses my cheek. "But I'll go get them. You deal with big guy here."

I look over and sigh, seeing him lying on the ground. I stop next to him and peer into his face. "Beast baby, what are you doing?"

"Sand angel!" he calls with a slur, moving his arms and legs to, yep, make an angel. I roll my lips inwards to stop myself from laughing. He's going to be so pissed tomorrow, but I've got to admit, he's cute like this. His eyes are hazy, and his hair is everywhere as he smiles unashamedly.

"You make a very good angel, but do you want to come with me?"

"Where to?" he asks, sitting up.

"Bed?" I offer, and he grins.

"Oh, hell yes!" He tries to get to his feet and falls with a giggle, so I help him up, propping myself under his arm with a grunt as I wave to Worth to let her know I'm going. She's laughing too, the dick.

Archel has managed to round up Clay and Evan, who are laughing and leaning on each other over at the entrance to the building. I drag Jago over, and between us, we manage to get them into the room and on the bed, though they are giggling like crazy.

"Shit, what is that stuff?"

"No one knows. Some guy named Conian found it and made it. He sells it for a high amount to warriors. Like I said, rite of passage, Princess."

"Uh-oh, so you did it?" I snap, turning to face him, ignoring the three giggling musketeers.

"Fuck yes. Dray made me and didn't tell me. That night, I tried to fight a brick wall for four hours and then passed out using my bike as a blanket. Good times."

"But you didn't let me take it." I frown.

He steps closer, making my breath catch as he presses his body to mine. He lowers his head until his cool eyes meet mine. "Princess, I wouldn't let you touch that shit. No one gets to see you like that but us," he growls out, and a shiver goes through me as he reaches out and pushes a strand of hair behind my ear. "I didn't know how it would affect you with your past, so I wasn't risking that."

Sighing, I lean into him, and he cranes his head down farther and kisses me softly. My shadow is always protecting me. "I love you."

"I love you too, Princess," he whispers, but the sound of Evan being sick interrupts us and we pull away. "I'll deal with him. Clay is already passed out. It's strong, but it wears off quickly enough. You are on your own with Jago though. Even drugged, that fucker scares me." He laughs and moves over to Evan, holding his hair away from his face and rubbing his back. "That's it, get it all out and then you can go to sleep, and tomorrow, Piper can laugh her ass off at your dancing."

"I'm a good" —heave— "dancer. Ain't I, Pip?"

"Yup, really good," I reply as I get into bed next to Jago, who's staring up at the ceiling, lifting and dropping his hands.

"Hey, big guy." I grin and then yelp when he suddenly moves, grabbing me and cuddling into my chest.

"Brawler, make the room stop spinning," he whines.

"Sure thing, baby," I coo quietly to calm him and start to stroke his hair.

"No, make it stop!" he yells, and I panic and say the first thing that comes to mind.

"Shh, you are the prettiest princess here. Yes, you are. The room is still, you are okay."

"Prettiest princess? Me?" he asks, relaxing into my chest. I share a giggle with Archel and stroke Jago's hair.

"Yes, you are the prettiest princess I've ever seen," I tell him and carry on saying it until he finally goes to sleep, snoring into my chest. Archel cleans up Evan and tucks him and Clay in before shaking his head. "You were right, not a good idea, Princess." He comes around to me, covers me up as much as he can, and helps me get comfy with a giant snoring on my chest. Crouching next to the bed, he kisses me softly. "But you never fail to make me smile. All I could think about tonight when I saw all those other warriors watching us with jealousy was how lucky I am to have you."

He looks over at the three others in the bed and shakes his head. "It's not what I would have imagined, but it's better. I have a family now as well as you."

"They are going to kick your ass tomorrow," I warn, and he grins, kissing me again.

"Let them try, Princess. You can even watch. I know how it gets you all hot and bothered, and after, you can kiss it better," he purrs against my lips.

Fuck.

Laughing, he kisses me again and sits on a chair next to me like he did when I was healing, only this time, his hand is in mine and he's watching over our family to make sure nothing happens while we sleep.

Our shadow, not just mine.

He's right—this isn't what I expected for my life...but it's so much better.

Chapter 17
#Womancrushwasteland

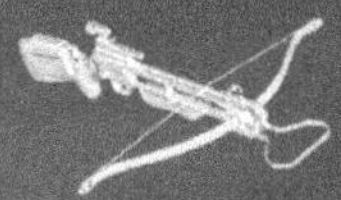

There doesn't seem to be any aftereffects from the drug, apart from their embarrassment and anger. Evan thanks Archel for helping him when he was sick, but he also punches him in the balls as he passes by to go check on people. Clay just laughs it off, and Jago? Well, I'm watching him chase Archel around The Ring right now. Jago may be strong, but he's tired, and Archel is a fast little fucker, laughing as he jumps and sprints away from him.

I sip my coffee as I watch. Finally, Jago gives up and lies next to me, his hand over his heaving chest. "Fucking little prick," he mutters.

"It's okay, pretty princess," I tease, and he glares at me, so for once, I shut up. Just then, Archel sneaks over. I don't think Jago has seen him, when suddenly, he springs up and punches Archel right in the face, knocking him out.

I watch him go down and glare at Jago. "That wasn't nice."

"He deserves it, Brawler," he argues as he sits next to me, both of us watching Archel.

"You didn't kill him, did you?" I snap.

"Nah, he'll get up... I think." He groans, resting his head on my shoulder. "My fucking body aches."

Archel groans and rolls over, and even with a bloody lip, he's grinning. "Now you can kiss it better, Princess." He winks and then looks at Jago. "We good?"

"Yeah, we're good. I'm too tired to kill you."

I sip my coffee as they sit on either side of me, enjoying the quiet, since most of the other warriors are still asleep or hungover. I spot Sascha coming my way and nod my greeting. "Worth wants to speak to you, boss, but did you have any missions for us?"

"In fact, I do. Can you go check on the scavs and Jon please? Worth said he's newly in control, and I'm betting he could use some backup. Also, please tell Vin I want him to arrange watch duty here for the others and then go on a food run. We ate a lot last night."

"Got it," she replies and then looks at Jago. "You handled it well last night. When they slipped it to me, I somehow locked myself in a fridge. When I finally managed to get out, I realised the fridge was actually in an enemy camp I snuck into before I decided to take a nap. Let's just say it was a bad hangover." She walks away, leaving us staring after her.

Seriously, how many woman crushes can I have?

Chapter 18
Yellow Brick Road

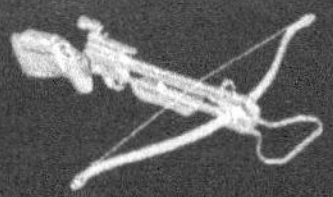

After making sure the guys aren't going to kill Archel or die from whatever drug they took, I leave them to go find Worth.

I locate her at the gate, and we sit and watch the sand as we talk.

"I have a task," she begins and then looks at me. "But I also have a bad feeling about it. I would normally go myself, but my fucking husbands said I need to trust you and let you do your job."

"Which is right," I agree with a smile. "I can handle it. Tell me what it is."

"There are rumours of a band of scavs causing trouble up north, past old Ivar's keep nearly at the top of The Wastes. I've never been up that far, but I've heard they are basically feral fuck- ers. They are traveling down and attacking people. I made a promise to protect The Wastes... We need to stop it."

"You want them dead." I shrug.

"Or reasoned with, but yeah, it probably will end up with their deaths."

"Got it. North. Kill. Back." "It won't be easy, Piper."

"I know, but when is life ever easy?" I grin. "Come on, Worth, give me some credit. Plus, I get to see up north. I've never really been up there, so it's sort of like a holiday but with more death and bloodshed than normal," I tease.

"Uh-huh, well, don't pack your swimsuit, but take your knife." She laughs.

"Oh my God, was that a joke? I'm rubbing off on you, aren't I? I knew it."

She stands, dusting off her ass and rolling her eyes. "Shut up, Piper, and get ready. You choose when you leave, but let me know before you do." Then she leaves me there, grinning.

Guess it's time to hit the Yellow Brick Road again. Standing, I skip my way back to the others, singing "Follow the Yellow Brick Road" the whole way...

Maybe I should change it to Red Brick Road? It seems more fitting for The Wastes.

"Grab your shit. We're going on an adventure!" I call as soon as I step into the room. Jago flips over, groaning at his obvious headache.

"Are you quoting *The Hobbit*?" Evvie snorts.

"Maybe, bet it made you hard though," I tease, and he winks at me. "But it was the truth. We are hitting the road again, so get your shit."

"When?" Clay groans. "My head hurts worse than my cock when you are around."

Pursing my lips, I look him over, specifically his cock, which, yep, is hard. Shit, I wonder if we have enough time for an orgy before we get on the road.

"Talking out loud, Princess," Archel calls from his spot at the table where he's sharpening his blades. Lifting it into the air, he checks the shine before smirking at me. "But I wouldn't say no to that kind of break."

"I need sleep," Jago grouses, and I become serious, knowing if he's complaining, it must be bad.

"You and Clay rest. Archel will get the bikes and weapons ready. Evan, grab the medical kit and check in with everyone. I will sort food, maps, and the other teams for when we are gone. When you are both feeling better, we will leave."

"You've got it, Pascha." Clay salutes.

"On it, Pip," Evan murmurs as he slides past me with a quick kiss.

"If you get bored and want that break, you know where I am," Archel purrs as he leaves too.

Jago gets to his feet and tumbles. "I was just whining. I'm fine. Let's get going—"

Rolling my eyes, I stomp over and push him back to the sofa. It's a testament to how weak he's feeling when he falls back with a grunt. I distract him by kissing him slowly until he groans and reaches up to drag me closer, but I pull away with a chuckle. "Rest for me, big guy?" I plead. "I'll make it up to you."

"You fucking better, or you could rest here with me," he whispers, grabbing for me again as I dance out of his grasp.

"Next time," I promise as I lean over and kiss Clay too. "Sleep," I order, and then I leave them before I'm tackled and forced into a warrior sandwich.

I manage to find some old maps from Nan who was hiding them with her underwear and knives—I didn't even question that one. "So you've been up there?" I ask as I sip my water in the canteen. I've put a request in for rations. The system here is changing thanks to Worth, and it works better now. Everyone has their allotted food, and you can always have extra, but it means no one goes hungry and no one has to fight for it.

"Once." She shrugs, tossing back her drink. I think nothing of it until she pulls a flask from her cardigan and grins at me. "Ya want some, girlie?"

"What is it?" I ask curiously.

"Fooking unicorn piss," she answers and tips some into my drink anyway. "It's good for ye."

I take a sip and cough all over her, making her cackle as others stare. "Fooking—I mean fucking hell, woman, that's like goddam tar."

"Aye, but it will put hair on ye chest." She nods seriously. "Why in the world would I want that? I have enough with the

hair that grows on my legs and even my toes."

She shrugs and keeps drinking. My mouth and throat still burn from the sip I took. No wonder her and Worth get on—they both drink the strong shit. "So up north," I prompt.

"Aye, go past the massive fooking castle that tosspot Ivar used to live in. Should be empty, but I wouldne recommend staying there... Maybe in the old houses around it. Too much death, too many fooking ghosts." She shivers. "Then ye keep fooking going, until ye don't think you can no more. Until ye think the world is almost ending and ye exhausted and sweating and about to give up."

"Sounds charming," I deadpan.

She shrugs. "It's a lawless world, kid. You only go up there to die or be left alone. If ye have men up there causing trouble, ye can bet they won't be as soft as these scavs."

"Soft?" I look around at the scavs in question, all massive fighters covered in more scars than even Worth.

"Aye, lass, soft. They are true survivors. Many stayed up there from when the world ended. They need no one or nothing. They live off the land and are almost feral, but not cannibals, I don't think. Just be careful and don't go in there cocky." She stands then, grabbing my glass and drinking it for me. "And don't get dead. Worth wouldn't like that, and that girl has been through enough."

I watch her waddle away, but when a scav accidentally falls against her, she turns quicker than a snake and punches him in the face, knocking him out cold before walking away.

I don't know about what she said, but she is the scariest son of a bitch out there.

Chapter 19
Love Shack Baby

After making sure the food is organised and double-checking the maps, I find myself drifting to the shop, which is basically a hut in the corner outside to repair bikes. Only Archel is in there. The sides and top are shielded from the sun, but the front is open to roll the bikes in. There's no one around as I stop and gawk, running my eyes over his naked torso. He's taken his shirt off, his muscles clenching as he does something to my bike. Sweat drips down his back and abs as he moves, and his hair is slicked back, his jeans tight.

My pussy takes that moment to remember the offer he made me.

He must feel my eyes on him, because he glances over his shoulder, his blue orbs sparkling when he sees me. "Hey, Princess, came to give me a hand?"

"No, that's your job—or mouth, or cock," I reply as I step into the hut and hop onto the workbench in the back.

He frowns for a minute in confusion and then it clicks. He surges to his feet and grabs my thighs, almost dragging them off the workbench as his lips crash onto mine.

We have to be quick so we don't get caught, but with the sun shining down on us and his lips on mine, I don't care about anything but being with my shadow. He groans into my mouth, the masculine sound so deep and rumbling, it makes me shiver. His hands slide up my thighs to the buttons of my jeans, and without even breaking the kiss, he flicks them open and pushes his hand inside. He quickly pushes my panties out of his way and strokes my pussy, making me moan into his mouth.

My shadow knows exactly where to touch, his thumb rubbing my clit before he teases me and strokes across my center and back up again. His caresses are soft, making me grind into his hand, but it's not enough.

Ripping my mouth away, I glare at him. "Stop messing around and fuck me."

"Always so demanding, Princess," he teases, nipping my lips. "You know it. Now get it out."

"How romantic," he deadpans. "It's a good thing you're cute." "Shut up and fuck me." I laugh, and he groans as he steps back,

unzipping his jeans and pulling out his hard cock. I swallow, word- less, as I stare at his huge length, wiggling on the table as I wait for him to fuck me hard and fast.

I want quick and hungry, not loving and slow, and in his eyes, I see the same. He wants to fuck, to rut, and I am down for it. He steps towards me and yanks on my jeans, and we get them off together, my panties too. He throws my clothes over my bike to stop them from getting dirty and then steps between my parted thighs.

He kisses me hard, making me lose myself in his mouth as his hand strokes my pussy again. But I don't want his hand, I want his cock. I reach down and palm it, squeezing it as he groans into my mouth. He takes the hint, pulling my thighs wider apart. Moving between them, Archel presses the head of his cock to my hole, slowly pushing in with a slow, measured thrust. He fights my tight channel as he pulls out and pushes back in over and over, sinking deeper each time until he's finally balls deep. His huge cock spears me, and he remains unmoving as I writhe.

He holds me there, on the verge of frustration, until I bite his lip hard, and then he finally relents. Archel pulls out and slams in, slowly at first as our mouths fight for dominance. My shadow always makes sure he never pushes me too far, never hurts me. He keeps me here with him as he speeds up, fucking me harder and faster. Our breaths mingle together as I pull back on a moan, my eyes closing as I lose myself in him.

"Stay with me, Princess," he snarls, and I force my eyes open, holding his gaze.

I drip down his dick, wild for his soft hands on my hips, even as he fucks me so hard, it almost hurts, only making me want it that much more. I know he will never take it too far. He will always protect me, even from himself and his desires.

But I want those desires.

He leans down, nipping and licking any skin he can reach. Each thrust hits that spot inside of me, pushing me higher and higher. The pleasure surges through me, making my heart race and clit throb, and then he finally touches it.

His fingers stroke across my thighs to my cunt, rubbing my clit, fast and quick, matching his thrusts. It throws me over the edge, and I cry out my release. My pussy clenches around him, but he doesn't stop, forcing his cock through my fluttering channel. His teeth dig into my shoulder, and one orgasm tumbles into another until he grunts and stills as he fills me with his release, and I slump in post orgasmic bliss. I wear a smile as Archel brushes his lips up my throat and kisses me softly.

"I love you," he breathes against them, and I smile wider.

"I love you too," I purr, leaning into him as we hold each other through the aftershocks. When we have calmed down, he pulls from my pussy, leaving me feeling good and fucked.

Kissing him softly, I grin and hop off the table to get dressed and back to work. "Thanks for the orgasm break, now back to work," I order, slapping his ass as I pass.

After cleaning up, I leave Archel to finish the bikes with a huge grin on his face as he whistles, the smug bastard. I would be mad at how cheery he is, but damn if I don't have a dopey, satisfied smile on my face.

It's scary how good that man is at everything. The big three— sex, killing, and...I forgot the last one.

I check on the others, and the day passes quickly. It's almost nightfall when everything is prepared, so we decide to just bite the bullet and leave tonight. It's going to be a long drive, and the sooner we can get there, the better. Less bodies, less chaos. Also, I was a little bored just sitting around here. I always have to be moving, or Jago says I get into trouble. It's usually with him, though, so I think he may be biased.

I say goodbye to Worth and, surprisingly, Clarissa, who is definitely starting to like me. She warns me to be careful up there, and as someone who has lived her life on the road, I take it seriously. She also gives me some good ideas of where to stop and search for supplies, and I nod my thanks before pulling down my goggles and peeling away from The Ring.

Our lights shine bright across the sand dunes as we carefully follow the roads. The heat is less pressing at night, thank God, but the echo of feral growls, guns, and screams is constant. You sorta get used to it though, like a relaxing lullaby of chaos.

I'm familiar with these roads by now, so I take point, turning north and heading through The Wastes of our world—the destroyed buildings and bloodstained pavements partially covered by debris and sand. The moon and stars shine brightly down on us, and it's honestly a nice drive. With my men at my back, it's freeing. The wind whips through my hair. Yeah, I'll have a bucket of sand filling my boots and clothes when we stop, but I'm going to look on the bright side and call it an exfoliant.

We drive for hours, since there's no point in stopping unless we need to. The Wastes are unchanging apart from the sand dunes. A bit later, Clay points out a petrol station, and we decide to chance it. Gasoline is hard to find nowadays and getting harder. Worth mentioned they once found a massive reserve, but it never hurts to check as we pass.

Pulling up to the edge of the lot, we keep our lights on. Jago smashes his hand into his bike, the resounding noise loud and echoing across the night. When nothing growls or leaps at us, I slip from my bike. With my crossbow in hand, I head towards the pumps. Jago follows, while Archel and Evan wait with our bikes, scanning the area for danger. Clay heads into the dirty, half destroyed building behind the pumps to check for supplies and anything else we could use.

"Don't go in there, Pascha," he warns, blocking the way. His face is drawn and sad, as sad as I have seen my warrior.

I go to walk past him. "I need—"

"No, I mean it. Do not look," he orders, and it's the first time he ever has.

I meet his eyes, the lights of the bikes illuminating us as Jago finishes using the canisters we found. "What is it?" I ask softly.

He frowns, and I step closer.

"Clay, you don't need to protect me. Tell me."

"It's a body. A woman." I stride past him then. He doesn't try to stop me again, but he follows, pausing behind me when I freeze at the door, staring at what he found.

It's a woman, a young woman. Probably barely even eighteen. She's obviously been here a while, because her body is starting to rot. I have to cover my mouth with my sleeve, the odour is so overwhelming. My eyes actually water from it, but I still stay.

She's tied to the ceiling fan above, and her neck is broken. Her head hangs to the left, and her eyes are open and unseeing, and completely filled with blood. Her mouth is gaping, showing rotten teeth. Her lips are cracked and cut up, her cheek too. She's naked, her body on display with a piece of old, yellow paper taped to her leg.

I move over and quickly pull it away, ignoring the way the body swings from the force, otherwise I will heave. Stepping back, I quickly read over the harshly written words. "I can't do this anymore, it's too hard. Tell my family I'm sorry. Hopefully, I'll see them in another life."

Fuck.

She did this. I'm betting someone stole her clothes after, since beggars can't be choosers. I stare at her sadly, wondering if this could have been me, could have been my family...could have been Clarissa. This world is a dark, hard place to survive in, especially alone, and sometimes that darkness gets to be too much. It doesn't matter how strong you are when you are sinking.

"We bury her," I murmur into my sleeve. I can already see some of her skin missing, and bones show where animals have tried to eat her. It doesn't matter why she did it or who she was, all that matters now is honouring her life. "Get Jago or Archel."

"I'll do it, Pascha," Clay murmurs. I turn and watch him pull his mask down, and then he moves over to the woman. He gently cuts the rope free and catches her. He holds her like a child, so gently I almost cry, and then he heads outside. I follow, and when they see us with the woman in our arms, they all leap up to help. Even Evan, stone-faced and sad, grabs a piece of wood and starts to dig into the sand. The whole time Clay stands there without a complaint at the smell or for the body he holds in his arms.

It only makes me love him more.

Leaping into the hole we dug, he gently lays her down in the sand, and then we work together to bury her. The ground is overturned where she is, in an unmarked grave. The idea that no one knows, no one is looking for her, or even worse, they are looking for her, makes me want to cry. Evan wraps his arm around me, kissing my head.

"You did all you could, Pip."

Scrunching the letter in my fists, I shove it into my pocket, needing to keep it for some reason. "I know, I just wish there was more we could do."

"What about a puole," Clay offers softly.

"Puole?" I repeat.

"Yes, Pascha. In my culture, it is a way of indicating a burial. It is also used to represent those among us who deserve recognition to help guide them from this life to the next and offer them a rite of passage."

"How do we do it?" I ask, liking that idea.

He searches around us before disappearing for a moment and coming back with a giant rock. He lays it on the upturned dirt and disappears again, coming back with a smaller rock. He starts to smash the rock into the bigger one, engraving it. He draws crudely done symbols across it, explaining each one.

One is for their life, a celebration.

The other is for their next life, where they will reside or be reborn.

Another is to allow them to pass from this world to the next.

Another is a beacon of love and sadness, of remembering but moving on.

It's beautiful, and when he sits back, holding the rock in his bloodied hand from carving, I know we did the right thing. We stay there for a moment, all silent. I don't know what they're thinking about, but for me, it's gratitude. I am beyond happy I have not just a new family after losing mine, but also a place to belong, a path that keeps me fighting, and men who pull me out of the dark when it gets to be too much.

Kneeling, I press my hand to the dirt. "I was lost in the darkness like you. I'm sorry no one was there to help. I would be like you if not for my men." I lift my head and meet their eyes. "They saved me from everything, even from myself when it was too hard to be in my body and head after what happened." I look back at the dirt. "I hope—no, that's the wrong word. I pray that whoever you are now, you are in a better place." With that, I stand and walk away.

My men stare after me, their eyes filled with love as I dash my tears away.

They saved me, they truly did, and every day since, I've promised to save them.

I hope I can keep it.

Chapter 20
Cowboys

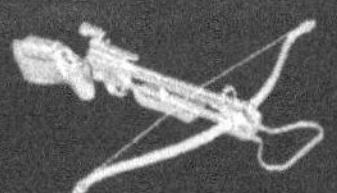

It's sombre as we ride. The woman we found was a stark reminder of just what this world is capable of. Not just the people in it, but how difficult it is trying to live on such a hard, unforgiving planet. There is no softness, no comfort. This is a place of survival, like the cavemen I was taught about as a child.

Every day could be your last, and every move is a risk. You don't fight or hunt for food? You die. You don't scavenge for water and supplies? You die. Even if you do all that, you still might meet your end. Each and every second is a constant battle of wills and a test of who you are. Many have fallen and failed, many still will. This world is not made for everyone, and although it's changing with Worth in charge, we will never be back to how it was before it all ended.

This is who we are now, and sometimes, it's easy to forget that with my men and friends surrounding me. I've seen the skills of the people who still linger in this place and call it home. I have survived such violations and attacks that I know my own limits and strengths now. It doesn't make it easier, and those events have scarred me, changed me.

I'm not the little girl from Paradise anymore. I'm Piper, the leader of The Damned.

A warrior, a lover, and sometimes, a crazy bitch.

But I can't let the darkness stain every part of me. If you only ever know survival—not just living, but existing—you'll never know what happiness is. I never want to fall too deep into those shadows where I forget how to love, how to laugh, and how to enjoy the little moments. Like Beast Jr., whom I left with Worth. He represented an innocence I wasn't used to out here, a chance to make a difference. He reminded me how easy it is to overlook and draw conclu- sions about people and things, because it's easier to.

My men remind me to love, and I like to think I remind them to laugh.

It works, and I hope it stays like that for a very long time.

Riding silently, I search the horizon, watching for assailants and the sunrise. The days are longer at the moment, since we're changing seasons, so it rises early, but it's a beautiful sight as the red and orange streak across the sky.

There was this old film I liked where it had a cowboy riding into the sunset on his horse after defeating the villain. It makes me think of that. Like we are cowboys riding off on our horses to save our land and people.

Let's just hope these cowboys don't end up bucked.

After another day of riding with only one break for a few hours of sleep, I see the castle Nan told me about, the one where Ivar used to live. It's now abandoned, and being this close to it has a shiver skating across my spine. It feels haunted, even from here, so instead of stop- ping like we want to, we keep going, hoping we will find something else to stay in—a place not haunted by the ghosts of the innocents he killed.

It's dark when we finally find a building that looks like it will protect us from the elements, give us shelter from passers-by, and not infested with murderers or ferals. Speaking of, I miss my baby. I didn't want to bring him on the road when we might not make it back since he is so small, but damn that fuzzy little cutie has wormed his way into my heart.

Clay and Jago check the building while I wait with the bikes, Archel, and Evvie.

They come out minutes later and wave us over, so we park the bikes around the corner near a backdoor they indicate. If someone comes in through the front, we can make a quick escape. Once through the door, we wander through a dark corridor before Jago pulls back a crusty curtain, and it finally clicks what we are standing in...or on, I should say.

A stage.

We are in a theatre. "Damn," I mutter, looking out at the rows and rows of seats, some missing and some ruined. There's a balcony up top, and boxes hanging to the left and right. The old gold fixtures were either ruined or stolen. There are some holes in the roof, but other than that, it's in okay condition.

"I'll find a way up to the balcony and take first watch," Archel murmurs and kisses my cheek as he brings his sniper rifle with him and slips into the wings.

He comes back out a minute later and sighs. "Stairs are destroyed, but where there's a will there's a way. Watch this, Princess. You can ogle my ass while I protect your pretty one." With that, he jumps from the stage and works through the chairs and seating, slinging the rifle over his shoulder as he grabs onto a post beneath the balcony and quickly climbs it. The ledge sticks out, and he has to jump back to grab onto the edge, dangling there as he effortlessly pulls himself up and over. Getting to his feet, he blows me a kiss as he sits down, his sniper rifle back out to watch us while we sleep.

Jago sets up our sleeping pads as Evan passes out water, and I choose food for us to eat. The floor is hard and worn, and scratched in places from years of use of performance and art. Now it's empty, forgotten like a lot in this world. No more plays, no more performances. No ballet or imagination. Just...surviving. It's sad really, how many stories these wooden boards could hold. How many years of dedication people had just to make it to this moment, only to be lost in the devastation of our world.

"I wonder what I would have been in the other world," I muse as I stroke along the floor. "A dancer? Probably not, I'm not graceful enough."

"Not a singer, you sound like a dying feral," Evan teases, and I grin at him.

"Something amazing. Like an inventor or an activist. A fighter, maybe even a soldier." Jago shrugs.

"Whatever it was, Pascha, you would have been remarkable and made a difference," Clay adds.

"Jago would be a soldier for sure. Evvie, would you still be a doctor?"

"Hmm, maybe. They always say doctors are born, but..." "But?" I prompt.

"I like drawing. I think I would have been an artist or even a tattooist." He smiles, and I can't help but smile back.

"I like that, I think so too." I lean into him, watching Clay. "What about you, my mountain man?"

"We do not speak of before, so I do not know. What do you think?" he asks, sipping his water. I run my eyes over him.

"Soldier," Evan offers.

"Nah, MMA fighter," Jago says.

"Serial killer!" Archel calls, making us all laugh.

"I think you would have been a bodyguard or maybe an architect. You like building things."

"Weapons. Hey, he could have been an arms dealer," Evan jokes, making me laugh.

"What about Archel?" I call, and we all share a look before laughing.

"Stalker for sure."

"Serial killer like he said," Jago grumbles. "Shady government agent," Evvie teases.

We laugh, even as Archel flips us off, and I settle back, still stroking the wood. I wonder what happened to the many talented people who walked or danced and performed on this stage. Where are they now? I wonder if one day we will ever get back to this, back to entertainment and talent that doesn't involve bloodshed and death.

Maybe one day, and that is why we fight—so we can reclaim as much as we can and live a life that is more than just killing.

So we can enjoy the little things.

We all sleep together on the stage with Archel watching our backs. We huddle together for comfort and warmth, the sound of old symphonies filling my head as I fall asleep to thoughts of art and dancers.

Chapter 21
I've Got A Bad Feeling Babe

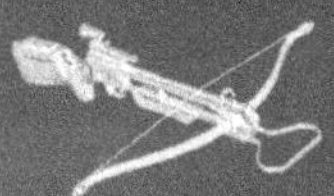

We get moving early. The sun is barely up when we are back on our bikes. We know the closer we get to the north, the more careful we need to be. This is new territory for all of us, and who knows where these scavs are hiding. But we will deal with them like we do everything else and protect our people and land like we promised.

The farther north we go, the quieter we get. Nan was right—even the terrain up here is rougher. The ground is filled with deep grooves and holes. The roads are broken halfway across bridges, just dropping off, and cars are still parked there like they tried to flee before it was destroyed. It makes finding a way true north hard, and we keep having to double back. Eventually, we get tired and take a break under an old, abandoned lorry. We sit in the back, eating and drinking. Clay perches on the top of the truck, watching the roads both front and back.

Archel has an hour power nap before we head back out again. We drive slowly, avoiding the holes that might pop our tires or trap us. There are signs of life, but they are old—tire tracks, bones, and blood littered around. We must be reaching the end of the land soon, so where are they hiding?

An hour later, we hit the coast. The land just disappears into the Dead Sea. We drive along it, making our own path as the land ascends into jagged cliffs, which are blocked by destroyed cars, making us head farther inland.

Where are they hiding?

Finding them might be harder than bloody killing them at this point.

Everywhere we look, there is empty, destroyed land, nothing more. We see no people, no ferals, and no cannibals...so where the fuck is everyone?

Could it be that the land is too destroyed to live up here? There is no shelter, no places for food or water, but Worth said her intel isn't usually wrong.

We stop the bikes near some devastated trees and sit down, debating what to do. I check the map, but it doesn't offer much. "We could set a trap," Evan suggests, and I blink and look at him.

"That's...pretty smart," I comment.

"I am known to be sometimes." He grins. "If they are up here, they must be watching or checking the land every now and again. We set a trap for them and wait, then draw them to us instead of driving around in circles."

"Any ideas for a trap?"

"The simpler the better. I'm betting they aren't very smart." Archel snorts. "Let's have Piper sit out in the open while we hide behind something, waiting to lure them in. Bam, we jump out, kill them all, then head home for some orgies and sleep."

"I mean...it's not a bad idea." I laugh.

"Then let's do it," Clay says and stands, looking for a good place to do it. "There is a load of abandoned train runners over there. We could easily hide behind and in them and keep an eye on you."

I follow his eye, and we quickly pack up and head over. We push the bikes behind the train carts and cover them with some scraps of fabrics and sand in case they come from that direction. Clay lies on the roof of one of the trains. Archel hides inside another with his rifle resting on a box, waiting. Evan and Jago are behind a different one, watching, as I just sit out in the open.

I feel exposed, and my eyes run across the area before Jago calls out, "Relax, Brawler, you look too alert."

He's right, so I close my eyes and breathe out before I bury a knife in the sand next to me, set my crossbow on the other side, and lean back on my bag like I'm resting. Who knows when they will turn up? But if they spot me waiting and watching, they might not take the bait.

I have to sit in the burning sun for hours, listening for any sign of scavs creeping up to kill me. Sweat drips down my face, and I wipe it away before closing my eyes. Let's hope I don't have to wait here all night too.

I doze off at some point, knowing my men are watching, but the rumble of the ground under me has me jerking awake. Luckily, I remember the plan and keep my eyes closed, even as I hear the engines drawing closer. And closer. I stay as still as I can, skidding my hand across the sand to land on top of my knee as I wait.

The engines stop, and then I hear boot steps.

"Well, look what we have here, boys!" comes a call with a thick accent.

I pretend to wake up and sit upright, acting scared as I dart my eyes between the men heading towards me—even though I'm checking their weapons and numbers. There are eight of them all looking worse for wear. One on the left is missing an eye, another an ear. Their clothes are tattered and covered in grime and blood. Their bodies are sweaty, and I can smell them from here, making me cringe as I swallow and fake scramble to my knees as they chuckle and call out rude remarks.

It's evident the one at the front is the leader of this gang. Is this all of them? Eight people are causing such chaos? Easy-peasy.

He's a big guy, but not huge. One of his arms is longer than the other, and one leg drags behind slightly, as if it was injured and didn't heal properly. His face is mean and squashed with his eyes spaced close together. His lips are thin, even when tilted up, and he licks his tongue along them. I shiver when I see it's split down the middle like a snake's. He has no eyebrows or hair at all, and sweat drips down his meaty face.

"All alone, little girl?" he sneers, stopping just before me. His men are laughing like fucking hyenas as they call out dirty remarks about my body, which I ignore. "Big fucking mistake. What do you think, men? Let's welcome the little dove to the north."

"Your first mistake was not checking the perimeter," I call, and then let out a whistle as I drop forward. Shots fire right over my head as I grab my crossbow and roll. Stopping near them, I get to my feet and fire. I hit one in the chest, making him scream as he falls back. Their calls are loud—they are unorganised. Some run, some stay. Engines start, and I see one in a golf cart covered in graffiti with spikes on the front and the name 'Crusher' on the side. Another gets in a similar cart with a shovel on the front with spikes on it.

Three men are already dead on the ground as Evan, Clay, and Jago rush out to meet me. Archel picks off those in the carts. I watch as one slumps, and the cart jerks to the side as he dies before the vehicle rolls, then explodes. I duck a punch from baldie and fire again, hitting him in the shoulder. He roars, and I have to reload. When I do, I swing my crossbow up, but he storms over, grabs it, rips it from my hand, and tosses it away. I snatch a knife from my side and slice it up with a snarl, cutting across his face. I duck another punch, but then someone grabs me from behind and jerks me back. With a grunt, I slam my head backwards, but it gives baldie enough time to take in the fight and realise he is losing.

He may not be smart, but he knows when he is outnumbered. He glares at me, turns, and rushes to an old police car waiting with the others' transports. It has the word 'Police' still written on it, but now it's covered in graffiti and skulls along the front hood, and it doesn't have a window. He revs the engine and peels away as I stamp on the foot of the man holding me. He spins us, and I spot Archel. He's standing in the doorway of the train cart, his eye to the scope, and I freeze as he fires, hitting the man behind me effortlessly. He falls away, and I scramble forward, grabbing my cross- bow. Turning, I scan my surroundings. Baldie and another scav on a bike got away, and they are speeding into the distance.

"We can't lose them!" I scream, slinging my crossbow and bag over my shoulder and racing to my bike.

I throw off the sand as best as I can, swing my leg over, and spin in the dirt as I rev the engine. Jago points at me. "Stay close," he orders as we peel after them, kicking up sand as we give chase.

We can't lose them and ruin the mission. They won't fall for another trap. We would have to spend weeks hunting them up here, and they have the advantage of knowing the land. No, we end this now.

I spot them on the horizon and push the bike to its limits. Luckily, our bikes are faster since we can cut across what they can't, and we catch up to them. They spot us and increase their speed, shooting forward as we race across the land. The hunt is on.

They twist and turn to avoid Clay's bombs and Archel's knives. I swing my crossbow up, and one-handed, I pull next to the other bike and fire right into his face. He goes down hard, his bike flip- ping into the distance. It's just us and the car now.

He turns so fast, he almost tips, his wheel squealing as he kicks up sand and dirt and then shoots forward. He's heading into a pass between dunes. We follow him down, and it gets darker and darker as we drive towards the cliffs on the coast.

I search the jagged edge, wondering what he's aiming for. It stretches into the sky, eclipsing the sun. Is he heading right for the rock to protect his back, trying to take us all down? That's suicide. Is he really that dumb? We follow either way, needing to kill him.

But he doesn't stop, gunning it faster and faster towards those rocks. I have to slow down, straining to see where he's going. It's only a moment before he shoots through the opening when I see it.

I skid to a stop at the top of the tunnel entrance, still in the sun. It's a fucking mine.

Its wooden entrance doesn't look too good, but it's wide enough to fit at least three bikes side by side or a car. There's a sign saying 'Active Mine,' with warning signs and a metal fence to the left and right. It dips in so we couldn't see it until we were nearly on it.

There's a crudely drawn skull above the entrance, and we hear the engine stop.

Fuck, we have to go in, don't we?

We park the bikes to the side and stare at the mine, waiting for him to come out. He can't have another exit, surely, so he's trapped in there. But we also can't stay awake out here forever. Fuck, he knows that. He knows this place better than us. There are too many variables.

"We can't go in." Clay sighs. "We ventured into an old mine once and lost a hundred of our men when it collapsed. It could be a trap and unsafe, not to mention gas leaks and the man currently hiding in there."

"Fuck," I mutter. "We have no choice. It's going to be dark soon, and we wouldn't see him coming. We need to end this now."

"This place gives me the creeps," Evan mutters. "I have a bad feeling, Brawler."

"Me too," I mumble, staring at the entrance. I really do, but I have no other idea. It's either this or we wait, and being out in the open doesn't sound appealing. Archel steps closer.

"There are five of us, one of him. We go in quiet and fast, watching each other's backs, kill him, and then get the fuck out of there. It will be okay as long as we stay smart," he murmurs.

Decision made, I grab a torch from my bag, and the others do the same, but all of us remain quiet. Going into the unknown is the usual in The Wastes, but they are right—I have a bad feeling about this. My heart hammers, my palms sweat, and my head screams at me that it's dumb. We could set a trap outside, but we could be waiting for days or even weeks. Who knows what supplies he has in there?

No, we need to end this now.

Crossbow held tight, I strap on more knives as well as my katana and wait for the others. Evan puts on a torch headband he found at the hospital and holds a knife. Archel grasps his sword, Jago an axe, and Clay a huge blade. All of us look around before we start towards the entrance together. We pause once inside in case he is waiting to leap out at us. Archel tosses a flare inside that lights up the entrance, reflecting back across orange rock, but nobody's there.

With the sun behind us, we head inside. Going deep into the earth.

Chapter 22
Mine Madness

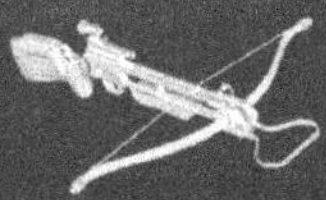

The mine is dark and hot, so hot, I feel sweat dripping down my spine as we slowly move into the huge, man-made tunnel. It tilts down with old, abandoned trolleys and tracks to the left, which we check to make sure he's not hiding in. Not too far in, we find his abandoned car. It clearly couldn't get any farther down, and after watching our front while Jago watches our back, the others check the car, and we conclude he must have moved deeper on foot.

He clearly knows this place. It must be a hiding area, or his scavs' home? Either way, we stay alert. My eyes skim the graffiti on the warm, dark rock walls. Words, phrases, skulls decorate the surface, all meant to scare, and it does the trick. I swallow but force my eyes to search the dark crevices before us. Our lights only pierce so far in front of us, leaving the rest in shadows and darkness, which I think I can see things moving in, but I know it's just my imag- ination.

"So creepy," Evan mutters, his voice echoing ominously.

"You can say that again," I reply, but go quiet after that. Our voices are too loud, and it will give us away. I'm honestly two seconds away from saying fuck this and just getting out of here and waiting outside. It may take longer, but I also won't feel like I'm in some sort of creepy horror movie with cave monsters waiting to eat me.

I like to be eaten as much as the next girl, but not to death, if you feel me.

That's when I hear shuffling, like feet along rocks. I freeze and hold my hand up before crouching. I hold my crossbow before me as I scan the rocks. Archel lights up another flare and tosses it, and I almost fall back in shock. There are at least ten men, all skinny, like fucking skeletons, bald and naked just standing in the dark waiting for us. Fuck! I fire and the others do too. They all laugh, a high tinkling sound, which is creepy as fuck as it echoes around. They try to dodge our bullets, and when they fall, others just take their place.

I keep firing and reloading, and eventually, they all are down. "What in the ever-loving fuck?" I hiss.

"That was fucking terrifying," Evan snarls. "Now can we get the fuck out of here?"

Just then, more laughter sounds, and we move forward slightly to see past the bodies. There are two tunnels. One is moving, and I realise men are crawling along the fucking floor, coming from cracks and other smaller tunnels.

Nope, fuck this.

Not today, God, Satan, or any other fucker who thinks this funny.

"We are out of here!" I yell.

There is no fucking way we are staying down here. It's like a goddamn nightmare. They can attack us in the sun where I can see the creepy fuckers and they can't crawl along the floor like some fucked-up worm.

We start backing away, firing into the mass as we go. "Fucking hell!" Jago barks.

I have to reload, and he yanks me back. I narrowly avoid one of them leaping out of a hole in a wall somewhere. Fuck!

"They are coming out of the fucking walls!" Archel yells, using his knives to hold them back.

"Behind us!" Clay shouts, and I see him turning to protect our backs as we move. I wish we could toss one of his bombs, but with us down here too, we would be trapping ourselves in a fucking mine with these…these creatures.

Instead, we just have to fight and slowly move backwards, falling over rocks in the dark as the flare starts to die. Jago is before me, swinging his axe and holding them back as much as he can. When they slip through, they leap at me, and I shoot them down mid-air. The sounds they make burrow into my head, and I know I'm going to have fucking nightmares about the creepy bastards.

"Pip!" Evan yells, and I turn, but I'm too late.

One of them scurries out of a tunnel opposite my head and leaps at me. I fall back, smacking into the wall. A sharp rock hits my head hard.

I fall with him on top of me. I am unable to move, feeling hot blood leak down my neck. Jago is suddenly there with a snarl, and with a fierce yell, he uses his axe like a battering ram, throwing the creepy fucker off me. Evan is beside me in an instant as my head lolls to the side. My fingers are cold and numb, and I release my crossbow. My vision blurs until I see two of everything, two of Jago still fighting the surge, even as they push him back. My ears ring, the high-pitched noise mixing with the sound of their panicked screams and Evan's directives.

"Fuck, we have to move!" Archel yells. "Princess!" "We can't move her!" Evan screams back.

"We have to!" Jago roars, and then I'm carefully picked up and cradled in Clay's arms. My head rests on his shoulder, and I watch as we move swiftly towards the exit. I see Evan grabbing my stuff and firing to help Jago as he backs towards us. It causes a separa- tion, and they surround Jago, cutting us and Evan off from him.

There are too many of them. He gets brought to his knees, but he quickly gets up. He looks back as we break into the sun to see we are free, then his eyes narrow as he rushes towards Evan.

"Love you, Brawler," he yells, and then grabs Evan, throwing him out of the cave and rushing into the horde, holding them back while we escape.

I want to scream. I want to fight and go back. But I can't move, and darkness claws at my vision. The pain in my head is indescribable, until I finally succumb with his name on my lips.

Jago.

When I blink, I'm on the front of a bike with arms holding me up as we gun it, and the world is dark around us. I realise someone's racing heart is pressed to my head, and then I pass out again. When I blink once more, I can tell time has passed, but not how much. My head aches, blood still drips from it, and my body is sluggish and cold. I am still unable to move. I hear yelling and arguing, and then a bright light shines in my eyes, sending agony through me. When I can blink enough to clear my eyes, I see the shape of someone walking towards us through those lights, but I promptly pass out.

When I wake again, I'm in someone's arms, swaying with the movement of walking. It makes bile rise in my throat, tangling with the pain pumping through me. My head is propped up and facing forward. There's a man before us—a stranger.

He has curly, shoulder-length grey hair. When he looks back, I see a grey beard and piercing eyes with glasses propped on his big red nose. He looks me over before returning his focus to the path we are on. Trees pass on either side of us as we seem to head up, but my head is spinning, so who knows.

I try to speak, to demand we go back, to ask for Jago, but my lips refuse to move.

I blink, and suddenly, we break through the trees, and I see a house standing on the edge of a cliff as the sun starts to rise behind it. I pass out again. Panic for Jago is still at the forefront of my mind, even as I fade into oblivion.

Chapter 23
The Man On The Cliff

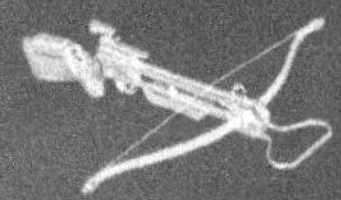

I'm warm, cosy almost, like I'm lying on a cloud. I'm comfortable, warm, and not wanting to move. It calls me back into the darkness, lulling me to forget my worries and just sleep, but something bugs me.

It pulls me back, wanting me to wake up. To get up.

What is it? It's like sand falling through my parted fingers—the harder I try to clench my fist, the more it escapes until I slip back into unconsciousness. When I wake again, my body aches, but the pain isn't as bad as before. My heart screams at me to get up, to wake up.

But why?

I hear voices then, but they seem far away, yet for some reason, they settle me. I can't understand the words, but the tone has me fighting through the fog. Something is wrong.

But what?

Then it comes crashing down on me like a ton of bricks. Jago!

I pry my eyes open. I'm still unable to move, like I'm trapped, as I move my eyes around desperately to see him or anyone. The room is dimly lit, and I'm in a bed in a random bedroom with exposed wood beams above me. There's a closed door at the end of the bed, and the noises are coming from behind it.

I try to open my lips, but nothing comes out. I try harder, and a trapped groan sounds from my throat. Jago! I scream internally as I struggle to lift my hand, my legs, anything. I keep trying to, and my head starts pounding again, but I manage to roll.

Only, I roll right off the bed, smacking into the cold wood floor. The voices stop and footsteps sound. I search for a weapon, and a moment later, the door opens with squeak to reveal Archel with Evan behind him. Their gazes are panicked, and when they see me on the floor, they rush in.

"Princess, what the hell? Are you okay?" "Pip, what happened?"

"Jago," I croak past my aching throat.

They share a look as they crouch before me and lift me back into the bed. "You need to rest. You have what I'm guessing is a fractured skull and a concussion," Evan starts, but I narrow my eyes.

"Jago—" I cough, and he helps me sit up and sip some water. Archel sits on my other side as a stranger, a man, appears in the doorway. He has white hair, he's the one I saw when I was passing out.

"Good, you're awake," he remarks, his voice low and slow. "Who are you?" I demand once I can and then look at Evan.

"Where's Jago?" Evvie's eyes drop to the bed as his lips turn down. I look at Archel, who scrubs at his head before sighing.

"Princess..." He trails off. "Where is he, and where's Clay?"

"Jago...Jago got trapped in there with them. He stayed so we could get you out. Clay is scouting the area now, trying to look for signs of him."

"You left him there?" I roar, jerking up, ignoring the pain it causes. "You left him?"

His eyes narrow. "It was that, or we all died, Princess, including you. He knew that, he gave us the signal. You always come first. We protect you, even if we die. Jago knew this, it was always his plan."

"He's not dead, he can't be," I whisper, and he sighs, his expression softening as he takes my hand and squeezes.

"If anyone can survive, it's Jago. Plus, why would they kill him right away? They would need information. It's only been around eight hours, so there's still a chance we can get him back. We didn't want to leave you while you were still unconscious though."

"Go, I'm awake, go get him!" I demand. "In fact, I'm coming." I move to the edge of the bed, but they stop me.

"You can't stand, Pip," Evvie snaps, in doctor mode now.

"He's right—you'll only be hurting yourself further. Those fools from the mine wouldn't have killed your friend yet, they like to enjoy taunting them first," the stranger informs me.

"That doesn't fucking help," I mutter and throw him a glare. "Who are you?"

"Manners, young one, this is my house, after all," he warns. "This is Abel, he saved us, Princess. We didn't know where to

go. We needed shelter and safety to lay you down and check you over. You were bleeding so badly. We drove around for hours until he found us. He lit the way and led us to his house here. He gave us supplies and shelter. Abel saved your life," Archel offers softly.

I swallow and look at the man, Able, who still appears grumpy. "I apologise, that was rude. Thank you for your home and assistance, but we really have to go now and retrieve Jago—"

"It's midday. They sleep now with only select scouts going out. As I told your friend, you ran into one of those scouts. They usually take you back to the mine for entertainment." He winces. "And then toss you into the sea out back when they are done. Your best bet is getting one of those scouts for information. Your friend, Clay, is doing that with my assistance right now. I implore you to wait instead of running in there with no plan again. I understand this may be hard—"

"Hard? You know nothing, old man," I snarl rudely, my worry and anger coming out full force on this stranger. "And why are you living up here alone? Why not kill them if you see what they are doing?"

"One man against a mine full of feral men? I may be good, but

I'm not that good," he snaps. "I've been here all my life. I was born here, and I will die here. You want to get yourself killed trying to save the world? Then be my guest, but do not ever disrespect me in my own walls again." He turns and storms away.

"Little harsh, Pip," Evvie chides.

"Fuck harsh," I mutter, staring at the floor and wiggling my toes where they hang above it. My head is killing me. "He saw them killing people and did nothing."

"Not everyone is a fighter, Princess. Some people are just trying to survive," Archel reminds me, kissing my shoulder. "We will get him back."

"We better, and then we are having a fucking word about this stupid save Piper rule, even if it's with all of you tied down while I yell at you."

"Sounds kinky, I'm in," Evvie teases. "Now let's get you lying down. He's right—you need to rest. If you want to save Jago, you need to save your energy and heal while we wait for information."

I can't argue with that logic, so I let them help me back into bed. They go to leave, but I grab Evan's hand. "Stay with me?" I look to Archel then and the door. "Both of you, please?"

"Anything you say, Princess." Archel bows, and instead of sitting in a chair this time like he did when I was first healing in a strange bed, he climbs over me and lies on my other side. Evan slips in next to me, and together, they hold me and help me fall back to sleep.

Jago's face in my mind.

His name across my broken, worried heart.

When I wake up again, Clay is not still back, but they don't seem concerned, so I settle down. They give me some food Abel dropped off and then check me over, washing me before they fall back to sleep next to me. But I can't, I'm awake and worried for my beast.

I slip from the bed on wobbly feet. I'm still in my jeans, but my jacket is gone, and my top is stained and stuck to me. My hair is matted and plaited to the side, and the back of my head is sore when I touch it, so I drop my hand and open the door.

"Princess," Archel murmurs, never truly sleeping.

"I need to pee," is all I say as I slip out and into a narrow hallway. There's a bathroom to the side, which I quickly use. There's a lamp burning, exposing the old-style mirror and claw foot tub. Using a bucket of water, I splash my face and my neck before leaving again. My eyes go to the bedroom door I was staying in and then focus farther into the house where I hear noises.

Wondering if it's Clay, I pad down a hallway to a black, winding spiral staircase. Taking them slowly, I get halfway down and have to stop, my head hurting something fierce again.

"You should be resting," Abel calls, and I open my eyes and lean over the edge. The steps go right into an old-fashioned country kitchen with a wood burning stove, copper sink, and dark wood cupboards. A huge, handmade table is placed across the room, facing a window that looks out onto the cliff. It has eight chairs and benches, and it's where I find Abel sitting with a teacup and saucer with a teapot before him.

"Can't sleep," I murmur as I head the rest of the way down and freeze at the bottom, meeting his eyes. "Is Clay back yet?"

"No," he answers, and I sigh, looking around. "Is your head hurting?"

I meet his eyes and find myself nodding. He seems less...angry, and I realise it was probably my fault. We disturbed his life, after all, and then I was rude to him. I'm betting he is used to being alone. "Yes."

"Come sit down." He gestures and pulls out a chair for me. I take it, and he pushes it back in.

"Thank you," I murmur, but I watch him closely as he moves around opening cupboards. There is some bread on the table with a knife for carving, and I quickly grab it and slip it under the table and onto my lap just in case. I know better, you can't trust anyone.

He comes back a moment later with a black clay mug with herbs inside and pours the water from the teapot into it before placing it in front of me. "It's a mix of herbs grown from my garden, a herbal painkiller. Try it, it will help." He sits back down, cupping his own, and his gaze goes to the window.

I look from him to the dark mixture and slowly take a sip with shaking hands. I almost gag, and he chuckles.

"Not the nicest tasting, but it does the trick. Down the hatch, young one," he orders. I keep sipping, and he's right—the pain starts to fade slightly and my body begins to ache less. I finish it off and wipe my mouth.

"Are you hungry? There is bread—" He looks at it and notices the knife is gone and then stares at me. I refuse to be ashamed as he searches my face. "I mean you no harm. In fact, I worry you will hurt me. I have no quarrel with you."

"I don't with you, but I've been tricked in the past, badly. Excuse me if I'm more cautious." I shrug.

"Understandable, as long as you don't use that knife on me."

"I won't if there is no reason to," I counter, and he nods. We have an understanding. He looks back to the window as I run my eyes around the homely, slightly askew house. It screams old, but it's also cosy and warm. No wonder he's never left if he was born here. It's all he knows.

"You were born here? Before the end?" I ask as he sips his tea. "I was. It feels like so long ago now. My mother raised me, we were farmers. When the end came, most of the farm was washed away, but the house survived...as did we. My mother died a few years later from a simple infection, and I was alone."

"Why not try to find others?"

"I did once or twice. Every time I went south and left the house, I found what this world had turned into. So much death. People killing everyone for scraps of food, for clothing or fun. It was feral—no, I was better here. So I came back and never left."

I nod. I can understand that. He's right—out there it's...a different world than in here. Here it seems almost separate from it, serene. Calm. "What about food and water?"

"I have a well. It only has slight signs of radiation like most of the water now. For food, I have gardens where I grow my own veg, and I still have a supply from when I went out a year or so ago and scouted." He looks to me then. "What about you? You're a fighter, that's for sure, but why are you here? Up north? How have you survived?"

"We are part of a collection of people surviving farther south but still in the north. We are rebuilding society as best as we can. We have a queen who was voted in with a council, and we are the enforcers of the new laws. We heard about the disturbances up here, and the queen asked if I would come and deal with it with my men," I murmur.

He blinks and sits back. "Well shit," he mutters. "A queen? A society? Maybe we aren't doing as bad as we once were. Good for you. But you should have left the north to itself. Those men aren't like freethinkers where you are from. You can't reason with them, they just want to kill and destroy."

"Then I'll destroy them." I shrug. "It's my job to keep our land and our people safe, and they are a threat."

"You really mean that," he murmurs. "You'd risk your life for everyone else. Why?"

"Because I can." I lean forward. "I've been hurt, betrayed, and left for dead. I know how weak it makes you, and how much I wished someone was there to save me. I won't let that happen to anyone else. I'll save as many as I can for as long as I can."

"Admirable." He nods. "But probably a short life." "But a meaningful one," I retort, and he grins. "Touché."

He pours me a normal tea this time, and we sit in silence as we drink it.

"So you've really been alone all the years?" I ask quickly.

"Not always. There was someone else once." He sighs. "But that's a story for a different time, not during the night where we call up ghosts of loved ones past."

Just then, we hear a bike. "That will be your man. Let's go see what he has to say."

"Thank you for telling me...and for the tea," I tell him as I stand, feeling stronger.

"You are welcome."

"Piper," I offer. "My name is Piper." "You are very welcome, Piper."

Chapter 24
Plant Your Tree

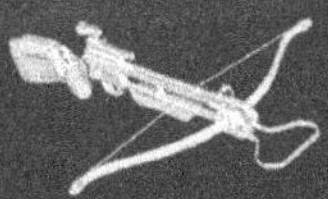

Clay is back. He sits down heavily at the table, and he's clearly tired, but he doesn't complain once. He pulls me into his arms and kisses me. "I'm sorry I failed you, Pascha. I should have gone back for him."

"No point in dwelling on the past," I murmur, knowing he is blaming himself. "Let's just get our beast home, okay?"

Pressing his head to mine, he searches my eyes for condemnation before he nods. "Bring him home."

"What did you find?" Archel calls as he and Evan come into the room with a yawn. They both take seats, and Abel quickly makes them all hot tea and puts more food on the table, bustling around silently while listening. This feels like a family matter, but this is his house, and he may have insight into these men, so I say nothing. Even if he was kind to me, helped me, I still have my reser- vations. Maybe it's because we are such different people and he's not a fighter. He stayed up here, all alone, with no inclination to explore or find more. We are opposites, but that doesn't mean I shouldn't trust him.

However, he has to earn that, and as of yet, he has not.

"I didn't see Jago, he must still be in the mines. I could hear voices coming from deep inside of it though." He grins at me and stands, setting me back down effortlessly. "They sent out a patrol just as I was about to give up." He disappears and then we hear a struggle. A moment later, he drags a bound and gagged man into the kitchen and tosses him to the floor. "A present, Pascha, to make up for my failure."

I glance at the hog-tied man and then to Clay with a smile. "You did good, babe. We can use him to get Jago back." I look at Archel and order, "Tie him to a chair, and let's find out everything we can about our new friends."

Archel's grin is definitely evil. He may be my shadow and protector, but he is also a Seeker, one of the best assassins in The Wastes. Right now, I'm going to use his skills as well as Evvie's, to keep this man alive long enough to find out what I need to know.

I need to learn if my beast is alive and how to get him back.

If he's not... No, I can't even think like that. Jago is invincible, untouchable, the strongest man I know. He's alive, and we will get him back. It's not a case of if, but when. There is no Brawler without Beast. That man saved my life over and over again and stole my heart. I'm not living without him. Even with an injured head and exhausted body, I know I'll walk through hell and back to get to him.

He would do the same for me. He would never stop, never give up until I was back in his arms. He already came for me, even when everyone else said I was dead. He never gave up hope, and I won't give up on him.

As I watch Archel effortlessly lift the man as he struggles, Evan leans closer and assures me, "We'll get him back, Pip, have faith. If there is one man in The Wastes who will always survive and make it back to your side, it's that big bastard."

It makes me smile. "Thank you," I murmur as he leans in and kisses my cheek. Abel notices, but he says nothing, and I turn my attention to the man Archel just tied to the chair in the middle of the room. Clay lifts me onto the table to sit and rest while Archel prowls around him.

His blue eyes dart around in fear and anger, his lips silenced by tape. He's half bald, and his eyebrows are gone like the others' were, but he seems bigger, more well fed. It makes sense if he's a scout, but I do wonder why they shave their heads. Less care maybe? I know shampooing can be a bitch, but damn, I don't think I could rock the bald look.

"You are not shaving your head, Princess," Archel remarks before he stops before the man and rips the tape away. His lips are bleeding, and his cheek is split open as well—I'm guessing from Clay. He rolls his lips as he runs his gaze around us, not saying a word.

"We will start easy. What is your name?" Archel asks, but the man doesn't respond, so he quickly back hands him.

"That was a warning, not even half of what I will do to you." He leans closer. "You see that woman? That sexy, smart as hell warrior sitting behind me?" The man looks and nods. "That's my princess, the love of my life, and you took her man from her. There is nothing in this world I won't do for her, no line I will not cross. I can guarantee you will be begging to give me information before the sun fully rises...or we could cut past all that bullshit of me ripping out your nails, cutting off limbs, burning out eyeballs, and slicing your skin, and you can tell me what I want to know now."

My heart melts. The speech is a little insane, but damn if it doesn't bring tears to my eyes. My shadow owns my heart like the others do, and yet again, he makes me fall in love with him all over again. He may be cocky, even scary to others at times, but to me, to our family, he's perfect, and right now, he's showing how far he is willing to go to protect our family, our lives, and my heart.

It only makes me love him more. "Gravel," he snaps. "My name is Gravel."

"Good, and how many of you are down in that mine?" Archel asks. He's testing if he's going to need to...influence him with pain. Honestly, I'm kinda hoping he does. I'm pissed, and watching my shadow work is weirdly hot. Like, I shouldn't be turned on, should I? Yet my secret garden is opening up like 'hey, you crazy fucker, plant your tree here.'

There's a pained sigh, and Archel looks back at me, but he's smiling. "Princess, you're talking out loud again. I'll happily plant my... tree." He coughs a laugh. "Another time though. Kinda hard to act tough with you talking about secret gardens."

I roll my lips inwards with a sorry expression as he turns back around. Evvie shakes his head and leans into me, chuckling. "Never change, Pip."

Abel just pretends he didn't hear, though he does come to my other side. "Is this necessary?" he inquires, and I throw him a glare.

"You want to protect him?"

"Because I don't wish to see a man tortured?" He frowns.

I sigh. "I used to feel the same way, but I've seen what's out there. That man" —I point to him— "would not hesitate to torture us, rape me, and eat us after they get bored."

"An eye for an eye. Those who seek revenge should dig two graves."

"Yes, one for this asshole and one for any other who touched my man," I snap. "You do not have to agree, but do not interfere. You can hate us and think we are terrible people, but like Archel said, I will do anything to get my man back. They have already broken the rules. I am simply playing the game they have set. Being a hero won't save Jago's life, even if it makes me feel like a better person. I can take a little stain on my soul if it means he's alive. What would you do to save those you love?"

"There are none of them left," he offers sadly and walks away without another protest. He's not stopping us, but he's not condoning it either. That's fine.

"You have not answered," Archel warns and pulls out a knife, twirling it through his fingers as the man watches. "Where would you like to be cut first?"

"Wait, fuck, okay. There are—were eighty of us. You killed a lot. There are around fifty left now."

"And those skinny bastards?" I prompt.

"They're half-dead, born with birth defects," he sneers. "We use them as fodder and send them out to get supplies. Most don't come back, but we don't care."

"What do you mean?" I ask with a frown.

"They are born from the women we keep down there," he hedges nervously and meets my eyes before looking away. "From male leaders over the years. Many have signs of radiation and weak- ness from lack of medicine or help." He shrugs. "Some grow up okay like me, but others like them are nothing better than slaves for us."

I almost snarl, but Archel slaps him for me. "How many women?"

"Ten at last count. Two died last week from bleeding out during birth," he answers honestly. "I've never touched them."

"How many...leaders, men like you, are there?" "About six, the rest are half-dead ones."

"Easy, Pascha," Clay cautions.

"It changes things, we have to free the women," I murmur. "We can't leave them there to be raped and used as fucking birthing machines."

"They won't go. Many have been down there all their lives. They know no other way. One of the half-dead tried to free his mother once, but she turned on him and killed him. They are loyal to our people."

"And who exactly is that?" I snap.

"We are the mine dwellers, we are the undead." He shrugs. "Our elders, who died, brought us there to survive, and we have not left since. This is our way of life—scavenging, killing, it is what we are taught to do."

"We are taught to kill, to train, but that doesn't make us fucking monsters like you," Clay snarls. "You are a disgrace, nothing but murderers and rapists."

"Maybe," the man concedes, "but you will not stop us."

"My man, Jago, the one you captured...is he alive?" I demand.

He meets my eyes again and smiles, his teeth covered in his own blood.

"Is he alive?" I yell, struggling to get to my feet, but Archel gets in his face.

"Answer her or I'll make you a eunuch," he hisses. "For now." He cackles.

"What does that mean?" I leap to my feet and almost fall. Evan and Clay catch me, but I still fight to get to the man. "What does that mean?"

"It means they are currently having fun trying to break him." He grins, spitting blood at me. "But once they get bored, he's dead meat."

I snap and fling myself at him. Luckily, Archel catches me with one arm before I can kill the bastard, and he hauls me back to his chest, holding me as he looks into my eyes. "Shh, we'll get him, Princess. Let me work, okay?"

He hands me back to Clay, who wraps me in his arms to protect the man...not me.

"Your man? He won't last long. They tortured him, and he wouldn't speak. He didn't utter even a word about who you are, where you're from or going, even when we made it hurt so bad, he passed out. You won't get him back. You'll all die trying."

Archel doesn't lose his cool, not once. Not even as the man's screams ring through the house when he won't tell us what we need to know. My shadow's expression is calm and cold, those icy eyes filled with determination, and when we are done, the man is passed out and coated in blood after telling us everything. Archel turns to me, blood splattered across his face, even as a cocky grin tips up his lips, making my pussy pulse at the sight.

"Ready to go get our beast?"

Archel and Clay pack up quickly, while Evan checks me over. The noise must draw Abel's attention, because he hovers at the door, watching us with a frown.

"Don't worry, we'll take him with us. Sorry about the blood," I say from the chair where my men placed me, wanting me to rest for as long as I can.

"I am not worried about that," Abel replies, regarding me worriedly. "You are not healed enough to leave yet."

It's my turn to frown then. "I'm fine, and we have to move to get Jago—"

"He said you will die if you go in now at night, and being injured only makes that more and more likely. You should wait until morning."

Why the hell is this man trying to keep us here? I don't have a bad feeling, but I do watch him carefully. "Why do you care?" I find myself asking. "Surely you want us gone? We have brought nothing but blood and chaos to your peaceful door."

"I also don't want you going out there to die, not when I could have stopped it," he answers sternly.

"You owe us nothing—"

"I do not care about that ether. This is stupid. At least wait until tomorrow—"

"Jago might not have until tomorrow," I argue before sucking in calming breaths. "I will never forgive myself if he dies during the night because I waited for sunrise."

"Then you will die there with him, is that what you want? Don't be so stupid!" Abel snaps. "Wait until you are more healed, until daylight, and then go—"

I lose it, done with his condescending lecture and advice. He's nothing but a stranger, but he's acting like I should listen to him simply because he's old and a man. Not a fucking chance. He doesn't know, he doesn't understand...

How could he?

"Do you even know what it feels like to love someone so deeply?" I snarl at him. My worry for Jago and my anger at Abel for calling me stupid flip the switch inside me. "So all-consuming that you would die for them? Would kill for them? Do anything for them, including burning the whole fucking world if you had to? Do you?" I step towards him, my eyes narrowed and nostrils flaring.

"I don't think you do," I accuse, staring him down as he flinches. "If you did, you would never ask me to leave him, to wait, because you would know how this feels. Each second that passes without him here next to me is another crack in my heart. I might die. I might not. But either way, I don't care because I will be with him."

"Pipe—"

I shake my head at him. "I would kill them all, ruin them, destroy them. I would wreck this world if that's what I had to do to get him back. There is nothing or no one that will keep me from my love. So don't you dare tell me what to do ever again. You speak of being smart, of being strong, but you don't know, not really. Walking away, even if it hurts, to save others isn't being strong. Not in this world. That's selfish and done out of self-preservation. You speak out of fear, as someone who has never had to fight every day of his life to find a glimpse of happiness only for it to be taken away. You hide up here on your cliff, you hide from the world, and I feel sorry for you."

I step closer again, and he flinches. "You will never have someone do for you what I will do for Jago. You'll never have to worry about death, but you'll also never truly live. Not really. You're like a ghost wandering across these rugged cliffs. Forgotten, lost, damned, and alone. You are everything others fight to never be, what I fight to never be, and I'll go out into the dark, into the fire of fucking hell. I'll head towards certain death just to be in his arms one more time, to have one last kiss, one last fucking second with my love. Dying isn't scary, but living with regrets is. If I die with him, then so fucking be it. At least I'll die with my family, with my loves. When the end comes, Abel, who will be by your side? What will you have left?"

"You don't know what you are speaking of—"

"No, *you* don't! Age does not always grant you wisdom! You have lost, you have suffered, but you let it turn you into this empty, lonely man. Well, here's some wisdom for you—everyone who has survived in this world has suffered. The key is to let it guide you, not stop you, and when you find a bit of hope or love in this fucked- up world, you hold onto it as hard as you can. I plan to do that. So don't you dare tell me what to do. You are a stranger, you are no one. That man waiting for me down in those mines is the love of my life. What do you know about sacrifice? What do you know about love?"

He stays quiet then, and I snort cruelly. "Exactly. If you did, you would never expect me to wait. Stay here, hiding on your cliff. I'm not asking for your help, but I'm asking you not to try and stop me as well." I turn away to see my men watching me. Clay nods in respect, Evan smiles in understanding, and Archel winks at me. They know, because they would do the same for me, and I them.

Life isn't about playing it safe. It's about taking chances, even when they are terrifying and the odds are stacked against you, because you find out what you are truly capable of through suffering.

We finish packing quickly without another word to Abel. Clay unties the man and takes him with us so he can show us the other way in he mentioned. It's still dark when we leave and head down the path between the trees. The water crashes into the cliff, and when I glance back, I see Abel framed in the doorway.

Turning forward, I ignore him as Clay shows me the path through the obstacles Abel has gathered to block off his house, so it looks like he isn't even there—including two buses and some cars, which is why we have to walk. There's also a chained gate with string and cans so he'll know when anyone tries to get in.

It's smart really. But lonely.

Once we reach our bikes, I take a deep breath. My head hurts, but that won't stop me.

It's time to get my beast back.

Chapter 25
Miner's Hell

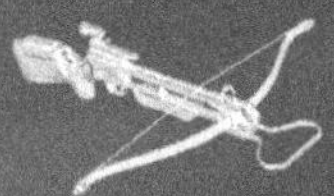

We don't head to the front entrance of the mine. No, Gravel takes us across a sharp incline, which then drops into another tunnel, where I see their bikes and cars. He explains this is their usual entrance, and it's unguarded because if you aren't one of them, then you won't know it's here. It's not easy to find, and I can agree with that.

We slip through the entrance and past the cars and bikes. We can hear talking, but he assures us it's way off, and their voices support that. We know we can't fully trust him, but at least if he gives us some direction we won't get lost in this fucking mine.

"Where?" Archel demands, his hand on the man's throat, keeping him in check while the rest of us are armed. I'm shoved in the middle, though, so they can protect me since I'm not fully healed yet.

At least they didn't try to stop me—they knew better.

"To the right," he murmurs, and we follow along the tunnel he directed us to. It gets dark, but there are lights strewn about, so luckily, we don't have to use our torches. It's still creepy though, and the places where the lights don't shine are in darkness and shadow, making me wonder if those half-dead men are waiting in cracks and crevices to jump out at us again.

We keep walking slowly, listening for anyone creeping up on us.

"Not much farther," he tells us softly. "He'll be in the main chamber, you'll have to fight to get to him."

"And the women?" I ask, wanting to save both Jago and the women.

"In the chamber before... I can take you there first?"

Fuck, Jago or the women? If we get Jago out first, they will all know, and we probably won't have time to save them. Can I live with myself if I leave them behind without trying?

"Women first," I order. The others don't argue, and we are quickly led through the maze to a rock wall with a piece of wood before it.

"They are in there, be quiet though. This is their room, which joins onto the main chamber."

Clay opens the door, and we rush in. Archel shuts it and stands guard as I look around in disgust. There are no beds, just blankets on the floor with ten women shoved in there together. Some are in various states of pregnancy, some are asleep. One is watching us as we come in, her eyes narrowed as she holds a baby in her arms, suckling on her naked breast.

"We are here to help," I whisper. "To set you free."

Her hair is tangled and matted, and her skin is dirty. How long has she been down here? Her body is bare, and there's blood between her legs, running down her thighs as if she was just hurt... or gave birth. What the fuck?

"Please, wake the others and let's get you out of here—" She opens her mouth and screams.

Loudly. Fuck.

"I told you. Now you're all dead." The man laughs and escapes Archel's hold. "They are in here!" he yells before Archel slips up behind him and knocks him out.

I rush over to the woman and press my hand over her mouth, but she tries to bite it. "Shit, stop, we want to help—"

I hear the thunder of footsteps and the shouts of the approaching men. I look to the others in panic. "We have to leave them and·get Jago."

The other women are waking up and yelling for the men. They don't want to be saved. I know it's brainwashing, but we don't have time to convince them otherwise. We will have to come back for them once we have Jago out and they aren't expecting it. They will be safe for now—not mentally, but at least they won't die. Not like Jago, who serves them no purpose.

"Side door! Go!" Evan barks and points at me. It's past the women and seems more like a hole than anything, but I rush through it with them following after me. Archel waits until last, holding the wooden door back as they slam into it to get to us and the women scream encouragement.

The side door opens into the main area of the mine, with raised platforms, ladders, and lowered sections going down. There's a giant well in the middle leading into the dark, and lights flood the entire space. It's filled to the brink with men. There must be forty or more of them here.

And right at the back, tied to a post with chains, is Jago. His head is lowered, and his eyes are closed. His top is missing, his chest is covered in blood, and he's unmoving. I scream his name.

My heart stops, and uncaring about the army between him and me, I rush forward. I hear my men chasing after me. I punch and kick those that get in my way. They are all half-dead, as Gravel explained, and are standing immobile, as if unsure what to do— until a roar of command sounds.

"Kill the intruders!"

They move then, surging around us. I fight them off, headbutting and kicking, ignoring my own pain. I pull a knife and stab and slash. Clay presses to my back, protecting it. Archel and Evan are next to us as we work our way through the room. Each step seems to take forever as more and more of them rush into the chamber. I spot the man whom we originally chased waiting next to Jago, watching us with a grin. There's another bald-headed man next to him, and three others wade towards us. They toss the half-dead away, and that's when I realise those we are fighting now have nearly no energy.

The approaching men are warriors. We don't stand a chance, but still, I don't stop.

Clay roars and starts ripping them to pieces. Archel slides through their masses, killing them before they can even turn. Clay leaps at one of the bald-headed men when they reach us, and Archel takes the other to protect me. Evan pushes against my back, fighting even though he's not the best at it. He keeps going as I slip and move through the half-dead, my entire focus on Jago.

I manage to get to the end where he is before I'm tackled. The half-dead pile onto me. I elbow, kick, and buck as the weight slowly lifts. I roll to see Evan holding them off. "Go!" he yells, giving me the opening I need to get to my beast. Even though he was always jealous, and even though he still struggles with the thought of me choosing another, he doesn't hesitate to risk his life to give me a chance to get to Jago.

I climb to my feet, stumbling as the pain blooms like hammers in my head down in this mining hell, but I don't give up. I climb up the rocks and rush to his side, using the opening as the other two leaders are shouting orders, their backs to me.

I reach Jago, tears in my eyes. "Jago," I whisper as a half-dead leaps next to me, crouching as he hisses like an animal. I kick him right in the face, and he tumbles down the rock. Lifting onto my toes, I cup Jago's chin. "Baby, talk to me," I beg, but he doesn't move.

No, he can't...

I turn his head and press my fingers to his neck. My own heart is thundering so loudly, I can barely hear over it as I wait... Then it comes—his throbbing pulse. He's alive but knocked out. I run my hands over his head as far as I can reach and pull them away to see my fingers coated in blood

Fuck, what did they do to him?

We need to get him out of here before it's too late.

The two bald men on this ledge turn and spot me. Without pause, they rush in my direction. Clay and Archel are split up now, fighting their way to me, while Evan is still holding back as many as he can.

I'm all alone, but they will not kill me, nor will they kill him.

Jago starts to wake up, the noise jarring him, and I cup his cheeks and lean in, having one moment of weakness. "I'm not leaving you. Do you hear me, Beast?" His eyes open and lock on mine. I kiss his lips, tasting his pain and hopelessness. I'm unwilling to flee, to leave without him. Live or die, we'll do it together. "I'm with you, I'm here, stay with us," I plead before I'm ripped away and tossed to the rock. The impact makes me groan as I roll and get to my feet, pulling my sword. Blood runs down my head again as I face off with both men.

"We knew you would come. Don't worry, we won't kill you. You'll do well as a breeder, I'm going first," one taunts, running his eyes across my body.

"Yeah, the only way you are ever touching me is when I rip out your throats," I snarl and look at Jago. "That's my man, and you're in my way." I spin my sword. "Do the math, assholes."

The one on the left jerks his head at me. "Get her, and you can have that little cunt first."

The one on the right turns to me with a smirk, and with a crack of his fists, he rushes me. I have more to fight for than he does. He only has his own desires. I will win, and his blood will run across my blade before the sun rises.

I duck his feral grab and get under his arms, slicing across his stomach and spinning away. He roars and turns. Blood covers the giant wound I made as he stumbles. He turns pale and sweaty, but he still lumbers towards me, unwilling to give up on his prize—me.

Arms wrap around me from behind and lift me into the air. I snarl as I kick and throw back my head, hitting something solid. Pain shoots through my already aching skull, but I ignore it. I am dropped to the floor, so I roll and slice as I get up. I gut the man facing me from his cock to his neck. Blood sprays me as I spin to face the remaining man.

Their followers have noticed me now. They're worried about their leaders and are fighting to get to me, even as my men try to hold them back to give me time to get our man, trusting me to save our family.

I wag my finger at the other man in a come here gesture. He snarls but waits for me, standing between Jago and me, learning from his friend's mistake. I hear others behind me and Archel's snarl as his attacks increase. Clay roars as he takes them on, while Evan is still trying his best to protect me. I have to kill this man fast and get Jago out of here. I don't know how, since the odds seem overwhelming, but I'll do it.

Kill man. Get Jago.

Get out of here.

Make untamed, dirty love to my beast.

With a twist of my lips, I rush across the rock. The man waits, bending slightly, and at the last moment, I turn, sprinting to the back wall. He follows, and I race up as high as I can and then flip over him. When I land, I want to whoop at my success, but I don't have time. I rush towards his unprotected back and slice his knees. He screams as he falls, and I grab his head, yank it back, and slice his throat. Blood squirts from the wound, and I push him away and turn.

No one is looking. Seriously? No one saw my badass worthy flip and kill?

Fine, I'll just regale them with my heroics later and be rewarded with orgasms. For now, I hurry towards Jago. His eyes are barely open, and they are fuzzy, like he can't focus. Blood covers nearly every inch of him, but there is fresh crimson trickling down his head, which could explain the confusion. He probably has a concussion like me.

How cute, matching wounds.

I debate how to get him down, but in the end, with the screams of the half-dead behind me, I slice the cords, and he falls forward. I try to catch him, but honestly, he's too big, and he doesn't even try to stop his fall, as if his limbs won't work. He just grunts as he plummets, pinning me to the rock floor, crushing the air from my lungs.

"A little help!" I squeak, but when I tilt my head back, I see my men are still fighting the half-dead, even though they are slowing, confused now that their leaders are deceased.

Shit, I'm on my own. Wrapping my legs around Jago, I start to rock, eventually getting enough momentum to tip and roll us until I'm sprawled across his chest. His eyes are shut now, and I start to panic, but his mouth is parted, and his breathing is slow and harsh. He's alive, but he needs Evan's help.

I hear a noise—the air moving—and quickly roll just as a blade goes over where I was moments before. It misses Jago, but it would have hit me in the side. I turn to Gravel as he smirks down at me with bloodied teeth. "Now you'll be wholly mine, or I can sell you." He shrugs. "Gotta thank you for clearing out these assholes for me. Less competition, less mouths to feed."

"Yeah, yeah, you're an evil man with an evil plan. Can we skip that shit? I'm getting tired, and big man isn't doing well."

"Skip it?" he repeats, frowning.

"Yeah, let's get straight to the killing." I laugh and leap at him. It takes him by surprise and we go down hard, his weapon spinning away across the rock. He snarls and smashes his head forward, hitting mine as I fall back, gripping it with a yell.

"Fucking nutsucker! Why is it always the head?" I grab my
blade and slam it into his leg over and over as he screams. "Don't"
—stab— "you" —stab— "know" —stab— "I have" —stab— "a concus- sion!" I yell in his face, but his eyes are closed, his mouth slack and face pale. He passed out. I stumble back, the pain making me wince as I turn, and the room spins.

"Let's get out of here!" I scream and then groan. My own voice hurts my aching head, but I try to push it back as quickly as I can to concentrate on our escape. But I'm slow, my ears are ringing again, and I feel like I might pass out. I fight it, but everything seems far away.

"No!" someone roars, and then I'm thrown over a shoulder. I yelp, closing my eyes as the world spins. When I open them again, I'm upside down... Now that's not right.

I'm on a rope, looking at the ground. I lift my head to see Clay climbing towards a hole in the ceiling. "Jago!" I cough.

Clay holds me tight, stopping my wiggling so he doesn't drop me. That's when I notice Archel perched before Jago's body below, and Evan is with him, holding back the surge. Clay climbs quickly, and when he's through the hole, he drops me on my ass and plunges back in. I scramble across the rock, ignoring my blurry vision, and gaze down to see him hauling Jago across his back. Archel helps strap him to Clay like a backpack, and then Clay is climbing again.

Eyes narrowed and determined, Clay holds Jago with one hand and climbs with the other. Evan follows him, and Archel is right behind him, but the half-dead are pursuing them. I search around me and find some sharp loose rocks. Grabbing them, I chuck them into the hole. Archel has to duck, and when he looks up, he grins at me as I throw more, hitting some of the half-dead. It stops the surge enough for him to climb the rope faster. A few leap to follow him, and one falls off almost instantly, not having enough strength to climb. The others are slower but still coming.

Clay makes it through the hole, and then Evan and finally Archel. As soon as he is through, I turn to Clay. "Bomb," I yell. He nods, pulls one from his pack, and starts to light it when I remember something. "Wait, the women!" I shout, shoving to my feet with a gasp.

"They already left," Archel mutters. "They saw their men losing and took off." He kicks one of the half-dead that's climbing through the hole. "They have a single-minded focus, they won't stop. Toss it!" Archel snarls at Clay, who lights it and throws it in.

Archel grabs my arm and yanks me after him, my weapons slung over his shoulder with his own as I'm pulled across the rock. I force my legs to work as we get as far away as we can. We reach an edge and slide down it, making me yell. It's over quickly, and when my feet hit the dirt, we are running again. The ground shakes with the first blast, and we finally stop. I look back to see smoke billowing from the rock.

"Yippee-ki-yeah-yeah, mother!" Clay calls and looks at me proudly. I smile, even as I shake my head. "That's the one you told me, right, Pascha?"

"Close enough, babe. Close enough," I tell him and sigh. "My head fucking hurts." I moan before looking at Jago. "Let's get him somewhere safe." As much as I don't want to, I know where we need to go, so do the others. It's the closest place, and it's safe enough for us to look after Jago.

"He needs to rest, and I need to check you both over. I agree, let's go back. Pip? Play nice this time," Evan mutters as we head towards our bikes.

"I always play nice." I pout, which makes them all laugh.

My head aches, my chest fills with worry for Jago, and my anger soars at having to go back to the man who would have made me leave him for dead.

Play nice... Yeah, I'll try as long as he does, but it seems when it comes to my family, I get a bit...stabby.

Chapter 26
Stranger's Eyes

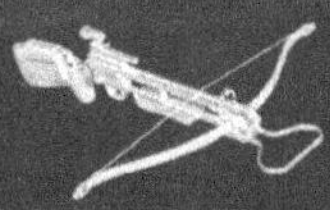

I struggle to drive my bike back, but I force myself to keep going for Jago's sake. He's slung over Clay's bike, and Evan and Archel are on their own. By the time we reach the blocked entrance to Abel's house, I slump on my ride. Archel scoops me up and carries me, and the fact that I don't complain is a testament to how tired and in pain I am. We wind up the dirt path, and the light comes on and the door opens to reveal Abel.

He peers at us, noticing Jago in Clay's arms, and then glances at me. I don't even say 'I told you so.' He just winces and looks down before moving back to let us in. Archel goes in first and sits me on the table. Jago is taken upstairs, and Evan hesitates, clearly wanting to check me over first.

"I'll get her some pain medication while you look at your man," Abel murmurs, and Evan nods but still waits until I give him a thumbs-up to go to Jago.

"I need to see if he's okay," I slur as Archel props me up against his side.

"Soon. Let Evan work. We need to treat you, or you'll be no use to anyone, Princess," he pleads, and then kisses my cheek. I sigh and nod, closing my eyes as I lean into him.

I hear Abel shuffling around, and then something warm and hard is pressed to my lips. "Drink," he orders, and despite my anger, I open my mouth and swallow as he tilts it, unable to open my eyes. "Good. That will lessen the pain and any swelling, but you need to be careful," he warns me before addressing Archel. "I'm sure your doctor will tell you this, but don't let her sleep for too long, and keep waking her up for her concussion. She can have more of this in four hours. Try not to let her exercise too much, and make sure she eats and drinks." He moves away after he finishes, and I finally force my eyes open.

"Thank you," I croak. Even though I'm annoyed, he let us in and helped again when he didn't have to. His shoulders hunch, and he looks back at me.

"No, thank you for ending those animals and stopping their reign of terror. You were right—I should have taken care of them a long time ago, but I can't change that. I'm just glad you were able to and I am in your debt for that, but we will speak again when you feel better. Until then, make yourself at home. There are beds and food and whatever else you need. I will be on the cliff." He heads out of a backdoor, and I watch through the window as he stops at the top of the cliff and sits on the bench I saw, staring out at the Dead Sea. He seems so alone and guilt creeps in for what I said, but my abused head can't handle too many emotions at the moment, so I push it away to deal with another day and instead close my eyes again.

"I'll wake you in an hour. Try to get some sleep, the medicine should work soon." He's not wrong—I can already feel it working. My muscles loosen, the pain is diminishing, and I sigh out a relieved breath as sleepiness winds through me.

Before I know it, I'm asleep, curled up against Archel.

Archel wakes me an hour later, and Evan looks me over, coming to the same conclusion—concussion and a reopened head wound. I can't have any more pain meds—which is okay, I'm used to pain— but they let me snooze. Jago is resting too. He has many wounds, but none are life threatening. He's got a huge gash on the back of his head, which Evan had to sew, and a few others. Evan gave him antibiotics and something to help him sleep and heal. As I fall asleep, he promises me I can see him later.

When I wake up, I'm in a bed with Evan awake next to me. Archel is with Jago, I am told as I blink through the haze of pain. "Is he okay?" I croak out, and Evan helps me sit up and sip water.

"He's still resting. I checked on him though. His bleeding has stopped, his heart rate is normal, and he's doing good," Evan informs me as he gets me comfortable. "Clay is securing the bikes and checking to make sure we were not followed."

"Abel?" I ask with a sigh as I snuggle closer.

"Still on the cliff watching the sun," Evan replies. "He's a strange man."

"He's lonely," I say without thought. "How do you know?"

"Because in his eyes, I see what I used to see in mine. He's lonely and doesn't know how to handle being surrounded by so many people now."

"You felt like that?" Evan queries, searching my face as he cups my cheek. "I was right there, Pip, always."

"And I was losing you. I lost my parents, and you were all I had left. I felt like I was losing that too. I was lonely and when...well, when I found you all, it was a lot. I love it, the noise and chaos, but I can understand how some people, especially if he's been alone that long, can find it a bit scary and overwhelming."

"Pip, you would have never lost me. No matter where you go in this world, I will always find you."

"Promise?" I whisper, feeling vulnerable.

"I promise," he murmurs, kissing me softly. "We were kids down there in that bunker, Pip. I was a stupid kid, but even then, I knew I loved you, and that love has only grown. I can't imagine my next breath, my next moment without being with you. The world never throws more at us than we can handle, and even through all the bad, I had hope... I had you in my heart leading me home. Leading me to you. The sun always rises on the darkness, Pip, and you're my sun."

"Soppy bastard," I tease, even though I nearly blush at how sweet he is. I waited so long for Evan to love me like I loved him, but he already did. I was just too young, too naïve and blinded by my own feelings to notice. He showed me in every little thing he did for me.

Maybe I wasn't as alone as I thought. I always had him.

"You'll never be alone again, Pip. You have all of us, mind, body, and soul, and not even The Wastes itself could tear us apart. We are family to the end," he vows before kissing me again.

"I love you." That's all I can say, no smart remark or sassy comment.

"That's tame for you," he teases as he chuckles and leans back. "I love you too, Pip."

"I blame the head wound. Give me a day or two, and I'll write a sonnet about your dick or something," I mutter, making him laugh and kiss me again.

"There's my girl."

I almost preen as I lean into his side with a grin, feeling better for simply being with him. "You're sure he'll be okay?" I ask worriedly. "His wounds looked bad."

"He hung on for you, Pip. He knew you would come for him, or that he would escape and find you, so don't give up on him now," he murmurs.

"Never." I nod as the door opens and Archel walks in. He looks sad, and when he meets my eyes, he looks to Evvie, as if he can't bear to see me, which isn't like my shadow. I sit up, a bad feeling starting in my stomach.

"Archel?"

He flinches at his name, his grasp tightening on the doorknob as he stares at Evan. "Jago is awak—"

I'm up instantly, ignoring the spinning room, but Archel blocks my way, still not meeting my eyes. "Piper, let Evan go check him—" He looks over my head at Evan, trying to communicate something. I push past him while he's not looking and rush to the slightly open door. It's dark inside when I step in. I frown when I see that Jago is bound. He has chains across his hands and arms, restraining him to the bed, but he's still struggling and thrashing, his hair blocking his face.

"Beast, it's okay, it's us—" I turn when I hear Archel. "Why is he chained?" I demand.

"Princess, I wanted Evan to see first. Please don't—"

I ignore him and step closer, and Jago's head snaps up. He snarls when he looks at me.

The usual fire in my beast is gone. His eyes are dark and empty as he watches me. "Who are you?" he growls out, yanking on the chains, his teeth bared like he would attack me if he was given the opportunity.

There's no recognition there.

Staring back at me are nothing but a stranger's eyes.

Chapter 27
Stranger

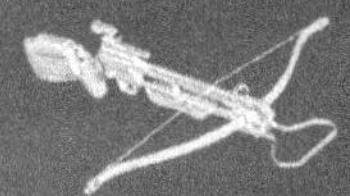

"Jago, Beast...it's me. It's your brawler," I soothe as Archel's hand lands on my shoulder, stopping me from moving forward. I don't shake it off as Jago jerks and yells like an animal.

"What's wrong with him?" I whisper brokenly.

"The head wound could be confusing him. He could have temporary amnesia," Evan offers, and I look at him. He appears worried.

"Could?" I ask, and he winces and meets my eyes.

"His head wound was severe, Pip. There are textbooks and evidence that some severe head wounds can cause permanent amnesia. Loss of memory, sometimes long or short term and some- times both. It's too early to tell. We need the swelling and confu- sion to go away first before we can fully asses—"

"He might never remember us, remember me?" I question, tears falling down my cheeks at the idea that Jago may never look at me with those fiery eyes again, never call me Brawler with such love that it makes my heart race, and may not remember how we fell in love, broke apart, and came back together. The man who fixed my broken heart and showed me my own strength may never remember us falling in love...

"I just don't know yet, Pip," Evan replies sadly. "All we can do is wait and treat the symptoms."

I can't look away from my love. It's him. He has the same face I've caressed a million times, the same lips I've kissed and whispered 'I love you' to. He has the same body and arms that held me so perfectly, keeping me safe...but he's not my Jago. This man is almost feral, roaring and tugging at the chains. The sight of me seems to enrage him, and I can't stand it anymore, so I turn and rush from the room. My tears blind me, so I don't know where I'm going other than fleeing the deafening shaking of the house. I rush downstairs, but I can still hear him, each sound hammering into my heart and cracking it open, so I race out the open back door. The breeze makes me gulp in fresh air, and the sun warms me instantly. I can still hear him, so I keep walking all the way to the cliff's edge and throw myself down on the bench.

I roll my lips inwards to stifle my sobs. Jago is in pain and probably afraid. I need to be there for him, not out here crying. He's the one who's lost his memories and is surrounded by strangers and frightened. I need to be strong, but right now, all I feel is weak.

My heart is ripped open, and questions stream through my head. What if I never get him back? What if he never remembers? Could I live without my beast? Even the thought makes me gasp in pain.

Jago, my beast, is my everything. He's my rock, my love, but if he doesn't remember, he could choose to leave me, to walk away, or even worse. Could I survive that? When each look at him fills me with love and pain?

Could our life really have been wiped out so quickly? Like it never really existed at all, just ghosts inside my head mocking me of what was and could have been?

The pain is too much. I want to scream, to rage at the unfair- ness of it all.

I jump when someone clears their throat. Lifting my head, I meet Abel's eyes, my lip trembling. He smiles sadly. "Are you okay?"

I shake my head, unable to speak in case it all flows out, but those kind eyes, those knowing looks as he patiently waits causes it all to just flow from my lips like word vomit.

"I should have been faster, should have stayed, should have—" "Should haves will not change the future, Piper." He sighs as he

sits, placing his hands on his knees as he stares across the water. "It won't change what happened. All it will do is hurt you more. Guilt has no place here. He needs you right now, he just doesn't know it. All you can do is deal with the present, with what happened. You're scared, you're hurt." He looks at me then. "That's okay. Don't bottle that up, but don't let it stop you either. What's done is done. You cannot change the past, and to keep trying will only make you live a half-life. I should know, like you said." I wince, but he smiles softly, reaches out, and clasps my hand. He holds it tightly before he looks back at the water. "I have faith it led you to that man and here for a reason. Whatever is to come, Piper, you are not alone, and that's all that he needs to know as well."

"But what if I never get him back?" I whisper. "Will you love him less?" he inquires curiously. "No. Never," I answer without hesitation.

"Deep down, he knows he loves you too. His brain might not remember, but his heart does. Be patient. You may get him back, you may not, but you can always start again, Piper. You can fall in love again, be together again. Wouldn't that be beautiful?" He looks at me with pain and sadness in his eyes. "To be given another chance, another life with your love?"

"It's...just unfair," I finish lamely.

"Life is." He shrugs, still holding my hand. "I loved before, Piper. I loved someone so deeply. Not the giant, roaring flame you have, but a slow gentle breeze. It was comforting, always there, keeping me upright. Reminding me I was not alone. It was slow and steady like the water, and that's why I love watching it, it reminds me of her. I didn't fight hard enough for it though, so broken by all those I had loved and lost before. My heart grew tired, and I was numb from trying to hold on. My own mind betrayed me. I didn't fight hard enough, and I lost it. I lost her. I let my own past, my own demons, stop me." He looks at me again. "Don't let that happen to you."

"I don't want to," I admit, "but looking into his eyes...I just want to scream, to rip this world apart until they give him back to me." I huff, wiping at my eyes and sniffling.

"Then scream, scream at the world, at what happened. Don't let it rot inside of you. Let it all out, but then come back and keep fighting for you and for him. Don't give up on something so beautiful. I saw what was between you, something so pure and meant to be. It's something people search their whole lives for and most never find it, but you did. Don't give up on that just because it's hard now. Be the woman who faced me down in my own kitchen, who taught this old dog a lesson, who stopped a mine full of feral murderers. Be the woman I know you are. Be the woman who made him fall in love in the first place. Even when it hurts to look at him, be there to remind him of who you are at every turn, and maybe, just maybe, Piper, you will get back what was forgotten, what was lost."

"Maybe I won't be damned," I finish ironically before wiping my face. He stands, and without a word, he leaves me. I gaze at the sea and realise he's right. My pain morphs into anger, ripping me apart like the thrashing waves below. I have to let it out, so I tip back my head and scream. My fury filled cry fills the air before it's stolen by the wind and taken out to sea.

Like a declaration to this world.

They may have taken my beast for now, but I'll get him back, and if not?

I'll love all the broken pieces of him, even as they hurt me.

Abel was right—I feel better after. I'm anchored, more put together. Once inside, I splash water on my red, puffy face and slick back my hair. I straighten my shoulders and turn to meet Archel's sad eyes. He opens his arms, and I rush into them. I fight back more tears. They are useless here, but he simply holds me.

My silent shadow always supports me. His embrace is home, my sanctuary.

The place I heal.

Jago is my rock, Archel is my healer, Evan is my home, and Clay is my bravery. I need them all, and I refuse to let one slip through my fingers. Jago saved me over and over, he gave me a purpose, and he never gave up on me. I won't ever give up on him. I press my head to Archel's chest, and he leans down and kisses my hair.

"We'll get him back, Princess, you can bring him back. I know that."

"You sure?" I murmur.

"If anyone could pull me from the fog, it would be you. I would fight through the pits of hell and the gates of heaven just to be in your arms again. We all would, including your beast, maybe even more so. I've never seen a man so dedicated to one person before. You are his entire world. He'll come back for you, because he cannot do anything but."

I nod as his words give me a strength I needed. I pull away a bit and tilt my head back. He smiles down at me, rubbing my chin softly before kissing me. "Bring our beast back, Princess," he whis- pers against my lips. "This world will be boring without him almost killing me all the time."

I laugh. I didn't think I was capable of it, but I do, and I kiss him back before pulling away. I straighten my back and head upstairs. Back to my love. Back to Jago.

At the door, I hesitate, my hand raised to open it. I hear murmuring on the other side, no more screaming, and just as I am about to turn the handle, Evan opens the door and steps out. I retreat, and he watches me. "Are you okay?" he asks.

"Sorry, I needed to..." He nods. "I know, Pip."

"How is he?" I ask, my voice stronger, more confident. "Physically, he's okay, healing fast, which is normal for him. His

brain is sluggish though. He seems to know he should recognise me, us, but he doesn't. Can't remember why. I've calmed him down. He thought we were enemies. I explained who we were...who you are."

"What did he say?"

He watches me and opens the door. "Why don't you see for yourself? Don't push him to remember, it might hurt. We will do that over the next few days as the swelling goes down, but maybe you being there, being around him, might slowly bring back memo- ries and assure him he's safe."

I nod, and Evan lets me past. I stand just beyond the threshold as the door shuts behind me and just stare. Jago is still in the bed, his chains loosened so he can move his hands and arms comfortably now. He's propped up, and he seems calmer. He's watching me with a mixture of curiosity and fear. It flickers through those muted depths, like he is waiting for us to attack or kill him.

It makes me sad, and when I step closer, he flinches, but I keep going until I can sit in the wooden chair near the bed. He doesn't look away, and I twist and tangle my hands, twirling my mum's ring like I do when I'm nervous, unsure what to say. I've never been speechless before. I don't want to make a joke or put my foot in my mouth, but I don't even know what to begin with.

"I'm Piper," I blurt. "I thought I should introduce myself." "I'm... Jago," he replies, but it seems like a question.

I nod and sit there awkwardly, unsure what to say. I never had that issue with my beast, but I don't want to upset or enrage him. What to talk about? Luckily, he starts to talk, filling the silence as he observes me with those piercing, if dimmed, eyes.

"It's strange," he mutters, staring at me. "I look at you and feel..."

"Feel?" I prompt softly.

"Whole," he finishes. "I feel whole, like you are supposed to be here at my side, like when you walked away, I needed to follow. The urge is so strong, I almost ripped myself from this bed. Why?"

"Did Evan tell you who I am?"

"He said I love you, that you're my girlfriend?"

I meet those almost flameless eyes and nod. This is hard. How much do I say? But as always, his eyes demand the truth. He may be a shadow of my beast, but he's still the same man. "I am, for a while now. We fell in love when you trained me to fight to be on patrol in our old home called Paradise."

"Paradise," he murmurs. "The name is familiar, I think. Continue." He settles back.

"Well, it's a long story, but we left there. We found new people, including Evan, Archel, and Clay."

"The others." He frowns. "Who are also your boyfriends?" "Yep." I nod quickly.

"And I'm okay with that?" he queries, not judgmentally, just out of confusion.

"You want to kill them every now and again like the other night. Remember when—" I cut off, ducking my head to conceal my pain. I don't want him to feel bad. It's not his fault he doesn't remember.

"I'm sorry," he mumbles, "that I don't remember."

"It's not your fault." I wipe my tears away and smile brightly at him. "You might remember one day."

"If I don't?" he questions worriedly, scanning the room on instinct.

"Then you don't." I shrug. "You are family. You can stay with us, and we can start again. No pressure on you, you don't even have to date me if you don't want to," I tell him hurriedly. It's true, I'd do anything for him, even give him up if that's what he needs. "Or I can take you to the capital, Worth's home, or help you get settled anywhere."

He observes me carefully. "You saved me down there." "It's what family does," I reply instantly.

"Family," he repeats, rolling it across his tongue. "I like that idea. Why was I down there?"

"You sacrificed yourself to save me, to get me out. We came back as soon as we could. We should have done it faster—" I cut off, hearing a warning in my head. "I'm sorry we didn't, but you're alive, and that's all that matters."

He nods, and I sit by his side, just talking and answering his questions about everything regarding the world, the past, people, and us. I don't keep anything a secret, answering honestly, even when it hurts when he doesn't remember.

A few hours later, Clay brings us food, demanding I eat. I do so, as does Jago. He hesitates briefly, but when he sees me take a bite, he does as well. The day passes quickly, and Evan checks on us every few hours. They make us eat and rest, and before I know it, it's almost night. I refuse to leave his side. Even if it doesn't trigger memories, I want him to know he's not alone.

Not ever.

"I'll let you sleep, I guess," I offer, my voice hoarse from talking so much. I go to stand, but I hesitate. I want to lean in and kiss him, to melt in his arms, but I refrain. I fist my hands to stop myself from reaching for him. Turning away before I do something stupid, I go to leave.

"Don't," he whispers, and when I look back, he's frowning, as if he's confused at his own words. "Please don't go. I feel safe with you here, like I can't let you out of my sight. I don't know who I am, who you are, or what this world is, but you...well, fuck, you calm that chaos in my head a little. Will you stay?"

"You never have to ask me twice, Beast," I reply. "Beast?" he repeats, and I nod.

"It's what I call you." "What do I call you?"

"Brawler," I grit out, my voice rough. Speaking the word nearly makes me cry again. "Trouble," I joke.

He smirks slightly. "I can see that. The doctor—" "Evan."

"Evan" —he nods— "says I need to rest, that I might get my memories back."

I nod and sit back down. He watches me as the darkness starts to filter into the room.

"I would like that."

"You would?" I ask, truly wondering. If I could forget everything that had happened to me, all that pain, would I really want those memories back?

The answer is yes, because even though I have those painful memories, if I didn't remember, didn't get that back, I wouldn't get the good either. Like memories of Evan fixing my cuts as a child, my mother's hug, and my father's smile. Jago's lovemaking and training, Archel making me laugh, and Clay teasing me. Worth... I would forget everything. I would not be as jaded, as scarred, but I would also lose all the good in my life that makes the pain worthwhile.

"I would like to remember you," he murmurs around a yawn before closing his eyes. "Remember why my heart feels like it might explode when I look at you, why it races and my palms sweat. I want to remember why I love you." He settles, and his head falls to the side, probably from a mix of exhaustion and medicine.

Hearing him admit that weakness makes my own heart race. My beast is always so strong, even in his love for me. I guess I never really knew that's how I made him feel—the same way he makes me feel even now. I look at him as if it's for the first time again, remembering the first day I saw him. He took my breath away and made my knees weak.

He made me feel alive.

He made me realise what love really was. Maybe, just maybe, we can find that again. Together.

Chapter 28
The Bench On The Cliff

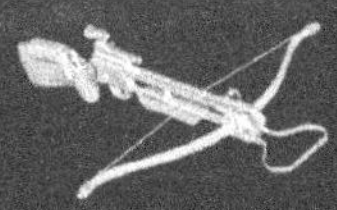

I have breakfast with my other men, not wanting them to worry or feel left out, then I check on Jago, but he's still snoring, so I back out quietly and hesitate, wondering where to go, before I decide to head to the cliff again.

It feels peaceful, like an escape, even for a moment, just like Abel said. He's already there with a cup of tea in his hand and one next to him. Smiling, I sit and take it. "How did you know I would come?" I ask as I sip the herbal liquid, sighing as the warmth flows through me, settling my nerves and worries.

"You are like me," is all he offers, watching the water below. It's calmer today, no churning dark sea, but Dray's words come back to me, and I wonder what hides under its depths.

"Have you ever been in it?" I inquire and nod my chin at the water.

"Once, on a dare, when I was a younger man." He laughs. "It's surprisingly hot."

"No monsters?" I joke.

He chuckles, sitting back and crossing his legs, resting the mug there. "Not that I saw, but it wouldn't surprise me in this world. I wouldn't worry about them though, plenty of human monsters to concern yourself with."

I guess that's true. I drink my tea and watch the water. The slow breeze, the sun, and the soft lapping of the water soothes me until I lean back, not realising there is a small smile on my lips. "The woman you loved, what happened?"

He flinches but sighs. "It's not a pretty story, nor a happy one."

"There aren't many of those left in this world, but I would still like to hear it if you want to tell it."

"Maybe one day," he hedges, and I nod, allowing him his privacy. I won't pry. If he wants to talk about it, he knows I'm here. If not, that's his choice too. But as the time passes, I realise he's happy. He enjoys the company. I cannot imagine living here alone for so long. He did what he thought was right by staying in his family home, while I sought out adventure, yet this world still brought us together.

Probably for a reason, like he said.

"Princess," comes a murmur, and I turn to see Archel looking slightly panicked. I instantly stand, my heart racing, and all the peace I absorbed disappears.

"Jago is going crazy, come quick," he urges.

I look at Abel, and he waves his hand. "Go, go, I'm fine."

I put the tea down and run after Archel. We race through the house, and I hear him thrashing and yelling. I hear my name and then a grunt, and I open the door just in time to see Clay being flung across the room, thrown by Jago, while Evan stands back, his eyes wide and hands up as he speaks quickly to calm him down.

"She's fine, just outside—"

I step in then, and Jago freezes, his gaze swinging to me. He stops fighting instantly and slumps as he looks me over. I rush to his side, sitting on the bed, and I reach for his hand before I drop mine. He probably doesn't want my touch. "Are you okay? What's wrong?"

"I couldn't find you," he mutters.

I relax, even as a bright smile covers my lips. That's good, right? "We'll leave you two alone. We told him you were fine, but he didn't believe us. He's okay. I've checked him over, but get the stub- born bastard to eat," Evan orders and drags the other two men from the room.

"Asshole," Clay grumbles. "When he's better, I'm kicking his ass for that." I hear him griping as he leaves with Evan and Archel, the door shutting softly behind them. Only then does Jago fully relax. He focuses on me, his eyes dropping a bit with embarrassment and confusion. He's probably wondering why he reacted like that. I know, deep down, his instincts towards me are still there. He's not used to having to control them, I should have thought of that.

Silly Piper.

"It's okay, I'm here. Please eat though, it will help you heal." I grab the plate and pass it over. He takes it and slowly eats, not meeting my eyes. I let him work through his thoughts. It must be hard to be in his head right now, his instincts and body knowing how to react before he does.

Once he's done, he passes the plate to me, and I place it on the chair. "I need to piss."

I jump to my feet. "Oh, of course! Erm, let me find the key—"

He jerks his hand, snapping the chain easily, and scoots to the end of the bed. My mouth drops and shock fills me as I gape. His chin lifts, and some of his fire returns to his eyes as he smirks at me—that cocky familiar one. "I'm strong," he teases.

"Erm, yeah." I turn away, hiding my blush and my annoying, throbbing body. I shouldn't be turned on right now, but my body doesn't care that he doesn't remember me. It remembers him and his strength, and the way he holds me as he eats my—

His hand catches mine, and my thoughts disappear as I jump, looking down at him. He searches my eyes, and his expression softens. "Will you help me get there? My legs feel weak."

"Mine too," I mutter before nodding. "Sure." I help him stand, and he leans into me. I grunt but hold his weight and slowly lead him to the other bathroom next door. Once there I go to leave, but he pulls his pants down and, uncaring about me, starts to wee. Some part of him is comfortable with me, even though he probably isn't aware.

After all, Jago has seen me in worse situations, and shyness while peeing is the least of my worries.

When he's done, he moves to the sink and quickly washes his hands and face before drooping there. His hair is greasy and hanging in his face. He blows it back and runs his hand through it and winces. I frown and then look to the bath behind him. The water won't run in it, but I could sit him down and wash his hair for him.

"Do you want me to wash your hair? I'll avoid the wound, but it might help, and I'll plait it back?"

He turns his head, and one eye locks on me. "You'll do that? For me?" he asks in confusion.

"I'd do anything for you," I reply instantly. He blinks before a soft smile curls up his lips.

"Please."

"Stay there," I murmur and rush away. I check with Evan, and he agrees it should be okay as long as I avoid the wound. I grab some supplies, and when I return, I help him sit with his back to the tub and hang his hair over it. He frowns, his eyes tightening as he watches me, clearly feeling vulnerable. He hates this weakness, hates his own injuries. I know, because I would too.

"It's okay. I promise I won't hurt you. Not ever," I vow as I get into the tub and start to fill the jug I found. He flinches when I run the first bit of lukewarm water over his hair but groans when I start to rub it gently.

Eventually, his head tips back, his eyes close, and his shoulders lose their tightness as I gently untangle his hair. I wash away the blood, dirt, and sand, combing my fingers through it.

I keep washing, and five jugs of water later, I've gotten rid of the blood. There are still bits around his covered wound, but I avoid it and only use a small portion of soap on his hair so it won't run into it before rinsing it again and massaging the injured parts. Once finished, I wring it out and comb his locks with my fingers again before plaiting it and tying it off.

He sighs softly. "Are you done?" he asks, but he seems sad. "Yes, come on, let's get you back to bed." I get out of the tub

and help him up. He leans into me as we walk back to the room, then he climbs into the bed. He grunts in pain before I rearrange his pillows. The door opens, and Evan comes in smiling.

"Pain relief time, they will make you sleepy." "No," Jago grumbles.

I grab his hand and squeeze. "He knows best. I trust him with my life, with yours. Please, I don't want you to be in pain." He looks down at my hand on his, and I try to take it back, but he turns his over and links our fingers.

"Okay," he murmurs without looking away from our clasped hands. Evan quickly passes them over, and Jago takes them. Evan looks at me, and I let him know I'm okay, then he leaves. I sit there, my hand in Jago's as he settles back and his eyes start to close. He tries to fight it, but I start to hum and then sing stupid, silly songs. He falls asleep with a smile on his face, his hand loosening in mine until it falls to the bed.

I miss his touch instantly, but it's a start, and I have hope.

Hope that we are going to be okay. I still want his memories to come back, but if they don't, I know we will be okay.

He will be okay.

He falls into a deep sleep, and I gently move away, shutting the door behind me. He won't wake for a while due to the medication, so I take the time to wash myself, re-plait my hair, and shove on some new panties and a shirt, which was kindly provided by Abel.

I spot him and Clay in the garden. Watching my big warrior delicately helping trim and look after the crops surprises me. Archel is napping in the sun, and Evan is looking through his medical bag. I kiss him on my way by and venture into the living room, down some steps, and to a white wooden door.

I gasp when I step in. The room is covered in plants, which hang and sit everywhere, with two matching green sofas pushed against the walls. There's an old-style fireplace and chimney to the left. On the side wall is a bay window with green cushioned seats. It looks over the cliff and a carved staircase to the water below. It's beautiful. I drift over, watching the waves before I turn. There, tucked in a corner, is an old-fashioned TV.

My curiosity gets the better of me. I move closer, stopping before it. There's a VHS player, and I press the button on the TV. Surprisingly, it turns on. I really need to ask where he gets power.

It loads to a paused video of a woman sitting in this room on the sofa, with a small, pained smile on her lips. She has crow's feet around her brown eyes, and lines across her sagging cheeks and lips. Her hair is greying and pulled back, and she wears a cardigan and a white top, but that's not what has me staring in shock.

I know her.

She's my mother.

My mother who I thought was dead. She's older...but it's her, and she's in the exact room I am in.

Alive and well.

Chapter 29
Blast From The Past

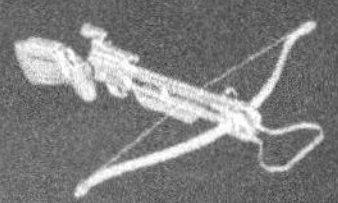

I just stare at the paused screen, my emotions roaring so loudly, I feel like I can't breathe. Staring at her face, I don't even notice the tears beginning to fall. I'm unwilling to blink or look away, afraid I might lose her again forever. Her visage had been dimming in my mind. I was only a child when I lost her, so I was starting to forget.

I lean forward and trace the shape of her face on the screen. It's her, I know it. We have the same eyes, same smile, same hair. I look so much like her, I hiccup, my heart slamming and stomach dropping.

They said they died... How? How is this possible?

Before I know it, I've hit play, and her soft, almost musical voice rings out.

"Hey there, bug, it's a nice sunny morning here." She grins. "You would love it, the sun I mean. Plenty of places to get lost in, to play hide and seek—" I pause it, unable to take hearing her voice. My own screams inside my head as I stare at the screen before I hit play again, a glutton for punishment.

"Abel and I are going to tend to the crops today. He's teaching me to have a green finger. I know! Me! Who would have guessed?" Her expression softens, her eyes shining. "I miss you so much, I wish you were here—"

I can't, I pause it.

I feel angry now, and I'm hurting.

I'm hurting more than I ever have. More than when I heard the news of their deaths. I was just a child then, with childish ways of thinking, but now I'm an adult. I thought I'd healed, thought I was over it, but I'm not. The wound is reopening as I stare at her, at the woman who was supposed to love me every day of my life, supposed to be at my side. Raise me, love me. Teach me right from wrong. Protect me.

And instead, it seems, she left.

I stare at the end screen, her eyes looking to the right, the doorway. She wears a smile on her lips, and she appears almost happy. I ache for her, to be held in her arms, to turn around and find her there, but when I do, all I see is Abel.

He's staring at the screen with heartbreak and love on his face.

"Abel," I croak. "How...how do you have this? How did you know her?"

He looks at me, frowning now. "Why did you play it?" he demands.

I turn to face him, crouched on my knees as my tears drip faster. I have so many questions. My world is crashing down around me. Everything I thought I knew...

She lived.

Which means...she left me.

"How did you know her?" I scream, pointing at the TV. My emotions are strong, and all that I've lost and suffered erupts in my scream.

He looks from her to me and back again, his face paling. "You looked familiar. I thought it was wishful thinking. It's you, isn't it?"

He steps closer, his mouth open and eyes wide. "She always called you..."

"Bug," I finish.

"It's you, her daughter."

"How?" I look back at the TV, already knowing deep down but needing to hear it. "How do you have this?"

"She recorded it, here in my house, just over ten years ago. It was a week before she died," he answers sadly. "Piper...I've wanted to meet you since the moment she told me about you. She told me so many stories—"

"Shut up!" I scream, and I hear racing footsteps as I get to my feet. "Don't you dare! Don't you dare talk about her! She left me! She was dead! She was supposed to be dead!" I scream, my heart splintering and breaking. I thought only my men could do that, but here she is. My own mother is breaking my heart. "She died, she died," I repeat brokenly.

"Piper," he murmurs.

I stumble back, laughing bitterly. "She didn't die, she just left me. She fucking left me."

Evan rips open the door, staring at me desperately, with Clay and Archel behind him. I hear a stumble, and then Jago is there too. I look at them with tears in my eyes. Their lips are moving, asking questions, and Clay is pinning Abel to the wall, but I can't speak.

I can't.

Evan rushes to my side, running his hands over me to see if I'm okay. His eyes flick to the TV, and he freezes before slowly looking back at me, knowing who that is. He knows better than anyone how much I loved her, how much I broke when they died. When she died. Evan knows how I cried for her every single night. How I begged the world to give my mum back. I missed her every day, and he knows that.

"She left me," I whisper raggedly.

I can't take the sadness and pain in his eyes. Their shouts, their demands, I can't take it. I run, needing to escape her voice, which is ringing through my head. I need air, I need to get away from the lies tangled around me.

My whole life is one big, tangled web.

I rush to the only place I can—the bench. Tears blind me as I drop down onto the seat, unsure what to do, what to say. My whole world is spinning. Everything I thought I knew is gone. My past burns away, like a tattered, destroyed picture.

I hear feet and panting, and then he's there. "My whole life is a lie," I whisper.

"No, Pip, it isn't. This is real, we are real. Everything you have achieved, everyone you have saved, is real. The only thing that isn't is what happened to them."

I raise my blurry, tear-filled eyes to him. My Evvie.

"She left me, Evvie. How could she do that? Was I not enough? What did I do wrong?" I sob, and he drags me closer, holding me, his own tears wetting my hair. "Why didn't she love me?"

He's the one person in the world who knows how I feel, who held me every night when I cried for her. Who was there for every achievement and every heartbreak. Who became my family after I lost my own. Who became my entire world when both of ours crumbled and we clung to each other.

"Why?" I beg, grabbing his chest and pulling him close as I sob. "Why didn't she love me?"

"She did, more than anything. More than I've ever seen anyone love anyone in this world. She fought to get back to you for so long." Abel's voice makes me jerk.

"Not now," Evan snaps.

"Please, I have to tell you. I promised her if I ever—"

"Shut up," Evan warns, getting to his feet, his fists clenched. "You speak one more fucking word, and I'll break your neck," he snarls. This is a side of him I've never seen.

I grab his hand and shake my head. He softens, sits, and pulls me onto his lap. A moment later, there's a soft touch on my shoulder, but I jerk away, raising my gaze to see Abel crouched before me. "Please, when you have had time to sort through your thoughts, please let me tell you what happened. I owe you that, and I promised her that. Even if you hate me, even if you hate her and want to leave, please just hear me out first. It's not what you think. Your mother didn't abandon you, Piper. She loved you more than anything in this world and died trying to get back to you."

With that, he stands. I let him go. The bench dips slightly, and more arms go around me as Clay and Archel hold me, kiss me.

"We are here, Princess."

"We have got you, my pascha."

But someone is missing. I lift my head and spot him standing off to the side, looking awkward. His hands fist, and his eyes flicker with flames. He's a stranger to my pain, even while he wants to help.

I ache for him to embrace me, to hold the broken pieces of me together, but he can't, he won't. He's just another person I am losing, just like her...

My mum... How? Why?

And even as broken and hurt as I am right now, I know I have to stay. I have to hear him out. I need to know the truth. I need to know what happened to my parents.

I need the painful truth over the pretty lie.

Chapter 30
Ghost Of A Mother

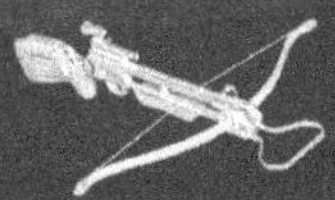

When I've calmed down enough to move, I get to my feet. I hold Evvie's hand in mine as we go back inside. Abel has poured a drink—not tea for once, something stronger—and he sits at the table nursing it as I stand there with my men behind me.

"She loved this table. She would sit here with me for hours at night and tell me stories of you." He sighs, and I sit as he lifts his head. "I want to tell you everything. Will you listen? It will hurt, I know that, and I'm sorry. Part of me wished you would never find out the truth, it's too painful, but I know loss is never easy, no matter the circumstances. You lost her, and you deserve an explana- tion. You desire to know your mother. The ghost of your mother is here always."

"Tell me," I croak out, taking my glass and knocking it back. Evvie sits next to me, holding my hand, and Archel takes the chair on my other side, stroking my thigh. Clay's comforting, anchoring hand rests on my shoulder, and even Jago, a stranger to me, stands behind me with his arms crossed. I want to protest. He should rest, he should sit, but even without his memories, he stands there, protecting my back like always.

Not for our lives, but for my heart.

My warriors guard it, ready to die for it.

"I found them out there. One day, I had gone farther than ever before, needing food. I was younger then, less scared of the world. I found them. Your father was severely hurt, and they were both starving and dehydrated. One look at her, and I knew I couldn't leave her. Those big brown eyes, so like yours, implored me. I brought them back here. I tried to heal your father but...he was too injured, Piper. The rot in his blood already set in from what should've been a killing blow. I learned after that he got it by protecting her, your mother. The people, your people, left them to die. They were ordered to kill them, feared they were traitors or some such. Anyway, she tended to him, but your father urged her to go back to get you, knowing he wouldn't make it. He wanted his baby girl saved. She refused to leave his side, promising they would get better and go together. He died that evening.

"When your father died, she retreated, becoming a shell of herself. She would sit upon that bench with a picture of you every day, from sunrise to sunset, barely eating or drinking. She never spoke a word. I sat with her all day, every day, talking just to fill the silence. A year later, she finally spoke. Home. That's all she said. Eventually I pried more out of her. She wanted to get back to you, to protect you and bring you above ground to start another life. She didn't know how to get back though, didn't know how to get down to Paradise without them killing her like they were supposed to. She was so tired, so weak and drained from surviving and fighting so long to get back to you. I warned her that trying would be her death. A woman out there? One who didn't know how to fight? It was certain death.

"The next day she ate and started to train to get stronger, faster, better. She was determined to get back to you. Even as we...even as we fell in love. We spent our days together, sitting on the bench every night as I consoled her while she cried for you. She never stopped dreaming of you. I had selfishly hoped I was enough. I knew she would die if she went back. It was selfish, but I couldn't bear the thought. At first, it was because I was lonely, but after, it was because I loved her. I loved her in a way I didn't know was possible. But I was never first place in her life, you were. You were always her priority, even as the years passed. She started leaving video messages for you, and I think it helped her, like you were there talking to her.

"One day a few years later, I came home and she was gone, leaving only a note behind on the bench. I knew she had gone back to you, so I went after her." He turns away for a moment. "I had to, I loved her. It terrified me, but I did. I left the only home I had, the only link I had to my family, for her. But when I found her... Piper, I'm so sorry. She died out there trying to get back to you. She was attacked and murdered. I brought her body back. I buried her before our bench. I hoped to find you one day. I'm not a fighter, Piper, but I knew I had to find a way to give you her message. To let you know she didn't leave. She hated that you would believe she just left, that you would miss her, need her, and she couldn't be there. She hated that she let you down, that she knew it would break your heart.

"I have lots of those messages if you want to see them. If not, I understand. I'm sorry, Piper, I really am. I tried to save them both. I did. I see her every day, her memory fills this house. She could never give me all of her, her heart was already yours, but I had a piece of it, and it was enough. Her ghost fills these walls and that bench—it's where I feel closest to her, the love of my life." He stops, licking his lips.

The whole time he spoke, I didn't say a word, didn't speak. I couldn't. The information flows through my head, whirling too rapidly for me to process. So much pain, so many lies. So many memories. All the years, the life I missed out on with my parents, all because of Paradise. It shouldn't surprise me, look what they did to me.

I rub my mother's ring as I stare at the table, unsure what to say.

"She didn't leave me," I mutter.

"Never. She lived and died to get back to you."

I lift my head. "She had a whole other life here with you…" "I would love to tell you about it…so would she, if you want."

"I-I think I would like that. I need a moment. I need to just think." I shake my head bitterly. "I don't know, maybe I need to sleep. I'm suddenly exhausted."

"Then let's sleep, Pip. It's okay. He'll be here to answer any questions whenever you want them answered, and we won't leave until you are happy."

I nod, and Abel smiles at me sadly. "I'll be here when you wake up. I'll tell you whatever you want or need. Please, stay as long as you like."

I stand silently and turn away.

"I'm so glad I got to meet you, Piper. I see now why she fought so hard, why she died to get back to you. You are worth it all. You, my child, are incredible. A miracle. Something worth fighting for. She would be so proud of you."

I flinch, but part of my heart settles at that. I'm just another girl searching for her parents' approval.

As I walk through the house, I swear I feel her here. The ghost of my mother.

Chapter 31
Learn To Love Again

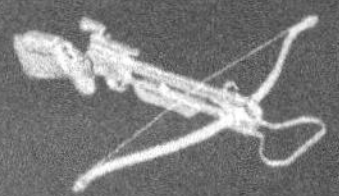

That night, my men hold me close between them. Their arms, their touches and love keep me together, but there's a hole where my beast should be, and all that separates us is a thin wall. Everyone snores around me as I stare at the wall, aching for him, wishing he was here. But he's not, because I'm a stranger to him.

I give the wall a longing look before I force my eyes away. He needs me too. This isn't just about me, he's lost his entire world. All I lost was my past. Everything I thought I knew was a lie, a mistake, but at least I know the truth now, and I know my future. I know the love between my men and me will stay true today, the next day, and the day after. I know me, my own mind, and my own life.

All he knows is what we tell him.

Both of us have lost a lot here on the cliff, but my beast...

My poor beast has lost it all. I'll try to put it back together for him, even if the jagged edges of his past, present, and future cut me. I'll do anything to get him back, and if I can't, if I lose him, I'll know I did everything to help.

It's up to him now.

All we can do is be there for him and hope it's enough.

With that hope in my heart, I close my eyes and snuggle closer to my men. The feel of their love is wrapped around me with their arms, while the ghost of my mother watches over me.

I sleep in for the first time ever, and when I wake up, Archel is there, wrapped around me, kissing my shoulder and stroking my hair. The sun streams in through the window and warms us. Evan and Clay are gone, but I can hear murmurs and their movements downstairs, so I settle back, knowing they are okay. I allow myself to relax for a moment, knowing if Evan is up, then Jago will be okay. He will be looking after him.

I need to check on Jago, but it can wait for a minute while I take in the moment of peace and the support in my lover's embrace. I turn to face him, and he smiles softly at me, stroking my cheek. It reminds me of a simpler time, when it was just the two of us sitting in a hut while I healed. Sometimes I wonder if it would be easier to just go back there, but I wouldn't have Evan, Clay, or Jago. I would lose so much just for some peace, but can there ever really be peace without love? I would be longing for them.

Missing them.

"Do you ever wish it was just us again? In that hut?" I whisper.

He blinks. I've clearly thrown him, but he recovers fast, and he doesn't speak without thinking. I see him mulling it over, and I know when he opens his mouth, it will be the truth. "Yes and no. Yes, because I had you all to myself. It was just us, falling in love."

"But no?"

"No, because you could never love just me, Princess." I wince, and he kisses me, silencing my pain. "I know that, and I wouldn't want it any other way now. Your heart's too big, too precious. It needs to be protected. It needs four men to fill it and hold it for you. It's not always easy." He cracks a smile, making me giggle at the thought of all the fights. "But it's worth it. I gained a family. These men…I know they will always protect you if something happens to me, and it helps me sleep easier knowing that. But they have become more. We fight, we argue, we get jealous, but doesn't every family?"

"We aren't whole anymore," I remind him, tears filling my eyes. "One day, we will be whole again, Princess, I can guarantee that. He's just lost in the smoke at the moment, but keep pulling, keep shining through it, and he'll find his way home." He kisses me softly. "And we will anchor you all the way, love you even when you are struggling to love yourself. Piper, you are the heart. Remember that no matter where we go, or how far away we are, you are home.

"Have faith, Princess, even when it's hard, because that's when you need it the most. You are my faith, my home, my world. I know no matter what is coming on that horizon, it was worth it to be with you, to love you for as long as I did. We all do. Jago does too, deep down. In a world full of death, Princess, you showed me how to live. So let's not live in the past. Let's learn from it and take its lessons… like how useless you are without coffee." I giggle as he wipes the tears away, those icy eyes soft on mine. My shadow is showing me his heart. "But live in the present right now. You've got us, Princess, always, now bring Jago home too."

I nod, closing my eyes as I press my head against him. I soak in some of his conviction, strength, and love. He's so sure I can bring him back, that we all made the right decision, that I can't do anything but try.

"Princess, about your mother… Whatever you want to do is the right decision, but I know you, I know your heart. You need the truth, even if it kills you. Jago can't be moved yet, so I think we should stay a while."

"I know, I do too. I'm just so…confused. So angry."

"You have every right to be, but you had a parent who loved you, Princess. She loved you so much, she died trying to get back to you. That's rare." I open my eyes then. He never speaks of his parents, but in his gaze, I see his pain. I see the truth. Whatever happened to them, it wasn't good, nor what they did to him.

I hold him closer, and we just cuddle and contemplate. He's right—I need to stay. I need to hear it all, watch those tapes, and let Abel tell me about my mother. I can never move forward without solidifying my past, now that it's up in the air. It will give Jago time to heal and hopefully get his memory back. I just need to ask the others and Abel to make sure that's okay.

Sighing, I lift my head. "We better get up before Jago busts in here and—" I wince and clear my throat. "Before the others look for us."

"Let's feed you, Princess, before you start getting all hangry."

"Hangry?" I laugh, sitting up.

"Yup, hungry and angry. You are quite scary then. Even more so than when you start talking about my dick in front of Dray." He winks, making me laugh like always.

"I do? Okay, I did that like one time..." He stares at me, and I sigh. "Five times. I can't help it. You have a very cute penis. Like, if there was modelling for penises, you would definitely be up there, you know? Like Vogue Cock. Photo shoots for the balls—" The door opens, Evan hears that, turns around, and just leaves again, making Archel laugh and chase after him.

"Save me! She's trying to fuck me, Doc!"

"Stop! I don't want your cute cock on me!" he yells, running away, and I shake my head. I know they did it to cheer me up, and when I head downstairs, I see Evan being chased around the table by Archel. Clay is sitting at it, eating and watching the show, and I can't help but laugh. I laugh so hard, I almost pee.

"Let me show you, you can decide!" Archel calls. "Get your cock out!"

"Get away from me, sex criminal!" Evan shouts back. I turn when I hear a noise and see Jago standing in the doorway, watching it all go down. His eyes go to me as I laugh, and I quiet down, but a small smile curves his lips.

"You have a beautiful laugh," he comments. I can't help the butterflies that take flight. I basically float—okay, stumble, to the table, since I fall over my own feet. I grab Evan as he runs past.

"Evan, you have a pretty dick too." I throw him a grin. "Archel, stop trying to show him your penis."

"Fine," he grumbles, winking at me as he grabs a seat, spins it, and sits. He grabs Clay's bowl, who snarls, reaches over, punches him, and takes it back. Rolling my eyes, I sit down, and Clay looks at me, noticing my lack of food, and without a moment's notice, he thrusts the bowl at me. Laughing, I accept it, eating the rest of the oats as he sits back.

"Oh, so she can have food? I see how it is," Archel whines.

"Get your own. She's my pascha, she eats before I do. It's respect." Clay looks at me then. "Which I forgot in my hunger. I apologise, Pascha." He places his fist over his chest, and I lean closer and kiss him.

"Forgiven, my mountain man," I tease.

A throat clears, and I look back to see Jago lingering on the threshold of the room. The sight hurts my heart. "Pascha?" he asks.

Clay kicks a chair out for him, and he sits gratefully. My heart soars at the thoughtfulness. "It's a term of respect for our leader, our queen. I met Piper when she stormed through my mountain—"

"Walked," I correct, rolling my eyes.

"Stole my heart, and defeated the ancient ritual."

I smile and eat while Clay regales Jago with the story of my trial, even though he embellishes a little bit, making us all laugh as he describes my incredible leaps and fighting skills. Each word is infused with respect and love, and I can't help but melt for my mountain man. He's helping Jago remember, but also showing me his love without realising it. In his eyes, I'm a hero, a true leader.

It makes me sit up taller, and I almost preen under their gazes. Jago watches me with a small, unguarded smile. It's so unlike him, but I suppose without his past, he has nothing to guard himself against. There's a gleam of respect in his eyes and…longing. I know I'm looking at him the same.

Clay finishes, and we share some tea made by Abel, who's sitting out on the cliff again.

"I remembered something last night," Jago remarks.

We all freeze and become silent as my eyes jerk up to him hopefully. He winces at my expression. "I'm sorry, that was thoughtless. It wasn't anything major…just my name. I remembered a male voice, I think my father, when I was younger, calling it to me as I ran through a house."

"That's great," I encourage him, not wilting at it not being about us. It's good news.

"If your memories are starting to return, even slowly, it means the pressure is going down, which is good."

"We still can't move yet." Archel looks at me. "Piper needs to learn about her mother, and Jago needs to heal…which is why I'm thinking of leaving."

My eyes widen, and he rushes on. "Not forever, Princess. You couldn't get rid of me even if you tried."

"And we've tried," Evan teases.

"It's just to report back to Worth to let her know we are okay before she sends an army. I'll check the explosion site for survivors as well, get supplies, and come back. It's a few days' journey if I push hard. This house is getting a little crowded." He's right—it is, though I don't say it. I know they feel useless and need to do some- thing, anything, and they are worried about Jago and me. "I'm in the way here. I can do this and be useful."

The others leave me to discuss it with Archel. I slide around the table and drop onto his lap, and he instantly wraps his arms around me. "I'll be back, Princess, I promise. We are just sitting here on top of each other and irritating the big guy more. He needs space, and you need time. I can provide that. The others will protect you and help you with him—"

"Jago doesn't need me anymore," I mutter.

"He does, Princess, he just doesn't know it yet, so show him that. Stick to him like glue, be the…endearing woman you are."

"You mean annoying."

"I mean relentless," he corrects, cupping my chin. "Just because you're strong, smart, and know what you want doesn't make you annoying. People fear strength, they fear what they can't under- stand or know, and they tear it down with the only thing they can— words. They called you annoying because you never gave up and they did. But Jago needs that now. He needs that strength, he needs you to not give up on him. He's returning to us. A memory is a good start. Bring them all back, and by the time we have our beast, I'll be back."

"I'll miss you," I mutter, and he laughs.

"Of course you will, Princess." He winks, and I roll my eyes. "Well, that makes this easier," I tease before I lean in and kiss

him. "Okay," I whisper against his lips. "But don't leave me for too long. I need my assassin to save me when I get into trouble."

"You never needed anyone to save you, Princess. You saved your- self and all of us, and one day, you'll save this world," he whis- pers before kissing me hard. My body pulses with desire, but he pulls back before we can do anything about it. "I'll pack up and be back before you know it."

"Tell Worth I said hi and nice rack." I sigh as I get up so he can prepare to leave.

"I'm not saying that. Dray will try to murder me, and then I'll have to kill him to keep my promise to come back to you," he teases. I watch him go before wrapping my arms around myself in the silence. I wait there, almost lost, while he packs, and when he comes back down, I follow him to the door. He kisses me so hard,

he leaves me breathless and aching for him, but now's not the time.

Down, man-eater, I warn my vagina.

"I'll be back before you know it. Try not to start a war or fall in love with anyone," he teases, making me laugh. I clutch his hand as he turns, holding on as long as I can. My fingers slip through his as he walks away. I watch his retreating back, and then he's gone, disappearing like the shadow he is. But he'll be back, I know that. My assassin would find me anywhere in this world.

He's trusting in me to save our beast, so I turn back to the house, my mission clear.

I let Archel go, concerned but trusting in my assassin, before I turn and head to the cliff, needing to watch those tapes. I'll tackle Mum first, then Jago. Time can heal almost anything, they tell me. I just hope it can help heal him.

⋙

I sit beside Abel as he silently views the water.

"I hope you don't mind, but we decided to stay for a while so Jago can heal, and I-I would like to watch the tapes. I want to know my mum the way you did—not as a hurt, abandoned child, but as the woman she raised and tried to get back to."

The smile he gives me is magnificent, and I help him to his feet. He leads me to the house and sets me up in the living room with a stack of tapes. "There is no rush. This is a home now for you as well. Take your time. I'll be here if you need anything." He shuts the door, and I settle before the TV with crisscrossed legs.

I swallow hard, unsure how to feel. I'm scared she won't be the woman I remember, but that's a child's thought. My mother was a complex living woman, and I want to know what she had to say. She suffered, she survived, and then she died to get me these messages. I owe it to her to watch them, even if they hurt. I have to know who she was.

Where I came from.

I have to know her end to understand my beginning.

I hit play and watch as her face comes onto screen. It's a different tape this time. She looks skinnier, paler. She has a huge scratch on her face, and her hair is almost ragged. It's definitely one of the earliest ones, I'm guessing. She looks sad, broken.

"Your dad died," she whispers, wiping at her eyes as she takes a shuddering breath. "I tried everything, bug, I really did. I know how much you loved him." She sobs before pushing it back. "I did too. He was my soulmate, and I miss him so much. I wish you were here so I could hold you. You always had a way of making every- thing better just by being you, just by making me smile when you didn't even know I needed it the most," she whispers brokenly, her voice uneven. Each word cuts into me as tears fill my eyes, so I blink to clear them and keep her in focus. My hands fist on my knee, wanting to reach out, to comfort her. She's obviously in pain, and my heart hurts for what she went through.

"I don't know why I'm recording this, other than you need to know. Maybe one day, you'll see these, maybe these will only ever be just for me, but you need to know the truth." She shivers, and a hand comes into the frame, draping a blanket around her. She wraps it tighter and smiles sadly to someone.

"Thank you, Abel," she murmurs, and then there's a click of the door closing. It makes me settle a little, knowing he was there helping her, looking after her. That she didn't have to go through that alone.

No child should watch their parents suffer, not without being able to help. I owe Abel for assisting her when I couldn't.

"This might be jumbled, since my brain is not what it used to be, but I need to get this out. He died because of this. You need to know, everyone needs to know," she states with fire in her eyes—the same fire I see in mine. Her back straightens, and she looks fierce. I take after her. She's so strong, so sure, always speaking her mind and standing up for others. My mother was a true warrior, and I see her struggling to rebuild that now. Her grief and pain fight with her sense of justice and hope.

She sighs. "Bear with me while I try to get this out. I—we went on patrol. It was supposed to be a normal one. I remember kissing you goodbye and promising to be back soon." She shivers. "But there was so much at play that you never knew, Piper. We protected you as a child. Paradise isn't the place we made it out to be, it isn't perfect.

Nowhere is, but there was darkness in those gleaming halls, corruption. We all knew it. We saw it more and more, even though they tried to hide it. With our station within the colony, we were granted certain knowledge, and we figured out some stuff we shouldn't have." She averts her gaze.

"Maybe if I had kept my mouth shut and looked the other way, maybe your father would be alive and we would be together." She looks down. "But what kind of mother would I have been? What kind of example would that have set? To see the true nature of someone, the evil they are capable of, and the lengths they were willing to go to and do nothing? If I did nothing, I was helping them, being a part of the problem. I wanted more for you. I wanted you to know you should stand up for what's wrong and protect what is right, and to fight for those who can't protect themselves. I wanted to raise you to be a good person." She looks up then, a fierce tilt to her lips. "To be strong, sure, and willing to fight and die for what is right in this world. If we weren't willing to do that, then we were nothing better than animals.

"But I digress. We knew things, Piper. Things we shouldn't have known about the real Paradise, and it got your father killed. They sent us on patrol, but it was a trap. They followed us and attacked. They knew I was investigating the corruption and trying to prove it. They wanted us dead to stop it, so no one would ever know. They attacked, and your father was badly hurt. I was injured, but I managed to get us away. We survived for days, wandering through The Wastes, then Abel found us. There are good people out there, Piper. Without him, I would be dead, or worse. He saved us, gave us a home, and tried to save your father. It's not a bad, dead place out here, not like they said. There's hope, love, and kindness. There is also plenty of destruction and death, but I have hope that we can heal from that, hope we can start again and do better than before, if only someone would step up and suggest it. I guess that doesn't matter anymore."

She shakes her head. "I'm sorry I can't be there to help you, to tell you who's bad and who's not and show you right from wrong, but I know your heart, my bug. It's pure, so pure. I just hope it doesn't get you killed. You were innocent, they knew that, just a child. I pray that protects you from them. One day, I will get back to you, I vow it. If it's that last thing I'll do, I will get back to you, and if they dare hurt you, I'll bring them all down. All the dirty, cheating, lying bastards. If no one else will, I'll remake this world into a better place for you. I need you to know I'll never give up. One day, I'll find you again, Piper, my daughter. I love you."

The tape cuts out. I wipe my tears and randomly grab another, greedy for her voice, her face. I thought I couldn't hate Paradise more, but I was wrong. They have paid for their sins, however. Who knew I was making them pay for my mother and father too? It's almost poetic that the child they made into an orphan was one of the people who brought them down and sought justice.

The tape starts halfway through, like it's been watched a lot. I can understand why. She looks healthy, happy almost. Her face is more rounded, and there's a smile on her lips. Her hair is lighter and tied back, and she wears a flowery blouse on her top half, although her hands are dirty from being in the garden. But there's something about her, a cheerfulness, a new hope, a new drive to live

—I see it in her eyes. She's not given up. She's not restarting her life, she is making a new one, even while trying to get back to me. In this moment, she's...alive.

"It's your sixteenth birthday today." I watch as she starts to cry, and my own tears trickle down my cheeks. "God, baby bug, I miss you. I hope you are okay. I pray that your ignorance to what those people are capable of saves you. I hope...I hope you're not alone. I hope you have somebody to celebrate with. I hope you are happy and loved. I ache to hug you, to hold you in my arms, but know I'm so proud of you. I love you so much."

She smiles through her tears, and I reach forward, running my hand across her face as the TV jumps from the contact. I wish I could tell her I wasn't alone, that I found love. That I spent the day with

Evan. I was happy, even though I missed her and wished she was there.

Abel comes into view then and places his hand on her shoulder, and I pause it. She's looking up at him with a wider smile on her face, her tears falling away like a shroud. Even in her pain and hopelessness, she found love again. I see it in her eyes. It's not the same as her love for my father. It's different, but no less or more. Just a different type, and it's brought her back. I see it giving her strength and energy, happiness. He provided her with happiness.

I don't even realise I'm completely crying now until a sob breaks free. I drop my hand and wipe my face before I hear a noise. Turning, I see Jago. "Hey, are you okay?" I ask automatically, but he ignores my concern. His eyes go to my mum and then return to me. I wonder how long he was watching.

He kneels before me, brushing my tears away with a frown. "Your pain called to me. Even without my memories, I knew I had to be here to help you, hold you. My heart knows what my brain doesn't. It tells me I'm not whole without you. Even deprived of my memories or a past, I know deep down you are meant to be mine... and me yours."

I hiccup as hope fills me while he searches my eyes, looking to me for answers. "I want that more than anything," I whisper. It's true—he's all I want. My beast is my love. Like my mother, my love for each of my men is different. Each one completes me in a different way, but without him, my rock, I'm falling apart. He said my pain called him, but his pain calls me too.

We're two broken souls once more, just trying to fit the jagged pieces of each other back together.

"Even if I never remember?" he whispers.

"Even if you never remember." I nod, leaning into his hand, his touch so familiar, it grounds me. I'll love him that much more even if he has no memories to fill his head when he looks at me.

He glances at the screen.

"Your mother learned to love again, so maybe we can as well," Jago observes.

I search his eyes, and he watches me back, unguarded and unashamed. He's offering me everything I want, but I have to be sure. "Are you certain? You don't have to because you think you owe me—" I gasp when his lips connect with mine. His kiss is soft and unsure but there, a slight pressure, before he pulls away.

"I may not know my past, my home, or my name, but I know you, Piper. I know my heart, and it belongs to you, so help me remember or show me how to love you again, because I cannot do anything but. I know I could leave, walk away, but my heart won't let me. I see you and I feel...good again, even in the chaos and confusion. You bring me a sense of home, and you make me want to fight for my memories so I can remember the way your eyes shine in triumph when you defeat an army like Clay said. I want to remember the way you smiled at me when I found you again like you told me. The way you cried when you thought you lost us. I want to remember it more than anything. I don't know who I am, Piper, or the type of man I am, but I want to be the one you love, the one you see when you look at me. Will you help me?"

"Always," I promise instantly. "If you never remember any of that, we'll start anew. We'll make new memories. We'll fall in love again, like you said."

"I'd like that." He smiles, bright and wide.

"Me too," I whisper, leaning into him, pressing my forehead against his as he holds me. My mother's smiling, loving face is still on the screen, almost watching us.

"Me too," I repeat.

Chapter 32
New And Old

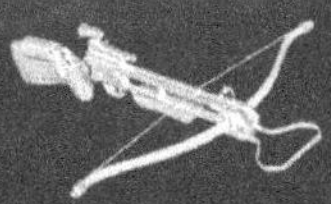

After my and Jago's declaration, I decide to take a break from the tapes. I need some air. They are hard to watch, and even though I need to view them all, there is no rush. They have been waiting for me for years, so they can wait a few days more. It's important to know the things to hold onto and things to drop in life. I once heard that it's like juggling balls, and some will break. You have to know which ones you can drop and which you can't. Jago is a breakable ball, he needs me right now.

My mother is a constant, strong ball waiting to be picked up whenever I have to drop it.

We find Clay helping Evan practise some moves outside. Clay steps back and nods. "Good. Again," he orders, and I watch as Evan attacks him using some new hand-to-hand moves I've never seen before.

"Do I fight?" Jago asks from my side.

"Yes." I snort. "You're one of the best, you taught me."

He nods and watches them before stepping forward. "Can I try?"

Evan moves back, panting. "Sure. Don't overdo it, but it might help jog your muscle memory."

Clay nods and turns to Jago, knowing he's a threat. Jago could beat anyone before, I just hope his body remembers some of it. It would be so hard for him to relearn how to fight, especially in a world where you have to fight every day. He steps up, watching Clay carefully. When Clay feints, he doesn't move, but when he does it again, he takes action. I watch the fight unfold. Clay goes easy at first, and Jago takes time to warm into it, but before long, he is on par with Clay, and then it really begins.

I watch as Jago loses himself in the fight. The moves are the same ones he used before he lost his memories—smooth, fast, and brutal. He pushes Clay back until Clay is winded and sweating. Eventually, Jago knocks him to his ass, and Clay quickly yanks him down too, and I clap and cheer.

When Jago looks up, he grins at me, and I just know everything is going to be okay.

⸻

After sparring, Abel and Evan cook for us, and we all sit down. We laugh and talk, and even Jago joins in. He's definitely different. There's a then Jago and a now Jago. He smiles more, laughs more. I like both versions of him, but I would be sad to see this openness disappear if he gets his memories back.

"What about that time Piper faced off with like ten scavs?"

"Oh, and the cannibals!" Evan adds while I grin, shaking my head at their story telling, but Abel encourages them, wanting to know us.

"Scavs?" Jago asks, frowning. "Cannibals?"

We share a look, and he sighs, staring down at the table.

"How the fuck can I help keep you safe when I can't remember this world?" he snaps, annoyed at himself.

"The past might shape the type of man you are, but it doesn't define you. Even without your memories, you are still you—a warrior, a lover, a fighter. You're a man who likes to protect people and be moving at all times. You like to sleep with the window open or outside, because you like to watch the sky. You like adventure and believe in love. You are still him, and I know one day, you'll find that. But we will be here the entire time, helping you when you need to be reminded of who you are. If there is anything you don't know, we are here," I tell him, reaching across the table for him, but he stands.

"Sorry. I didn't mean to make a scene. Carry on, I just need a moment." I watch as he leaves, heading to the bench and sitting heavily. I sigh and the others sober up. Maybe we were talking about the past too much. It must be hard to hear about yourself in stories and not remember every moment of them, to feel like everyone else knows you better than you do.

I wipe my mouth and get to my feet. Clay reaches out, and I squeeze his hand. "I've got it, keep eating. Why don't you tell Abel about that time we went into war?"

"Oh, that is a good one," Clay remarks, turning to tell the story as I slip out and across the cliff. I sit next to Jago, and he sighs, his head in his hands. He sits upright and looks at me, and I see frustra- tion and sadness mixing in those once fiery eyes.

"I want to be him so badly," he admits. "The man they see when they look at me."

"All they want is for you to be happy. They care for you," I assure him, nudging him with my shoulder. "No matter what, that's all we want. They came with me into that mine to save you because you're family. I can't even imagine how hard it is, but when you are scared, when you don't remember, or it's too much, lean on us, ask us. That's what family does."

I lay my head on his shoulder. He rests his on mine, our hands tangling. He stares at them as he plays with my fingers. I stay silent, offering comfort.

"Old and new," he whispers.

"A mix." I nod. "I can do that."

I know he can. If anyone can recover from this, it's Jago. Maybe I need to stop hoping for his memories to come back and just...be happy he's here. I almost lost him, and even though it's not my whole Jago sitting next to me, I have a piece of him, and that's enough.

Just like my mother and father.

<h1 style="text-align:center">Chapter 33
The Dick Cure</h1>

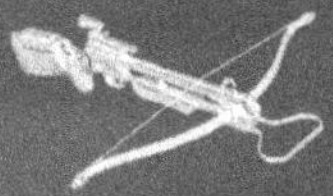

A rchel is gone for several days, like he promised. I spend those days watching my mother's tapes in bits and pieces. It's too much to watch them in their entirety, and it depresses me and makes me cry, which none of my men like. During that time, Jago sits with Evan and Clay. They check him over and remind him of things he might have forgotten, filling him in on the world as he asks everything and anything. They are patient and kind, and it only makes me love them more.

I spend the rest of the time with him. Each day, I remember more and more why I fell in love with this man. Even without his memories, he's still that person. He opens doors for me, laughs with me, encourages my silliness, and has a unique way of looking at everything. At night, we all sit on the cliff, and he holds my hand before I go to bed with my two other men, knowing he probably isn't ready for that.

I fall more and more in love with them. He's piecing his life back together, and after the first few days, he no longer gets annoyed with himself—well, not as much. He trusts us and allows us to help fill in the gaps. He learns he's rubbish at cooking and almost burns the

213

house down as we laugh. Jago discovers he likes to run and be outside. He's learning who he is again, and me along with it.

He asks me everything and anything. Some of his inquiries are hard ones that hit home, but that's my beast, after all, asking the deep questions and not letting me shy away. Each day, the space around us fills with more tension. Desire builds between us. Our bodies know each other better than anyone in this world, and it reminds me of when we used to have to try to fight it.

And how we exploded in passion.

It keeps me up at night. My thighs clench as the memories tumble through my head. I could take my frustration out on Clay or Evan, both would be willing, but it almost seems wrong. When I'm with them, I want it to be for them, not because I can't have Jago. They know that and still love me, holding and kissing me, even though I can't take it further right now. It's not fair to them, Jago, or me.

I feel Jago's eyes on me at all times, tracking me around the room like prey. His body knows what his mind doesn't. He watches me hungrily, refusing to look away when I catch him. I find his eyes on my ass, legs, hips, breasts, and everything in between, making me shiver at the intensity of his gaze.

The wonder in it, the question I can't answer, not yet.

Like now, he's watching me spar with Evan. I need to keep up my own training, after all. He watches me so intensely, not just analysing my moves and shouting pointers, which feels like old times, but raking his eyes across me. I'm so filled with lust, I feel like I might explode.

I turn away, trying to focus on Evan as he moves towards me, but my entire focus is on Jago. It's why I don't see his punch until it's too late. Usually, I would move, since he's not exactly fast and I'm definitely the better fighter.

Stupid horny pussy and hormones distracting me with thoughts of cocks and orgasms.

It slams into the side of my face, knocking me to my ass in shock. I just gape up at him, my mouth open as he freezes. He stares down at me, his fist still poised mid-air, before blinking slowly and letting out an adorable squeal. He drops to his knees, his hands hovering over my face. I hear Clay and Jago rushing over.

"Are you okay?" "Pascha?"

"Piper?"

But I just laugh, I can't help it. It's that hysterical kind of laughter built up over days of stress, desire, and pain. It flows out of me, high and loud, as I lie on the ground with an aching face. I see their worry, the exchange of looks.

"Do you think the lack of dick is getting to her?" Clay asks seriously. "Is that a thing? Does she need orgasms to be made sane again?"

"She's never been sane," Evan murmurs.

"Yes, orgasms fix all." I giggle. "I'm in cock hysteria," I joke and laugh harder as Clay's eyes widen, seriously worried as he scoops me up.

"Fuck, okay, Pascha, let's get you the dick."

I laugh even harder, and Evan and Jago are laughing now. Clay's actual worry is hilarious, the poor guy. He seems almost frantic as he holds me in his arms and stares at the others.

"What? Do you guys have it too? I'm not fucking you—"

I snort, I'm laughing so hard, and Evan tumbles onto his back, tears rolling down his face, while Jago laughs so hard, he can't even speak. I guess we all needed this. It's probably not even that funny, but I think we all needed an outlet, and this is it. It's that type of laugh you can't stop, and when anyone tries to, we make eye contact and it sets us off all over again.

"What is happening?" Clay mutters. "I saw poisoning once when we went into an abandoned building. Is it that?" he asks himself, making me laugh harder like a seal. When he starts to yell for Abel, I manage to control myself and touch his chest.

"I'm okay," I wheeze. "Just needed to laugh."

"Are you sure? You don't need my dick to be okay?"

I roll my lip inwards to stop the chuckles from escaping. "Always, but I promise I'm fine, really."

"Okay, then it's time to eat, and Evan can look at your face." "Wait." Evan gets to his feet. "She needs a free shot, payback." "Evvie," I protest, but he insists. "We aren't kids anymore—"

"It still counts, Pip. Free shot." Clay puts me down, and before Evan can speak, I punch him in the face. He stumbles back with a groan. "Good one," he rasps in pain as I laugh and lean in, kissing it better.

"Now we match. Come on, I'm hungry."

"When aren't you? I swear, I don't know where you hide the food," he mutters as I drag him after me.

Abel joins us for dinner and provides Evan and me with a home-made salve to lessen the bruising on our faces, which I thank him for.

After dinner, we spend the evening relaxing, just being together. Clay helps gather some firewood, and I assist Abel in the garden outside. Evan watches him make some healing supplies, learning from him, while Jago watches everyone.

It's nice, homey, and feels right...if only my shadow were here. That night, I'm about to head into my room with Clay and

Evan when I see Jago's open door. I hesitate before moving towards it and peeking inside. He's staring out of the window. "Are you okay?" I ask softly, stepping in and closing the door. He shivers at my voice and turns slightly.

"I can't sleep for some reason. It feels too empty."

I grin. "You are used to fighting with the others to sleep at my side."

"Probably," he murmurs, watching me. In the dark room, the moonlight illuminates half of his face, and he looks dangerous, so dangerous and sexy. His soft hair falls around his shoulders in waves, and those fiery eyes light up a little, his lips curving in a smile. His muscles are on display in the tank and jeans he's in, and his feet are bare. He's still my beast and so fucking beautiful, it hurts. My body flushes, and my breathing picks up from the elec- tricity filling the dim space. The need to speak, to move, fills me, even as I remain speechless. I'm lost in him, wishing I was in his arms. Desire surges through me so hard, I have to squeeze my thighs together to stop from tackling him. His eyes drop to my body and slowly drag across my curves before he meets my gaze again, and in them, I see pure fucking desire.

I explode.

I step forward, and the tension breaks like I thought it would. He rushes across the room, and I do the same, colliding in the middle. His hands cup my ass and lift me like old times. I slide my fingers into his hair, careful of his wound, and hold on as our lips meet in a flurry of hard, quick kisses. A groan escapes my throat, and Jago growls, the sound vibrating his body as he pulls me closer. I wrap my legs around his waist, feeling his hardness pressed against me, and he sweeps his tongue between my lips, deepening the kiss.

He might not remember how perfectly we come together, where to touch, or how to kiss and touch me, but his body does. I'm wild for him.

We fall backwards. My back hits the bed, and the breath is knocked out of me, which he swallows before pulling away. Both of us are panting, our bodies locked together as I arch my chest, rubbing against his solid one. His hips thrust slightly as he shivers.

"This feels so right," he whispers as he kisses me again. "Like every moment I'm not kissing you is wrong. Like I should be here at all times, with you in my arms and your lips on mine. As if every moment I'm apart from you is a fucking tragedy. Like I was made to kiss you, fuck you, love you."

His words nearly make me come apart as I chase his moving lips, desperate for his touch.

"You were," I whisper, and he groans.

"I don't remember being with you, but you remember."

"Then it will be the first time all over again, and I can show you my mad moves and make you lose control like I did then." I grin as he chuckles.

"Mad moves? Bring it," he teases, nipping my lip and making me rub against him harder. "Show me what I'm forgetting."

"With pleasure." I grin and then grab him, flipping us. He lands on his back with an *oomph* as I straddle his waist. Usually, he would be in control, he would be pinning me down with his hand on my throat and his cock pummelling into me, but this is new Jago, and he's unsure, like he's a virgin again. For some reason, I find that really fucking hot. My pussy drips as I imagine showing him every- thing for the first time all over again.

It's going to be fast. It's been too long since we've been together, but I will cherish every brush of his fingers, every sharp inhale, and the look in those muted eyes as he stares up at me, so trusting and ready.

I wind my hips, grinding against his cock, and he moans. Leaning forward, I place my hands on his chest as I roll my hips. "I want you too much. I've been craving you for days. Next time, I'll show you my mouth, my ass, and everything else, but for now, I need to feel you inside of me."

"You better. I feel like I'm about to fucking burst," he growls out, grabbing my hips to still my movements as I chuckle. Apparently, there's still some of my dominant man in there, and I can't wait to bring him out by playing the brat and making him control me.

Sliding down his legs, I stand at the edge of the bed and slowly undress. He watches me the entire time, unblinking, like he's seeing me for the first time...which I guess he is. I turn around and bend over to pull my jeans down, and I hear him scrambling across the bed before I'm tossed onto it. The rest of my clothes are ripped away, and he explores me with his hands as his lips meet mine again.

I moan into our kiss as he grabs my thigh and hikes it over his, pressing his hard body against mine as I shiver and arch. "Too many clothes," I mutter against his lips, and he rears his head back before looking down as if remembering his clothes, and with a snarl, he quickly stands and sheds them. Seeing him naked steals my breath, just as it does every time I see his bare body. His muscles shine in the moonlight, and he's so fucking ripped and strong, I get to my knees and reach for him. I need him against me, inside of me, tasting me.

Fucking me.

He tackles me to the bed, making me laugh before he makes me moan again. His lips wrap confidently around my nipple. I thought he would be hesitant, but it seems like he still knows how to make me scream, especially when his hand drags down my stomach to my pussy, cupping it. Then, though, he does hesitate slightly, and I decide to take over again.

"Let me," I murmur as he raises his head. I roll us again so he's beneath me. Hovering above him, I trace my hands down his body, feeling him tremble beneath me as I circle his huge cock and stroke the hard length. He groans, his abs clenching and hips lifting.

"The first time I saw you, you stole my breath," I tell him as I slide my hand across his length before poising above him. He watches me, his eyes wide and lips parted. "The first time you kissed me, I knew I was yours." I lean down and kiss him then, and when I pull away, I press the head of his cock to my pussy. "The first time you fucked me, I vowed I would do anything to be yours forever." Holding him still as he trembles, I work my way down his cock, gasping. I'm wet as hell from all the teasing and tension, but he's big, stretching me as I shiver. Clenching around him, I lift slightly to drop again, burying another inch of him inside of me each time until there is no more. "When you told me you loved me," I continue breathlessly, "my heart knew that there was nowhere else in this world I would rather be than at your side, no matter what."

I start to move, and I can't speak anymore, not with the way his thick cock feels inside of me as I roll and swivel my hips. He hits that spot that has me moaning, and I dig my nails into his pecs. I wind, roll, lift, and drop, starting out slow, but soon his hands drift down to urge me on. His grunts fill the air as he clenches his teeth.

"Like that," I rasp as he thrusts up to meet me. He starts off slowly, watching my movements to time his. The slow roll and thrust has me gasping and dripping down his cock.

His nervous strokes disappear, changing into a pounding rhythm, as he catches on.

"Oh fuck," I mutter, digging my nails in as he fucks me from below.

His neck is corded as he throws his head back, clutching my ass cheeks, helping me ride his huge cock as he writhes beneath me. The power is heady as I lift my hands and cup my swaying breasts, feeling so strong and confident.

"I-I'm almost there," I cry out, gripping my breasts harder as he lifts and drops me faster. We race to reach our orgasms, and when he lets go of one of my ass cheeks and pinches my clit, I fall into it with a scream. I shudder above him as my pussy milks his cock. The pleasure flows through me so strongly, my vision goes black. Days of going without it has only made it that much stronger as I ride through the pleasure, then he stills beneath me, yelling as I feel him fill me with his release.

When I can finally open my eyes, it's to see him with his head thrown back, his eyes closed, and his mouth slack in pleasure. His muscles glisten with sweat, and his cock still fills me as I continue to pulse around him.

Fuck, I love this man.

Flopping across his chest, I just pant, trying to calm my breathing. I feel our releases dripping from me, and his heart races in time with mine as his arms wrap around me.

"Holy fuck," he whispers with worship in his tone. "Yeah, we are doing that again." I can't help but laugh as I sit up slightly, purposely squeezing my pussy around his cock. His eyes narrow, and he grasps my waist hard.

"Piper," he warns as I roll my hips, feeling his cock starting to harden within me again. I tease him, sliding my hands up my stomach and across my throat to my mouth, pressing my thumb there.

"Want to fuck here next?" I purr. "You love that, love slamming down my throat."

His breath hitches, and his eyes darken with hunger as I keep up that constant roll, but when he goes to meet me, I stop with a giggle. He snarls and grabs me tighter, and suddenly, I'm flipped. My face smashes into the bed, and my hips are dragged into the air before his hand comes down on my ass.

"Fuck yes," I mutter, pushing back. "I'm yours. Do whatever the hell you want to me."

"Oh, I plan to. Especially for that little show…"

"Brat," I supply as his fingers drag down my ass to my pussy. "That's the word you are looking for."

"Brat," he repeats and then chuckles. "I like that. Well then, brat…" His hand comes down on my ass again. "Let's see if I can make you scream again."

He does, over and over, until I can't even open my eyes.

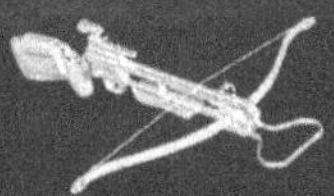

Well, sex didn't magically heal Jago. It put him in a good mood, though, and he's actually whistling, but it didn't bring back his memories. It did help lessen the desire between us— not all the way, however, because all it takes is a look from him and I'm wet and ready to climb him like a tree—but it's not so bad where I can't function.

"Lucky bastard," Evan mutters as he watches Jago flit around the kitchen, helping with breakfast.

"At least she won't be dick insane." Clay shrugs unashamedly as my face flames.

We eat breakfast together, and after, I decide to go and watch more of my tapes while Clay and Evan help Jago. I make sure he is okay first, but he's laughing and joking with them, fitting in well. He seems...happier today.

Pussy power for the win.

I've just settled down in front of the TV when someone clears their throat. Abel stands on the threshold, glancing from the TV to me. "I wanted to make sure you were okay with the tapes and, er—"

"You can stay and watch if you like," I offer softly.

He winces but smiles. "That transparent, am I?" I nod, and he laughs, stepping in. "Thank you. You don't have to let me stay, it's... it's just been so long since I've seen her face. I didn't want to watch the few tapes I knew about too much and ruin the order of them, and the others... Well, I thought they were private."

I nod in understanding and get up to sit next to him on the sofa. "You loved my mother. I saw that she loved you too. She would want you to see, plus it can be hard watching them alone, so please stay."

When he settles back, I hit play.

"It's so sunny here today, bug," she starts with a smile, wearing a tank top and a skirt with a scarf wrapped around her hair. She looks older here, happier. "The garden is growing really well. I swear I even saw a butterfly yesterday. Abel says it's impossible, but I know I did. I named it Piper. It was here to tell me that you are okay, that you're happy and safe. I know it." She looks down, tugging at her skirt before she sighs sadly. "I miss you so much. I feel so guilty. The days pass so quickly here with laughter and happiness, yet in the back of my mind, there is so much pain, knowing that each hour, each day that passes is another away from you. Another of you growing up without me there. While I'm happy here...you're alone in Paradise, wondering if I left you."

She shakes her head, peering into the camera. "Abel doesn't know, I dare not tell him because I'm afraid to hurt him, but as happy as I am, it's tainted by pain, by longing. I wish you were here. It's a foolish wish, but I know each day that passes is another away from you. I think...I think I have to try to find my way back, even if it breaks both of our hearts."

My hand darts out and grabs Abel's, wrapping around his fist before I even realise what I'm doing. He doesn't complain, he just lets me squeeze and take out my anger. His face is shadowed and sad, but he can't tear his gaze away from her. I realise how much it must hurt, knowing these tapes are here, knowing he could see her, hear her at any time, yet he didn't out of respect and loyalty for her and me. I wish I could reach in and scream at her to stay and be happy and in love, and that one day, I would find her myself. She could wait at the door with that smile, and everything would be okay.

But that's a childish wish. I cannot change the past, I can only be present for it and watch, love, and learn.

"I know it will be dangerous. He won't come with me, although he would if I asked. He would leave his home and the life he has built here for me, but I can't ask that. I love him too much to do that, Piper. No, this is my journey, not his. I hope you can under- stand. I loved your father very much, so much, but some things just happen, even when you don't expect them to. Abel's an amazing man. He taught me to heal. He held me when life got hard and put the broken pieces of me back together again, asking for nothing in return. He's an incredible soul, so kind and loving, I couldn't do anything but fall in love with him. I always thought your father was my soulmate, but maybe the heart can love more than one person. Maybe there is more than one perfect soul made for everyone. I don't know, I just hope one day you find someone who loves you as selflessly as he loves me."

I look at the side of his face, seeing tears on his lashes as his mouth moves. I see the words 'I love you' form silently on his lips.

"Either way, I have a decision to make. Half of my heart wants to stay, but the other wants to try to find you. I don't know how yet or when, but I have to try. I can't give up." I shake my head as she sighs. "One day, I'll get back to you, Piper. It's time. I'll see you soon."

Turning away with a sob, I lean into Abel's shoulder, still grip-ping his hand. She was so happy, so settled here, and she gave it up for me. She abandoned her second chance at a life, at love, and there is nothing I can do to change that. I can only be here with the man who stole her heart, his broken pieces matching mine.

Pulling back, I stare into his broken face as he gazes at the screen, at the woman he loved. The woman who left him for me.

"You must hate me," I whisper.

"What?" he asks, frowning down at me as I wipe my face. "She left you, she died trying to get back to me."

He inhales and shakes his head before reaching out and taking my hand. "No, never. When I fell in love with her, I knew I was always second place. I was okay with that because it meant I still got a piece of her heart. I don't hate you, Piper. How could I? I spent, days, hours, weeks listening to stories about you growing up. It felt like I knew you too, like I was there, like I loved you like she did. I was angry at first, so angry at her for going alone, but never for going. I always knew our time was borrowed. I was just happy to have her for so long. But she was always yours, always destined to go back to you. I knew that, and I didn't hate you for that. I was grateful for the time I had with the love of my life, and beyond grateful to her for introducing you to me, because, Piper, you are a brilliant person. You truly are, and I know you and your men are going to make this world a better place. If I didn't meet her, I would never have met you. As much as I loved your mother, you've pushed me to be better, to want to fight again and be a part of this world, where before, your mother made me want to hide from it with her by my side."

"Abel." I hiccup, and he smiles at me softly, wiping away my tears like a father would. The soft, gentle gesture sends a pang of longing through my heart for the parents I lost. Through him, I have a connection to them, and although it's selfish, I want that, him, in my life for the memories he has of her, to keep her alive for me...and that has made me realise that he is a good person too. He's worthy of love and companionship, this world just did him wrong. He deserves to be happy, to live again, and to be able to go into the world and feel safe. He has no one here. He's alone and cut off...

Maybe, just maybe, we can find our way back home together, or better yet, we can make a new home.

"I have to leave at some point," I begin, and he nods, dropping his hand. "Come with me, with us, you can start anew. You could help us with the crops." The words are rushed, excited. I can't stay here forever, and once Jago is okay to travel, we need to return to Worth, Evan's medical equipment, and the people relying on me.

"Piper, I can't. This is my home. This is where I was born, where

I fell in love. This is where your mother is buried. As much as I would like to, and I would, I cannot leave her."

I blink, staring at the floor sadly. "I understand." I do, and I admire his loyalty. My mind whirrs before I settle on something. "Maybe I could visit again?"

"I'd like that," he answers quickly, smiling at me widely. "I'd like that a lot. I'll make more tea in preparation."

I laugh, wiping my face as I share his grin. "I'll bring you some proper tea and food, maybe even coffee."

"Deal," he agrees.

Sharing a nod, an understanding, we turn back to the TV and watch the woman we both loved.

Needing a break from the pain and memories, I head outside to see the guys working. Jago is exercising under Evan's supervision, while Clay does tasks around the house, like things that need fixing or sorting that Abel probably can't do anymore. Clay reinforces the roof and the traps at the gate, fixes the rain catchers, checks the structural integrity of the bench and house, and goes out on the roof and fixes holes. It makes me love him even more as I watch, knowing he's doing this because he saw the need and wanted to help, not out of boredom. Clay knows this man helped us, so he is helping him in return.

Without being asked or told.

Tying my shirt up and donning a hat I find inside, I head up the rickety old ladders to the roof to help him. This was my mother's house with Abel, and it deserves to be preserved so he can remember her and be happy. It shielded her and my father, and then saved her. I need to help keep it in good condition.

"Can I help?" I ask, the cap shielding my eyes from the sun, which instantly heats my skin and makes me sweat.

"Sure, Pascha, here." He hands over some of the tiles he's holding and shows me how to fit them. He doesn't tell me to be careful or second-guess my request, he just trusts me to help and be smart about it. I lean in and kiss him, and he grins as he gets back to work. We work side by side for hours, stopping only to chug some water before carrying on. My arms start to ache in the best way, the kind of pain that comes from working hard. Sweat pours down my body, soaking my shirt, but we still carry on. Halfway across the roof, when we are straddling the peak, Clay rips his shirt off, wipes his face with it, and ties it to his jeans, and I swear I almost tumble off the roof. My mouth drops open and my pussy clenches as I stare at the muscles.

"Abs," I murmur, almost like zombies call for brains. It makes him grin, and he flexes his arms and chest as I watch. "You're like a Ken doll on steroids, but not. Like if Ken was a bodybuilder and lived under a mountain, only you don't have the shiny no man bits, you know?"

"Not a clue, Pascha," he replies casually, used to my rambling by now.

"It's a compliment." I nod, and he grins. "It usually is."

"Can I touch them?" I reach out like a greedy kid. Laughing, he scoots closer, and I drag my hand down his stomach.

"So hard," I mutter.

"That's what he said," Clay retorts. I blink in shock, and he frowns. "Did I say that right? Archel taught me."

I can't help but giggle, and then as Clay starts to turn away, a strange compulsion takes over me. I lean in and lick a line down his abs. He freezes and turns back to blink at me as I quickly sit up and grin sweetly.

"Did you just lick me, Pascha?" he rasps. "I—erm, yes," I hedge. "You looked yummy."

"It's only fair I lick you then," he warns, and then tackles me back. He pins me to the roof as I laugh and fake scream. He tickles me as his head burrows into my hair, and then his tongue slides up my neck, over and over, until my laughter turns into a moan.

"I can think of somewhere else you can lick," I taunt, gripping his shoulders.

A whistle sounds, and I lift my head. "Are you two about to fuck on a roof? That doesn't seem safe, but I'm down for dangerous sex!" Archel calls.

Archel!

I jerk upright, almost falling off the roof, but Clay catches me as I peer over the edge to see a grinning Archel. "Shadow!" I scream.

"Hi, Princess, miss me?"

I scramble down the ladder as I hear him laugh and race through the house and out of the front door. I fling myself at him. He grunts but catches me, swinging me around as I grin and pepper kisses on his face.

"If this is the greeting I get, I need to leave more often. I brought you a surprise."

"Coffee?" I plead.

"Better." He puts me on my feet, and I see it then. Beast Jr.!

I grab him and cuddle him closer, kissing all over his furry face. He's got bigger for sure. "Oh my God, Mummy missed you, yes she did, missed you so much."

"I am both turned on and disturbed," Archel mutters. "And my homecoming attention has been stolen by a dog." I ignore him as Beast Jr. yips in my arms and slobbers all over my face as he kisses and licks me.

"I missed you too. Come on, let's see Beast Daddy..." I sigh. "I'm sorry, baby, he probably won't remember you, but the others missed you. Come on." I put him on the floor, and he jumps at my legs as I walk, following me happily. His huge ears are still floppy, but he's definitely bigger.

Inside of the house, I find the rest of my men, and Beast Jr. instantly runs up to Jago, who steps back, his eyes darting to me in confusion. When he doesn't pick him up or kneel down, Beast Jr. whines, then hurries back to hide behind me. Sighing, I bend down. "Baby, Daddy doesn't know what to do, okay?"

"Daddy?" Jago repeats.

"This is Beast Jr., our son," I tell him proudly, grinning.

He peeks around me at the puppy before getting to his knees and slapping them. "Come here, boy."

"Puppy? He's a feral," Evan scoffs, but he leans down and kisses and strokes our puppy on his way back outside. Clay cuddles him then sets him down before Jago. We all watch, waiting, and then Archel comes to my side.

"Still nothing?" I shake my head as he wraps his arms around me. "Give it time, Princess."

With a whimper, Beast Jr. slowly walks towards Jago, who waits patiently. Once the pup is before him, he reaches out slowly to let him sniff his hands, and as soon as he does, he barks and jumps at Jago, realising it's him. Laughing, Jago catches him and lets him lick his face as he strokes and talks to the pup. Jago is unashamed and fussing over him like he used to when he thought no one was watching.

"Not really a beast anymore, is he?" Archel jokes, but it hits home.

Jago has changed, he's different. He said we could fall in love again, and he's right. I need to find out who this new Jago is to see if I still feel the same. Everything hasn't just changed for him...

But for all of us.

Chapter 35
The Shadow And The Princess

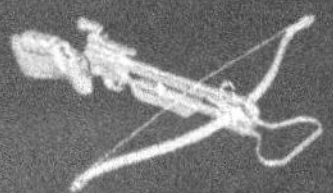

Feeling confused and lost, I find myself on the bench on the cliff. Jago is inside playing with Beast Jr., laughing freely and talking so much, it almost gives me a headache. When I look at him, he's the same man...but he's not. It's giving me whiplash, and my heart is confused as well as my brain.

"Mum, what do I do?" I whisper, stroking the bench. "It's him, it's still him, and I love him...but when I look at him, I see a stranger in my love's body. He talks differently, acts differently. How can it still be him? I'm scared he will never get his memory back. I'm scared I won't like this new him as much or that I'll like him too much. I'm just...lost. I need you." I hiccup on a sob. "I need you, and you're not here to tell me what to do." Wiping away my tears, I lift my head and suck in clean air. "How did you do it, Mom? How did you fall in love with someone again? Give them your heart, knowing it might get hurt, broken, dropped? When I thought I had lost him, I would have done anything to get him back, and now he's here and I feel like I lost him all over again down in that mine."

Wiping at my face, I smile bitterly. "I'm being stupid, aren't I?

He's here, he's alive and well, and he wants to know me, to fall in love with me again, and I'm being a big baby sitting out here complaining because he smiles more. Fucking hell, Piper. If it was the other way, he would never give up on me. Right? So how can I abandon him? Just because he's different doesn't mean I don't and won't love him. Maybe it was for the best, maybe not, but I guess only time will tell."

"I think you have your answer, Princess," comes a smooth voice, and I turn to see Archel, my shadow. I should have known he would follow me. He moves around the bench and sits, taking my hand. "You know, deep down in your heart, you will love him no matter what. It won't be easy, nothing ever is, but you've never backed down from a fight yet, and you won't now, it's why we love you." With that declaration, he leans in, kissing me softly. His lips drag along mine as my heart fills with love for this man.

When he pulls away, I lean into his shoulder, just being with him.

The shadow and the princess.

"How was everything back home?" I ask, unable to stay quiet too long and needing to know.

"Fine. Worth was worried, but I explained everything. She told us to take as much time as we need, and she will give orders to your people for now, but she was sorry. She also told me to tell you something..."

"Yeah, about how great my ass is?" I joke as he laughs and kisses my hair.

"She told me to tell you that a great woman loves despite the pain, but a queen loves the pain or some shit like that. Basically, she told you to keep fighting, and to remember where you came from and what you have achieved. It's okay to be hurt, but you still need to fight and love."

"She is a smart cookie."

He tuts and pulls away. "Hey, I said that."

"Okay, you're a smart cookie too, and a good cookie as well.

You'd be like one of those fancy chocolate ones everyone fights over in the box, you know?"

He ignores my rambling and leans in, kissing me again. "I love you too, now let's get back before we have all those idiots out here."

Holding my hand, he pulls me back inside, where I see Jago hovering over Abel's shoulder as he teaches him to cook. When he sees me come in, he watches me carefully, probably knowing something was up, so I purposely go up to him and lean on my tiptoes and kiss his cheek. The smile he directs at me is huge and happy and settles any doubts that I might be doing the wrong thing.

We eat together, and after, I excuse myself to wash. The sweat on my skin is making me feel dirty, and I need a moment to myself after the multitude of emotions today. The sun has set, so I light the candles in the bathroom and lean into the sink, breathing slowly as I close my eyes.

I turn away when I feel calmer and draw some water into the bath and shed my clothes. Getting in, I grab them and soak the fabric with me, wringing them out and scrubbing them before rinsing and hanging them over the side as I wash my hair and body. Once clean, I get out and dry off, and then I put on the clean dry clothes I brought with me. Re-plaiting my hair, I instantly feel better, but when I open the door, I hear a commotion.

Walking downstairs, I stop at the bottom with a frown, looking at my men who are yelling at each other. "Guys, what's happening?" I call.

They all turn, all apart from Jago, who is missing.

"It's Jago. He mentioned something about knowing how to ride still. He could remember, and he wanted to go get you a present to prove he could. I thought I talked him out of it," Evan growls out, "but when I came in, he was gone."

"I checked, his bike is gone too," Archel murmurs. "Fuck! Get your bikes, we are going after him."

"He could be anywhere, Pascha," Clay cautions softly.

"He could be hurt. Let's go," I snap, grabbing my boots and storming from the house.

We rush to our bikes, and I don't wait for them. As soon as I swing my leg over it, I'm roaring into the distance. I yell his name, uncaring who hears. Let them attack me if they dare. All I care about is getting to him. My heart pounds, and all those previous worries disappear. I love him, of course I do, with or without his memories.

It's us against the world.

Brawler and Beast forever, even if the beast is more like the Disney version now.

We spread out, staying within view of each other while trying to cover as much ground as we can. Our lights pierce the night, our yells echoed by the howls of creatures in the distance, but they don't scare me as much as losing Jago does.

Not again.

I start to panic, thinking of all the things that could happen to him. I need to stay smart and in control, because one wrong move out here means death, but I can't. Not with terror filling me.

Then I see a light shining across the sand. I quickly turn to it and gun the engine. The others follow, and we race towards the light that, as we get closer, we realise is the same as ours—a bike light.

It's Jago's headlight, and it's on the ground. Fuck!

I stop my bike. In my haste, it falls over as I sprint across the sand, covering the remaining distance between us. He's on his back, crushed under the weight of the bike. Clay moves past me, yanking the bike up with a snarl, while Archel and Evan pull him free and Evan starts to check him over. He's got cuts and scrapes, but he's also hit his head again and the wound has reopened. Evan's hand hesitates over it, combing the hair aside to see the bleeding injury is deeper than before.

"Fuck, he hit it again." He begins to work to stop the bleeding, and I slide under his head like a cushion just as he instructs. Tears fill my eyes as I stroke his tranquil face.

"Jago," I whisper as everyone waits with bated breath for him to wake up.

"His pulse is slow, but he's okay. I don't know about the head wound."

"Jago," I say louder, leaning over him as I press my hand against his chest to feel his beating heart. "Jago!"

He groans and his lashes flutter, but his eyes remain closed, his legs twisting. "That's it, baby, it's me, wake up," I plead, curling my hands into his chest as I lean over further. Clay and Archel watch our backs, while Evan waits to evaluate the damage.

"Jago, please!" I yell, and he groans louder, his eyes nearly opening. "Please, please, I can't lose you. Not again."

"You could bever lose me, Brawler," he murmurs with his eyes closed. I freeze, my heart slamming in my chest as I stare down at him.

"What...what did you call me?" I whisper.

"Brawler, of course." He groans as his eyes blink open before he's staring up at me. The fire in them is back. "Why, what else would I call you?"

"Beast?" I whisper, staring into those fiery eyes. He frowns, then winces. "Fuck, my head hurts."

"That's what happens when you fall from a bike, dumbass," Archel calls. "We need to get moving. All this commotion is attracting predators, so is the scent of his blood."

"Can he move?" I ask Evan.

"I—shit, maybe," he mutters. "We have no choice, he can't ride though."

"I'll hold him against me on the bike," Clay volunteers while I just stare into Jago's confused gaze as he looks up at me. His hand drifts across my jaw and captures a tear rolling down my chin.

"What's wrong, Brawler?" he demands, his voice thick with pain and confusion, but also anger on my behalf.

"It's you, it's really you... You're back."

"Back? What did I miss?" he mutters in confusion, and I just laugh as I lean in and kiss him swiftly.

"Well shit, I kinda liked the new smiley Jago. He didn't try to kill me as much," Archel jokes. "Okay, big guy, time to go."

"Go where?" he asks, letting them help him up with his arms over their shoulders.

"Anywhere, just as long as you're there." I rush to my feet before him, unable to take my eyes off those fiery orbs as he smiles widely.

"Always, Brawler."

Chapter 36

Our Love Is Like A Condom

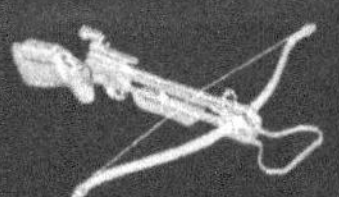

Between us, we manage to get Jago back. Clay and Archel help walk him to the house, where Abel waits. As soon as we are there, they carefully sit him down as Evan goes about cleaning and dressing the wound and asking questions. He tests Jago's eyesight, memory, and much more. I stand at the back with my arms crossed, trying to refrain from rushing over there. I want to shake sense into him for leaving, but if he didn't, I wouldn't have my Jago back—and he is back. Before Evan asks if he knows us, I see the answer in his eyes.

"Why wouldn't I?" he snaps and looks at me. "Brawler, what's going on? Everything is fuzzy. I remember the cave... Shit, how did I get out of there? Did I escape?"

"You didn't," I croak out hoarsely and shake off the memories of almost losing him—again. "We rescued you. You had been... tortured. You had a head injury, and it gave you amnesia. You couldn't remember anything or anyone, even yourself...or me."

His expression drops as he stares at me. "I forgot you?" "And yourself," I add.

"I don't give a fuck about that." He surges to his feet and wobbles.

Evan tries to restrain him, but Jago throws off his hands and hurries to me on unsteady feet. He cups my face reassuringly, like always, and I lean into his touch. I feel tears in my eyes as he searches my gaze. "Brawler, I'm so sorry."

"It wasn't your fault," I whisper.

He rests his forehead on mine. "I don't care, I don't even know how I could forget you. You are so ingrained in me, into every thought, action, and every inch of my body."

"Deep down, I think you remembered some of me," I reassure him.

"You tried to protect her," Clay offers.

"You got pissed when she wasn't next to you," Archel adds. "You couldn't pull yourself away from her, and even without

your memories, you wanted to fall in love with her again...but you said your heart was already there," Evan finishes.

"You were still you, just different."

"I didn't sing, did I?" he jokes, and I smack his chest.

"Never joke again. Fuck, you smiled and joked way too often to be you." I almost cry with happiness then as he laughs and kisses me softly.

"Then I'll be stern and angry at all times. You will never lose me, Brawler. With or without my memories, I knew you were mine. This heart is yours, always has been and always will be," he vows, making me nod as the tears fall. He stumbles again, and Evan and Clay catch him before he takes us both down.

"Okay, big guy, enough love confessions for now. Let's get you better so you can go back to kicking Archel's ass," Evan teases as he guides him into a chair.

Abel comes in and looks at Jago, sighing in relief. "Good, you found him."

"Not just him, but his memories." I grin, wiping my face. "Abel, I would like you to meet Jago, the real Jago...my beast."

He's confused, but it looks like that blow to the head helped restart his brain. Will he remember forgetting? Who knows, his brain is hard and complicated, and he has a thick skull, thank God.

"It's nice to meet you." Abel sticks his hand out. "I am Abel, a friend."

"And my mother's lover," I add, and Jago frowns. "It's a long story. Let Evan check you over and get some fluid and food in you, and then I'll tell you everything."

"Would you like some of the healing tea, Doctor?" Abel asks Evan.

"Yes, thank you." Evvie almost preens at being called 'Doctor.'

Abel instantly hops to it, moving with purpose to swiftly brew and hand Evan anything he might need as he inspects Jago's wound and continues his tests. Jago keeps his eyes on me the entire time, so I smile reassuringly, and only then does he relax a little. Did I really look that bad?

"You ripped open your head wound. I'm going to need to stitch and dress it, it will hurt," Evan warns before talking him through it as he lays out what he needs, while Abel passes over the drink.

"Down the hatch," he instructs, and when I nod, Jago drains the drink with pursed lips, then hands the mug back, being polite as Evan moves his hair, clipping it back so he can see the wound.

"Pip, get your fine ass over here and make sure he doesn't kill me."

Grinning, I move closer and straddle Jago's lap, keeping him pinned as Evan starts to sew. He knows if he moves too fast with Beast, his first reaction to pain is to fight. Jago grunts, holding me tighter as his lips twist in pain. I stroke his shoulders and face, humming to him as Evan finishes up and then dresses the lesion before stepping back.

"There, all done," I coo, tipping his head up and kissing him gently. "Now you need to eat and drink something, okay? Then we'll rest."

"I want to know everything that happened." "Tomorrow, once you've slept," I promise.

He concedes for once, and after getting him settled, Abel and I quickly hand out drinks and cook some warm food for everyone.

All the while, my brain whirls and turns, always landing on the same thought.

I'm happy he's back.

Once we've eaten, I force Jago to rest, but the only way he will is if I lie down with him, and of course my other men think that's an invitation, so we all pile into the room he was staying in. I curl up into Jago's side, while Archel is wrapped around my legs from behind. Evan is between them, and Clay is draped along the bottom, his head and legs hanging off in a very uncomfortable angle, not that he seems to mind.

"Now that he has his memories back, can we tell him all the embarrassing shit he did?" Archel teases into the dark.

Jago's chest moves with a deep sigh before he pulls me closer. "Any more embarrassing than you doing and enjoying sand face-masks with Brawler?"

"Princess!" Archel whines. "That was one time, and you told me you wouldn't tell anyone."

"Oops." I giggle, snuggling closer to Jago, content to just be with them. The hole in my heart is filled once more, and I feel completely full and loved.

It goes quiet for a moment as I stroke my beast's chest, mulling over everything that has happened, how we handled him losing his memories, and how we adapted. As usual, my thoughts come out like word vomit. "It's like our love is a condom, it stretches, changes, and adapts. Altering to fit us all and keep us safe."

"What a weird metaphor, but I guess so," Evan replies, smiling against my skin, unbothered by my random outburst.

"I mean we were going to do whatever it took," I finish lamely.

"Yeah, you were even willing to give Jago up," Clay scoffs.

"Give me up?" he repeats, and I wince.

"I offered to let you find another life, since you couldn't remember this one. I didn't want you to feel trapped," I mutter.

"You were going to let me go?" Jago demands, glaring down at me. I smile sweetly, innocently, even though he knows better than to trust it.

"You're so pretty," I tell him, making him roll his eyes. "She was," Archel inserts, so I kick him, making him grunt.

"Shut the fuck up. I wouldn't have really let him go. I would have stalked him like a weirdo until he loved me and fucked my brains out again—oops." I roll my lips inwards to keep myself from talking.

They all groan, then laugh, and I flip to see Jago's fiery eyes on me. He strokes my side like he can't bear not to touch me. My heart flips from that look, and my whole body heats up. It's possessive, caring, and so fucking hungry, I actually swallow my next words. We just stare at each other in the dark.

"All right. Up we go, boys. These two clearly want to fuck," Archel announces and kicks Evan off the bed.

"I'm hungry anyway. Evan can make me a sandwich," Clay decides as he climbs from the bed, kisses my cheek, and leaves the room. Evan follows, rubbing his ass and grumbling at them both. Archel chuckles and kisses my cheek, breaking the staring contest. "Good humping, Princess."

Jago snarls, and before he can punch him, Archel is out of the door with the others, closing it behind him.

"I missed you so much," I whisper.

"It feels like I've had no time apart from you, but I'm sorry I hurt you, Brawler."

"You have nothing to be sorry for, it was an accident. It happened, and we will grow stronger because of it. Now we know we can survive absolutely anything," I whisper, leaning in to kiss him softly. I keep it chaste, despite Archel's comments—he's hurt, after all, and he needs to rest.

"He is right though—I need to feel you and wipe that sad, hurt look from your eyes. I want to replace it with so much pleasure, you scream for them all to hear and I will never forget again. How could I?"

"That sounds like a plan." I gasp as I rub against him. Jago and I were together without the memories. It was beautiful, and I had resigned myself to always knowing what he did not, but with my beast here, holding me so tightly and promising me the world...I need him again. I need to feel that fire in his eyes washing across my skin until I can't breathe or think.

Just feel.

He lowers his head, giving me no chance to escape as he captures my lips. He claims them once more before he quickly flips us, pinning me to the bed as he decimates my mouth. His tongue tangles with mine, controlling the pace.

He's reclaiming me, and I'm okay with that. I'll do the same to him. I pull back and gasp for air. He kisses across my cheek to my ear, growling out, "Never try to let me go again," before kissing down my throat. My eyes slip close, and my head drops back to the pillow. I'm drugged by him. By his warmth, the strength of his body, and the conviction in his words. By the assurance in his kisses. I need everything he's promising.

Need him. My beast.

His mouth descends across my shoulder, leaving no inch of skin unkissed as he gently nudges my top down. His lips wrap around my nipple, sucking as his fingers pluck my free nipple before he lets go and gives the other the same treatment. His rough touch makes me whimper and tug on his hair as I drag him closer. My legs are wrapped around his waist, and I grind into him. He kisses down my belly to my pussy before parting my lips and covering my clit with his mouth.

I cry out as I lift my hips into his mouth. Lust surges through me so fiercely, I claw at him, needing him inside of me, needing to feel my beast. When he lets go, he licks down my pussy and spears his tongue inside of me, tasting my cream. He fucks me with it as I whimper and roll in the sheets. It's too much, and when his fingers join in, I can't take anymore. I come all over them.

He surges above me, grabs one leg, and presses my foot against his chest as he lines his cock up with my hole and slams all the way in. I scream, my orgasm still rolling through me as he starts to move. He fucks me softly at first, keeping his eyes locked on mine. He watches me, assuring himself I'm here, just as I'm doing with him. I clutch his shoulders and hold on.

He fucks me hard and fast. Each thrust pushes me higher on the bed, the angle hitting me so deep that it nearly hurts, but I crave his brand of painful love. It's feral and raw like my beast.

"I missed your fire so much. Never leave me again," I rasp, my eyes sliding shut. He snarls and leans down, biting my neck hard.

"Eyes on me, Brawler," he orders with a snarl as he pulls away. I force them open, my gaze clashing with his. Our eyes remain locked together as the pleasure builds with each stroke of his huge cock. "You are mine. This mouth." He leans down and kisses me, biting my lip until it bleeds. "These breasts." He twists one of my nipples so hard, I clench around him. His hand drags down my stomach and pinches my clit. "This pussy, and even that tight little ass. All of you is mine, don't you ever forget that."

His name leaves my lips on a moan as I listen to his possessive, dirty words. I plant my other foot on the bed beside his, lifting myself to meet his hard thrusts. I take everything he has and more. He snarls and clenches his teeth as he powers into me, and the wet noise of our bodies joining makes me all that hotter for him.

I can't take any more, and I come all across his dick as he growls and fights my tight channel. Pulling out, he flips me and drags my ass back into the air, and in one smooth thrust, he buries himself back inside of me. I scream and clutch at the bedding as he rams into me, forcing his cock deeper, harder, faster. His grip on my hips is bruising, just the way I like it.

I close my eyes, pressing my face to the bed as I pant, sweat coating my skin. "I can't come again, I can't—"

"You can and you fucking will," he snarls. His palm lands on my ass cheek in punishment over and over in time with his thrusts. The burn of it elicits a whimper from my lips as I push back to meet him.

"Can't!" I cry out, even as the pleasure builds again. It's so strong this time, I feel like I might pass out, and when his slap lands on my pussy, catching my clit, I scream.

I come again like he promised, pulling him with me as he snarls and fights, filling me with his cum. I nearly pass out, and when I come to, he's pulling his softening cock from my sore pussy. He places a gentle kiss on my back, and I almost weep, before he cleans me up and tucks me into bed with him. I'm barely able to keep my eyes open, he fucked me that good.

"Love you," I whisper into his chest, feeling his heart race in time with mine.

"I love you forever, Brawler," he vows, kissing me tenderly.

I fall asleep in my beast's arms with his kiss on my lips and his hands on my heart, knowing that whatever tomorrow brings, we can handle it.

Together.

Chapter 37
Goodbye Finally

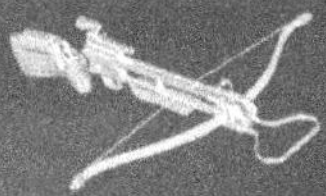

Over breakfast, we take turns filling Jago in on everything he has missed. By the time we are done, he looks like his head is about to explode. Beast Jr. has been exploring while we talk, but when he hears us moving around, he rushes back in just in time to see Evan forcing Jago to rest again. I help Jago to the sofa in the living room, and for the first time, I tell them all to stay as I place the next tape in the player.

It loads up to her smiling but stern face. Her hair is tied back, and she's wearing a pair of jeans and a tucked-in blouse. By her knees is a full backpack, and she seems almost frantic as she takes in a deep breath as she kneels on the carpet.

"Hi, bug. Today is the day—the day I come back to you. I couldn't sleep last night. Something in me knew you needed me, so I got up and packed, and I'm ready to go. Abel...he's out gathering food. I couldn't bear to tell him." She looks down. "It's selfish, I know. I love him, but I love you more. I left a note, and I hope one day, he will understand or that we may even get to be here together, and you can meet the man who saved my life." She glances over her shoulder. "I don't have much time, but I needed you to know I'm coming and I love you."

Panic fills me as a sick feeling churns in my stomach. This was the day she died trying to get back to me. She could have had all this, yet she threw it away for me. But wouldn't I do the same for my friends and family? For my loves?

Yes, without question.

Her eyes close for a moment, and I see the pain and indecision on her face. Clay takes my hand, and Evan grasps the other as we sit on the floor before the sofa. Jago's hand comes down on my shoulder, and Archel's on the other. Beast Jr. has his head on my lap, always at my side. They ground me as tears fill my eyes. That's all I seem to be doing recently—crying.

"I hope you never have to see these. I hope I'll get to hold you in my arms again soon and tell you everything I did in these tapes... but if not, if I don't make it back to you..." Her eyes open, shining with tears as her lips curl up. "Know that I love you so very much, my daughter. You are so loved, and I am so proud of you. Be kind, be daring, but most of all, stay strong and be the person I know you are. The one so filled with questions, the need to explore, and the desire to save people...to save this world. I love you. Goodbye." The video cuts off, and tears roll down my cheeks as I stare at her face.

"Goodbye, Mum," I whisper.

Closing my eyes, I let my men comfort me as I say goodbye. I let her go. I let all the anger and pain at losing her, at thinking she didn't want me, go. All that is left is the sparkling love and memo- ries she provided me with. It will still hurt, loss doesn't just go away because you will it, and I will always have my dark times when I feel like I can't breathe because I miss her and my dad so much, but...watching these tapes and getting to say goodbye has helped.

No matter if they are gone or not, I will cherish the time I had with them, and even if it hurts, it just means that my love for them is still there. In that love and their memories, they will live on.

"She loved you so much, Pip," Evvie murmurs.

"She would be so proud of the woman you have become," Jago soothes.

"I know." I do, and I'll spend the rest of my life striving to ensure she's proud and be the woman she died for, the woman she expected me to be. I won't always get it right, since I'm not perfect, but no one is. Life is all about making mistakes and learning from them. Life is about taking chances, even if it might get you hurt.

And my men will be with me the entire way.

***

I find Abel on the bench on the cliff. I sit next to him and admire the sun cresting across the dark, deep ocean.

"You're leaving soon, aren't you?" he questions.

"As soon as Jago can travel. I need to get back to my job," I reply honestly. I've been debating it all morning, but the others agree. "I want to come back though...if you'll have me. Not just because I feel close to my mum here, but it feels right and I enjoy your company."

He looks at me and smiles. "I'd like that. You are welcome here anytime."

"Good." I look back at the sunrise. "Depending how Jago is, we will aim to leave tomorrow. I'd like to have a celebration tonight, if that's okay? For my mum, for you, for us. I feel like we need to."

"That sounds like a great idea. I actually have some homemade spirits," he teases, making me laugh.

"Oh God, maybe we should leave the day after then," I retort as I smile at him. "Thank you for giving me the time and space I needed. Thank you for letting us invade your life, and thank you for loving her."

"She was the one I should be thanking. She gave me a purpose, and now she brought you to me. She was an incredible woman, and she created an incredible daughter—one this world needs. I might never be the strongest, smartest, or bravest, but you make me believe in a world outside these walls again. You give me hope for the future of this world."

"It's bigger than me. One day, I hope you get to see it and all of the incredible people out there fighting for a future, trying to protect people, and restarting a new life. A better one."

"One day." He nods, and we become quiet again, looking at the water. "It will seem so empty here with you gone."

"You won't miss all the noise, trust me." I laugh. "But we'll be back. I've been told I'm like a bad rash, you can't get rid of me, but now that I think about it, it doesn't sound like the compliment I thought it was."

"Life is meant to be noisy. I'll make some food to last you through your journey and give Evan some of those herbs and seeds so you may grow some at The Ring, as he calls it." He stands and smiles down at me. "I'm glad we met, Piper. I'm glad life led you back to your mum." With those parting words, he leaves, and I watch him go before looking back at the water.

Peace fills me. I know my life is only just beginning. We have so much to do to settle The Wastes and make it a place to be proud of again. But with his trust in me, my mother's trust in me, I know it's worthwhile.

No matter what is to come, I cannot forget I am fighting so no other child has to grow up without a mum or a dad, so that they feel safe and their lives are filled with happiness and love.

The world may have ended, but that doesn't mean we have to break with it.

Like Worth said, it's time to start anew, fresh, like the flowers that grow here on the cliff with my mother's memory.

Chapter 38

Hump And Run

The food may not be a feast like in Paradise, but it sure is for The Wastes. It covers the table. There are vegetables Abel grew, which were added to some fresh meat Clay managed to catch. I don't ask what it is, I don't care. We have home brewed spir- its, water, and sweets. We laugh and talk and drink, our bellies full as we enjoy the night. The more booze we consume, the fuzzier my head gets and the lighter I feel.

"What about the time Clay tried to make a new bomb to impress Piper, but she distracted him with her boobs and he almost blew up the entire building?" Archel roars with laughter, I grin, and Clay howls, smacking the table and the empty plates.

"No, no, the time Piper chased Jago around singing Disney songs until he kept accidentally singing them after," Evan offers, struggling to breathe through his laughter.

"No! I've got it!" I yell, spilling my glass as I gesture with it. "Oops." I grin. "The time when they took drugs and made sand angels, oh my dicking God, it was so funny." Archel starts to laugh, while Jago grins and rolls his eyes. Beast Jr. barks with us as if laughing, running around the table and playing with a toy Abel made for him.

Evan leans into me, his eyes bright with happiness and booze. His arm is draped around my shoulder, holding me to him. I don't know if it's the alcohol or his proximity, but my pussy suddenly wakes up with ferocity, pulsing and demanding I lead one of them away to fuck them.

Definitely the alcohol.

When Abel gets up to grab more booze from outside, I make my move. I think I'm being stealthy, but they all hear as I lean in and try to whisper, "I want to ride your ding-a-ling." I hiccup loudly and cover my mouth. "Oops, that wasn't sexy. I mean let's fuck." I get to my feet, stumble, grab his hand, and drag him after me. With his arm over my shoulder, I giggle and weave upstairs, Evan following behind me.

Hoots and whistles trail after us, but I ignore them as I rush to the bathroom, throw him inside, and shut the door, my hands going to my pants. "Trousers off, Evvie."

"Jeez, Pip." He grins but reaches down, managing to undo his trousers before pushing them down. I kick mine off and pounce on him. I smash my lips to his as I circle his hardening cock and squeeze. He groans into my mouth as we fall back with a laugh— right into the bath. He groans from the impact but quickly returns to kissing me before breaking away. "You're drunk—"

"You are too. Shut up and fuck me," I mumble into his lips, squeezing his cock harder as his hips jerk.

He moans into my mouth before untangling himself from my arms and climbing from the tub without falling. I kneel, my lips sore and eyes wide.

"What—" I start before he grabs me, yanks me from the tub, and bends me over it.

"I'm shutting up," he snaps, "like you said." He pulls my panties aside and slides his fingers along my wet pussy before stopping at my clit and rubbing. I push back into him, needing more, needing his cock. Like he can hear me, his fingers glide down and push into me with none of his usual teasing.

He pulls a gasp from my mouth as his talented fingers curl inside of me, rubbing my walls before pulling out and pushing back in. He moves in a slow rhythm at first before he speeds up. With his other hand, he circles my clit, over and over. It quickly sends me over the edge, and I come all over his fingers with a groan. Evan moans, pulling free of my fluttering channel and replacing his digits with the head of his cock.

In one smooth thrust, he fills me, fighting through my after-shocks to bury himself inside of me. We still for a moment as I shiver in pleasure from being stretched around his cock. His breath blows across my sweaty neck, and my breasts heave as he keeps me there, impaled. He grasps my hips and then starts to move, working his dick deep inside of me with each punishing thrust. When my brain finally kicks into gear, I push back, moving with him.

"Fuck, I love your pussy." He nips at my neck before pushing me down farther until I'm bent all the way over, and he's just smashing into me. Each slide of his cock drags along the nerves in my channel, making me whimper and cry out. I grip the porcelain bath hard to stay on my feet. "Love you so fucking much. Love the way you feel, the way you taste, the way you come for me." The words are almost snarled out, and his tone is filled with his desire, which only spurs me on. I purposely clench around him, and with a yell, he loses all restraint.

His tattooed hand reaches out, grips my neck, and pulls me up until my back meets his chest. I wear his hand like a necklace as he powers into me. The sound of our heavy breathing mixes together over the slap of our skin. Everyone downstairs knows exactly what's happening, and for some reason, that only spurs me on. My pussy drips so much, I feel it on my thighs as he snarls, his hips snapping forward over and over as he fucks me relentlessly.

"So" —thrust— "fucking" —thrust— "good," he snarls, squeezing my throat harder than he normally would. Using me, fucking me.

The small, dim room only adds to our pleasure, our voices echoing slightly as I cry out his name. I try to hold back the surge of pleasure working its way through me, caused by his cock and hands.

He slips his free hand across my hip and pinches my clit between two fingers.

Hard.

I jerk as a scream leaves my throat, and I'm sent soaring over the precipice again. My orgasm smashes through me so hard, I fall. It doesn't stop him, though, he fucks me hard and fast, chasing his own release. My tight cunt milks him as his hips stutter, and he comes with a groan and a squeeze of my throat, filling me with his release.

"Holy shit," I mutter, still shivering, my body exhausted in the best way. "You were like some kind of dick god, pussy obsessed feral. I loved it," I tease, and he chuckles, stroking my throat before kissing away the sting of his hand.

We lean into each other and the bath as we catch our breath before he pulls free of me. Turning on the tap, he cleans me before I can move.

"Hey, hurry up, you two. Archel made a bet he can swim in the ocean without dying!" someone calls.

Shit. I move past Evan and grab my clothes and start to dress. "Sorry to hump and run," I tell him as I pull up my trousers.

"But I want to see Archel swim!"

My head is pounding. I blame the alcohol and Archel, who threw me into the Dead Sea. We swam for hours before stumbling to bed and promptly passing out. Now the sun is up and shining onto my face, demanding I wake. We are leaving today, so I need to pack and get ready, but my mouth is thick and cottony, my head is

pounding, and my muscles ache so badly, I don't even want to move.

"Oh God, I'm dying, Pascha," Clay calls from the floor, where he fell from the bed last night, with Beast Jr. sleeping on him like a blanket.

Evan flops over and covers his pale face. "No more booze, ever," he mumbles.

Jago grins, sitting near the window as he puts on his boots. Unlike us, he didn't drink too much, worried about medication interactions. "Feeling rough?" he calls.

I lift my head and glare at him before dropping down and turning to Archel, who is naked and lying across the bed diagonally. "I blame you."

"I blame myself too." He groans. "Princess, make the room stop spinning."

"Only if you make my head stop pounding," I mutter. "I'll pound something else. I'm too hungover for this."

"Really? I feel fine. Even my head doesn't hurt that bad anymore," Jago comments as he stands and stretches. Despite my hangover, I still check him out because come on, that man is fine with capital F. If F was for fuck me like you hate me, deep, dirty sex like the type we had—

"I'm going to be sick if you carry on," Evan warns. "Oops," I chirp as Jago comes over and kisses me.

"I appreciate it. Let me get some food cooked and see if Abel has any more of that tea that might help you guys," he offers like the hero he is, which the hero always gets the girl, and honestly, even with my hangover, he could still have me—

"Nope, I'm out." Evan groans and tries to climb off the bed, but he falls onto Clay, who grunts and punches him. They start to fight, which, of course, a naked Archel has to get in on. I leave them to it with a roll of my eyes. After washing off the grime that always coats my body after drinking, I head down to Jago and Abel, but I freeze near the bottom step when I hear them speaking. My eyes flicker to

Beast Jr. as he happily trots out of the back door after Jago fed him. I don't worry about him, since I know he will be back and won't venture too far. Instead, I focus on the conversation.

"You really love her, don't you?" Abel asks.

There's a pause where I don't think Jago will answer, and Abel clearly doesn't think he will either, because he continues, "Sorry, I didn't mean to speak so bluntly. It's just that I love—loved her mother so much, and she worried for Piper. To see her so happy is comforting. I wish I could tell her mother. They are so easy to love, aren't they?"

"Yes, I love her, more than anything in this world. Before her, I never loved anything or anyone. She gave me a purpose, a life, a family," Jago murmurs, and my heart pounds. I duck so they won't see me when I hear them bustling around the kitchen. Jago is hard to read. He tells me he loves me, and I see it in his actions, but he never bares his heart, especially to a stranger, so I find myself interested in their conversation.

"Good, she deserves it. She reminds me a lot of her mother—a deep soul with a kind heart. Too trusting, but always finding the joy in life."

"With a laugh that can make anyone smile," Jago adds. "You're not wrong. She's a lot more jaded than she used to be, but she still loves so deeply and tries to save everyone. She feels everything so intensely, it's why she has us—to protect that fragile, strong heart."

"Good, I'm glad," Abel replies, and I cover my mouth, blinking back my tears.

"Might as well come out, Brawler. You are not sneaky," Jago calls.

Fuck.

I pop out and grin like I wasn't listening in. "Oh, hey there, I didn't see you. Come here often?"

"Sure you didn't." He smiles but welcomes me with a kiss, not embarrassed or worried I was listening in on his soppy conversation.

Eventually, the others come down, and after drinking some of what I am dubbing as Abel's miracle tea, our heads are clear enough to think and pack. Abel gives us some seeds, food, and water. He even had some gas, which Archel and Clay use to fuel the bikes. Evan checks Jago over once more and tells us that if we take plenty of breaks, we should be good to go.

While they take the bags to the bikes and Beast Jr. has one last exploration, I find Abel sitting on the cliff. He seems sad as I sit down, so I reach over and squeeze his hand. "We'll be back."

"I know. It's just, with you here, I have finally realised how much I have missed company. Missed noise and laughter. But that's my problem, not yours." He seems to shake himself out of it and then turns to me with a little velvet box. "Here, this is for you. It was your mother's. I want you to have it, and so would she."

I gently take the soft box that fits in the palm of my hand before cracking it open. I exhale sharply once I see what is nestled in the blue silk material inside. It's a locket. The smooth oval sides are a shiny silver, and the front is the same but with intricate designs inlaid with blue. Reaching out carefully, I pull it free of the box and softly put it down on the bench beside me as I turn the locket around, the long silver chain dangling over my hand.

"Open it," he encourages softly.

I spare him a quick glance before turning the locket and gently prying open the clasp with my nail. The two halves fall open, and for the second time since I sat down, my breath is stolen and all of my words with it. Inside is a picture of me, my mum, and my dad. His arm is wrapped around me as he grins down at me. She's smiling at me, her hands tickling my sides as I laugh. I remember when this was taken, it was the happiest day of my life. I never thought I'd see my dad again, nor my mum, and now I have a locket with their picture to keep forever.

"She wore it every day. When I buried her, I knew I had to keep it. Something told me it was important, and now I know it was for you."

I feel tears well in my eyes and try to blink them away, but they flow down my cheeks as I reach out and run a soft finger down my father's face. I thought I had forgotten what he looked like, the way he smiled. "He smelled like cedar all the time. He had a comb for his brush, and every time he laughed, he would end it with a little giggle. He hated pie but loved ice cream. His favourite colour was blue, not like the sky, but the deep blue that used to be the ocean." Looking up with the tears running down my face, I smile at him. "I remember him, I remember everything. Thank you. I never thought I would see them again, and you have given them both back to me."

"They were always with you, Piper. This is just an anchor for them. They will follow you through this life. The lessons they taught you make you the woman you are today, and wherever they are, I know they are proud of you and waiting for the day you will be together again." He closes the box, takes the necklace, and gestures for me to turn. I do, and he moves my hair, drapes the necklace over my neck, and clasps it. Turning to face him, I watch it fall to lie right over my heart. I cover it with my hand. Like he said, it's as if they are right here with me.

"Now they get to see the world with you. Carry them with you, and they will be with you on your lowest and highest days. That's what family is for." He looks to the house then. "A family comes in all shapes, sizes, and ages. Blood or not blood, family is who you choose to love, who stays with you. Celebrate your highs, hold hands at your lows. Family is whatever you want to make it, and you, Piper? You have made an incredible family."

"I have, haven't I?" I whisper, holding her necklace. "And you are part of that now."

He smiles at me, and I lean in and kiss his cheek. "She was lucky to be loved by you." I stand and look into his eyes again. "We'll meet again, but until then, enjoy the quiet."

He doesn't follow, but that's okay. I head back inside and linger in the kitchen. "Look after him for me, Mum," I murmur, dragging

my hand along the table. "I'll be back. Goodbye." I turn to see my men in the doorway, waiting for me.

"Are you ready, Princess?" Archel asks, probably knowing how hard this is for me. Here on this cliff, I found my mother again. I feel close to her, and I'm walking away, but the locket helps. When we set off up north, I expected adventure, but instead I found my past...and myself.

"Yeah," I whisper before clearing my throat. "Let's do it. Piper's Penis Pals for the win!" I call, and they laugh as we head down to our bikes, Beast Jr. in tow. Before we fade into the trees, I turn back and spot Abel at the door, watching us go with a wave and a smile, and I know we will be back, but until then, it's time to return to The Ring.

It's time to go back to being damned.

Chapter 39
Big Dicked Assassin

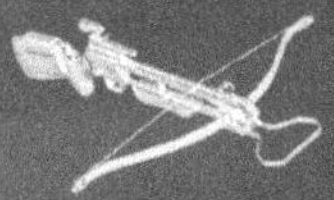

We make frequent stops, as directed by Evan, and each time, he checks Jago over and occasionally makes him drink or eat something and take more pain medicine. Archel and I play with Beast Jr. while Jago rests, stretching his legs before he has to get back on the bike again.

We don't want to stop up north for the night in case there are any stragglers waiting for us, so we push the bikes to their limits, and just as night sets in, we find ourselves past Ivar's castle. After searching for another twenty or thirty minutes, we discover an old, broken motorway bridge. The road cuts off halfway across, but the edge seems safe, and after Clay and Jago jump on it to make sure it doesn't collapse, we set up camp. No one can sneak up on us this way.

Archel and Clay make a barricade with the bikes and some old burnt cars by pushing them in the way. We would hear anyone trying to get to us before they even got close. We are in the open, more so than we would normally be, but it doesn't feel too exposed. The land around us is flat, and there is nothing but destroyed build- ings on the horizon and more sand.

Everywhere.

We build a fire just in case there are any ferals around, and I force Jago to lie down and rest while I take first watch after eating. "Protect," I order Beast Jr. He whines but lies down by Jago, easily remembering some of the commands we have taught him.

I perch on the roof of a decayed, sand-covered four-wheeler, my legs stretched across where the windshield used to be. My boots clear the sand from the hood as I keep my crossbow on my lap and scan the horizon. I can hear Jago's snores, although he protested he was tired. Today took it out of him—not that he would ever complain—Evan too. I saw it in his eyes, and when I glance over, he's watching Jago again, keeping an eye on our injured beast.

Clay is asleep by the fire, while Archel sits by it, polishing his weapons. Turning forward, I let my mind wander, even as I keep my eyes sharp. The land around is silent apart from the crackle of the flames and my men's breathing.

"You okay?" comes a whisper, making me jump out of my skin and almost fall from the vehicle. Archel chuckles as he hops up behind me, his legs spread on either side, before he yanks me into his chest.

"Motherfucking silent asshole," I grumble, even as I relax into his embrace. "I warned you, one more time and you are wearing a bell."

"I'm not that bad." He chuckles as he kisses my neck.

"I almost cut off my lips when shaving because you snuck up on me." I turn my head and meet his laughing gaze. "And not the lips on my head, Archel."

"Okay, I'll be louder." He grins, only saying it to make me shut up. With a huff, I turn back to observe as he leans into me.

"You should be asleep," I murmur.

"I can never sleep without you in my arms, Princess, you know that. We'll watch together, take turns napping here," he tells me when he thinks I'm about to complain about him needing his rest.

"Fine, you sleep first," I mutter, making him laugh again.

"Tell me a story then." He sighs as he leans further into me, each of us holding the other up. I don't worry, because I know if we were attacked, he would react before me, even if he was asleep.

"There once was a sneaky assassin with a big dick..." I begin, and he starts to laugh as I dive into the story, getting more and more over the top. He's laughing so hard, he's shaking.

"Okay, okay, stop, Princess. Jesus." He grins, kissing my neck. "I fucking love you."

"I know." I snigger. "Who wouldn't? Now go to sleep, my big dicked assassin."

"Goodnight, Princess," he murmurs as he settles back. I keep my eyes on the horizon, even as I smile.

"Goodnight, my love."

The next morning, we get on the road early after kicking sand over the fire and cleaning up after ourselves. We have only been driving for thirty minutes before a scream cuts through the air. I turn my head and skid to a stop. The bike rumbles under me as I cock my head and listen. My men stop around me, listening too, and a moment later, a male yell and a high-pitched, ragged female shriek sounds.

I hear genuine terror in their voices. I turn towards the sound, and without a second's hesitation, I race towards it. As we get closer, I hear their screams getting louder and more desperate, and accompanying it is...laughter.

Human laughter.

This isn't a cannibal or feral attack. This is a fucking human on human attack.

Not on my fucking watch. In my haste, I almost barrel over the cliff that suddenly appears out of nowhere. The ground just stops. I quickly leave my bike, grab my crossbow, and peek over the edge, scanning the situation. There's a woman on the ground fighting off two huge, dirty men who are above her, ripping at her dress.

There's a male who's pinned down, but other men laugh as they watch her struggle. The restrained man screams and tries to break free.

"Piper, no!" Evan yells as I leap over the edge and slide down, firing as I go. I hit the one who rips her dress free right through his ear. He stumbles back with the arrow sticking from his skull, and when he turns, I fire into his throat. He drops to his knees as I land at the bottom, getting to my feet and aiming at the other assailant. He roars and turns to me, ignoring the woman who scrambles away, trying to cover herself. I hear my men's footsteps as they hit the ground.

"Get the man," I order. "This bastard is mine," I snarl, my own past coming to mind. I fight through the memories, through my own screams and pleas that fell on deaf ears. It enrages me more, and when I meet her empty, numb eyes, I lose it. It's how I felt with their dirty hands on my body—traumatised, hollow, disconnected. No. I won't let that happen here.

I storm towards him, letting go of my crossbow. This fucker deserves to have a long, drawn-out death.

I pull a knife from my boot as I move. The blade is long enough to hurt, but not kill. No he will bleed out, and it will be agony. He rushes me, grabbing for me with his meaty hands. I duck and slice across his stomach as he howls. Whirling around him, I cut across his back and then his legs. He spins wildly, bleeding.

"Want to play with women? Fucking try me, asshole," I hiss.

In my head, it's them—the men who attacked me. Their sneering faces, dirty touches, and violations crowd my vision until I can barely see nor hear. My whole focus narrows down to this man

—this man who thinks he has a right to lay a hand on an nonconsenting woman, who thinks her body is his to take. He's fucking wrong. So fucking wrong. This world is filled with rapists like him. Ones who play the victim, the ones who blame the victims, the ones who get angry, those who deny it, and those who blame the world and their upbringing. But they are fucking adults, and they know right from wrong, they just don't care.

They think they are worth more, think women's bodies are only made for their pleasure. They don't give a fuck about the aftereffects, and they don't care about anything but achieving what they want. It's a sick fucking world where women don't even feel safe to exist simply for being born with a vagina. This isn't a man's fucking world, and they have no right.

No fucking right.

Women owe nothing to no one.

We deserve to feel safe. We deserve for our daughters to have a better life than us, to never have to know the pain, the pure numbing terror, the guilt, and the blame we put on ourselves. It's time men understood they can't get away with it any longer. That this isn't their world anymore. This isn't about equality, this is about pure fucking right from wrong. This is about our bodies being our own.

They are in the wrong, and there are too many of them. Each man is a potential attacker. I know the feeling, I struggled for so long. I still do. In every eye, I expect a promise. In every hand, I expect pain. I expect to be forced, taken. They not only stole my body, but my mind. They stole my confidence, my trust, and that's hard to earn back while they walk away without a backwards glance.

Not anymore.

Not to this woman or any other. I don't care if it means I'm aggressive, or if I have to cover myself in their blood. This world is being taken back. If I have to wipe all of them out for someone to feel safe enough to walk alone, I will.

The percentage stops here, with me. With her. With them.

They might have taken my body, but they didn't take my voice or my feet, which I stand on right now. I reclaimed my body, and I'll reclaim this world. For my mother. For Worth. For Clarissa. For

the stranger huddled behind me with dirty handprints covering her soft skin.

Showing him the bloody knife, I bare my teeth at him. "How about I fucking bend you over and shove this up your ass and see how you like it?" I snarl. I rush him again, and this time, I slice off his shirt like he did her. He stumbles back for a moment, and I use it to stab into his belly, twisting and twirling away as he screams. He falls to his knees, and I grab his head, forcing him to look at her. "Look at her, it will be the last thing you ever fucking see." I stab his neck over and over. Fury has taken over. I can feel my movements and the blood splashing across me. I can hear talking, footsteps, and the yelps of Beast Jr. as he tries to get my attention.

But I'm lost.

Arms wrap around me, pulling me away as the man falls forward, choking on his blood. But it's not enough. It's never enough. He needs to know how it feels to have your own body taken away from you.

He deserves to suffer. They all do.

"He's dead, Brawler," Jago coos, holding me in mid-air as I struggle to get back to him. "He's dead, they are safe." He turns me to see the man cradling the woman, who is crying and holding onto him dearly, but Jago's right. I settle, and he releases me. Sucking in a deep breath, I move closer before getting to my knees.

"Are you okay?" I ask as softly as I can.

The man looks at me and nods. "Thanks to you. How can I ever repay you?"

"No need. Look, I don't know where you're going, but there is a safe zone—"

"We can't," the woman cries, wiping her face. "We are grateful, but we have to find our daughter."

Archel hands me a cloth, and I wipe my face. Beast Jr. is there at my side, tugging on my pants and licking me like he's trying to help me. He lopes away, and I watch him run to one of the bodies and start biting, making me smile. "Your daughter?" I ask, turning back to them.

"Yes. She left a couple of weeks ago, leaving us a note. We have to find her. Maybe you've seen her?" She scrambles to her bag before freezing as her dress falls away. She flinches, and I look up as my men instantly turn away, surrounding them to protect her from anyone that might come along. In that moment, I fall in love all over again.

These men right here always restore my faith in the world, in goodness and love, and when Clay drags his shirt off and tosses it back to me, I melt. I grab it and hand it over, but her arms refuse to work and she cries. Between the man and me, we manage to get it on her, and she instantly straightens a bit. "Thank you," she murmurs, before the man I think is her husband roots around in her bag and pulls out a tattered, tiny piece of paper and hands it over.

I freeze and my blood turns cold. It's a picture, a polaroid, of a young, smiling girl. She's beautiful. There is such joy in her eyes and face, but it's not her expression that has me wanting to sob—it's because I know her. The note she wrote is burning a hole my pocket.

"She was going south, but we think we can—Is everything okay?" she asks, and I lift my head numbly to stare at her. I don't know if she sees it in my eyes, but she disintegrates, sobbing, shaking her head, and shuddering.

"I'm sorry," I offer. "I do know her. We found her body a week ago."

"What? No, that can't be right. Not her," her dad snaps, but I ignore the anger, knowing it's not directed at me.

"I'm sorry, it was. We buried her. We didn't want to leave her there. Here, we found this in her possession, it's a note to you." I carefully pull it free and hand it back with the picture before moving away to give them privacy. I head over to my men and instantly melt into their embraces, needing their comfort. I don't know why I kept the note until now, but a part of me is glad they will know, that they don't have to wonder for so long like I did.

I hear their sobs as we stand stoically for an hour or so. Eventually, we hear the clearing of a throat. "Thank you for giving us this." We turn and meet the man's eyes. He's holding the woman again, who is shaking her head with the note clutched in her grip.

"You should know we buried her with as much respect as we

could. We even had a small ceremony. If you wish, we could take you there."

"I-I would like that, to say goodbye." He nods, tears filling his eyes.

"Of course," I murmur and look to my men, feeling helpless.

Their pain is so palpable.

What are the odds that in all of this deserted world, I would run into them? Her parents? As if her note called them to me. For some reason, the fact I was able to save them resonates with me. I couldn't save her, but I saved her parents, and her legacy will live on with them. It will live on in the change in this world. Her death fans the flames that burn inside of me, driving me to tackle this world one person at a time until it's a safe place to live.

"If you ever feel like you can share, I'd love to know more about your daughter. She seemed like an incredible person. She deserves to be remembered, to be known."

"You...you care about her?" her dad questions quickly. "Why? We are strangers."

"Everyone's a stranger at first." I shrug. "This world is chang- ing. We aren't all like those monsters out there. I'm sorry your daughter isn't around to see it, but there are people out there who care. People who will want to remember her name."

"It's happening, just like she said," her mother whispers. "People are fighting back. Did you hear that, Steve? It's finally changing." She sniffs and looks at me. "She always said it would, that the world couldn't stay this way forever. She always believed there was some- where out there that was safe and thriving. It's why she left, to find us a better life. Can we come with you?"

"Of course. Let me show you the new world."

We leave with the couple. They have their own bike, but it's slower and rusted, so we surround them and stay at their speed. When we stop for the night, they cry, and we give them protection and privacy. On the third day, we reach the girl's grave. They weep over her resting spot, telling stories to us the whole time. We listen, storing them with our own. We will never forget this brave girl who set out into the world just like me.

When they are ready, we drive back to The Ring with them in tow. I assure them they can come back whenever they want, and we will even escort them, but they seem exhausted, and they need to be checked over, so it's The Ring for now. We don't stop that night, riding until the sun rises as we reach the gates to my home.

"Welcome to The Nations," I murmur as we stop before the gates to The Ring. "Welcome to the future your daughter dreamed of."

Chapter 40
Helping Hand

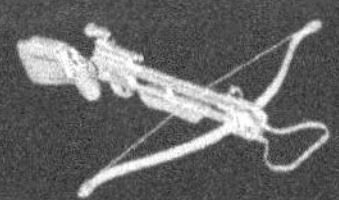

Worth is busy in a meeting, so I direct some of the guards to find a suitable room for the couple. Once they have, I escort them there with the guards. I walk inside and check it out. It's in the main house near Worth, therefore safer and probably quieter—apart from her sex parties. It's got a bed and a bathroom, and not much else, but it's liveable.

"Here you go," I offer, pulling back the curtains to let some light in. "It's not a five-star hotel, but it's what we have. Feel free to wander anywhere. We have food in the cafeteria, as well as anything you want to drink. I could order some to your room if you like?"

The mum is standing with her arms wrapped around herself, looking at the floor. The dad glances at her and then nods at me. "That would be great, thank you so much. I'm sorry, we are just both so tired. We have been searching for what seems like forever, so scared and hopeful and now—"

"You are empty." I nod. "I can understand that. I will leave you to sleep and ask them to bring you food. If you need anything, find any of the guards and ask for me." With that, I leave them to sleep. The guard is still outside, and I nod at him as I pass.

"Thank you. Can you bring them some food and drink please?" I ask politely.

"Of course, General." He nods and rushes off to do just that. I want to make sure they are okay, but they probably need someone to talk to, someone who can understand their pain and the trauma from the attack. There is only one person I can think of who offers that calming, understanding presence.

Mother. AKA Clarissa.

"I'll go check the bikes in and get an update on everything to relay to you, Princess," Archel says and kisses my cheek.

"I'm going to take Jago to examine his head. Clay, can you come hold him down?" Evan asks.

"I don't need holding down," Jago snaps.

Laughing, I lean into his chest and kiss him. "Yes, you do, big guy. Go, and find me after," I murmur. I watch them leave and turn to locate Clarissa. I find her wandering around with a few other women, and when she spots me, she smiles at them and heads over. I lean into The Ring's fence and wait. She steps up next to me, looking me over.

"Well, at least you're not dead," she deadpans.

"Charming, truly you are. You kiss Worth with that mouth?" I tease.

"You wish, because you want to watch," she mutters.

"Oh my God, did you make a joke? It's truly the end of the world." I gasp, my hand over my heart, as she snorts and scans the area around us.

"Archel said something happened up there. You okay?" Her eyes bore into me. "Seriously?"

Clarissa and I didn't have the best start, but she truly is a great, caring person, and to survive out there through everything she did? Yeah, she has my respect. "I will be. It was..." I look away then, searching for a way to encapsulate everything that has happened. "A lot, but I think we are okay now, thank you."

"Good. Now I'm guessing you didn't search me out for my charming presence?"

"Nope, I need your help." I push from the fence and turn to fully face her.

She shields her eyes from the sun to see me.

"We found a couple on the road. They were...being attacked." I meet her eyes, and she instantly knows what I am alluding to. "We helped them before anything too bad could happen, but they don't know anyone here. I got the feeling they haven't been out in the world much." I suck in a breath and forge ahead.

"Clarissa, they lost their daughter." She flinches, but I push on. "We found her body on the way up north. We didn't know she was theirs. We buried her, and when we saved them on the way back, they showed us a picture of her. They are grieving the loss, and I'm betting they feel really alone. We both know what that feels like. They need friends, they need support. You are caring, understanding, and calm, and I thought maybe you could help."

"Of course," she promises. "God, they must be in so much pain."

It's good you brought them here and saved them." "I did what everyone would do."

She meets my eyes. "No, you did more. Most would have watched it happen. Most wouldn't have interfered or tried to help them, never mind bring them here and try to build them a new home and family. Don't talk down on yourself, Piper. You are an incredible person, even if you are inappropriate a lot of the time."

"Don't lie, you love it when I check your rack out," I murmur, looking away shyly. She laughs and squeezes my shoulder.

"Well then, check out my ass while I walk away. I'll look after them." She wanders off, and I do check her out ass out—dammit. You can't mention it and not expect me to.

"Very peachy!" I call after her, making her laugh.

Standing there alone, I wrap my arms around myself, shivering despite the heat. I feel cold after the events of the trip. From the young girl, to Jago, then the attack on the couple... If I'm being honest, it was a lot to deal with, and my mind is screaming at me. Not just that, but seeing the attack and my own reaction brought back a lot of painful memories that still linger. Still have me in their sharp, painful clutches. It's not healthy to bury pain. Those things...my past, it happened. Sometimes I forget, sometimes it's like it never occurred, but then some days, it's all I can think about as I remember the way their hands felt and the way they smelled until it's like I'm right back there again. I'm good at holding it at bay, at fighting the dark- ness that accompanies those memories, but sometimes I just have to be weak, to cry and release all of the pain. It's therapeutic. I can feel the pressure growing in me now, like an explosion ready to detonate.

I hurry back to our rooms, not wanting anyone else to see, not wanting to be labelled as weak, even though I know it's not. Some- times being strong is knowing when you need to be weak. It's about being caring and kind, but knowing when to stand up tall. It's about knowing how to bend and how to deal with your mind and heart so it's all in sync.

Strength isn't just an external attribute, like muscles. Strength comes from deep inside you.

Once in our room, I can still feel their hands, and although I know it's not healthy, I strip and crank on the shower as hot as it will go before I step inside, letting the boiling water wash it away. I manage not to scrub my skin like I used to, but I do let it run across my body and face as I lean into the wall. Closing my eyes, I try to mentally push the memories back into the box where I keep them so I can function.

I don't even hear the sound of the opening door over the roar of my own emotions. Only when arms wrap around me and pull me against a huge chest do I realise I'm not alone.

"Let it out, Brawler," Jago murmurs, resting his head on my shoul- der. He holds me tightly. I cry, letting him hold me up, and when I slip to the floor, he follows me down, holding me in his lap.

"I thought I was okay. I thought I was better. I thought I was healed," I say raggedly as I raise my head, my lips trembling and my hair plastered to my naked body.

"Healing isn't a straight line, Brawler. It's like life, it has its ups and downs. Sometimes you are high and happy, almost like it never happened. Sometimes you are low, and that's okay too. Memories stay forever, but the feel of them will fade with time. You aren't failing by getting upset, by suffering. You could never fail us and certainly not yourself. Healing is healing, Brawler, it's like a wound. The outer wound recovers, but there is still a scar inside."

I've never felt so seen. That's exactly what it is. Although the outward wound healed, the scars still remain, and sometimes they consume me. Other times, they are so closed, I can function without even thinking about it. It's okay not to be okay, and as he holds me, I settle back and let the emotions wash over me. He holds me the entire time, not rushing me, just being there. He supports me like always, my rock.

"All right, fuckers," comes a yell, and then the door slams inwards. "Out, you." I turn to meet Worth's angry eyes, her hands on her hips as she glares at Jago. "Girl time."

"Since when are you a girl?" he teases and looks at me. When I nod, he stands and leans over and kisses me. "If you need me, I'll be outside. I'll kick her ass if you need me to." He sweeps past her as she laughs.

"Like he could," she mutters as she kicks the door shut behind her. Reaching up, I turn off the shower and climb out, huddling on the floor before it. I'm unable to move farther, to look at her. I feel so weak right now, especially in her eyes. She suffered, probably more than me, and yet she's so strong.

She sighs. "Here," Worth murmurs and thrusts a towel at me.

Wiping my face, I snigger slightly.

"Afraid you can't control yourself?" I tease, even as I wrap it around my nakedness and shiver.

"You know it." She grins before she sinks to her ass next to me, her back to the shower cubicle. We sit side by side, her hands on her raised knees. She doesn't speak, just sits.

"I'm weak," I eventually mutter.

"Who the fuck told you that? I'll gut them," she snarls, turning to me in her anger.

I laugh bitterly, turning my face to wipe my tears on the towel as I draw my legs to my chest. "No one, but I am. So fucking weak. I should be over this by now, not crying in the shower because I saw the way he touched her and all I could think about was the—" I hiccup.

"Way they touched you," she finishes. "The first time I slept with someone after, I saw them over and over. I couldn't even come. I forced myself to finish him, though, to prove I could, and after I felt so bad, I almost drank myself into a coma."

I shake my head. "But your past is worse than mine, yet you are so fucking strong. I'm weak," I argue, slamming my fists onto my knees in my anger.

"My trauma does not lessen yours. I'm not as strong as you think I am, Piper. It's a mask. I struggled a lot before I met my men. I drowned my demons in booze and girls and men. You handle it healthily by letting it out, and that makes you so much stronger than me. You face it, you don't run or hide. You...feel it. I ran. I ran so far, I almost couldn't get back."

I turn my head, and she meets my eyes, her gaze filled with ghosts.

"I felt each scar on my body again when I came back. My men saved me from those flames, but it came with a cost. Running doesn't help because it will always catch up with you. So let it out, let it free. Be sad, be angry, be what you need to be. But know you are never alone...and that I—" She inhales. "I am in awe of your strength."

I stare, and she reaches out, covering my hand.

"You hear me? I don't lie, you know that. You astound me. It's okay to let it guide you, but you even let it control you. You are better than that, than them, any of them. You have survived what others cannot even imagine. You are so strong, and when you don't feel it, we are here to remind you. Sometimes you just need someone who has been through what you have," she murmurs. "Archel saw you running, that's why I'm here. I was with him, and I saw the look in your eyes—haunted, chased. It's the same one I saw in my eyes for years."

"Worth," I whisper, and she smiles sadly.

"Learn from my mistakes, Piper. Don't waste so much time, not like I did. You have incredible men out there who love you. You have friends, family, and a home. I know it's not always enough in those darkest times, but they will guide you back, no matter how long it takes, and I will be waiting in the light with a helping hand, always."

I turn away again, but a smile covers my lips. "Okay." I take a deep breath, the first one in many minutes, as if I can breathe again. "Good." She squeezes and lets go. "And don't let me ever hear you say you are weak again, or I'll kick your ass," she mutters, making me laugh.

I drop my head to her shoulder, and she sits still, holding me up as I rebuild myself. I am like this world. I'm scarred from my past, from what's happening, but slowly, with the help of others, I am healing.

I am becoming something new. Like The Nations, I'm evolving.

Chapter 41
LoveShack-Er Reptile-Shack

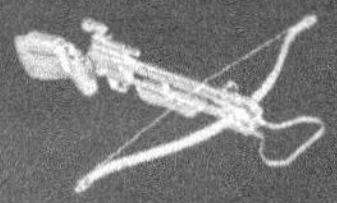

That night, I eat in my room with my men. Archel brushes my hair, and Clay plaits it. Evan holds me while I sleep like old times, and Jago lies on my other side. They put me back together again. The next morning, I wake before them and dress, slipping from the room. In the sun, I take some deep breaths. Last night I felt fragile and raw, but today I feel better, and when I see Clarissa leaning against the building with Worth beside her, I smile.

"Was wondering if you were coming, lazy." Clarissa smirks, pushing upright. "Let's walk before it gets too fucking warm."

I fall into step with them, and we stroll around The Ring as the sun fully rises. It's quiet and hardly anyone is out aside from us, but I spot Evvie a little while later going to check on patients. He blows me a kiss, and I wave. Archel is probably around somewhere too, following me, but it's nice to be with Worth and Clarissa to get a bit of air and space.

"How was it up there?" Worth asks. "I got a report from your men, but I'm curious."

"It was…different, like it had been forgotten, but there was something so achingly beautiful about the untouched land." I smile at her. "I guess they told you about Abel?" I clutch my necklace, looking down at it. "I found a tie to my mother through him. It felt right. Even now, my heart aches to go back, to be with her, even though I'm happy here. Can you feel like two places are your home?"

"Of course. Home doesn't even need to be a place, it can be a feeling or a person—or persons." Clarissa smirks. "Follow it, split your time." She shrugs casually like it's that easy.

"Yeah, you're right." I drop the necklace, tucking it back in my shirt. "I never thought I would ever see them again. I guess now that I have, I'm greedy for more."

"Any sane person would feel the same, though you aren't really sane," Worth teases.

"Ass eater," I mutter, making her bark out a laugh.

"It's been way too quiet around here without you," she remarks. "No one insults me to my face while checking out my breasts." I jerk my eyes up with a guilty smile.

"Oops." I wink. "I can't help it, they are just so…up. How do you keep them so high? Do they get sweaty?" I blurt.

"My ass does, it's killer," Clarissa inserts.

"Pussy too." I nod. "And when I'm on my period at the same time?" I groan. "Killer. Last time, I punched Clay because he told me I looked glowy. He meant it as a compliment, but I didn't take it as such."

"What did he do after you punched him?" Worth asks as we stop before The Ring.

"He smiled and asked me to stay forever. They are all insane."
"They match you well." They both nod.

Maybe they aren't wrong, especially when I see Clay trying to hide behind a table with Archel right next to him. If it wasn't for the hulking giant struggling to duck, I wouldn't have seen them.

Stalkers.

The Damned

The next few days pass in a blur. I work with some scavs to update the map of the north. I also give new orders to my teams after inspecting our scouting plan, and then I go with Worth to meet with Jon and a representative of The Cities. Usually by the evening, I'm exhausted and fall into a deep sleep. My guys are keeping busy too, settling into life easily enough. Archel works with Dray on...well, I'm scared to ask. Clay teaches the guards to fight and build explosives, and Jago helps him. Evan has returned to attending to his patients and looking after everyone.

It means we don't get to spend a lot of time together. They make sure to check in with me, and I get stolen kisses, hugs, and laughs—a reminder they are there to love and miss me. I never knew being a general, Worth's left-hand woman, would come with so many boring meetings, but as the final one of the day finishes, I recline with a groan.

"Fooking hell, if I wasn't buzzed right now, I'd be fast asleep." Nan groans. "All this chatter, fooking hell."

"Wait, you're drunk? I didn't get invited to pre-drink council meetings." I pout.

"Nah, 'cause ye a wee spragger and would tell your girlfriend here," Nan mutters, jerking her head at Worth, who just sighs.

"Share," I demand, holding my hand out. With a grumble, she pulls a half empty bottle from behind her cardigan.

"Thieves," she spits. "Can't leave an old lady with her booze."
"Shut up. You probably have another bottle stashed somewhere. Dray told me you've been stealing the guys' stash."

"Such liars," she grumbles as I take a swig and pass it to Worth. "So the trade lines with The Cities are sorted now. The teams
know their schedules and are working well. What else is there to do?" I ask Worth.

She frowns, musing it over. "More food production. We need to expand safe zones and clear routes, but...we are doing good. Really good."

There's a knock on the door, and Archel sticks his head in. "You done, Princess? I came to walk back with you."

"Go." Worth waves me off. I down my drink and smile at them both before skipping to the door. Once outside, he leans in and kisses me softly.

"Hi, Princess," he murmurs.

I swallow my groan as he takes my hand and starts to tug me out of the building and back towards the others, but that one kiss has ignited the passion in me for my assassin. I want some one-on- one time, so I start to pull him the other way.

"I want to show you something." I grin back at him.

"What's that?" he inquires with a smile, going along with it happily.

"The reptile house. It's part of the old zoo. They are expanding it for housing, but it's empty at the moment."

"You want me all to yourself?"

"You know it. I want to see your reptile," I tease, making him groan at my bad joke, but he speeds up, nearly pulling me along, so it couldn't have been too bad.

We move through the other enclosures and away from the noise of The Ring, through the old, reinforced underground tunnel, and out the other side. The timeworn, cracked pavement leads in each direction. The reptile house sign is still up somehow, and he throws me over his shoulder and races over as I laugh, smacking his ass. The hexagonal hut comes into view. The door is partially open, and he kicks it the rest of the way before spinning and slamming me against it to shut it.

His lips come down on mine as I groan and wrap my legs around his waist. I don't try to look around, not that I wanted to. My eyes close as I lose myself in him and the silence around us.

"Fuck, I've missed you, Princess."

"You saw me this morning," I whisper against his lips as I nip them.

"Too long," he growls, dragging his hands up my legs to my hips then under my shirt. "And you weren't naked."

"I'm not now," I tease, tipping my head back as his lips glide down my chin to my neck, licking and nipping, as his hands burrow under my bra and cup my breasts. Hard. I groan as his fingers tweak and twist my nipples as he licks along my neck.

"You will be soon, and my cock will be buried inside you as you scream for me loud enough for everyone to hear, even from here," he whispers against my skin, the promise sinking in until I shiver. My pussy clamps, and my clit throbs for his attention. He turns, holding me up, and I quickly look around. Each wall has a sunken glass enclosure—all empty of course—although most of the glass is gone. In the middle is a large, flat sign with all the animals on it, and there's a door at the back too. That's all I see before I'm laid out on the sign with my legs dangling off the edge before he forces himself between them.

He lowers his head and cups my hips before dragging his fingers up my sides. His lips brush up and across my stomach before meeting my bra. I shiver below him, my eyes rolling down to meet his as he smirks and darts his tongue out to lick a long, teasing line across my skin just under my bra.

"Stop teasing," I demand, and he chuckles in response before bringing his hands down to unbuckle my trousers. As he straightens, he steps back and pulls them off. He carefully undoes my boots and tugs my jeans the rest of the way off, and then he folds them on the floor. Sitting up, I grab the bottom of my shirt, but he reaches out and helps me, working my shirt off and over my head before I unhook my bra. I let it fall down my arms as he groans, staring at my breasts and body like it's the first time he has ever seen me. Hunger and love sparkle in his eyes as he gently leans down and places a protective kiss above my heart.

A promise.

That alone makes my pussy clench. I lie back, watching as his lips drift down again, kissing across my chest and between my breasts.

With a knowing smirk, he kisses each nipple before moving farther down, kissing my belly and then lower still, kissing my pussy.

"Archel," I whine like a brat.

He meets my gaze, his eyes icy and determined. "Oh no, Princess, I won't rush this. I have all the time in the world to devour every inch of your body and have you screaming for me and coming so many times, you can't even walk, never mind talk."

I suck in a breath at that, my heart pounding as I swallow and lick my lips, unsure what to say, but before I can come back with a witty retort, his lips slide down my pussy again with fluttering, teasing kisses. The pressure is not enough to relieve my ache, but it makes me crazy with lust.

I arch my chest into the air and drape my legs over his shoulders before reaching above me to grab the edge of the sign. I let him have his way with me. He's right—this isn't a quick fuck. No, Archel is showing me that he loves me all over again, reminding me that I'm his and he is mine.

This isn't fucking for the sake of finding release, this is love, this is forever, and we have all the time in the world.

Parting my lips, he cuts off all my rambling thoughts as his tongue darts out and tastes me. Humming, he savours my flavour before he goes lower, burying his head between my thighs. He slides his tongue along my cleft, back and forth, licking up my cream before flicking my clit. My eyes close as my head falls back, and I lift my hips to grind into his mouth as the pleasure winding through me grows, stealing every thought other than how good his talented mouth feels.

"Archel," I whisper, his name like a prayer on my lips. The world is silent around us, empty apart from us and this desire burning between us.

He murmurs against my intimate flesh before sucking my clit into his mouth, making me jerk and cry out. His fingers trail up my thigh before pressing against my hole, and then I grind down, trying

to get them inside of me, and he finally relents. Slowly, he thrusts two into my channel, curling them up and stroking as he sucks. My eyes cross behind my eyelids, my breaths coming out hard and ragged. Releasing my clit, he licks the pulsing bud as he pulls his fingers out and then adds a third, spearing them into me.

He fucks me with quick, hard thrusts as his tongue curls around my clit, driving me wild as I lift my hips to match his rhythm. His fingers feel good, so fucking good, but his dick would feel better. He's giving me this for now, though, and when he finally touches my clit again, I come like a bomb going off. Screams leave my lips as the pleasure, which was slowly growing, suddenly bursts through me. My vision goes completely black, like fireworks going off behind my eyes, my thighs jerking and pussy clamping down. He licks and fucks me through it, even as my pussy flutters and clenches. He doesn't stop until I reach down and push his head away, and then he laughs. As he straightens, I can see his cream- covered face. With a cocky smirk, he wipes his lips with two fingers and then sucks them into his mouth as I watch, still panting.

"Fucking perfect," he praises, and I can't deal. I reach for him, and he stops playing.

His wet fingers grip my thighs firmly and pull me farther down as he frees his cock and presses it against my pussy. He drags it back and forth, covering it in my release as I groan. I clutch my breasts, tweaking my nipples and sending arcs of pleasure straight to my aching core.

"Hold on, Princess, wouldn't want you to hurt yourself." He winks, and as I open my mouth to reply, he slams into me. I scream and shudder as he forces his length through my fluttering channel until he's balls deep. I wrap my legs around his waist as he leans down, covering my body with his, and encircles my nipple with his lips and sucks. His hips never lose their pace, pulling out and pushing back in. His firm, rapid thrusts hinder my body from coming down from the last orgasm. He's intent on making me come again without a breather between them.

I'm down for that.

Releasing my breasts, I tunnel my hands into his hair and drag his head closer. His teeth press into my skin, making me moan as I clench around his cock. Scraping my nails down his scalp, I feel him pummel into me harder, so with a grin of my own, I scratch them down his neck and back.

"Harder," he mumbles as he pulls back from my nipple. "Cut it to ribbons, scar me. Let them all see, Princess."

Fuck. Me.

The thought almost makes me come again, so I do it. I rake my nails down his back, all the way to his ass before cupping his flexing cheeks and urging him on. He slams into me harder and harder, grinding into my clit after each one. The solid pressure steals my screams until I'm writhing beneath him. Releasing his ass, I drag my nails up, pressing so hard, I feel his skin bleed under my touch. He yells, and his hips stutter, then with a snarl, he straightens, grabs my hips, and lifts me. He turns us and slams me into the closest exhibit. The blow steals my breath as I stare into his twisted, snarling, feral face.

Gripping his shoulders, I claw my nails in and hold on as I use the leverage to ride his huge dick. The pain and pleasure from our joining mixes until I'm melting and just as wild as he is.

He slams me back against the exhibit wall again. I blindly search with my lips until ours connect. We eat each other hungrily, our bodies slapping together from the force of our fucking. He holds me effortlessly, helping me ride his dick.

Each thrust brings me closer to another spiralling orgasm. Over and over, he fucks me, and I feel his blood under my nails as I cut his skin. It only urges him on, and he fucks me so hard, I know it will hurt later, but I love every painful inch.

Ripping his mouth away, he bites my chin and neck. "Princess," he growls. The sound makes me whimper as I drop my head back to the wall. "I fucking love you."

"Love you," I reply, but it ends in a cry as he slams into me and twists his hips, hitting that spot that sends me over the edge with a scream.

"Love you," he snarls, fighting my tight body, fighting my pussy to keep going. "Love you," he snarls again, slamming into me. The force shatters the remaining glass behind me. One orgasm tumbles into the next, and I'm almost lifeless against him as it flows through me. "Love you!" he howls as he stills, filling me with his release and sealing his declaration with a kiss.

A promise of forever.

Chapter 42
Forever?

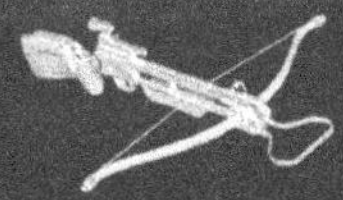

My days are filled with meetings and short day runs with my teams to check their control and how they work together.

It's a lot of fun, and we settle into a routine. My men come with me sometimes, and sometimes they stay behind to help around The Ring, and we sleep in each other's arms every night, falling more and more in love.

But I ache. I dream of a bench on a cliff and a man who sits on it.

I never knew I was missing a father figure in my life, nor that Abel would come to mean so much to me. Maybe it's the link to my mother, or maybe it's because I feel safe when I'm there. I feel like young Piper, with no worries or responsibilities, *and* new Piper, the leader of The Damned.

It is undeniable, I miss it.

I know my men see that. I couldn't explain why I feel this way if I tried, but they don't ask because they know. Up there on that cliff, I found a piece of my soul. I found my mother, my father, and my heritage. It's where Jago and I found ourselves again, and it will always hold a special place in my heart.

Leaning against the edge of The Ring, I watch Worth as she spars with her man Maxen. Jago and Clay are teaching self-defence moves to some of the women Clarissa brought in, and I smile when Jago barks at a woman, only to hesitate when she jerks back. He softens instantly and reassures her, something I like to think I taught him. He never did that before. He had the softness, the kind- ness in him, but he never knew how to show it.

"We are going on a run, a local job for your doctor. You want in?" Sascha asks as she leans in next to me, observing the training too. She wears some round black sunglasses, which she pulls down as she watches Worth knock her man to his ass, making us both laugh. I face her, looking her over. She looks fucking badass in her shorts and crop top, and she knows it.

"Sure, when are you leaving?"

"Now. I'll meet you at the gate." She winks as she pushes her glasses back up and strolls away. Some of the guards rush out of her path and watch her go with a wary but hungry look. Good luck to any man or woman who tries to capture that one.

With one last glance at my men, I push away and grab one of Worth's twins as he passes—I think it's Jax. "Hey, will you let my men and Worth know I've gone on a run please? I'll be back later today."

"Sure." He nods, and with a grateful smile, I jog back to our rooms to get my stuff. Once I've changed into some longer trousers and reloaded and checked my crossbow, knives, and katana, I grab my goggles and bandana and sling a pack over my shoulder before I hurry to the infirmary wing Evan established. I want to check if he needs anything in particular and say goodbye before I go. I know Archel is with Dray on the road, placing some traps and wires, so I don't worry about him. Evan will tell him when I'll be back, if he doesn't already know, the stalker.

His bay is empty for once, and he's staring at something as I step behind him and cover his eyes.

"Guess who?" I chirp. He jolts, jumping away and spinning as I blink.

"Hi, erm, hi," he rushes out, his wide eyes darting around.

"Evvie, you okay?" I ask when he still doesn't look at me.

"Sure, fine, you?" he squeaks out.

"If you were pulling your wood, you don't have to hide it," I tease, and he blinks. "Taming the serpent? Stroking the stick?" I carry on when he doesn't speak. Sighing, I move closer. "Just maybe not in here, since it's not very hygienic." I wink, and when he still doesn't speak, I frown. "Okay, well, I'm going on a run and just wanted to check in. I'll be back later—"

"Okay, sounds good, be safe." He kisses me before turning away.

"Evan, what's going on?" I snap.

"Nothing," he mutters, hunching before he sighs. He peers at me over his shoulder. "Sorry, just stressed about an, erm, diagnosis." He's lying, but Evan is stubborn, so I leave him to it, knowing he will tell me when he's ready.

"Okay, well, I love you. I'll see you later," I call and turn away, my heart sinking a little.

"Pip, wait." He grabs me, spins me, and kisses me. "I love you so much. I'm sorry, be safe, and I'll see you later," he promises.

Happier, I smile and skip from the room, rushing through The Ring to see Sascha and some of her men waiting at the gate on their bikes with mine parked next to them.

"There you are, come on, trouble!" she hollers.

Securing my pack to my bike, I swing my leg over and don my goggles before revving the engine. "Yeah, yeah. Keep up, won't you?" I taunt as I spin, spraying sand at them as I race away from The Ring. I hear them laugh and then gun it. Eventually, Sascha catches up to me, and I slow down so she can lead—after all, it's her run. I'm just here to help and watch. Plus, I don't know where the fuck we are going.

"What the fuck does this even say?" Sascha groans and thrusts the list at me. I stand in the shadows, channelling my assassin as I watch them move around the doctor's surgery. Half of it is buried in sand, and we had to enter through a window on what used to be the second floor, but we got lucky, most of it was still intact because the rooms were locked.

There will be enough equipment to set up a new center for Evan, and we found a lot of what he was still looking for. Sascha and I are in a treatment room off a long hallway. The lights don't work, so we have our torches on, and the wooden door is splintered from where we kicked it in. There's an old, dirty curtain pulled halfway across a leather bed, with a desk in one corner and two chairs opposite it. There are even some drawings and medical posters on the walls. I take the list, and Sascha grumbles as she opens cupboards and throws everything in her bag. I hear the others doing the same, the boom of doors being forced open echoing around. It's a good job we brought a big crew, but I think they will still need to come back to get some of it. As long as we can get as many items on Evvie's list as possible, we will be good, but as I peer down at it, I see why she is so frustrated.

His writing is like chicken scratch, but luckily, I have years of sneaking glimpses of his notes to cheat off of him, so I understand it. "It says stethoscope," I tell her, and then rattle off the rest. A whistle comes from down the hallway, and I peek out to see a torch sweeping back and forth.

"Yo, look at this!" someone calls.

"Stay here," I command Sascha. "Finish up, I'll see what's wrong." I hand the list back and leave the room. I move carefully over the broken door debris as I step into the hallway, my torch piercing the dark, but it's still creepy down here for sure. The man moves out of my way as I peer into what seems to be another

waiting room, shining my torch around to see what's piqued his interest.

The ceiling is falling down in places, the old white tiles left to decay. The carpet is a godawful dirty blue, and to the left is a curved desk with a room behind it. Beyond that are some old wooden doors with glass in them—the entrance, no doubt—but they are blacked out from the sand and newspapers which have been taped to them.

I keep scanning, the beam of my torch only illuminating so much. I spot some turned over chairs, empty sofas, and coffee tables, and then I turn back to him. "What?" I ask in confusion.

He grabs his light, one that's bigger and brighter than mine, and he shines it to the right, an area I didn't bother to check.

What I see shouldn't surprise me, but it makes me sigh in sadness. Skeletons are huddled together in the corner. Clearly, they have been here since the beginning. I'm betting this is where they hid to ride it out. Maybe they even worked here. They are wrapped around each other—two big ones with a little kid in the middle. I can't help but sigh again and turn away. "Leave them, at least they are together here and undisturbed."

"Got it," he replies.

As I walk away, passing rooms being pillaged and emptied, I can't help but feel like this place is a ghost town, untouched since the end. How many places are like this? Filled with the bodies of the lost, forgotten, or just the plain damned?

Is this my duty to bear? To find them all as I try to make the world a better place? To learn their stories, to remember their ending, and to make sure they are never disturbed or lost in what this world once was? If so, I will endure it, my heart heavy with their losses, but I won't let them be lost like so much of the world has been. Not every story has a happy ending. Some have the endings you never expected, like the girl and her parents. They lost her, but at least they got to say goodbye.

I never thought I would find my parents again. I thought I would wander The Wastes, always wondering how they really died. Yet I did. It wasn't in the way I wanted, but at least I have the truth, and sometimes, a painful truth is better than a pretty lie. Life will test you, it will make you wonder if you are truly strong enough to shoulder everything it throws at you, but glimpses of happiness make it worth- while. All that you suffer pales when you think of all the good days. After all, how could you see the rainbow in the sun without the rain?

Life is like that, a rainbow—fleeting, beautiful, and oh so fucking unpredictable.

I wouldn't have my life any other way. Although there are bodies, pain, and unknowns thrown in, at least I'm truly living, truly free. One day, this world will be a better place, and the stories I have will be all that is left from before, so I memorise them as I wander through this empty apparition of what once was.

For my kids, for their kids, and for the generations beyond that.

When we get back to The Ring, the sun is setting, throwing beautiful shades of orange and red across the sky and sand. I let Sascha and her men unload everything, while I go tell my men I'm back so they don't worry.

I wander through the community we built as people wave and greet me. I spot Clarissa gardening with some of the guards and women. There are people eating and drinking outside, while others lounge about. Everyone is happy and safe, thanks to Worth...and us. All the death and pain is worth it. This little haven, sanctuary... oasis in the middle of all this agony.

That's like me and my men—an oasis.

I don't see them out here, so I head to our rooms, the place where we have spent so many hours together, learning to grieve, to love. It's where we are free from prying eyes, where we can be together forever.

When I open the door, I gawk. My heart lodges in my throat, and I freeze as my stomach flips. I sweep my eyes around the room repeatedly, disbelief filling me.

The whole space is alight with candles, throwing the room into a sultry, beautiful haze, and in the middle of it are my men, waiting in a line. Clay looks nervous, Archel smiles, Jago is expressionless, and Evan is wincing.

"What—" I whisper, swallowing the frog in my throat as I stare at them, wondering what is happening. "What is it? Did I forget a birthday? An anniversary?" I ask with a grimace.

"No, Brawler." Jago grins and then looks at Evan. "Go ahead."

I watch him take a deep breath as I stare at him in confusion, my heart racing as if it knows something I don't.

"I've never been very good at lying to you, Pip," Evan whispers, then he clears his throat and shares a look with the others. "I have loved you since I was just a boy. I'm not perfect, we both know that. I'll piss you off and you'll kick my ass, but I'll love you with every fibre of my being." He takes a deep breath and gets down on one knee. "You're my best friend, Pip, my lover, my life, and the reason I am the man kneeling before you today. Without you, there is no me, so I'm asking you, begging you, if you will do me the honour of making me your husband?" he inquires with tears in his eyes. His hands shake before him as he presents a box and opens it. It's a band, a golden one, with a traditional diamond offset from the ring.

"I—" I gasp, wide-eyed.

"Not yet, Princess," Archel jokes.

Jago clears his throat and drops to his knee as well, holding his fist up.

"You drive me wild. You used to infuriate me so much, with your loud, rude babbling…and yet you're so fucking beautiful and amazing that I can't even think when I'm around you. You make me want to be a better man, the man you deserve, and I will spend the rest of my life trying, even when you tell people about my dick." He grins, making me choke on a laugh. "Be mine forever?" he finishes and uncurls his palm, exposing another ring. This one is thicker than the other, strong, sturdy, and simple like our love, with another diamond in the side.

"Princess," Archel begins, and he bows before dropping to his knee with a flourish. "You stole my heart the moment I saw your ass

—" He grunts when Jago elbows him. "I mean face. You smiled at me, and I swear I finally understood everything Dray talked about when he mentioned soulmates. I searched, waited, and loved you from afar."

"Stalker," I tease, and he winks.

"I'll spend the rest of my life being your shadow, loving you, making you laugh, and killing those who dare to hurt you. I'll bring you coffee, even if I have to search the world for it just to see your smile. I'll hold you when you struggle, and I'll be whatever you need, because I love you more than I ever knew I was capable of. You gave me back my heart and yours with it, and I will guard them for eternity. Princess, marry me?" He exposes a ring. The band is black and matte, and it has another diamond in it.

Clay kneels with his hands over his heart in a respectful gesture. "You never have to be alone again, Pascha," he says as I stare into those bright eyes. "I was alone, nearly all my life, until you came along and brought joy, laughter, and love back into it. You made me want to fight for something other than my land—my pascha, a true leader. I will never tire of your strength, beauty, and madness. We fell in love under the stars, and now I'm asking you to take me as yours forever. To trust me to heal you, protect you, and fight with you. I'm asking you to be mine..." He looks at the others. "To be ours. Our pascha."

"Princess," Archel adds. "Brawler." Jago smiles.

"Pip," Evan finishes. "For the rest of our days?"

I look back at Clay as he produces two rings. One is silver, like that of his mask, with a diamond off one side, and the other is a very thin delicate mix of all the metal colours with a stone in the middle.

"When they are put together, they make one beautiful ring, with you in the centre like that stone. Four chambers of a heart, with you as the beat. Apart, we are alone. Together, we are whole," Archel explains.

Tears fill my eyes as I stare at them, truly, utterly speechless for once.

"We finally did it," Archel jokes and then swallows. "But, Princess, we are going to need an answer," he urges nervously. It's the first time I've ever seen him so. Jago too, he's practically as pale as a ghost.

It's what makes me step closer. It's what makes me open my mouth and finally speak. Because like they said, when they cannot, I will, and when I cannot, they will. We are one, we are whole, we are soulmates.

"Yes, yes, yes. I'll be yours," I tell them softly and then laugh. "You're stuck with me forever now!" I almost yell as they rush to their feet.

They embrace me, pass me around, and kiss and hug me. There are laughter and tears and so much happiness, I almost choke on it. I can barely breathe around it as they put me down and slide the rings onto my finger, and I finally see how they slot together. Each one is different, yet they fit together perfectly to make a stunning ring that climbs all the way to my knuckle.

Sturdy, strong, beautiful, and lasting, just like our love.

Chapter 43
Celebration Nation

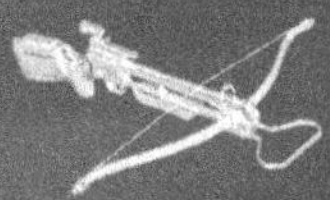

Someone knocks on the door as I'm kissing Jago, and I turn as it's ripped open. "Did she say yes yet?" two voices yell, and then Worth and Clarissa are there, staring at me hopefully.

"I said yes!" I squeal, and then I rush into their arms as they laugh and hug me. Worth's men come in behind her, and they congratulate my guys. Dray smacks Archel so hard, he falls. I pull back and smile. "Were you in on this?"

"Like they could do this alone," Clarissa scoffs. "We even got Sascha in on it to get you out of here so we could get ready."

"And William made the rings for them, even though he threatened to make one into a dick to get back at you," Worth tells me as I laugh. "Now let's celebrate!" she calls and drags me outside. I glance back at my men before I turn forward, and outside, it seems like all of The Ring is gathered.

Worth lifts my hand into the air.

"My general is to be married! Let's celebrate!" she shouts, and cheers instantly go up. Music is played, and alcohol and food are passed around. As I stand here, with my men behind me and their rings on my finger, I can't help but grin. I wish my mum were here to

297

see this, but I know she would be so proud of me and the life I've built thanks to them. I turn to see them grinning widely, accepting people's congratulations.

They are so getting laid tonight.

I'm given a bottle and offered my own congratulations. I say more thank yous than I can count. I dance with my men, drink, and eat, and at the end of the night, I sit in their arms, staring up at the stars. Clarissa and Worth are with us, as are their men. Sascha is even here, sitting back and sipping a bottle with Nan.

"I want to get married on the cliff," I murmur, and then look around at my men. "It's where my mother found herself and where she was buried. It's also where Jago and I fell in love again, and where we all agreed to never leave each other no matter what. There on the cliff, in that house, are memories of my past, present, and future. It seems only right that it's the place we choose to share our vows, our love... It's the last place my father was alive. It's almost like he is there too. I want to do it on the cliff so my mother and father can be with me." I look to Worth. "I understand you probably wouldn't be able to come—"

"Just fucking try to stop me." She snorts. "The Ring will be okay for a while. We'll sneak away."

"We can invite only those you want to attend. I'll arrange transport and security. You guys can go first to alert any residents and get it ready." Sascha nods. "Whatever you want, boss, we can do it."

"I'm coming too, if that's okay?" Clarissa calls. "I expected no less."

"Aye, fuck it, guess I'll be there too. There will be booze, right?" Nan hollers, making us all laugh.

"Plenty of booze," I assure her. "And probably some men you can hit on."

She teases me then. "Knew I liked you. I will be there."

"So it's settled." I nod and look over at my men. "Is that okay?"

"Pip, wherever you want to get married is fine with us, we just want to marry you."

"He's right, Pascha—wherever you want, we are there."

I nearly cry again, and Jago groans, leans in, and kisses me to distract me. "No more crying, you know I hate it," he grumbles as he pulls away, but he's smiling. "Now...I'm thinking we need to celebrate ourselves?"

I leap to my feet, almost stumbling in my rush. "Sorry, gotta go, ladies, it's orgy time!" I yell and grab my closest man, Archel, who laughs and smacks my ass. "Your fiancée needs her orgasms, so remind me why I'm marrying you," I taunt. I ignore the catcalls and whispers as I drag my other men up, and then they chase me back to our rooms, laughing the entire time.

My heart is so full, it might explode, and then my pussy is filled too.

The key to a happy marriage, I'm betting.

The preparations begin the next day. We don't see any point in wasting time. We pack everything we might need, and with Clarissa and Nan and a few guards, we set off towards the north and Abel. The guards have their own gear to camp with, and Worth will follow in a few days as long as Abel is okay with it, but it feels right. Excitement fills me, just like last time I was heading up there, but now it's not for adventure or to hunt, it's for my happily ever after. I don't see why he wouldn't be okay with it, but I make sure the guards know they might have to sleep outside. After all, there is only so much room in Abel's house, and I want him to feel comfort- able. After so many years alone, it may be too much for him to have all these people around him.

The trip should take a day or two. We want to make enough stops for Nan and the others—though Nan could probably outride all of us as she speeds past us with a whoop, her cardigan flying in the wind as she guns her bike. She drives a huge motorcycle, with a big seat and an attached sidecar.

We manage to reach Ivar's before stopping for the night, and then the next day, we camp out in the open. When the sun rises, we start moving. Today we will reach the cliff and Abel, and nerves run through me. For some reason, I'm worried about what he will think. I'm hoping he will be happy we chose to have it with him. As the miles pass and we get closer and closer, I find myself second- guessing my decision, but when we stop at the end of the hidden entryway and I see him waiting with a wide smile—obviously hearing our arrival—all my fear disappears. I shut down my bike and get off, walking over with a large smile. He hugs me instantly.

"You're back so soon," he says as he pulls away and grins at me. "Not that I'm complaining, and you brought company?"

I block his view and take his hands, holding them as I lick my lips. I think about what to ask before I just blurt it out. "I'm getting married." I turn my hand to show him the ring.

"How wonderful, Piper!" He grins widely. "Why do you look worried?"

"I want to do it here. I want to get married here, where my mum lived, so she can be a part of it," I whisper and swallow as he stares at me, his lips tilting down in understanding. "Is that okay?"

"Of course it is. This is as much your home as it is mine. How many people are we talking?" He looks us over. "I need more beds and food—"

"Don't worry about that, we will figure it out and not intrude as much as we can, but Abel...I have one more question."

He blinks, meeting my eyes again as I take a deep sigh. "My father isn't here, my mother isn't either, and you are the closest thing I have to a parent. I was hoping, praying really, that you would be a part of the wedding. I know you never expected to find or know me, but I feel like we were brought together for a reason. I understand why you might say no, but I want you to be a part of it, part of my new life—"

"Piper, just ask." He smiles.

"Will you walk me down the aisle?" I rush out and swallow.

"Nothing, I mean nothing, would make me happier," he vows, and then leans down to kiss my hand. "Your mother would be so proud and honoured you are having it here. Let's go inside and get you all settled."

I turn back to the others and wave them in. It's a rush of bodies and people. We get Nan settled in a room, Clarissa in another, and we take the one we shared before. The others are happy to camp outside in the sun, since they are used to it.

Abel puts out plenty of food for the hungry warriors, and the kitchen is crowded with men and women. I see him smiling, taking it all in, and I feel like we are healing Abel one step at a time. After eating, my men and the guards under Clarissa's command start on the area outside. She won't let me help, forcing me to stay indoors. I find Nan at the table, working her way through Abel's booze, as she orders people around. He's sitting with her, drinking as she regales him with stories of me and The Wastes. I leave her to it as I head to the living room. I find my mother's face frozen in one of her videos on the screen and kneel before it, smiling.

"I'm getting married, Mum," I whisper. "You would love them. They are incredibly sweet, strong, and so perfect for me, it almost hurts. They laugh with me, cry with me, and hold me up when I feel like I can't stand anymore. They...they are my soulmates." I wipe away a stray tear, smiling through it.

"I wish you were here so badly to help me get ready, to laugh and hold my hand. But a part of you is here, and I know I'm doing the right thing. Abel said he will give me away. I know Dad would have liked that, you too, and I know you'll both be watching when I say I do." I close my eyes, pressing my hand to the screen. "It doesn't make up for you being gone though. It hurts knowing you won't be here, but it's enough, it has to be. I love you so much. Thank you for bringing me to a new home, for giving me an amazing life, a life which brought me to my soulmates. Thank you for being my mum."

I lean in and kiss her cheek before standing, my heart sturdy, if a little sad. She will be with me. It's time to look to my future.

That night, we gather outside, although I'm not allowed to see what they did. We eat, drink, and laugh. Worth will be here in the morning, and the wedding will be in the afternoon. They have everything covered. All I have to do is relax, and I do, in the company of my men and Abel.

I celebrate my last night of being single—not of being free, because they would never restrict that—of being alone, because no matter what is to come, I will never be alone again. My men will be there, our life an adventure.

Chapter 44
Soulmates

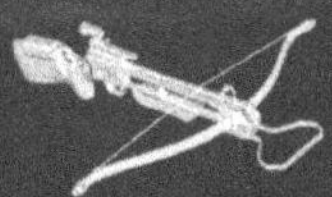

I can't sleep that night. My men surround me, but I'm too excited. I sneak downstairs, make myself a cup of tea, and nurse it at the table, watching the sun begin to rise out of the window. There's a creak, and I turn to see Abel making his way towards me.

"Couldn't sleep?"

"Too excited," I admit. He chuckles and makes himself a cup before sitting. I warm my hands around my mug as I smile, meeting his eyes. "Most girls dream of their wedding since they were a kid, but I never did. My mum always said any man that ever tried to marry me would have to be both crazy and stupid." We both laugh as I look down at my cup. "I think they all are."

"And she would love them," he murmurs, nodding at me. "And be more than happy to see them vow themselves to you and the life you lead forever."

"It's silly, a child's wish that she was here." I swallow back my sadness. "I want to be happy. I am happy, but it's tainted. Being here, it reminds me of her and how she should be here today."

"She is," he tells me, and then takes my hand. "She's here, and you are not alone. You are surrounded by family and friends. Those who love you and want to see you happy. That in itself is something to be excited about. Miss her, of course, but today is about you, about starting your new life with your loves. It's unconventional, I will give you that, but so are you. When you are up there today, searching the crowd for a face you wish you could see one more time, remember she is right here." He lays his hand over the neck- lace. "Watching, listening, and supporting you. Unconventional, like you."

"Thank you." I smile and sip my tea. "I'm glad you are walking me down the aisle."

"As am I. I'm honoured, actually, to be a part of your day." He tops up my tea and nods at it. "Have another drink. I'm betting today is going to be fast and filled with madness, so this may be the last second of quiet you have before then."

"I wouldn't want to spend it with anyone else."

Worth arrives in a whirlwind as I am staring at myself in the mirror, wondering what to wear. I remembered the grooms, I remembered the location...but I forgot the dress. Fucking hell, I can't get married in my underwear...can I?

But no, Nan and Worth march into the room, push me to the bed, and get started. Nan works on my hair, though she takes more breaks to drink than I think a hairstylist should. Worth produces a bowl of red and black paint, and then carefully presses it along my face, her own features twisted in concentration.

"What are you doing?" I ask out of immobile lips, my question mumbled.

"What Clay showed me was traditional for a pascha," she replies distractedly, "when they take the throne. It seemed fitting."

Clarissa comes into the room and grins at me. "Never fear, mother is here."

"Corny." I snort, and she narrows her eyes.

"Shut up and be nice, or I won't save your ass by saying I found you an amazing garment to wear," she warns.

Grinning, I mime zipping my lips shut. "That would be the day," Worth teases.

I fake gasp and jerk away, placing my hand over my heart. "To think I was going to add you to my list."

"List?" she asks, wincing as if unsure if she actually wants to know.

"You know, the list, the people I can still fuck." I shrug.

"Erm, yeah, that's not a thing, Piper," she tells me around a laugh.

"It totally is, they just don't know it yet." Looking at Clarissa, I smile nicely. "What did you find?"

She pulls a hanger from behind her back, and I suck in a breath, all teasing and laughter leaving me as I stare at it. She steps forward, holding it out delicately. "Your mother never remarried, but she wore this when Abel and her swore their love for each other. I think she would very much want you to wear it."

"It's beautiful," I whisper, my eyes filling with tears. It's something my mother would wear, and knowing she did means that much more to me.

"We can Piper it up if you are okay with me altering it a little?" Clarissa suggests nervously. "I will make sure not to change it too much, just enough to make it yours."

I nod, trusting her, and I blink as I stare at the dress again. It's white, a bright white which you don't see anymore. The hem reaches the floor, and it has long sleeves and a square neckline. It's made of lace, intricate and beautiful. It's ethereal and stunning, honestly.

Clarissa leaves as Worth and Nan return to my hair and makeup. Worth slowly and delicately paints my face, neck, arms, and nearly my entire body. About an hour or so later, Worth hands me some trousers from her pack. "Here, I had them made for you. I'd love it if you could wear them."

"You big softie." I grin as I quickly slip from the ones I'm wearing and into the pair she gave me, pulling on my boots after just as Clarissa returns. I stand, and together they help me dress. Worth attaches something to the left side of the top and eyes it as they step back.

"There, perfect," Clarissa murmurs. "Take a look."

I turn to face the mirror, and what I see steals my breath. They did an amazing job, especially Clarissa. She cut some of it away, saving the trimmings, so it's now a shirt. The sleeves are gone to show my arms, and the neckline is the same, but the dress ends just above my stomach to expose the intricate tribal paintings Worth did. The rest of the dress has been used to make a cape of sorts. It's similar to what Worth wore at her own wedding, but this one drapes over my right shoulder, opposite of where I wear my weapons, and I know that was done on purpose. It flows down my arm and side, finishing in a waterfall around my knee. On the left shoulder is what I can only describe as a medal. There are three symbols, those of The Nations, The Lost, then The Damned, dangling and shining gold. A general's medallion.

The trousers Worth gave me cling to my skin, the hand stitched leather comfortable and cupping every inch of me. My usual kick- ass boots have been shined and almost gleam. My entire left arm has been painted in tribal paints, more of Clay's designs, I'm betting, and they extend up my neck to my face, swirling around it like a person's touch in shades of reds, blacks, and oranges. My hair is braided to the same side as my cape, with feathers, jewels, and a handmade metal pin with my damned symbol on it worked into the strands. I look...so fucking badass and beautiful. I feel stronger too.

I look like a pascha, a leader, a woman willing to walk this earth with her four men at her side. The woman they all say they see, and now, I finally do too.

"You are a true pasha today," Worth murmurs as she stands next to me. Clarissa joins us on my left side and smiles.

"You are the perfect mixture of beauty and danger, just like in real life."

Nan peeks around us and leans next to Worth. "Aye, they will be tearing it off of her later for sure." I grin, and she softens. "Ya look lovely girlie, ya mam would be proud."

I tear up before settling down and looking back at the mirror. I reach up to touch the necklace as I smile, noticing them all standing around me. No matter what, Abel is right—I am never alone. My mother might not be here in person, but the rest of my family is.

"I-I never imagined this is where I would end up," I whisper, meeting their eyes. "I was always so lonely as a child after I lost my family, especially when Evvie pulled away. I was so lost, and now look at me. I have friends, family, lovers. I'm the richest, luckiest person in this world. I am so grateful to have met each and every one of you and call you a friend." Tears fill my eyes again, and I try not to let them fall and ruin the makeup. "For you to be here today with me, at my side…"

"You will never walk alone," Clarissa murmurs. "To the edges of this land, to the depths of the sea, we are with you," she finishes. "It's a proverb of our people, of our families, of which you belong, Piper. You brought us together, and you're saving this world. It's us who are honoured to be at your side."

"To see you grow, love, learn. To see the incredible leader and woman you've become," Worth adds.

"To know that when the winds take me away from this place, it's in good hands. Am grateful I gotta see this world as it once was, thanks to you," Nan says.

"Fuckity fuck," I mutter, sniffling.

"No crying!" They laugh, and I chuckle as I shake the tears away.

"I feel like we should hug or some shit after that." I sigh and turn to them. They step back. Right, body paint. No hugging.

"Let's rock this shit," I mutter, making them laugh. "Let's get me hitched to four dicks forever." I turn to Worth and wink. "Apart from you, of course. The list still stands."

"All right, time to go." She chuckles. "Before Archel breaks the door down looking for you."

I tread confidently to the door, my head held high as I walk down the corridor to the stairs, knowing my men are outside waiting for me.

Standing at the bottom of the staircase is Abel—in a full suit. That's something I haven't seen since Paradise. He tugs at it with a grin. "I have had it since I was a boy, it's a little tight."

Laughing, I step down next to him. There's a bark as Beast Jr. hops out from behind him, wagging his tail with his tongue out. Around his neck is a bow, like that around Abel's.

"It wouldn't be a wedding without your fur child," Worth calls as I lean down and kiss him.

"Good boy," I murmur as he licks my hands. "Let's go see your daddies."

Worth, Clarissa, and Nan pass me, all squeezing my shoulder in support. The door stays open, and I hear some soft music. Abel lays my hand on his arm and turns to face the door. "Are you ready?"

I stare at the cliff and smile widely. "Never been more sure of anything in my life," I state.

He leans down and kisses my cheek. "Good."

Arm in arm, with Beast Jr. following happily behind us, we step outside, and I see all the hard work everyone has put in. The sun is shining down on the cliff, lighting it up so beautifully, and I can feel my mother's love in the warmth of the slight breeze. There are makeshift chairs and boxes where everyone sits. Between them is an aisle, and standing just before my mother's bench are my men. Next to them, ready and smiling, is Trev. I gasp and still, and Abel chuckles.

"Nice man. Apparently, when he heard of the ceremony, he insisted on being here to conduct it for you."

I smile at him gratefully, and he nods in return. In the stands, I see Priest, Jon, Nan, Worth, and Clarissa. I see my friends. I see people I've saved, and people I've met along my journey in The Wastes. And waiting for me at the end is my future.

My husbands.

I don't think I'll ever get used to that, maybe I'll just call them my bitches instead.

They turn to face me and steal my heart—and yes, vagina—all over again.

Clay stands at the end as the tallest, closest to the cliff. He's wearing his mask around his throat like the first time I saw him. His hair is braided similarly to mine, and across his neck and chin is a handprint, a red one. He's shirtless, showing off his muscles and tattoos, and his whole chest and back are covered in tribal ink like me. His legs are encased in some leather trousers, which make him look like a snack, and his feet are bare and digging into the grass.

Next to him stands Archel, who grins widely as he checks me out. He's wearing all black, of course, and the only pop of colour on his frame is a red handprint across the skin of his chest, which is exposed by his half-unbuttoned shirt. His trousers are skintight, his usual hunting trousers, just fancier. His hair is combed and pushed back, and he's standing with his hands behind his back, no doubt concealing some form of weapon.

Jago is next, with an open leather jacket, loose cargo trousers, and boots. His chest is exposed to show the red handprint over his lower stomach, towards his pants. His hair is braided like mine, some of the shoulder-length curls falling into his fiery eyes as he smirks at me.

At the end, with a soft look in his eyes and a smile on his pierced lips, is my Evvie. His black hair is tamed and controlled for once, and his tattoos sparkle in the sun, revealed by his traditional, sleeveless black shirt from Paradise. I don't even know where he managed to find it. It's from ceremonies we used to perform down there that we watched as kids. It has a black collar, which is partly sticking up, thick black material, and buttons down the front. He's also wearing matching pants, and I almost cry at the reminder of our home, knowing he found them just for me—it's also what my father would have worn. Across his cheek and eye is a red handprint.

That's when I realise I have a matching red handprint across my chest and heart, and I almost cry at how cute that is.

The music changes to something slower, the cooing words sung by a woman to my left as Abel starts to slowly lead me down the aisle, Beast Jr. trotting behind us. When I reach them, I have to refrain from flinging myself into their arms. I want to make a joke, but for once, I swallow it down and turn to face Trev, who grins at me, standing before my mother's bench.

Abel kisses my cheek and steps back, and Trev begins as my men spread out next to me. "We are gathered here today to cele- brate the union between Piper and her men—"

"Piper's pied dicks," I mutter softly, and I hear Archel snigger as Trev ignores me and carries on.

I get distracted, my eyes roving hungrily across my men. They just look so fucking good, and by the time I zone in, it's to Trev prompting me.

"Piper?"

"Huh?" I ask, jerking my head up, and everyone laughs as I grin. "Whoops."

"Do you take these men in sickness and in health? In death and survival? Do you promise to love them, support them, and fight with them for eternity? Do you pledge your heart to theirs? Do you take them as yours?"

"I do," I answer without hesitation.

Trev asks every single one of my men separately, and they all say 'I do' so strongly and assuredly that my heart explodes.

"Then you may kiss your bride." I am passed around, kissed, and hugged. When I'm spun back into position, my head is hazy and my lips are bruised, but I'm grinning widely.

"I now pronounce you wife and husbands. May your future be long and fruitful," Trev finishes and then bows to me. "General."

Turning, I grin at our audience. "That's right! We are married!" I whoop. "Time to party!"

The music kicks up a notch, and the ceremony location is rearranged slightly so people can dance and eat all the food Abel and others cooked. I dance and drink. I lounge in my new husbands' laps

—a surreal saying. I let them pamper and tease me as the day goes on. I watch Jago dance with Beast Jr., and I see Clarissa swaying to the melody with the lurking giant.

Above it all, I feel my mother watching me and smiling, and my heart finally fully heals. The sun warms me, the necklace against my chest heating with it, and I know it's my mother telling me she is here and she is happy.

A little while later, Clay scoops me into his arms, and with a grin, he turns and leaves, ignoring the hollers and hoots of the drunken guests and those celebrating with us. "Clay!" I gasp as he rushes through the house and down the pathway to our bikes.

"Where are we going?" I laugh as I'm thrown onto the back of Archel's bike, which has 'Just hitched, bitch,' scrawled on a sign tied to the back.

"Secret, Princess, you'll see." He laughs as he guns it.

I don't have to wait long. After five minutes of me laughing without a worry in the world, we pull up to our location, and they cut the engine. Jago grabs me from the back and hauls me into his arms, not letting me see much of the outside.

But what I did see stole my breath. It was a cute little one-story cottage, with vines crawling along the stone walls and roof. I don't even know how they found this place, but I don't question it as I'm carried inside.

There's one large room, with a kitchen to the left and a table in the middle. To the right on a raised platform is a huge bed, which looks freshly made and almost too perfect to be true as the sun shines through the window, illuminating it. The window is open, letting in the sound of the waves.

Once inside, Evan turns me and lays me softly down on the bed. I stare up at him as he grins down at me. "Is this the orgy part?" I tease.

"Pip." He groans as I sit up and reach for him. He holds my hands, and Archel climbs onto the bed, slowly and softly stripping off my cape. I watch him fold it and pack it away in one of our bags so as not to damage it, and I can't hold back anymore. I turn and dive at him, tackling him to the bed as he laughs. The sound soon turns into a moan as my lips crash into his.

Another pair of lips meet my skin, brushing along my shoulders. More lips graze my hand, and another glides along my leg. There are hands and mouths everywhere, touching everything, until every inch of my skin has been caressed and kissed. I pull away from Archel's lips, panting, my eyes wide as I stare into his lust filled gaze.

"I want you to scream for us," he whispers. "Then make me," I reply, equally as quiet.

No more words are exchanged as I'm turned and made to sit on my heels as they finish stripping me. Their hands move too quickly for me to see who is where. I pant, my belly quivering, my heart racing, and my pussy aching.

"Who do you want first?" Clay questions as he crouches next to me, cupping my chin and tilting it up so I stare into his eyes. Licking my lips, I catch his finger with my tongue, and he groans, stroking my lips before pushing his thumb into my mouth.

"First?" I mumble around it.

"Tonight, you get all of us, Brawler," Jago clarifies from somewhere behind me.

"I want her mouth," Clay states, narrowing his eyes as I suck on his thumb, lapping the salty scarred skin.

"Then I want that beautiful ass she is always teasing me with." Archel chuckles as he does a sexy as hell sit-up before crawling to me, licking up my leg to my stomach. "And you'll love every moment, Princess."

"Fine with me, I'd hurt her anyway. I'll take that addictive pussy," Jago growls.

"Erm...there are four cocks," Evan says, and I grin as I pop Clay free from my mouth and turn to him.

"Then you can be my last, the way you wish you were my first," I offer, and his face lights up as a smile curves his lips.

Clay grabs my face as he towers over me, bending down to kiss me hard, rough—a promise. I groan into his mouth as he lies back, taking me with him so I'm on all fours. Only then does he break the kiss and move out from under my body to kneel before me. He unfastens his trousers as I pant, my face flushed with excitement. I'm not the least bit embarrassed, even with my pussy and ass spread and aimed at my other men. No, I feel their hungry gazes, and it's empowering. I flip my hair over my shoulder and look at them.

"Well?" I prompt. "Going to leave your wife waiting?" "Never," Archel promises.

Jago strips and then moves behind me, kissing up my back until his lips meet my ear. "I'm going to let your shadow fuck this tight little cunt and get his dick nice and wet for your little ass, and only when you are almost coming, begging, will I bury my big dick inside you."

I think I just came from his words alone. My pussy clenches from his dark tone and the hungry promise as Archel chuckles, coming closer as Jago moves away. Evan pulls up a chair and sits back, watching me with a wide grin.

Archel's teasing hands slide up my pussy, back and forth, in a light caress. "Be a good girl, won't you, wife?" he purrs before plunging a finger into me. I gasp, clenching around him as I push back. I am so fucking wet from just thinking about what's to come that my juices drip out of me.

"Princess," he growls, leaning down and licking my ass cheeks.

"I want to taste you, to have my wife's cream be the last thing I ever taste."

Dropping my head, I roll my hips as he keeps up that slow pace with his finger, then he adds another and another, stretching me. He maintains that slow burning desire as I feel the warmth of his breath across my pussy, making me whimper. He chuckles, turns his head, and kisses my thigh before kissing my pussy right above my aching, throbbing clit.

"Please," I beg.

His tongue slides out, flicking my clit in time with his fingers. I fuck myself on them, desperately reaching for my release, but I should have known better. Just as I am about to reach the precipice, he pulls away, his wet fingers gripping my hips.

I groan, fisting the covers in my anger, and lift my head to meet Clay's eyes. He watches me with a smile, reaching down to stroke my hair as I feel Archel's cock at my entrance.

"P—" He pushes into me, stealing my words. Archel only pushes in a few inches, slowly stretching me around his cock, before he pulls out and thrusts back in, all the way to the hilt. I moan, keeping my eyes locked with Clay's as he strokes me. Archel fucks me, his fingers spasming on my hips as he pulls out and pushes back in. He starts off soft, gentle, and loving, but it's not long before he's pounding into me and I'm pushing back to meet him.

I reach for that orgasm again. I'm so close, and just when I'm about to fall into the abyss, he pulls out, leaving my pussy empty and cold. I cry out with frustration.

"Clay, fill her mouth, shut her up," Jago orders. I turn my glare to him as I'm lifted, and he slides below me, my breasts pressing against his solid chest. He strokes my hips as he holds me above his hard cock.

"You son of a—"

He slams me down onto his cock, impaling me, and I scream, tossing my head back, but my hair gets caught in someone's grip. It's

ripped forward and to the side where another cock presses against my lips—Clay's.

Jago buries himself inside me, holding me still as Clay bumps my lips with his tip until I open for him, and then he surges inside. His huge, stiff cock slowly slides out and in, my saliva dripping down his shaft as he holds his dick for me. Jago starts to move with a slow roll of his hips, establishing a rhythm to keep me on the edge of release.

I feel my ass parted, and then Archel's wet fingers touch my other hole. I relax, and he slowly works one inside me, making me cry out at the pressure. They work together to fuck me as Archel adds another finger, and then they pick up speed. I greedily suck on Clay's cock, swallowing him all the way to the back of my throat. I glance at Evan, who watches me hungrily.

I put on a show for my usually jealous lover, sucking and pushing back until my orgasm finally crests and they let it. I come all over Jago's huge cock and open my mouth wider, letting Clay's wet dick slip out. Archel pulls free of my ass as I shiver and shake, and as I ride the high, his cock presses against my ass.

He goes slow, pushing in past the ring of muscles. I try to relax, to hold still as he thrusts in an inch and pulls out before pushing back in. The sting soon dissipates as Jago begins to move, thrusting up in time with Archel's movements. Finally, Archel is buried all the way inside me, his huge cock stretching me. Caught between them, I can do nothing but whimper and work with them as they fuck me.

Clay presses his cock against my mouth once again, and I suck it hard, taking out my pleasure on him as he snarls. He snaps his hips forward, plunging into my mouth over and over.

All my holes are filled, and it feels so good. I'm so full, so loved... Evvie.

I open my eyes to see him moving closer. He steps around my other side, and I reach out blindly, accidentally hitting his hard cock before I wrap my hand around it.

"Piper," he gasps, jerking in my grip as I suck on Clay and start to stroke my Evvie.

I rub him in time to the others' rhythm, letting them take over. Clay controls my head, angling it to swallow him deeper. Archel and Jago slam into me, chasing their releases and mine. Evan grunts, his eyes closing as I stroke his hard cock, but I falter when I feel another orgasm rolling through me.

"That's right, come for me, wife," Jago coos.

Taken by surprise, I scream around Clay's cock. He growls, slamming down my throat before coming. I swallow it as I clamp down on Jago and Archel. Archel groans, clutches my ass cheeks, and stills, filling my ass with his cum. Jago manages two more thrusts, even as I clamp around his cock, before he snarls below me, his release surging inside me. I droop forward for a moment, trying to catch my breath. Hands stroke me, and I lift my head, meeting Evan's hungry gaze.

"Pip, you don't have—"

Jago helps lift me off his and Archel's cocks, and I turn to Evan and crawl towards him as he lies against the pillows.

I ignore his protests about me being tired and grab his cock. This time, I line it up with my pussy and slam down onto it. We both groan. His hands automatically go to my hips as I roll and circle them. I start to ride him, bouncing on his dick.

"I love you," he murmurs, thrusting up into me. He fucks me hard and fast, uncaring about the others being before him because he knows he's mine as well. He's not my only, but he is my forever.

I meet his eyes as I lean forward, pressing my lips to his. I kiss him hard, our teeth clashing as we fuck. His dick fills me with each thrust, and although I didn't think it was possible, I feel my plea- sure building again.

Slow and soft but there.

We work towards our orgasms together, our bodies in sync. We were made for each other. He rips his lips away, panting as he stares up at me, and I lean back. I grip his thighs as I roll my body, taking control while I stare into those worshipful eyes.

My Evvie, my first love. One of my lasts.

My husband.

I force my eyes to stay open as I ride him. His hands trail down my body before flicking my clit, and then they glide back up, tweaking my nipples—down, rub, up, flick—until his hands grab my ass cheeks and he flips us. I grin as he takes over, groaning when he slams into me. My legs wrap around his waist as he pounds into my body.

"Pip," he snarls, fighting my tight pussy, fighting to keep his rhythm, but it's no use. We are both so close that when he slams into me, grinding into my clit, I scream my release again, and he follows.

It's one of those mind-blowing, all-consuming orgasms that you can only try to breathe through as it takes over your entire body and mind. When it finally subsides, I collapse.

They shuffle around me, stroking my sweaty hair and body. They dot kisses across my skin, telling me they love me, that I'm beautiful, and a smile curves my lips, even as my eyes stay closed.

When the sun rises, there are more palm prints on my body, the best kind, and I fall into an exhausted sleep in my husbands' arms.

Chapter 45
Oops!

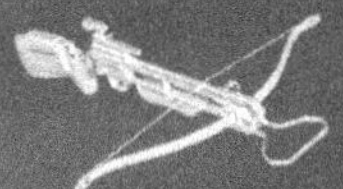

The few days following the wedding are a blur of roaming hands and orgasms. We spend our time in the little cottage, with Abel dropping off food and looking after Beast Jr., until we decide to see him on our way to The Ring. Our honeymoon is over, after all, and we need to get back to work. We need to finish what we started and make The Wastes a better place to live.

I leave the men in the kitchen with Able as they speak about converting the cottage so we can make it a home for when we visit the north. Beast Jr. barks and follows me out to the cliff as I sit down on the bench. I watch him yip and chase his tail, laughing at his antics. He leaps up next to me, his tongue lolling out of his mouth as he pants and stares across the ocean.

It's peaceful.

"Hi, Mum," I whisper, turning to watch the waves like my fur baby is. "I hope you didn't watch the after wedding cockathon," I tease. "But I'm glad you were here, watching us say I do. You were right, Mum. I found someone, or someones, to love me, to make me happy, and they do. They make me so happy..." My words trail off as I think of the reason I came here, the reason I've been so quiet.

"I missed my period," I admit. "I didn't even realise it until yesterday morning when I was thinking about it," I murmur, placing my hand on my belly. "I don't know if I am or even can after...after everything my body went through. I still have scars, after all, but if I am...can I? Can I bring a baby into this world, Mum? It's so filled with anger and death. Every day's a fight for survival. And what if I'm no good at it? What if I'm a terrible mother? They would make amazing daddies, and although I wouldn't know whose they were biologically, it wouldn't matter. Mum, what do I do?"

I lift my head, taking a deep breath of the warm, salty sea air. "How do you know if you are ready? I guess you never do. All I know is that I would love this baby more than anyone ever could. I would die to protect it, like you did for me. I would do anything to ensure they were happy and safe. Is that enough? I did say I wanted adventure, but damn, I'm scared, Mummy. I wish you were here to walk me through this...and how do I tell them? I don't even know if it's real yet..." I swallow, looking at Beast Jr.

"But as soon as I considered it, I knew I wanted it to be true. I want to see a baby Archel running around with a fake blade, a stern, funny baby Evvie, a strong, wild Jago, and a crazy, huge baby Clay... maybe not the last. That baby would be so big, it would rip me apart, and I'm not down for that," I joke with a laugh as I reach out and rub Beast's head before covering my belly again, feeling for anything, any change, to tell me what I so desperately want to know and not know.

The truth.

"I'll protect them so they will never have to go through what I did, like so many others have. It only makes what Worth and I are doing up here all that more important for this baby and all the babies to come. I always thought the world ended, but what if this is just the beginning, Mum? What if to start anew, to be reborn, this world first needed to fall apart? There is such elegance in it now, such simplicity." I shake off my strange thoughts. "I'm rambling, not a surprise... When I thought that I could be pregnant, I was happy, Mum. Not scared, not worried or shocked...happy. Like it was right, meant to be."

Beast Jr. whines and lays his head on my lap, his face turned to my belly, and that's answer enough for me. "If you're in there, if...if I'm going to be a mum, I want you to know how very loved you are. You aren't even born yet, and you will have a whole army of people fawning over you, protecting you, loving you. I'll tell you stories of your grandmother, of the incredible woman who raised me. She would have loved you more than anything in this world." I sniffle back tears as I look to the sea with a smile. "I guess that's answer enough, isn't it, Mum? Whatever is to happen, to come, I'm ready for it, and I'll try to be a good mum, as good as you. I'll learn. I'll probably make mistakes, but who doesn't?"

Closing my eyes, I stroke my belly. "I'll wait to tell them until I know for sure. Until then, I may as well make the most of it. It's not like I can get more pregnant...although that thing we did last night definitely could have knocked me up, if you know what I mean."

Beast Jr. barks, and I laugh. "Yeah, too much info, baby, sorry."

"Pascha, we are ready, you coming?" comes a yell, and I look over my shoulder to see my men peering at me through the door.

"Coming!" I call, and then I sigh, turning back to the sea. "I can do this, I can do anything," I whisper before looking down at my stomach and smiling. "If you are in there, if you are real, I'm ready." I inhale. "I'm ready for you, for this, and when it's time, I'll be a good mum. I promise I'll love you so deeply, you will never want for anything. I'll protect you, hold you when you cry, and kiss your scrapes better. I'll be everything she was. I'll be a good mother," I vow, and the wind blows again, letting me know I'm right, and a mixture of fear and excitement fills me.

"I guess I'm ready to jump in, as always... Thank you. I know you are listening" —I stroke my stomach— "watching all of us. Goodbye, Mum. I'll see you soon."

I stand and pat my leg. "Come on, Beast Jr., let's go see your daddies, but don't tell them yet." I grin, and we wander back to the house. I see my men carrying the bags and food to the bikes, and I meet Abel at the door where he is watching. He turns to see me with a smile.

"Thank you for letting me be a part of your life," he murmurs. "Thank you for wanting to be." I lean up and kiss his cheek.

"Look after the place and her for me, won't you?"

"Always," he promises. I step out of the door, grab my jacket with The Damned symbol on the back, and put it on before pulling down my goggles. "You'll be back, right?"

"Couldn't stop me if you tried. Plus next time, there might be one more of us." I wink. "See you soon, Abel." I follow after my men, heading towards my bike, my husbands, and my new life.

"Ready, Princess?" Archel calls, leaning against his bike.

"More than I have ever been," I reply as I swing my leg over the bike and rev the engine. Beast Jr. hops up onto his homemade seat on Jago's ride. "Keep up if you can."

"Better ride fast then, Brawler, 'cause when I catch you, you're mine," he teases with a smirk.

"I don't know, I think I'm faster than you all, you're all too muscley," Evan teases as he winks at me, striding to his own bike. "Let's go home."

"Home," I agree.

As they pull down their shades and helmets, I look down at my stomach once again and smile softly. At what is to come, at the possibilities.

At the adventure that awaits.

Epilogue

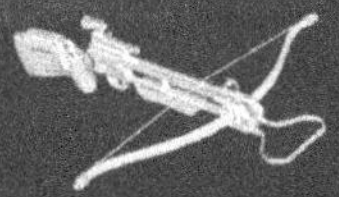

The last few months have been crazy in the best possible way.

I was right—I am pregnant. I waited a few days before I talked to Worth and asked for her advice. Together with Clarissa, they managed to convince me to talk to my men.

I expected some fear, but instead they were just...excited. Evan did a test, and we found out the truth that night, and ever since, everything has changed. We are married and in love, and now we have a baby on the way.

Worth has already started building us a bigger place to sleep, and Dray is building us a crib with Archel. Everyone in The Ring is excited, and when the baby is born, there will be a huge celebra- tion, with the godmothers, Worth and Clarissa, leading the pack— not to mention the godfather, Abel, who has started to venture out. I showed him The Wastes, The Ring, and my life. He's become a huge part of my world, and he's been so much help, as have the other women here. They help me with morning sickness, the pains and aches, and talk me through what's to come so I'm not scared.

We are visiting Abel this time though, because I want to speak to my mother. Beast Jr. follows as I waddle my huge, pregnant ass up to the bench, dropping with a sigh. "Fuck, my boobs are sweating, my ass too," I mutter, and then laugh as Beast Jr., who's huge now, plops onto the grass and starts rolling around on his back.

"Hi, Mum," I start with a smile. "It's me, but you know that. Sorry it's been a while, it's been, well...insane. I was right—I'm pregnant, as you can see since I'm the size of a house. Though Jago says he likes the boob part of the pregnancy, and Archel appreciates my ass. I swear they can't keep their hands off me, not that I'm complaining."

With my hand over my stomach, I tell her, "Evan thinks it's a girl. He's so excited, he almost fainted when he heard her heart- beat, the others too. Jago is already planning on killing anyone who comes close to her. Clay was talking about making her a mini bike, and Archel was thinking about some mini swords. I swear, Mum, she is going to have her hands full with them. I chose her name. They don't know yet, but it feels right. Hope. I want to call her Hope, because that's what she is. She's my hope for a future, for a better life. She's the hope of this world, so meet Hope, Mum, your grandchild." I lean down, and to my belly, I whisper, "Hope, meet your grandmother. I'll tell you as much as I can about her, and when you're ready, you can come here and talk to her."

I lose my vision for a moment, letting the sun wash away the nausea from being on the bike. Soon I'll be too big to ride, but I won't stop doing my job until I'm actually giving birth. Sure, I've stepped back from some duties, and I let the men do most of the fighting now, but I get in fistfights now and again and help with diplomacy and hunting. My teams have taken on a lot of the burden while we stay at The Ring to allow me to nap and pee.

"Pip, you okay?" Evan calls, and I can't help but grin wider.

"I got all of two minutes alone," I tease as I open my eyes to see him crouched before me. His hand automatically covers my stomach, and he wears a smile on his face that he reserves for his daughter, one I've never seen before. "Did you rock-paper-scissors?"

"Yep, and I won." Evan chuckles as he leans in and kisses my huge belly just as Hope kicks.

"She likes you. She's going to have you wrapped around her finger," I murmur as I reach down and run my hands through his hair.

"Just like her mum then," he replies and lays his head on my lap. I hear footsteps, and soon enough, my men are there. Jago picks me up and places me on his lap, as if the bench is not good enough for me to sit on. Clay grabs my legs and starts massaging my feet, while Archel rubs my legs as he sits next to Jago.

"I could get used to this," I tell them. "Not being huge and needing to pee all the time, but this? Yeah."

"Uh-oh, one baby at a time," Evan teases.

"Oh God, there will be more?" Archel groans. "I'm going to have to kill so many boys."

"I'll help," Clay offers with a smile.

I look up to see Jago grinning widely, an expression that's new as well. "Our family is perfect," he whispers as he gazes down at me. "You are perfect, Brawler. Thank you for loving me, for giving us a reason to fight, to love, and now more than ever." He looks at my belly. "I'll love our little bean so much, just as much as I love her mother."

"I love you all." I sniff, crying again. Archel groans.

"Oh God, not the tears again. I prefer horny, pregnant Princess."

That makes me giggle, and then I wince. "Shit, Shadow, now you made me pee." I groan and peer at Jago guiltily. "Only a little."

He just shrugs. "I better get used to it." He holds me closer, and I relax into his hold. All of us watch the sunset, while Beast Jr. lies before us in the grass.

"We all will, together," I murmur.

They call us The Damned, but in reality, we are the total opposite. We are so blessed. I've been many things in this life—Paradise, Forgotten, Lost...Damned. Now, I'm a mother. I can be all that and more. Life is a complex thing, and people grow. They learn and change, and I can't wait to see what the rest of my life holds.

Together, with my men.
Loving and living in The Wastes. In The Nations.
Forever.

About K.A. Knight

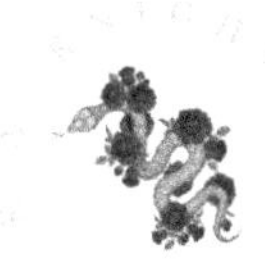

K.A Knight is an USA Today bestselling indie author trying to get all of the stories and characters out of her head, writing the monsters that you love to hate. She loves reading and devours every book she can get her hands on, and she also has a worrying caffeine addiction.

She leads her double life in a sleepy English town, where she spends her days writing like a crazy person.

Read more at K.A Knight's website or join her Facebook Reader Group.
Sign up for exclusive content and my newsletter here
http://eepurl.com/drLLoj

Other Books by K.A. Knight

CONTEMPORARY

LEGENDS AND LOVE *CONTEMPORARY RH*

Revolt

Rebel

Riot - coming soon..

PRETTY LIARS *CONTEMPORARY RH*

Unstoppable

Unbreakable

PINE VALLEY COLLEGE *CONTEMPORARY*

Racing Hearts

DEN OF VIPERS UNIVERSE STANDALONES

Scarlett Limerence *CONTEMPORARY*

Nadia's Salvation *CONTEMPORARY*

Alena's Revenge *CONTEMPORARY*

Den of Vipers *CONTEMPORARY RH*

Gangsters and Guns (Co-Write with Loxley Savage) *CONTEMPORARY RH*

FORBIDDEN READS *(STANDALONES)*

Daddy's Angel *CONTEMPORARY*

Stepbrothers' Darling *CONTEMPORARY RH*

STANDALONES

The Standby *CONTEMPORARY*

Diver's Heart *CONTEMPORARY RH*

DYSTOPIAN

THEIR CHAMPION SERIES *Dystopian RH*

The Wasteland

The Summit

The Cities

The Nations

Their Champion Coloring Book

Their Champion - the omnibus

The Forgotten

The Lost

The Damned

Their Champion Companion - the omnibus

PARANORMAL

THE LOST COVEN SERIES *PNR RH*

Aurora's Coven

Aurora's Betrayal

HER MONSTERS SERIES *PNR RH*

Rage

Hate

Book 3 - *coming soon..*

COURTS AND KINGS *PNR RH*

Court of Nightmares

Court of Death

Court of Beasts

Court of Heathens - coming soon..

THE FALLEN GODS SERIES *PNR*

Pretty Painful

Pretty Bloody

Pretty Stormy

Pretty Wild

Pretty Hot

Pretty Faces

Pretty Spelled

Fallen Gods - the omnibus 1

Fallen Gods - the omnibus 2

FORGOTTEN CITY *PNR*

Monstrous Lies

Monstrous Truths

Monstrous Ends

SCIENCE FICTION

DAWNBREAKER SERIES *SCI FI RH*

Voyage to Ayama

Dreaming of Ayama

STANDALONES

Crown of Stars *SCI FI RH*

SHARED WORLD PROJECTS

Blade of Iris - Mafia Wars *CONTEMPORARY RH*

CO-WRITES

CO-AUTHOR PROJECTS - *Erin O'Kane*

HER FREAKS SERIES *PNR Dystopian RH*

Circus Save Me

Taming The Ringmaster

Walking the Tightrope

Her Freaks Series - the omnibus

STANDALONES

The Hero Complex *PNR RH*

Dark Temptations *Collection of Short Stories, ft. One Night Only & Circus Saves Christmas*

THE WILD BOYS SERIES *CONTEMPORARY RH*

The Wild Interview

The Wild Tour

The Wild Finale

The Wild Boys - the omnibus

CO-AUTHOR PROJECTS - *Ivy Fox*

Deadly Love Series *CONTEMPORARY*

Deadly Affair

Deadly Match

Deadly Encounter

CO-AUTHOR PROJECTS - *Kendra Moreno*

STANDALONES

Stolen Trophy *CONTEMPORARY RH*

Fractured Shadows *PNR RH*

Shadowed Heart

Burn Me *PNR*

Cirque Obscurum *PNR RH*

CO-AUTHOR PROJECTS - *Loxley Savage*

THE FORSAKEN SERIES *SCI FI RH*

Capturing Carmen

Stealing Shiloh

Harboring Harlow

STANDALONES

Gangsters and Guns *CONTEMPORARY*, IN DEN OF VIPERS' UNIVERSE

OTHER CO-WRITES

Shipwreck Souls (*with Kendra Moreno & Poppy Woods*)

The Horror Emporium (*with Kendra Moreno & Poppy Woods*)

AUDIOBOOKS

The Wasteland

The Summit

The Cities

The Nations - *coming soon*

Rage

Hate

Den of Vipers (*From Podium Audio*)

Gangsters and Guns (*From Podium Audio*)

Daddy's Angel (*From Podium Audio*)

Stepbrothers' Darling (*From Podium Audio*)

Blade of Iris (*From Podium Audio*)

Deadly Affair (*From Podium Audio*)

Deadly Match (*From Podium Audio*)

Deadly Encounter (*From Podium Audio*)

Stolen Trophy (*From Podium Audio*)

Crown of Stars (*From Podium Audio*)

Monstrous Lies (*From Podium Audio*)

Monstrous Truth (*From Podium Audio*)

Monstrous Ends (*From Podium Audio*)

Court of Nightmares (*From Podium Audio*)

Court of Death (*From Podium Audio*)

Unstoppable (*From Podium Audio*)

Unbreakable (*From Podium Audio*)

Fractured Shadows (*From Podium Audio*)

Shadowed Heart (*From Podium Audio*)

Revolt (*From Podium Audio*)

Rebel (*From Podium Audio*) - *coming soon*

Find an error?

Please email this information to thenuttyformatter1@gmail.com:

- *the author name*
- *title of the book*
- *screenshot of the error*
- *suggested correction*